The Doctor's Suit

A Novel

SUSAN HERRON

authorHOUSE®

AuthorHouse™
1663 Liberty Drive
Bloomington, IN 47403
www.authorhouse.com
Phone: 1-800-839-8640

All the characters in this book are fictitious. Their names are all taken from the names of islands along the shores of Massachusetts and off'n the coast a Maine.

Published by AuthorHouse 2/28/2013

ISBN: 978-1-4772-9200-6 (sc)
ISBN: 978-1-4772-9201-3 (hc)
ISBN: 978-1-4772-9202-0 (e)

Library of Congress Control Number: 2012921734

Chapter 1

To err is human; to forgive, divine.
—Alexander Pope

Sally Gardiner simply could not believe it when she realized what was starting to happen. Her eyes closed for a moment as a dense cloud of fog descended across her mind, obstructing all her thought processing. First a shiver. Then a tear. She opened her eyes and saw the sun glistening in through her tears. Then slowly, from out of nowhere, sadness and depression began to envelop her. How could this happen? And on such a beautiful sunny afternoon in May.

All hunched over on her knees, with dirt under her fingernails, Sally had almost finished the lengthy and enjoyable process of planning and planting a flower garden. It was the first time she had done this in her adult life. Throughout her whole time on the medical school faculty back in Philadelphia, she had always lived in apartments. She had neither time nor opportunity for gardening, a pleasure she never really missed that much. The ever-increasing prestige and fame from her blossoming career gave her all she needed for a happy, satisfying life. It also helped sustain her through difficult times: her divorce and, later, the sadness of her son's scary problems in high school.

Now that she was practicing in rural Maine, she found new things to bring her satisfaction. She finally owned her own home—a historic sea captain's house, which she thoroughly renovated and restored, after much research into Federal–period architecture. It was a totally engaging project that brought much happiness and satisfaction and helped to fill up the hole in her life caused by the loss of her career. Practicing medicine in Maine turned out to be not very satisfying. It was merely a job. Not a career.

But, at least, in Maine doctors still took Wednesday afternoons off, just like her grandfather used to do when he practiced back in rural Illinois. It was probably the thing she liked best about practicing in Maine. Wednesday afternoons in the garden were supposed to be happy and relaxing. But an unhappy, lonely feeling began seeping in after she realized that when she finished putting in her dahlias, everything would be done. No more projects left. Nothing to make life satisfying. She tried to figure it out.

I've lived in Maine for nearly a year now. I finally have my own house and everything, but I still don't have the slightest idea how to get a happy and satisfying life in this backward rural community on the coast of Maine. Why did I ever move here? She could not stop herself from thinking about the overpowering problem that caused her to decide to move up to Maine in the first place.

Sally's son, Sam, began having troubles when he entered high school. The gang culture and drug use in his school were growing problems. The local PTA had tried to inform parents about the problem. They invited parents to meetings where they could learn how to deal with it. Sally had been able to attend only once. They told her that boys with single moms were at a much greater risk.

A brief revue of the psychology literature on adolescent developmental problems gave her the impression that in today's culture, teens developed an emotional accelerator much earlier, before they learned to steer or use the brakes.

At first Sam didn't seem to be affected. But gradually, after he entered puberty, his devotion to class work began to fade, and his grades fell to the C-minus level. His participation on the junior swim team, thanks to training at the YMCA, was the only positive thing in his life.

Throughout his freshman year, Sally toyed with the idea of private school. Her ex-husband was not very supportive of that idea. Things remained the same until near the end of his sophomore year, when one of Sam's friends was murdered by a gang. Sam was terrified of school. In desperation, Sally decided to move as soon as possible.

She researched extensively and checked out most of the places advertising to hire an ophthalmologist. Then, she went online and found out which places in the United States had low gang culture rates. The job opening in coastal Maine looked like the best choice, despite the sacrifice of her academic career.

Seeing her son, Sam, get away from the gang and drug environment in Philly and settle into a new high school was very satisfying. Getting accepted to the high school swim team seemed to restore his motivation and self-esteem. This alone was enough to justify her decision to move up to Maine. Plus, she had the joyous task of restoring the historic old house, with endless reading and studying about Federal–period houses, so she could furnish it with style and dignity. A pleasant endeavor that completely filled all of her spare time and brought her enough satisfaction and happiness to fill the void in her ego caused by the loss of her promising career. But that task was finished a few weeks ago.

And now she was just completing the last project on her list: designing and creating a splendid garden to complement the house. A job she had been planning and looking forward to all winter long. Almost done. What next? She took a moment to ponder what she might find to do, now that the garden was almost finished. Sally could not see a single new, or interesting, project on the horizon. Just fog. And a feeling of emptiness.

She managed to plant the last pansy before she realized that, without the prestige and esteem of the medical faculty, life in Maine might even become lonely and boring. *No more projects on the horizon to occupy my mind. Hardly any friends. No women I'd care to hang out with. And no men educated and sophisticated enough for any personal relationship. Just a bunch of redneck lobstermen. That's the downside of living in Maine. I haven't the faintest idea of how to get a life. And what's gonna happen if Sam goes off to college and leaves me all alone in the house?*

Sally felt like she really needed to get out of this fog. It was all too depressing to even think about. She went inside and made herself a glass of iced tea. Sitting out on her sunny back porch, the birch trees in full blossom, blue jays squawking at the bird feeder, she tried to cope with the idea that she might be getting depressed. *Hmm. Strange noises those birds were making.* She shook her head. *Ahh!* It was the new ring on her cell phone. *That's it.*

"Hello, Mom! I didn't expect you'd be calling," Sally said as she answered the phone.

"Well, since doctors in Maine still take Wednesday afternoons off, I figured this might be a good time to catch you."

"Well, you didn't catch me at a very good time. I'm having sort of a down day today."

"Oh, yeah? What seems to be the problem?"

"I think it's because I've finally run out of interesting projects to occupy my mind and keep me happy. With Memorial Day coming up, I'll be on call all weekend, with nothing to do. I realize it's really kinda lonely up here in Maine. And my medical practice, here in Maine, doesn't bring much satisfaction. It's just a job."

"Gee! That's too bad. But I'm sure you'll figure out something. So how is Sam making out these days?"

"Sam is doing better, but he still has a long way to go. His senior year in high school is coming up. That's a critical turning point in the destiny of his life. It's like he shifted out of reverse and into neutral. But I can't get him to shift into drive, so he can start going forward. He doesn't have much interest in class work or getting good grades. So far, being on the swim team is all he cares about."

"Well, keep working on it. I know you can do it, if you try. Besides, it's your duty as a mom."

"Mom, I know all that. And I have been working on it, but I haven't come up with a plan yet. I figured that he'd just blossom once I transplanted him into a more fertile environment. But it's not happening. That's just part of what's getting me down. I'm also getting pretty lonely here in Maine."

"Well, now that you have more time on your hands, maybe you'll find a chance to make some friends. You know, get involved with community activities. If you look around, I'm sure you'll find some things that interest you."

"Well, it doesn't look too promising right now. I didn't even consider social issues when I made the hasty decision to move up to Maine. At the time, all I cared about was getting Sam away from the druggies and into a more wholesome high school environment. And making certain it was in a place where I could find a job in ophthalmology. Turns out, folks around here are a lot like the farmers back home in Illinois. Here, they're all lobstermen. Uneducated and not very interesting."

"Sally, if that's true, just look around a bit. I'm sure you'll be able to find pleasant people to socialize with."

"Mom! I didn't spend all those years going through medical school and residency training just so I could spend the rest of my life going to knitting clubs and dating some guy in a pickup truck. It really bothers me that my career has hit the skids. And I really miss my life as a professor in a medical school. In our society, women get a bum rap. Men don't have any responsibility for bearing children and raising them. I wouldn't be in this mess if I didn't have to raise a child. It's not fair. Men don't have to choose between having children and having a career. And without my career, I just don't see any way for me to find happiness and satisfaction in life here in Maine."

"Get a life, Sally! You just can't see the forest for the trees."

"Bye, Mom." *Click.*

Sally just shook her head in amazement. Somehow, anger at her mom had forced the depressive feelings completely out of her consciousness. Anger seemed a lot easier to handle than depression. A few minutes later, Sally decided she should really call her mom back and apologize. Then she happened to glance at her watch, and reality set in. She needed to get on the road right away if she wanted to have enough time to stop off at the greenhouse and buy some dahlia bulbs before she picked up Sam at the YMCA, after swim practice. She needed to have some extra time because of all the construction delays on the road. In the driver's seat she forced herself to concentrate on which dahlia bulbs would best complement her garden plan.

That seemed to work. Both the anger and depression vanished by the time she got to the top of the Pitch Pine Hill and saw that, at last, all the roadwork and one-way traffic were finally gone. The new scenic turnout and rest stop had been completed. Sally couldn't resist the urge to turn left into the rest stop and check the place out.

What a *view!* Out on the road, the huge trees next to the pavement totally blocked the view. *You could never see any of this breathtaking landscape.* Now, at last, the forest was really visible—a vast expanse, covering a scenic peninsula, extending out to sea. *Mom was right. Until now, I couldn't see the forest for the trees. I need to find some way to get this kind of perspective on my personal life.*

Sally quickly spotted her own house, near the left side of the peninsula. . *Oh my God! There is a large cove, not far from the front of my house. I never realized it was so close. The heavy forest across the road from my house blocks that view too. Guess I also can't see the ocean for the trees. I'll have to check that out. Looks like there might be some interesting exploring to do this summer. But right now it's time to get back on the road and get my errands done.*

While waiting for a break in traffic and an opportunity to get back onto the highway, Sally was pleased that her sense of loneliness had somehow disappeared. Then suddenly, an old pickup truck came to a stop, holding up the traffic and blinking its lights, signaling that it was okay for her to pull back onto the road. To her surprise, the truck made a right turn and pulled in just as she was pulling out. The driver, somehow, looked familiar to her. Quite a handsome hunk, he was. Probably no one she would know, driving a rusty old pickup truck, loaded with lobster traps. *Damnit! Why is it the only guys I find attractive are always driving around in old pickups? I gotta do something about that.*

Tom MacMahan could not believe the scenery before his eyes when he parked his pickup in the rest area. Eager to check the place out, he switched off the engine and just shook his head as the reality sunk in. *I've lived here since I was a kid, but I've never been able to see this view before. Now I can finally understand why they built this scenic turnout. I always thought they were nuts, especially whenever I'd get caught in the traffic delays during all that construction.*

The panorama of a broad, wooded peninsula, stretching out to sea, was romantic, with islands nestled all around. The eastern shore bordered the banks of a large river, flowing from deep in the heart of Maine and out into the Atlantic Ocean. The western shore bordered on a broad, deep-water cove, which opened out to sea.

Breathtaking! This spot is so awesome. You could never see this from the road because of all the trees. Probably a good thing. A view like this would take a driver's eyes off the road and probably cause a lotta accidents.

Tom took a moment to savor this inspiring new perspective of the Maine coast, which then seemed to trigger an inspiring new perspective on his own life. He took a moment to think about that.

No doubt about it. He could feel something exciting happening inside. This was the first time since his wife died, eight months ago, that he had bothered to take a Wednesday afternoon off. After her death, working full time at his medical practice was the only thing left in life that still gave him any satisfaction. Somehow, walking into his office and putting on the white coat and tie completely changed the way he felt about life. Drape the stethoscope around his neck, and he was a whole new person—no longer a lonely widower with no life to live. With the doctor's suit on, he was still able to get a life.

Tom kept on trying to analyze what was happening, but the scenery in front of him displaced all other thoughts. He slowly scanned all the houses, most of them over two hundred years old, scattered across the land on sites that were once working farms. Like the rest of Maine, most of the land was no longer cultivated and had returned to forest, just as it was when the first settlers arrived. In the quaint little village of Snug

Harbor, snuggled along the western shore, houses were much closer together. Tom felt a certain satisfaction from knowing the residents of almost every single house on the peninsula.

He rolled down the windows to let in the warm southwest wind, blowing in from the sea. After several deep breaths, he became even more aware of something stirring inside himself.

It was the first time, since his wife died, that he felt "in the moment." Alive again. Kind of like a dahlia bulb, after spending all winter in the cold dark basement, suddenly feeling the sprouts of life. Eager to be placed back in the moist warm soil of a garden in spring. And how nice it was to be a doctor and be able to take Wednesday afternoons off. The perfect opportunity for replanting the dahlias in his own garden. *I was wondering what I was gonna do this afternoon.*

He took another deep breath and looked out to sea. Lobster boats were everywhere, putting out their traps and getting ready for lobster season. *Ahh. There she blows.* The *Shady Lady,* his own lobster boat, was just off Mark Island. Arthur Prince at the helm. *Better git on goin'.*

Tom cranked up the engine and pulled back onto the road. Both cab windows were open, left elbow out the window. In truckin' mode. Near the bottom of the hill he detected the aroma of the mud flats over on First Creek. Must be low tide. He savored another aromatic whiff of the flats and felt a twinge of happiness as he drove across the bridge. It had been a long time since he had felt this good. He couldn't help wondering what might happen, in his life, now that the grieving had finally started to go.

He reached the village of Snug Harbor, drove on past his dock, and stopped at the general store. He went inside, picked up a six-pack of beer (to help with his gardening chores), and looked around for something he could heat and eat for supper. *Oh my god! Fiddleheads. Can't pass them up.* He threw a mess of 'em in a plastic bag, grabbed a package of frozen Lean Cuisine, and checked out.

When he got back home, the *Shady Lady* was already tied up to the dock. Arthur Prince, dressed in his yellow oilskin overalls, was starting to unload crates of lobsters. Tom went on down to the dock and offered a beer to Arthur, and then they shared the chores of servicing the boat.

"Today's gotta be Wednesday," Arthur commented. "The doctor's day off. Whatcha got goin' this afternoon, Tom?"

"Plantin' my dahlias," Tom replied. "I promised Caroline, before she died, I'd keep 'em going every spring, so long as I am alive. They were her favorite flower. I'm plantin' 'em this afternoon. After supper I'm watching the Red Sox."

"Well, ya got a good day for it. I might could plant my dahlias this afternoon. Noticed the bulbs already startin' t' sprout down in the basement. Ellie's been after me to git 'em in the ground."

"I picked up that load o' lobster traps you ordered. Thought I'd save ya a trip."

"Thanks a bunch, Tom. Gimme a hand, and we'll git 'em unloaded."

"By the way," Tom said as they left the dock and started up the hill toward the road, "fiddleheads are in, over at the general store, in case you're interested."

"Finest kind. I'll pick some up on the way home."

Tom succeeded in planting all the dahlias and completely weeding two flower beds before the sun slipped off the horizon and into the ocean, still radiating an abundance of pink and red light up into the patchy clouds overhead. *A dramatic display,* Tom thought. *Life is good again!*

Somehow, getting his fingers into the soil helped to complete the process of reconnecting himself with life. It seemed like his batteries had finally been recharged. He was even motivated to start back again with his daily swim at the YMCA during lunch hour. He packed up his tote bag with a bathing suit, goggles, and a towel, and set it by the door so he would not forget them in the morning. Then he turned on the Red Sox, opened a beer, and started fixing his fiddleheads.

Later on, during the festivities of the seventh-inning stretch, it occurred to Tom that this was the first time in over a year that he had enjoyed watching a baseball game. With the Sox in the lead, the announcer raved on with wild expectations for the coming months of this season. This prompted Tom to wonder what kind of great things might be in store for him in the coming months. A fresh, new way of thinking for Tom. Since Caroline's death, he lived mostly in the past. It had been a long time since he had even bothered to contemplate the future. What was about to happen would be beyond his wildest expectations.

~

Cathy Dyer's glasses fogged up when she reached the steamy atmosphere of the YMCA hot tub, late on Thursday morning. She took off the glasses, grabbed the handrail, and began her descent into the bubbling, thermal waters. Her first time in a hot tub, she was somewhat anxious about how it might feel. With her eyes closed, she lowered herself into the water. She savored the sensuous warmth, slowly moving up over her thighs and hips, oozing in around her breasts. *Ahhh!* It felt so good. What a release! Only after she opened her eyes did Cathy recognize the other person in the hot tub with her.

"Cathy. What an unexpected pleasure, having you share the hot tub with me today."

"Mrs. Norton? Oh my God! I'm so nearsighted, I almost didn't recognize you without my glasses on," Cathy answered, embarrassed for having ignored her boss, the vice president of nursing services at the local hospital. Nothing was going right today.

Cathy adjusted her position slightly and let the hot water jet massage her lower back. She could feel the muscle spasm begin to release. She was gradually able to pull her knees up to her chest. *Ahh!* Relief at last. Now, maybe, she could work on repairing her social faux pas.

"I didn't intend to ignore you, Mrs. Norton. It's just that my back was really killing me, and this is my first time in a hot tub. It's a pretty overwhelming experience, if you know what I mean."

"Please call me Betty," she replied with a warm, motherly smile. "And I know exactly what you mean, Cathy. Hot tubs are supposed to be like that. So tell me. What's going on with your back?"

"It happened when I was lifting my daughter onto the school bus this morning. She gets very clingy when she knows she has to leave me to go and stay with her father for a week. I couldn't make her climb into the bus by herself, so I lifted her. Rather awkwardly, it seems. I got a really bad spasm in the lumbar muscles. The pain hung on all morning. I could barely walk. My neighbor suggested the hot tub. So here I am."

"Well, you've come to the right place. I can see you already look a lot more comfortable."

"Oh, yes. It really helped a lot. I'm amazed," Cathy said. "So, what brings you here today, Mrs. Norton?"

"I'm in here almost every day," Betty replied, "after I finish my daily workout. Usually the hot tub is pretty busy at noon. But I guess all this nice weather has people exercising outside. But—come to think of it, Cathy—I'm amazed that you haven't ever used the hot tub before."

"I just joined the YMCA. Well, rejoined, I guess, is more like it. We had a family membership back when we first came to town. Brought my daughter here for swim lessons and used the workout room occasionally. But then, after the divorce, I couldn't afford a membership, and, besides, I was too busy with school, finishing up my B.S. in nursing to come here anyway. But now that I'm back working at the hospital again, with a much better-paying job, I can afford a membership at the YMCA, among other things."

"That's nice to hear. Especially that you're happy with your salary at the hospital. It's very important to me, you know, that our nurses are happy."

"Well, Mrs. Norton, I did do some checking after I graduated from nursing school, and I was surprised to find that you pay the highest salaries in the whole state of Maine, in case you didn't already know."

"Please, just call me Betty. I know you're new around here, but nearly everyone in a small Maine town goes by their first name. Formality is kinda useless when you know each other as well as we all do. But you are right about the pay. With the shortage of health-care workers in Maine, high pay is the only way to keep the place fully staffed. I sure hope you're not intending to leave us any time soon, Cathy."

"Not hardly. I'm stuck in this town for a good ten years or more. My ex-husband and I share custody of our daughter, Britney. I have to live around here so I can be with her. Know what I mean?"

"Well, sort of. I never had any kids, so—"

"Well, she needs her mother here until she's old enough to go off to college. So I've got to figure out some kind of a life for myself, right here in Maine."

"I'm sure you'll figure it out. Most people really enjoy living in Maine, once they get the hang of it."

"Honestly, Betty, rural Maine is not the place for a single woman to live a decent life. Career opportunities are very limited. And the social scene is dead. At least for me. I should have listened to my mother."

"Is that right? What did she say?"

"Well, first you have to understand my mother. She was a confirmed feminist. Totally against traditional marriage. When she found out I was pregnant, she told me to get an abortion and finish college. She thought I should get a good start on my career before I thought about having children. And not to bother getting married. If a woman wants to live a full life, it was her opinion that men were not necessary."

"Interesting ideas your mom had. Do you agree with her views?" Betty asked with an engaging smile.

"Well, not entirely," Cathy responded, pleased at seeing the smile. Feeling a little more relaxed, Cathy was now able to appreciate Betty's slim figure and stylish hairdo. "At least, not for me. I'm still undecided on some of her big issues."

"Your mom sounds like a fascinating person. What kind of social life did she enjoy?"

"Well, for one thing, she was an operaholic."

"An alcoholic?"

"Well, she was that too. But I said opera-holic. She loved opera. It was the centerpiece of her social life. She saw life as one big dramatic tragedy. She dragged my sister and me to so many operas, we're kinda hooked too."

"I know what that's like. My husband drags me to operas. But I never get hooked," Betty said with a sigh. "So tell me, Cathy, what did your mother do for a living?"

"For a living? Well, my mother had her PhD in history, and she taught at a number of women's colleges over the years. Women's rights were her special field of interest. And to set an example for her students, she made a point of never getting married, Raising her family without a husband."

"But you're not saying she was a lesbian, I take it?"

"Oh, no. She had relationships with all kinds of men. She just wanted to demonstrate that women were capable of much more prominent, you know, independent, leadership roles in society than our culture traditionally allows," Cathy proudly reported. "And without a husband to lead the way. Know what I mean?"

"Sounds like an interesting lady. What kinda guy was your father?"

"Well, I never knew my dad. Mom thought it was better if I didn't know who he was."

"That seems a bit strange."

"Yeah. Unless you knew my mom. But she did reassure me that he was a really great guy. She dated him specifically to have him be the father of her child. Had a PhD in mathematics and taught at one of the Boston colleges. Mom says she ran a careful check on his family and his children before she made her selection."

"Isn't that amazing? Told you all that but wouldn't say who he actually was?"

"Right," Cathy responded. "Mom said it was important for me to know that I had inherited great genes, but if my father's wife and children ever found out that he had had an affair, it would cause a lot of unnecessary trouble."

"Wow! Your mom sounds like an amazing person."

"Yeah. She's amazing. If I had only just listened to her, I wouldn't be in this mess." Cathy sighed and thought for a moment. "Oh my God! I can't believe I just said that. If I had done what my mother said, I wouldn't have Britney."

"Britney? That's your daughter?"

Cathy nodded.

"And how old is Britney?"

"Nine."

"I see. And what was it that brought you up to Maine in the first place?"

"My ex-husband is from Maine. After he got out of the army, we moved here."

"And when did you go to school to get your LPN?"

"After my daughter was born." Cathy, starting to tear up, stopped and thought for a moment. Betty kept on looking straight at her with a sympathetic smile. When Cathy looked up and saw the smile, she continued. "See what I'm up against, Betty? It's just not fair. Men are free to do whatever they want in life. They don't have to worry about taking care of kids. Women have an unfair disadvantage in our society. Only, in Maine, it's worse."

"Cathy, dear, I can sure see you have a problem there. But things may not be as glum as they seem. There are some career opportunities out there that might interest you. Stop by the office some time, and I'll fill you in. There is also opera. Down in Portland, from time to time. My husband loves to go. I'll have him put your name on their mailing list. As for your social life, you're on your own in that department. Right now, I've got to be getting out of this tub and heading back to the office. I've got a meeting this afternoon."

"Yeah! I've got to go too. Whew, it's getting hot in here."

"You're right about that," Betty agreed. "It helps if you exit slowly. Sit on the edge and dangle your calves in the hot water jets." She crawled out and repositioned herself.

Cathy crawled out too. But she sat on the deck and began some stretching exercises, now that her back had loosened up. *Oh my God!* she thought in the middle of a stretch. On the other side of the plate glass wall, she saw a man climb out of the swimming pool. She reached for her glasses, wiped off the fog, and put them on in time to see him bend over and pick up a towel.

"Wow! Look at that," she said.

"Where?" Betty asked.

"In there, by the edge of the swimming pool. That guy, starting to dry himself off. What a build!"

Cathy felt something happen inside as she watched him flex his pecs and lats, rubbing the towel back and forth across his back. A rare specimen.

"That's Tom MacMahan. You know. From the hospital."

"You mean Dr. MacMahan? Oh my God, yes. I can see his blue eyes. Looking right at me." Instinctively, she sucked in her stomach, turned slightly, and, without even realizing it, stuck out her breasts. "Even with my glasses on, I would never have recognized him by myself," Cathy went on. "At the hospital, he's always covered up with that white coat and tie. Who'd ever guess he could have abs like that? Does he come here often?"

"Tom has been swimming here since he was a kid. In fact, we were on the high school swim team together. Helluva swimmer, he was. And he's been pretty regular, swimming here ever since he opened his practice here in town. Except after his wife died last year. He laid off for quite a while. But it looks like he's back swimming again."

Cathy said nothing.

Betty picked up her towel and started to leave. "Listen, Cathy, if you have any interest in furthering your academic career in the future, do stop by my office sometime."

Cathy nodded an acknowledgment and thanked her, never taking her eyes off the gorgeous masculine specimen, strolling toward the men's locker-room door.

Chapter 2

During her lunch break on Thursday, Sally dialed up her mom. "Hi, Mom. Sorry about hanging up on you yesterday. Guess I was having a down day."

"It's okay. I could tell you were already upset when you answered the phone. But thanks for calling and apologizing. I hope you are feeling better now."

"Not really. Sam got arrested for drunk driving last night."

"I can't believe it! I didn't even know he was into alcohol. When did he take up boozing?"

"Last night, if you can believe what he says. He swore that it was his first time, and he didn't realize what a strange effect it would have on him. Said he didn't like the taste of it and he'll never drink again."

"Well, that's too bad, Sally. What do you reckon they're gonna do to him?"

"The policeman I talked to last night said he'll probably lose his driver's license for six months. That's going to cause us some big transportation problems."

"I'm sure you'll figure it out. Stay in touch, and keep me posted on how things turn out, okay?"

"I'll try. Bye, Mom." Sally was at her wit's end. *Guess I should never have moved to Maine. Nothing's going my way.*

~

Sitting at her desk in the ICU nursing station later that Thursday afternoon, Cathy felt an exciting touch of joy when she saw the white coat and tie, complete with stethoscope around the neck, come strolling into the ward. "Good afternoon, Dr. MacMahan! Surprised to see you in here so early."

"Well, my last cardiac stress test got rescheduled, so I'm getting off early, for a change. Care to join me on rounds?"

"Be delighted. I was hoping you'd ask. The girls say you make everything so interesting."

"Humph!" Tom grunted as he pawed through the chart rack. "Just part of the job. Kinda surprised to see you in here though. Didn't you used to work in OB?"

"That was back when I was only an LPN. Now that I've got my BS in nursing, they put me on the medical ward."

"Excellent!" Tom replied as he began reviewing his first chart. "Are you familiar with this lady's problem? She's pretty interesting."

Cathy's fascination blossomed. The privilege of participating in rounds with a doctor was never extended to her when she was an LPN. She was still getting used to her new role. Now it was her first opportunity to make patient rounds with Dr. MacMahan.

"I notice her fever has finally come down," Tom said, looking at the chart, as they entered the patient's room. "And look! Her heart is back in normal sinus rhythm. That's encouraging."

"Very nice. Do you think we could stop her nasal oxygen and let her go to the bathroom?" Cathy proposed.

"Good idea. Just keep her cardiac monitor on, in case she goes back into heart block. "How are you feeling this morning?" he asked the patient.

"Much, much better, thank you. My headache is almost gone. Thank God! Or maybe I should be thanking you, Dr. MacMahan."

"The thanks should go to the nurses. They provide most of the care. The doctor's job is to create the most effective guidelines for giving the care."

When the examination was finished, they left the patient's room.

"I didn't know Lyme disease could cause heart block," Cathy said after they left the room. "How did you figure that out?"

"It wasn't easy. At first, they thought she had chronic fatigue syndrome, or maybe fibromyalgia. Then she developed a severe headache, stiff neck, and fever, like you see with meningitis. So they put her in the hospital. They called me in when they discovered the heart block. I had seen a few cases like this, back when I was in Boston. Lyme disease is more common down there."

"*Borrelia burgdorferi,*" Cathy piped up. "Isn't that what causes Lyme disease?"

"Exactly," Tom replied. "I'm impressed that you know that."

"I went and looked it up when they found out that's what she had. I've never had a patient with Lyme disease, so I checked it out on the hospital computer. It's really a handy resource for looking up information about patients' diseases, and treatments, and all kinds of things. All the nurses use it."

"Good job! Things go a lot better when nurses are well informed."

Cathy spent the next half hour with Dr. MacMahan, visiting patients, discussing their illnesses, and refining treatment strategies. Near the end of their rounds she realized that this was the most intellectually satisfying experience in all of her medical career. *Going back to school was worth it. When you get your RN degree, doctors treat you like you know something. It feels good to really be a part of the team. Not just a bat boy, anymore. And Dr. MacMahan has a very collaborative manner. Nice just to be around him.* She left him at the desk for a while. It was hard to believe the man in the white coat was the same well-built man she saw at the YMCA pool this morning. She could hardly wait for him to finish writing all his orders.

After he had finished all his charts, Tom looked up and noticed Cathy, still standing close to his desk, studying him, with a smile on her face.

"Whatcha got coming up for Memorial Day?" Tom asked, feeling surprised at himself for even asking.

"I'm doing evening shift in the ICU, Saturday, Sunday, and Monday," Cathy answered with a downcast look. "Did you have something in mind?"

"No, not really. I mean, I don't know," he said, running his fingers through a full head of hair. "It's just that Memorial Day is kinda special for us Mainers. The only warm holiday we get before the summer people arrive. Got the state all to ourselves. A good time to go up to camp and do some fishing. Know what I mean?"

"Not exactly. I was planning to spend the holiday in Boston, for some R & R. Maybe take in an opera. But a lot of the nurses are off on family trips for Memorial Day weekend, so, being the low gal on the totem pole, I got tapped for extra duty. But I must say, they do give me a nice overtime bonus for the effort, which is something I really need right now."

"Yes. They are pretty careful about how they treat nurses at this hospital. But I'm curious why it is you need to go all the way back to

Boston to have fun." His blue eyes sparkled as he cocked his head in an inquisitive manner. "I used to live in Boston, and I always came up to Maine whenever I needed R & R."

"Well, for a single woman, the pickings are rather slim around here. Still, I mean, like if you're asking, I am off the next two evenings. Are you on call?"

"Not 'til Sunday morning. I split the weekend call with Dr. Cousins. Why do you ask?"

She took a silent breath. *Well, here goes.* "Since I'm off the social horizon in Boston this weekend, I wondered if you might be interested in getting together some evening. That's all."

Tom's dark brows shot up. "Me?"

"Yes," she teased, enjoying Tom's sudden discomfort. "You're single now. Are you seeing anyone?"

"Well, no, but I'm not sure we'd have a lot in common. After all, I'm a good bit older than you. Besides, I'm sort of out of it these days. I pretty much lost interest in women after my wife died."

"Maybe I could help you get over that." She smiled coyly.

"What makes you so interested in my problems anyway?"

"I saw you in the YMCA pool today," Cathy said, rolling her eyes upward with a dreamy smile. "Quite the hunk, you are. Tucked away under that white coat and tie you wear all the time."

"Humph! I had no idea I was under surveillance," Tom said, taking a moment to reassess his feelings. "That wasn't you in the hot tub room, was it?"

"Sure was."

"You know? We might could give it a try. I'm not on call for the next three nights. Take your choice."

Three nights later, on Saturday, the house was dark. Not even a back-door light was on. But a couple of drinks had wiped out all of Cathy's inhibitions. She went ahead and tried the back door. Unlocked. She went inside, turned on the kitchen light, and easily found a cocktail glass, which she filled with ice and a premixed manhattan. On a shelf she spotted a candle with matches on the holder. She grabbed that and headed up the back stairs, as quietly as she could.

Cathy managed to place the candle holder on the bedside table without spilling the drink in her other hand. She struck the match. *Scrritcch!*

What the devil was that? Sounded like a match? Rousing from a deep sleep, Tom struggled to reboot his mind as the shadowy, flickering image of someone standing by his bed slowly formatted in his brain. "Cathy? What's with the candle?" He glanced at the antique Seth Thomas clock hanging on the wall. "Christ! It's after midnight. I figured you probably changed your mind about comin' again tonight."

"After all the kindness and pleasure you shared with me the past two nights, there's no way I would let us waste your last night off call. I'm late because the girls wanted to stop off at Eddy's after we finished our shift and enjoy a couple of drinks."

Cathy set the cocktail on the table and stood there. The smoothness of her skin, her seductive brown eyes, the long sable hair, glistening in the shimmering light—it took Tom's breath away. Then, when she lay down alongside him on the old four-poster bed and pounced on him with a passionate kiss, Tom felt himself completely awaken. His response changed from passivity to desire. That's when Cathy interrupted the kiss and stood up.

"Guess what I've got for you," she said.

"What?"

"A double manhattan, on ice."

"But I'm on call in the morning," he protested.

"Not until 8:00 a.m. Here, drink it. You're going to need it. Making love is much better when you get rid of some of your inhibitions."

"Well, okay. If you say so." He took a sip. "How come you're so late gettin' here?"

"I just told you. A bunch of nurses went over to Eddy's for drinks after our shift ended. I knew you'd be sleeping anyway."

Tom sat up and sipped his drink, listening to Cathy, clinking around in the bathroom and filling up the bathtub. "You mix a pretty good manhattan," he shouted to her through the bathroom door. "Where did you learn that?"

"It's called a perfect manhattan. The bartender at Eddy's mixed it for me."

Clad only in his pajama bottoms, Tom laid his head back against the pillows and kept on sipping, basking in his cozy surroundings. Even though he had slept in this room for more than five years, he was still in awe of its tasteful decor. But his life, in the past year or so, had become so hectic the bedroom had become just a place to crash. Who cared how it looked?

Now that things in life were starting to shape up again, his appreciation for the finer things was recovering. Soft candlelight lent a romantic charm to the elegant bedchamber. It was amazing what artistic and technical skills they had at the end of the eighteenth century. The graceful old toile de Jouy, hanging from reeded posts of the canopy bed, a feature his mother-in-law had raved about, finally made an impression in some remote, artistic corner of his brain. The well-proportioned chimney breast and fireplace extended into the room across from the foot of the bed. *Mmm. Might be nice having a fire in the fireplace. Nah, too warm for that.* A gentle breeze, coming in through the window, blew across him, ruffling all the hairs on his chest. Lilac bushes bloomed out in the yard. Their aromatic scent poured in through the window, filling the room and complementing the effects of a well-mixed manhattan. *Mmm! A man doesn't get many moments like this in his life.*

The sound of water, sloshing into the tub, finally stopped, and a quiet air of enchantment crept into the atmosphere. Suddenly, Tom became aware of the peepers, their rhythmic peeping like a coded fax transmission. Peepers. Little tree frogs, barely an inch long. They could blow up their little lips like balloons. He had studied them back in high school. Hyla crucifer was not a member of the true frog family. That's about all he could remember.

He listened for a while and tried to eavesdrop on their froggy communications. His mind drifted back to when he and his brother used to visit their grandmother in the summertime. Usually, they slept out on the screened porch, where it was cool, and often they stayed up late, talking. Grandmother would encourage them to be quiet and listen to the frogs peeping.

"If you listen carefully and concentrate on the peeping," she said, "the frogs will tell you what's going to happen in the future. The Indians used to foretell the future by listening to the peepers."

The possibility of foretelling the future fascinated Tom. Still as a mouse, he would lie in his cot and totally concentrate on the rhythm of the peepers. Usually, just when he had the code almost figured out, he would fall off to sleep. As they grew older, Tom and his brother eventually concluded that the whole thing was an old wives' tale to make kids quiet down and fall asleep. But he still enjoyed hearing the peepers at night, even though he no longer believed in the messages.

The effects of the manhattan helped suspend his disbelief enough so that, by the time he was munching on the cherry from the bottom of his drink, he realized the frogs were telling him that something important was about to happen in his life. At long last, he was able to decipher their code. The frogs were just beginning to reveal their secret, when suddenly the bathroom door opened. Cathy came over to the foot of the bed, reached under the covers, and pulled off Tom's pajama bottoms.

"We won't be needing these," she said as she dropped her towel and slid herself under the covers.

Chapter 3

*I*t was 6:00 a.m. Tom was wide awake, as usual. He retrieved his pajama bottoms from the corner of the bedroom floor and tiptoed down the back stairs to the kitchen so as not to awaken Cathy.

Coffee. Industrial-strength coffee. That's what he needed. He built a pot with two extra scoops and went into the bathroom while it brewed. Tom had always kept his personal things in the downstairs bathroom so his early-morning ablutions would not disturb the rest of the family. Besides, it was his favorite bathroom. His father-in-law had devoted much of his fortune and time to preserving the grandeur and style of the old Federal house, even in the details of the bathrooms. The reproduction, antique plumbing fixtures were a complement to the beaded oak wainscoting. Starting his day in this room was always a pleasure.

The electric shaver buzzed, and Tom looked in the mirror. No sagging skin folds yet. His sideburns were starting to turn gray, but his hair was still mostly dark, and his hairline was not receding. For the first time in months, Tom had bothered to survey himself. Not that bad for a guy who just turned fifty. Suddenly, it dawned on him. *Three times in one night.* Tom couldn't even remember the last time he'd done it three times in a row. *Amazing.* And at his age. *Truly amazing. So that's what the frogs were trying to tell me last night. Or is something else about to happen?*

The coffee was ready. He poured out a cup and let it cool while he fetched the morning paper. After he finished the funnies and a cup of coffee, his mind drifted back to last night. There was no doubt about it. Something inside had changed. It was like waking up after a nine-month hibernation. Rip van MacMahan. Ever since his wife's death last year, Tom had resigned himself to spending the rest of his life feeling sorry for himself as a lonely widower. It seemed to him he had, more or less, quit paddling in the stream of life, floating along with the current, waiting for grandchildren. Maybe a dog to keep him company. After last night, he didn't seem quite as old as he used to be. Maybe there was someone out there who could wipe away the curse of loneliness in his life? Wouldn't that be great?

What a morning, Tom thought as his mind shifted back to reality. The present. *I am here.* He was no longer living in the past. Suddenly aware again of the world around him, he noticed the brilliant morning sun, shining down on the blooming tulips and daffodils around the border of the patio. They had been in blossom for weeks, but until now Tom had barely noticed them. He opened the window, and the fragrance of lilacs came pouring into the kitchen. *Mmmmm. That does it.* He went out on the patio for the rest of breakfast.

Considering the fact that he had slept very little, Tom was surprised at how rested and ambitious he felt this morning. He felt better than he had felt in months. Good thing he had a couple hours of sleep before Cathy came in. Cathy, on the other hand, having worked late last night, would no doubt sleep in. *Gosh. What a shame to miss such a beautiful spring morning. Don't get many days like this in a year.* It was perfect weather for a morning run. It was Sunday, and he was on call. But he didn't have to go into the hospital early on Sundays. There was plenty of time to run and be back before call started at eight thirty.

Tom's exercise routine—run four miles one day and swim a mile the next—had ended abruptly when Caroline died. He just started swimming again last week. Now it was time to get back into running.

Where in hell did I leave all my running clothes? He dug around in the bottom of the closet until he found his jogging shoes. Then he clipped his beeper and cell phone onto his sweatpants and set off. The satisfying, familiar anticipation of cardiovascular exercise came immediately back to him. He was like an addict—getting a hit and anticipating a high. The time had finally come to put some discipline and order back into his life. Eager with anticipation, Tom stopped off at the barn long enough to put some oats in the horse stable for Jerry. Then he started off.

He jogged at a gentle pace at first, along the riding trail that ran adjacent to the back pasture fence. *Oh, Jesus!* The spell was broken. Noise from a chain saw came roaring up from somewhere across the road. *How annoying on a Sunday morning. No self-respecting Mainer would run a chain saw on Sunday morning, except maybe up at camp.*

At the end of the pasture, the trail went into the quiet solitude of the

Hundred Acre Woods, a name he and his brother had given that area of forest back when they were children and enchanted by Winnie-the-Pooh. He smiled inwardly, remembering how his own kids had enjoyed the same fantasy about these woods when they were young.

The trail went up a long grade, and Tom was pretty much out of breath by the time he reached Pooh's house. He walked most of the way to Piglet's. The fragrant scents of spring filled his brain with pleasure as he caught his breath. Without thinking, he scanned the ground, searching for familiar, comforting plant life found in the woods. Bunchberries, already in bloom, crept over the woodland floor. Lady's slipper budded out and was ready to blossom. *I wonder if the trillium is out yet. Ahh! Yes. There it is. Just like when I was a kid.*

Shortly he emerged from the woods onto the upper meadow near the top of the hill. He went over to a large boulder, crawled up on it, and sat down to rest for a few minutes. He was not in very good shape these days. He leaned back on his elbows, propped up his legs, and took in the panorama from the top of the hill.

Down across the large meadow, shoots of green were pushing up through the tall, tawny brown hay that Tom had neglected to bale last summer. That would not happen again. This year, he would make hay. The lupine was up around the edges of the field, just getting ready to bloom. A few devil's paintbrushes were also in blossom—orange dandelion-like flowers with hairy leaves. A decorative finishing touch for a pastoral setting.

Down beyond the meadow and over a vast stretch of woods, Tom could barely see the cupola on his barn with its ornate wind vane. *Cheeyer! Cheeyer!* The unmistakable call of a cardinal distracted him for a minute. He scanned the treetops but could not locate the bird, only ubiquitous chickadees darting about. *Chicka dee dee dee.* The right kind of Sunday morning noise. Adjacent to the barn was an open green pasture with a surrounding white fence. Jerry was out grazing in the new spring grass, ignoring the breakfast oats Tom had placed in his stall.

Beyond the barn was his house. He still admired the classic Federal-period architecture, complete with widow's walk and all. Rebuilding the widow's walk was what had bonded Tom to the house. His father-in-law was recovering from a stroke when the roof first began to leak. The cost of a new roof, on top of college tuitions, inspired Tom to attempt the job himself: double-coverage roll roofing on a shallow pitched roof. It was fairly simple to apply but required lots of labor. With some help from his daughter, and technical advice from his father-in-law, Tom had a deeply satisfying summer vacation project. But the widow's walk was in ruin. The ornate wooden railing, nearly two hundred years old, was rotten and crumbling. Over the next year Tom reproduced the railing, with much mentoring and assistance in the wood shop from his recovering father-in-law. The collaborative and creative process formed a new bond between them and further cemented Tom's psychological investment in the historic old house.

It was nicely shaded to the south and west by huge old hardwood trees, including a few surviving elms. The lilac hedge on the north was in full bloom. It really could stand some pruning. Someday he would get to it. One more thing on his list.

The vegetable garden lay fallow, just like the large cornfield that stretched some twenty acres along the road. There was still time to plant. No reason to let another season go by. The pleasant task of planting the garden flashed briefly through his mind. His to-do list was growing. The honey-do list, as he used to call it, was a constant, heavy burden on his back. Strange, how good it was to feel that weight again. So much better than wandering aimlessly through life, living from day to day, as he had been doing the past nine months. Totally without purpose or goals. It felt good to be reengaged in life.

Across the road was a more modest house, where he had grown up. It was once the office building for the old shipyard, with property sloping gently down to the shore. Most of the other buildings had been taken down, except for a small shingled shack on the dock that his father had used as his fish house. The *Shady Lady* was tied to the dock.

Out in the harbor most of the fishing boats were at anchor. Pretty normal for a Sunday. A two-masted sailboat, fastened to a mooring over in First Cove, caught his attention. Was it a ketch or a yawl? Didn't really matter. Tom never cared much for sailboats anyway.

Besides, the hull was painted blue. That's a big no-no. All lobstermen are superstitious about blue boats. Blue always brings bad luck. Tom's rational brain knew this was nonsense, but something inside kept him totally biased against blue boats. Never would he own one. No use taking a chance on bad luck. *Must belong to some out-o'-stater who sailed up for the Memorial Day weekend. No gettin' round it.* The tourist season has begun, right on schedule.

With the morning sun warming everything up, and a fresh breeze to keep away the black flies, it would have been a perfect moment if it wasn't for the annoying whine of that chain saw. There was no doubt it was coming from somewhere down near the cove at First Creek. Probably that jerk with the blue sailboat.

No longer out of breath, Tom resumed jogging on the trail that ran along the upper border of the meadow. The one nice thing was that, with nobody riding Jerry these days, he no longer had to dodge all the horse poop on the trail. He passed by the cellar hole of the original York homestead, built back in the seventeen hundreds. There were still some mayflowers blooming around the old foundation. He stopped to pick a small bouquet and then continued running along the trail across the top of the meadow until he came to the stone wall surrounding the York family graveyard. He slipped in through a gap in the wall and walked respectfully past the markers of Yorks who had fought in the Revolutionary War, the Civil War, and both World Wars. The cemetery was bordered by a row of ancient oak trees. Tom wondered if he might somehow be related to some of the people in those graves. He sat down beside a headstone with the name Caroline York MacMahan engraved on it.

> Death is nothing at all.
> I have only slipped away into the next room.
> I am I and you are you.
> Whatever we were to each other,
> That, we still are.

That stanza from a poem by Henry Scott Holland was engraved beneath her name. The rest of the poem ran through Tom's mind as he sat there. He remembered the mayflowers. They used to be her favorite. Traditionally, they were given on the first of May. Tom used to leave them at the front door, ring the bell, and go hide in the bushes.

When Caroline answered the door and spotted the mayflowers, she began shouting out her favorite poem.

> Hooray, hooray,
> It's the first of May.
> Outside screwing
> Starts today!

Then she would pick up the flowers and run out to chase Tom around the yard. Sometimes, if it was a warm sunny day, she had even insisted they make love outdoors. He laid the flowers on her grave.

"Hi! It's me. Sorry I haven't been up to visit for a while, but I have been pretty busy all spring, it seems. Trying, you know, to get my life in order again. Swimming at the Y at lunchtime. Started back joggin' today. And I got the dahlias planted. That should help. Also, you might be happy to know, you were right. It looks like things may be happening just the way you said they should."

Shortly before she died, Caroline had presented him with a framed copy of Holland's poem and had told him that she did not wish for his life to stop just because her life was ending. She sincerely wanted him to find another woman with whom to share the rest of his life. "And it had better not be some worn-out old hussy either." A mature woman was what she envisioned. Someone who could form a close relationship, both physically and emotionally, with Tom. And with her daughters too. And someday, maybe, be a loving grandmother for her grandchildren.

At the time, Tom couldn't see how it would ever be possible for someone to fill that enormous void. But he promised he would try. And he hung the poem on the wall above their bed. The next morning he found a small sticker, proclaiming, "Make love, not war!" stuck onto the bottom edge of the poem. Caroline died that afternoon.

"Mind if I sit over here?" Tom asked as he moved out of the cool shadow of an oak tree and into a warmer, sunny nook in the stone wall next to her grave where the breeze kept away the black flies. Tom customarily did most of his visiting on that perch. He looked down at his father's dock and thought about the first time he met Caroline. It felt like it could have been yesterday.

It was the long red hair, glistening in the sunlight, that first caught Tom's eye as he gently guided his father's lobster boat into the dock. But it was the perfectly formed hips, displayed in tight-fitting jean shorts, that diverted his attention long enough to cause a wharf-rattling crash as he slammed the boat into the dock.

"Hey, buddy," said the redhead. "Is this your boat?"

"No, it ain't," shouted Tom's father from the stern of the boat. "And it ain't never gonna be if he don't start payin' more 'tention how he brings it into the dock."

"Don't mind him," Tom said. "Wanna come aboard and look around?"

"Sure."

She climbed aboard and introduced herself. Tom gave her an educational tour of lobster boats while he continued his work—putting the day's catch into the lobster car, cleaning out the bait boxes, and swabbing the gurry off of the deck.

"Gurry? What the hell is gurry?"

"Scraps of fish bait and stuff off the traps," Tom replied. "If you don't scrub it off while it's fresh, it gits all gormy and stinks like hell in the morning."

While he finished the deck, Caroline asked him about the local high school and if he went there. He could see her carefully appraising his muscular physique and could not stop himself from flexing into a virile pose as he reached for his T-shirt and pulled it down over his head and torso. He told her he was finished with high school. In fact, he was starting his senior year at Yale and was applying to medical school. She didn't seem particularly impressed.

"Where ya gonna be livin' around here?" Tom inquired.

"In that house across the street."

"The old York house? Are you serious?"

"Well, yes. Is that okay?"

"Finest kind! It's really a beautiful place."

"Boy, that's a crock. The place is a dump. My mom says Dad is going through a midlife crisis. He sold our house in Connecticut and his business, and we're moving up here so he can become a farmer."

"Is that so? Are you guys part of the original York family that used to own that place?"

"Unfortunately, yes." She went on to describe how unfair it was that she had been forced to leave all her friends back home in Connecticut, just because her dad had some lunatic idea of moving back to Snug Harbor, Maine, and reestablishing the family in its ancestral home.

"Oh, you might like it here, once you get used to it," he assured her. "York Farm is a wonderful place. It was abandoned the whole time I was growing up. My brother and I used to play in those woods all the time when we were kids. We had forts and hideouts all over the place. Later on we used to go partridge hunting in the old orchard. Be kinda nice to have someone livin' in it again. We used ta think there were ghosts livin' there when I was a kid."

"Well, just be glad you don't have to live there," she spit back. "Nobody has lived in that house for years, except maybe a bunch of spiders and mice. There's no dishwasher, so I have to help do dishes by hand. And, worst of all, there's no shower. I have to take a bath in a tub. How can I do my hair in a tub? They don't even care. It's just not fair."

"Well, I've never been inside the place," Tom replied, "only peeped in through the windows. But my mom and all her historical society friends always raved about that house because of the classic colonial architecture. They want to recommend that it be placed on the National Register of Historic Places. I'm sure your parents will put in modern appliances and bathrooms. All these old houses have been fixed up pretty nice. We have two showers at home. Be patient. Life ain't always fair. So try an' figure out how to make the best of all the bad things in life, so you can enjoy all the good things that come along."

The disdainful sneer on Caroline's face made Tom suddenly realize he had gone a little overboard in response to her helpless posturing. By then, it was too late.

"You sound just like my dad. I don't care how many bathrooms they put in that house. All I know is one more year of high school and I'm out of here," she proclaimed and stormed off the boat.

Tom didn't see her again for several years, but the image of her long red hair and the perfectly filled shorts, as she marched up the wharf, was permanently etched in his memory.

"I don't know if you are keeping track of what's going on around here or not," Tom said to Caroline, when his remembrance was finished. "Maybe you already know this, but here's the latest. Our girls are doing great. Kristen is applying to medical school, and Sherry has just moved in with her boyfriend. And I finally started seeing someone. Her name is Cathy. I think you'd like her. She's an ICU nurse at the hospital. Really smart. Kinda cute too. Probably not anyone you might have known. She's not from around here. Was an LPN on OB a while back, but she went back and got her bachelor's in nursing. Now she's in the ICU, working the evening shift. Turns out she's one of the smartest nurses I've ever seen. Probably could have gone to med school. Her ability to evaluate patients and understand the pathophysiology of their illness is amazing.

"Anyway. The other night, we had a few over at Eddy's and ended up spending the night together. Well, last night, she really showed me how much passion I still had left inside of me. Almost as good as you. Well, maybe not that good, but I'm kinda hopeful, you know? About myself. Maybe I'm not all washed up after all.

"Oh, yeah. She's got this tattoo on her left breast. *Liebestod* is what it says. Means 'love's death' in German. She said it comes from an opera, *Tristan und Isolde*. Don't think we ever saw that one. I didn't ask her what it meant to her personally. Didn't want to get too personal.

"Which reminds me. Sherry's got a tattoo too. She's too embarrassed to show it to me." Tom shrugged. "What can we do about it anyway?"

Tom started to get up but sat down again. "You know? I'm startin' to get tired of feeling lonely all the time. The way I've got it figured, having someone you really like, and knowing what they're thinking and how they're feeling, and knowing they know the same things about you, is what keeps people from feeling lonely in life. I'm hoping someday, maybe, Cathy 'n I will be able to get close. You know? Like we did.

"But I haven't figured out yet how to make that happen. With you, it was a piece of cake. I knew how you were feeling the first time I met you. We always talked. You know? Told each other how we felt inside. Cathy is a little more reserved. She's divorced and has one kid. A girl. That's about all she's told me so far.

"Who knows? Time will tell. But it sure is nice, still having you to talk over things."

The chain saw finally stopped. *What a relief!* Tom stood up again. "Sorry. Gotta get going. I'll stop in more often now that I'm back running again."

The trail continued on through the apple orchard. Running felt good now that he was somewhat rested. Besides, it was all downhill to the road. The rows of neatly pruned trees had been restored to productivity and profitability during the years after Caroline's father took over the farm. All the trees were in full blossom. Bees buzzed everywhere, preparing for a full harvest next fall. Tom subcontracted management of the orchard out to a nearby grower. There was a warm spot in his heart for the orchard, left over from years of partridge hunting here with his brother, back when they were in high school. He passed by his favorite spot and savored the memory of hitting a partridge in midair—after his brother, a much better shot than Tom, had missed it.

At the end of the apples was another stretch of woods before the trail came out on a dirt road that bordered the northern edge of the farm. Two partridges flew up from the side of the road and into the trees just as Tom stepped out into the open. He peered up into the branches to see if he could spot them. The only thing he saw was a sign. POSTED, NO HUNTING. He climbed up on the stone wall, tore down the sign, and threw it in the woods. Tom hated those signs. Posting the land was the only thing that Caroline's father had done to the place that Tom didn't approve of. But what else could he expect from out-of-staters?

Now that Tom had inherited the farm, it was time to unpost it. As he ran along the road, Tom took great pleasure in removing every POSTED sign he came to. He figured most of the folks lying in the cemetery would approve.

A smooth dirt country road is soft and gentle on a runner's joints and muscles. The urge to sprint was irresistible. His stride lengthened. Feeling the satisfying contractions in his gluteal muscles, he added even more kick to his stride. His arms swung in synchrony with his forward momentum, and his lungs pumped great volumes as he made the final stretch toward the finish line. It all came back to him in a rush of endorphins. Almost as satisfying as last night's sex. He pushed himself as long as he could, until he knew his brain had exhausted its supply of opiate enkephalins. Also, he was out of breath.

He slowed down to jogging pace. His mind was in the winner's circle. Tom caught his breath and savored a runner's high. As he came around a bend in the road, Tom spotted another jogger up ahead. *How unusual.* He almost never ran into anyone else running on these back roads. And especially a woman. Black spandex displayed her perfect anatomy. Well-defined gluteal muscles rippled temptingly with every stride. Poking out through the hole in the back of her baseball cap was a blonde ponytail, bobbing up and down. Tom felt a surge of testosterone and picked up his pace a little to overtake her.

Much to his surprise, he knew her. It was Sally Gardiner, the new doctor with the ophthalmology group. She had come to town over a year ago, but their separate specialties offered rare occasions for professional interaction. Besides, he could tell she was definitely not his type: baggy dresses and professorial aloofness. He never dreamed of what was underneath all that veneer.

The sound of footsteps, coming up behind her, altered Sally's awareness. She looked back apprehensively to see who might be stalking her. Much to her relief, she recognized him. Tom MacMahan, a doctor from the hospital. *Whew!* "Why hello, Tom. Jeez, I almost didn't recognize you without your white coat and stethoscope! You scared me there for a minute."

"Good morning, Miss Sally. Sorry, didn't mean to scare you. I saw someone running up ahead, and curiosity got the better of me. So seldom do I see other runners out this way. I just had to find out who it was."

"Gee, that's funny. I've been running here all spring. Ever since I moved into that house down the road, back in April. Surprising we didn't run into each other before now."

"That's probably because I stopped running for a while. Just started back today," Tom replied. "So, you must have bought the old Bennings place. I wondered who bought it. I've been a little out of touch for a while so I haven't done much snooping. How do you like it.?"

"Well, I really love it now. Great location. The yard has a lot of potential. But it took six months of renovations before we could move in." Sally cleared her throat and sniffed. "And you live close by, I presume?"

"Oh, yes. That's my property on the right. We own all the way over to the bay."

"No kidding. That's a gorgeous piece of real estate."

"Yes," Tom acknowledged, shaking his head in agreement. "Been in my wife's family for over two hundred years."

"Really! And are you originally from around here too?"

"Ayeah. Born and bred."

They lapsed into silence while Sally reprogrammed her mental image of Dr. MacMahan. Since first coming to the hospital nearly a year ago, this was the only time she had seen him without his white coat and stethoscope. As an ophthalmologist, she rarely had occasion for professional interaction with cardiologists. She had seen him at staff meetings and spoken to him occasionally in the doctors' lounge. He always seemed courteous but rather shy and distant. How different he appeared, all disguised as a normal human being.

"What a great morning for running, don'tcha think?" Sally observed, just to break the silence.

"That's for sure. I'm just getting back into running again. So—"

"Oh, look!" Sally interrupted. "An eagle! See him?"

"Oh, yeah. I see him, only that's not an eagle. It's an osprey."

"Really? An osprey? How can you tell?"

"It's hard to believe, but eagles are even bigger than that. Also, an eagle has a dark brown body with an all-white head. See, the osprey has a grayish, almost white, chest. And, I don't know if you can see it or not, but the osprey has a dark streak running up to its eye."

"Wow, an osprey. I've been seeing that bird almost every day for weeks. I always thought it was an eagle. I heard ospreys had all been wiped out by DDT?"

"Oh, God, no. They're everywhere. Wanna see his nest?" Tom asked. "It's not very far. Maybe a quarter of a mile down that dirt road, comin' up on the right. Here. It'll only take a minute."

"I'm game," Sally replied, following Tom down the narrow dirt road. "Where does this road go anyway?"

"It comes out on Back Cove, just around the corner, up ahead. You'll see in a minute. This road marks the back border to our farm, but I don't get over here very often anymore, so I'm a bit curious to see how things look."

"Back Cove? So that's what they call it," Sally said. "I never knew that cove was there until a couple of days ago. I drove into the new scenic turnout at the top of Pitch Pine Hill. When I scoped out everything and saw the cove right in front of my house, it blew my mind. I've been planning to explore around and check it out ever since."

The view opened up as they rounded the corner. A narrow cove led into a small bay. Out beyond several scattered islands was the open ocean. Sally slowed down a bit, trying to navigate the rocky, rutted, two-track, dirt road. Carefully watching where she stepped made it difficult for her to scope out the breathtaking scenery.

"Sorry about the lousy shape this road is in, but you gotta keep moving in here," Tom explained. "The black flies are wicked."

"I'll say. How do people manage working outdoors with all these damn things anyway?"

"Fly dope. Only I forgot to put it on this morning."

"Fly dope? Never heard of it."

"Insect repellent. Only, round here, we call it fly dope. Works great."

"Phewie!" Sally exclaimed. "What is that smell?"

"Clam flats. The tide is out."

Sally turned her attention away from the sea and gazed off to the east at the extensive flats. "It's no wonder there aren't any houses around here. Who could stand that smell?"

"Funny," Tom replied, "I like that smell. Reminds me of diggin' clams."

"You dig clams? Out there in all that smell?" She shook her head in disbelief.

"I used to dig clams on these flats when I was a kid. Somehow, I learned to like that smell. My kids liked to clam too. We all like that smell."

"Unbelievable."

"I'll tell you. Back when we were living down in Boston, I kinda forgot about that smell. But whenever we would come back home for a visit, as soon as I smelled a clam flat, I would feel at home. It's almost like a tranquilizer."

"It's hard to believe a smell as bad as that could ever make someone feel happy."

"I guess it's all according to what you're used to. Across there," Tom pointed out, "is where the Back River dumps into the cove. First Creek comes in on the left there."

"And all that flat mud out there." Sally nodded. "Those are clam flats too?"

"Ayeah!"

"And what's that big banking out there between those two points of land? Looks like a dike or a levee."

"That was once a dam for an old tide mill."

"A tide mill?"

"Well, a sawmill, to be more precise. Powered by the tides. You see, the dam—or dike, as we call it—held back the flow of the tide. We got eight foot tides round here. And the force of all that backed-up water came flowing through the opening in the dike. Well, that strong tidal flow, rushing through the hole in the dike, was what turned the water wheel that powered the sawmill."

"Fascinating."

"You can see where they built the sawmill. Look. There's still a lot of the old pilings that supported it, left over from the sixteen hundreds, when they first built it."

"Amazing! And do you know who those early settlers were?"

"The York family. My wife's ancestors. Their original home was up on that hill, overlooking this bay. Later they moved the ship-building part of the operation over to Snug Harbor. The water is deeper there, and it allowed them to build much larger boats—ocean-going ships. And they built themselves another house, across from the new shipyard. That's the house we live in now."

"Did they keep on running the sawmill?"

"Oh, yeah. Right up into the late eighteen hundreds, when the steam engine was developed. Timber was harvested inland, and the logs were floated down the river to the mill and turned into lumber. They used the lumber from here to build boats, which they then used to transport the rest of their lumber down to Boston."

"No kidding! Ouch! Damn black flies. And that's how the early settlers made their living?"

"Yeah. Well, yes, some of them anyway. Mills like this were pretty common all along the coast. The York family did pretty well at it. Later on, when they started making square riggers and larger ocean-going vessels in the new boatyard in the cove where I live, they built this road to transport the lumber over to the new yard. During the early eighteen hundreds, they sold lumber and barrel staves to the Caribbean islands for the rum trade. It was a prosperous business."

"Wow! You really know a lot about the history of this place."

"Well, I went to school here. Local history was an important subject. They ground it into us. Anyway, you see that big post with the sign on it, sticking out of the water? That's a navigational marker. The nest is on top. See? The osprey is taking something to the nest. He's feeding the babies."

"Look! Here comes the other one. She's got something to eat also. How can you tell which one is the female?" Sally asked.

"Humph! I'm not really certain. It's hard to tell them apart."

"Gee. I wish I had my binoculars. I might have to come back later and look around more. I'm starting to get interested in bird watching. How did you know the nest was there?"

"That osprey nest was there when I was a kid."

"No kidding! Do they nest there every year?"

"Ayeah. Every year for as long as I can remember. I doubt if it's always the same birds, but every spring, someone's always nesting there."

"That's amazing. Where do they go in the winter?"

"South. I don't know exactly where. But they come back every spring. Eagles don't migrate. They hang around all winter. They're great to see, but I'm fond of ospreys. I guess because you see them a lot more down here along the coast. You ought to have dinner sometime over at Eddy's Wharf. They have a couple of osprey nests around the restaurant, out in the harbor. 'N there are field glasses on all the tables, so the guests can watch the ospreys while they dine."

"Boy," Sally said, once they resumed jogging back out toward the main road, "those birds are amazing. Both of them were hard at work feeding those chicks."

"I think that's what fascinates everyone about ospreys. Watching them tend their nests."

"Such devoted parents, ospreys are."

"Yeah, Then, at the end of summer, they teach the kids how to fly and kick 'em out of the nest. Never see them again. Imagine, never seeing your children anymore. Or your grandchildren either. I guess they're not that connected."

Sally just shook her head in silence. "Do ospreys mate for life?" she finally asked.

"Ayeah, just like geese. Funny how some birds can bond for life and others pick and choose."

"Humph. Sure is strange, isn't it?" Sally opined, scanning the lush green horizon all the way out to the point where the blue ocean began. Many varieties of birds occupied the varied habitats along the shore and adjacent hills. "I can't get over all the birds there are in Maine. Lots more than I can ever remember back in Illinois. You know, bird watching is pretty interesting. It's great fun, learning about them and their habits. And this really is an interesting place. I'm coming back sometime with binoculars and my bird book. But right now, I've gotta be getting back home. I'm on call at eight o'clock, and I'm not wearing my beeper."

Jogging on the narrow road, with Tom behind her, Sally could not stop thinking about the ospreys. *Somehow, they have learned to bond for life, but humans, apparently, still don't quite have the hang of it. Maybe that's why Charlie and I got divorced. Strange. It felt like we were in love. At least, in the beginning. But maybe being in love is not quite the same as bonding for life. Maybe it's only the first step. Who knows?*

Now Tom turns out to be completely different from what I expected. Kinda cute. Not what you'd expect for an older guy. She got the impression that under that baggy sweatshirt he could be a real hunk. *And not at all put on or cultured, once you see him in his natural environment. Reminds me, in some ways, of the small-town guys I grew up with back in Illinois. Nice, but definitely, not my type. Damn! What's wrong with me? Every time I meet a new guy, some primitive program inside my brain has to try him on and see how he fits. It's not like I'm out there shopping around. Now is not the right time for me to be looking for another man*

in my life. Period. I've managed to keep out of the dating scene now for
nearly two years. I need to keep focused on getting Sam back on track,
more interested in school and getting better grades. So he can, maybe, get
accepted to college.

I can resist the urge to chase after men. Still, the proper thing, if you
want to be decent and neighborly, would be to invite Tom in for a bit.

They arrived at her house shortly. Tom accepted her invitation.

"Oh my God! What happened to the widow's watch?" Tom asked in disbelief when they got to the house.

"What do you mean, widow's watch?" Sally asked.

"On the top of the roof, there used to be this elegant, white structure, enclosed with windows, where you could sit and view out to sea. Supposedly, wives would have a cup of tea while they waited and watched and hoped to see their husbands' ship return from a voyage. While the men were gone, their wives were, sort of, temporary widows. Whatever made you get rid of it?"

"Well, it turns out there was this huge leak in the roof next to the widow's watch that I didn't know about when I bought the place. The contractor found all this rotten wood supporting the roof, and the stairway going up to the widow's watch. I saved a lot of money by not having to rebuild that structure."

"That's terrible," Tom replied. "You know, I was up there years ago. And I can tell you, if you had that widow's watch, you'd be able to see the whole cove we just saw and all the way out to sea."

"Rats! If I had known that, I would have borrowed more money and paid to keep it there. Now I can't even see the ocean for the trees, to paraphrase one of my mom's old sayings. But I still have the widow's watch in the garage. The contractor suggested I save it in case I change my mind and decide to reinstall it later on."

"That makes sense," Tom replied. "Putting the widow's watch back up there would restore the historic integrity of this place and make it much more valuable when it comes time to sell it."

"Sell this house? No way! After what I put into this place, I plan to die here," Sally replied, totally amazed that she had said that. Or even thought it.

They went around behind the house and entered through the kitchen. Sally's son, Sam, was busy at the open refrigerator.

"What are you doing, Sam?" she asked.

"Like, I haven't had any breakfast, in case anyone wants to know," he said.

"Oh, bother!" Sally said, her face lighting up in a smile. Tom was surprised to see the effect that the presence her child brought to Sally's face. She actually seemed beautiful for a second or two. "Tigger, there's someone here I'd like you to meet."

"Sounds like a line from Winnie-the-Pooh," Tom observed. "You folks must be Pooh fans too."

"Exactly," Sally returned. "Sam was always a Pooh fan. Sometimes, he still thinks he's Tigger."

"Sam, this is Dr. MacMahan. He lives on that farm on the left-hand side of the road, just before you get into Snug Harbor. And, it turns out, he is also a runner, like me."

Sam shook his hand and made bashful, polite conversation for a few moments and then excused himself. A friend was coming by to pick him up.

"Would you care to look around for a minute?" Sally asked.

"Sure would. Gosh, I haven't been in this place in years. I can see you've put in a whole new kitchen. And you put back the wainscoting in the dining room. I like that. Boy! You put a lot into this place."

"Yes. We tore out everything, insulated the walls, redid the plumbing and the electric. It took nearly a year by the time we finished all the furnishing and interior decorating. But it's been worth all the effort."

"Definitely. Wherever did you find all this great period furniture? I thought it had all been bought up."

"I spent all last year, it seems, in antique stores. That was an adventure. Of course, some of it's reproduction. An interior decorator down in Portland helped me a lot, finding stuff and putting it all together in a tasteful decor."

"Very nice job. I love it when people restore these historic old houses. This place is actually older than mine. Did you know?"

"Well, not exactly. I think the deed said 1790 or thereabouts. Anyway, I want to put a deck out back, and there's still a bit of gardening to do. But for now I've run out of money, so the rest of it's still in my dreams."

"I know what that's like. But it makes life more fun to always have some project in your head that you're working on. It's one of the joys of owning these old homes," Tom said, finishing off the last gulp of water in his glass. "I could use a refill, if you could spare a little more."

"Sure," Sally replied, opening the fridge and pouring out some cold, bottled spring water for both of them. "Shall we drink it out on the porch? I can show you what I've got planned for the backyard."

"Oh! And I see you have a bird feeder," Tom said, holding the door open for Sally.

"Sam gave it to me for Christmas. He made it himself in shop class."

"Nice job he did, building it."

"You're right," Sally answered. "They really do a good job motivating and teaching kids in the shop class." *Too bad,* Sally thought to herself, *they couldn't motivate him in the rest of his schoolwork.* "You wouldn't believe the birds we get. They are a real pleasure."

"Do you have much trouble with squirrels? They pretty much kept our feeders cleaned out most of the time. I haven't bothered to fill them lately."

"This feeder is pretty well designed. The squirrels don't have much of a chance. But we do have chipmunks."

"Chipmunks?"

"Yeah. Let me show you." She disappeared inside and returned with a handful of sunflower seeds. Sitting on the steps, she dropped a few seeds beside the porch steps. A chipmunk appeared almost instantly. She put a few seeds in the palm of her hand and held it out. "Come and get 'em, Freddie."

Freddie scampered up the steps, hopped right into her lap, reached out, and took a sunflower seed from Sally's hand. He stuffed it in his mouth, little dark eyes peering up at her. He had pale puffy lines above and below the eyes, and his whiskers twitched.

"Isn't he cute? Freddie the freeloader is what we call him. Sam gave him that name. He loves to feed him even more than me. He was the one who tamed the little critter."

Freddie kept on stuffing his cheeks with seeds from Sally's hand. All the while, his long fluffy tail, black and grizzled, twitched behind him like a metronome. When his cheeks would hold no more, he dashed down the steps and disappeared under the porch.

"He's a charming fellow," Tom said, glancing at his watch. "'Fraid I can't stay any longer. Gotta get movin' on. I'm on call today too. Gotta go in an' make rounds."

"Well, thanks for showing me the osprey nest. I really enjoyed having someone to run with for a change. Give me a call sometime. Maybe we could do it again."

"Good idea. I'll be in touch. Bye," Tom shouted as he headed down the road.

Sally felt a touch of satisfaction from her brief connection with Tom. Not at all her kinda guy. But still, nice to have as a neighbor.

Tom had two more miles of running to get back home. He could not believe how good it felt to run again after laying off for so long. He would probably be sore tomorrow. *In a way, that might feel good.*

What a pleasure, having someone to run with. Sally sure turned out to be a lot different from the way I had her figured. And surprising to see how nice she's restoring the Bennings' place instead of modernizing it or tearing it down, like folks seem to be doing on down the coast. And she's not that bad looking either, without all the frumpy clothes she wears around the hospital. And especially when she got a look at Sam. What a smile. When she smiles at him, she's actually pretty. Funny, how Sam can do that. Reminds me a lot of Mark, just before he died. I wonder if Mark ever made Caroline smile like that. You'd think I would have noticed if my son made my wife smile. How stupid can you get? I never really appreciated all the connections people have with each other until after I got disconnected. Wonder if I'll ever be able to reconnect again.

The smell of spring was in the air—bayberry, juniper, and spruce, coming back to life again after a winter of dormancy. Their pungent fragrance blended with the moist clean air, blowing in from the sea. In the swampy areas, the coiled heads of fiddlehead ferns were starting to emerge through layers of dead leaves. Maybe tomorrow he would have time to run over to Second Creek and see if he could get another mess of 'em. They were even tastier when he picked them himself and cooked them right away. Tom hoped no one had discovered his secret spot, over on Second Creek. He knew that this spring Granville Bailey had set up his alewife weir in Second Creek. *Sure hope Granville hasn't already cleaned out all the fiddleheads.*

At the top of the hill the road took a sharp turn. He looked over at the corner maple, a significant tree in Tom's life. The old Norway maple was already three feet in diameter when he was a child. He and his brother loved to climb it because it branched dramatically, close to the ground, and was easy to climb. It was under that tree that he drank his first beer. A momentous occasion. Liz Cross, Art Libby, and Lorna Bailey were with him that night. They were seniors in high school. Lorna had sneaked the beer out of her father's general store. It only took two six-packs to get everyone loaded.

But the most memorable event at that location, was the night, a few years back, when lightning struck the corner maple. The ambulance had just picked up Luther Drisko's boy, Clyde, and was rushing him to the hospital with severe difficulty breathing. Turned out he had acute epiglottitis. Just before the ambulance reached the top of the hill, lightning hit the corner tree and sent it sprawling across the road. With that huge tree blocking the road, there was no way of reaching the hospital. And Clyde barely had any airway left. He was turning dusky. The ambulance radioed the ER, and the ER doc called Tom on the phone because he knew Tom lived close by. Tom rushed to the scene, climbed over the tree, and managed to perform an emergency tracheostomy on Clyde in time to save the boy's life.

The cutoff stump of the old tree was still there after twelve years. Only it refused to die. Next spring, the root system sent up new shoots from around the perimeter of the stump, and many of them survived. Now the tree had a cluster of trunks, four to five inches in diameter, and was nearly thirty feet high. In some ways Tom felt as if lightning had struck him when Caroline died. There was nothing left of him but a stump and his roots. Tom wondered if he could ever grow some new branches. *If a maple tree can do it, so can I.*

By the time he was back on the paved road, the idea of a nice hot shower and a cold beer wiped out all other thoughts. Too bad he was on call. No beer. *Ahh, but maybe Cathy will be awake when I get back.*

Tom's fantasy was interrupted by a siren, wailing up from somewhere down in the harbor. Tom dreaded sirens. Too often it meant he might be called into the emergency room to treat someone sick or dying from a heart attack. Soon, the ambulance passed him. Arthur Prince was driving. He waved at Tom as he passed. Tom hoped whoever was inside had some injury that didn't require a cardiologist. Sirens were bad omens that sent shivers down his spine. He could hardly wait to get home and see Cathy.

When he got back home, a note on the kitchen table said that Cathy couldn't wait. She had to pick up her daughter and take her to the YMCA for her swim class. "And thanks for an unforgettable night." Tom drank a tall glass of ice water and headed for the shower.

Chapter 4

*O*n Sunday morning, George Gurnet woke up with the sun and hit the deck. His poor wife groaned loudly, rolled over, pulled the pillow up around her head, and then grumbled a protest about being so rudely awakened in the middle of the night.

"Sweet is the breath of morn. Her rising sweet, with charm of earliest birds." Whispering Milton's verse in her ear evoked yet another mournful moan, further invigorating his mood. He chuckled to himself as he quietly strutted out to the kitchen.

Eager to get to work on his project, he started a pot of coffee. Then he went into the bathroom to clean up and take all his medicines. George decided not to shave that morning and began opening the package containing his new Filson work clothes. He could hardly wait to get into them. A momentary pause in front of the mirror brought a satisfying self-appraisal. His unshaved face fit perfectly with the rugged, but still elegant, clothes. No wonder people said he resembled Teddy Roosevelt.

George proceeded into the kitchen and started breakfast. A man needed a solid breakfast if he expected to accomplish a day's work. Nothing but bacon and eggs would do.

After breakfast, George sipped his coffee and reread the instruction manual to his new chain saw. The salesman had assured him that this model was the best chain saw on the market. The preferred saw among woodcutters in the North Maine Woods. He saw no reason to spend his hard-earned money on anything but the best. It was one of the Gurnet family guiding principles.

The aromatic fragrance of fir and spruce trees blended with the pleasant odor of fuel mix and bar oil as George filled the tank of his chain saw in the warm morning sun. *This is the way a man should spend his Sunday mornings,* he thought to himself. Much better than swinging a golf club or hanging around the yacht club. He consulted the instruction manual one more time to make certain he had everything right. The saw roared to a start on the second pull. He revved the engine several times to get the feel of it. The salesman was right. Definitely a precision machine. Very nice balance. And it really wasn't all that loud. He put on his earmuffs just the same and stepped over to a large fir tree. The cuts were made precisely as he had envisioned them, over and over, ever since he had purchased the chain saw and the handbook on logging technique.

The tree came crashing down exactly where he had planned. Very nice. It confirmed what George had always believed. A man could do anything if he put his mind to it. And carefully read the instruction book. Three more trees, felled with the same satisfying precision. Now, the process of limbing, converting each tree into a log. The fragrance of Christmas trees enhanced the pleasure of this job. When the logs were all neatly trimmed, he drove the Range Rover over to the edge of the embankment and used his brand-new winch to haul the logs up onto the edge of the road.

George looked at his watch. Nine thirty. *Time flies when you're having fun.* A coffee break was in order. He walked back to the cottage and went into the kitchen. The pot was empty. He stepped out onto the porch. "You guys drink all the coffee?"

"Sorry," his wife, Arlene, replied, "but we've been up for hours."

"Yeah. Who could sleep with that stupid chain saw going?" his daughter chimed in.

Arlene offered him some bagels and got up to make another pot of coffee, but by then George had a better idea. He went over to the refrigerator and took out a beer. He had earned it. He picked up a stack of catalogs and went out on the porch to browse. His granddaughter crawled up into his lap to help.

"George Jr.," his wife said, "what are you doing drinking beer? It's not even ten o'clock in the morning."

"Don't worry about it, Arlene. Back when we first got married, the two-martini lunch was an everyday practice. This is nothing," he reassured her.

"Well, at least you could find something better than Budweiser to drink," his daughter inserted. "I'm sure they must sell microbrews around here. Whatever made you buy Budweiser? That's what all the rednecks drink."

"I really don't know what came over me. Guess I was in a hurry, and they didn't have much of a selection," he responded, hoping to end the interrogation.

In truth, George knew exactly why he had picked up Bud. He took a sip and recalled with pleasure his experience yesterday evening, after he and his son-in-law, Adrian, had sailed all the way up from Boston and had secured the yawl to its mooring. No sooner had he set foot on solid ground, before he was even permitted to have a proper cocktail, George was commissioned to drive over to Snug Harbor and pick up some fresh milk and other miscellaneous supplies at the general store.

He parked the Rover in a space next to the store. The bumper jutted out over the steep, rocky shore. A shiny, new, black Dodge pickup truck was parked in front of the store, with its engine running. George made a short detour around the truck and took in all the details. Unmistakably a diesel, with loud clacking pistons and aromatic exhaust. Big rugged front end too. And a solid suspension that gave the truck plenty of height. He resisted the urge to climb up and peek into the cab.

About then, a hefty woman and her daughter, their arms filled with groceries, emerged from the store. George stepped over and held the door for them. He watched as they disappeared around the corner and went down behind the store. George was curious to see where they could be going. The store was built on the rocky shore of a narrow cove, across from an island. For want of land, the store was built like a pier, with the front of the building anchored on the solid ground along the shore, but the main part of the building extended out over the water, supported by huge pilings. A ramp alongside the store led down to a floating dock, where the woman and a man were loading her purchases onto a lobster boat.

Being a newcomer to the harbor, George looked over the adjacent buildings to see how they were constructed. A lobster pound and fish wholesaler next door was built in the same manner. What little land that was available between the road and the shore was used for parking. A nearby restaurant was built entirely on a pier, with several picnic tables outside on the dock. At first glance, it did not seem like a very secure way to construct public buildings. But the buildings were quite old and obviously had stood the test of time. George went on inside the store.

It was totally unlike anything he had ever seen. Half the store was crammed to the ceiling with groceries, frozen foods, dairy, and produce. The aisles were narrow. There was no room at all for shopping carts. The other half was filled with marine supplies. George scanned the entire inventory: clamming gloves, rubber fishing boots, spark plugs, pot warp, diesel fuel additive, and a selection of fish hooks. Some were nearly three inches long and sturdy enough to lift a truck. At the checkout counter was a young man in jeans, a T-shirt, and a lobsterman's hat.

"I see you gotcha a new truck theyah, Bert," said the old man behind the counter.

"Ah, yeah. She's a diesel."

"Oh, we know that. Can hear her good in here, can't we, Martha?" The old man glanced over at his wife. "I bet she's got some powah."

"Oh, she's got plenty of power, alright."

"Man had a truck like that, wouldn't need Viagra." The old man snickered. They all laughed, and the young lobsterman picked up his six-pack of Budweiser and walked out.

It occurred to George that in this environment, a six-pack of Bud might be an appropriate addition to his own basket. So he picked one up for himself. In fact, at nine thirty the next morning, it still seemed like a good idea. So he went to the fridge and got himself another one.

"Why are you cutting down all those trees anyway, Daddy?" his daughter, Karen, inquired.

"Well, your mother and I got the idea when we were up here last month, closing the deal on this place. We wanted to create a glade of birch trees in front of all those evergreens that will run from the road all the way down to the beach. We just needed to take out a few odd fir trees, scattered amongst the birches, and plant in a few more birches in the open spaces. Sitting on the porch here or in the living room, what you'll see is a classic birch glade, with all their white trunks, against a background of evergreens, just like you're always seeing in paintings and magazines."

"Excuse me, Daddy. You said *beach*. What beach are you talking about? There's nothing on the shore but a disgusting pile of oyster shells. The place is a dump. What kind of people would dump their shells on a beach anyway? Of all places."

"I have no idea who dumped them there. Apparently, Maine does not have very strict environmental laws, I guess. Or maybe they just don't enforce them. Who knows? Anyway, I'm having them all dug up and trucked to the dump. We'll haul in a few loads of sand and have a nice beach again," George said as he popped open his second Bud and hauled his granddaughter up onto his lap.

"Why are we looking at trucks, Grampy?" she asked with obvious delight.

"Grampy is thinking about buying a pickup truck, Arly. See. This is the new Super Duty Ford F-350. That's the one I was planning to buy. It's tall and massive and very macho. Grampy was afraid the Ford might raise his serum testosterone levels too high, so he decided to buy a Dodge instead. With a diesel engine. Here, I'll show you one." He began leafing through the paper to find the Dodge advertisements.

"What's macho, Grampy?"

"Never mind." He ran his fingers through her curly blonde hair. "See here. There are the Dodges. Don't they look rugged? I'd like the standard cab, but because of you, Arly, I'm going to get the extended cab, with a backseat. Then there will be plenty of room for Arly to ride with Grampy. How about that?" he asked, giving her a big hug.

"George, don't tell me you're going to trade in that Rover for a pickup truck. It's practically brand-new," his wife complained.

"Arlene, since we bought this place I keep thinking about retiring early and moving up to Maine full-time. Next year, after we get this place fixed up and winterized, I just might turn in my resignation at the bank. Living up here, I'll be needing a pickup truck."

"Why in the world would you need a pickup truck if you move to Maine, Daddy?"

"To go to the dump. A man needs a truck to go to the dump."

"The dump? Why would you want to go to a dump?"

"Because around here they don't have trash pickup service. Everyone takes their own trash to the dump."

"Just forget about that, George," Arlene interrupted. "I'm not living in a tiny little cottage like this for the rest of my life. I don't care how cute it is."

"It's not going to be a tiny little cottage much longer. I took the photos and drawings of this place over to a client of mine who is an architect. He says we can build onto this place and make it into a totally modern building, inside and out. He's coming up next month to do an on-site survey. After that we can all get together and plan a really grand place where we can live year-round."

"That's okay for you, George," said Arlene, "but what about me? Nobody lives up here. Nobody you can talk to or with whom one might care to socialize. You have to drive forever to find a golf course or a country club. What will I do when we don't have family visiting?"

"Arlene, people from Massachusetts are moving up here all the time," he replied. "They're buying up the choice properties at bargain prices and developing the coast of Maine into a civilized place where anyone would want to live. Maine was once a very civilized place. You can tell that by looking at all the magnificent old homes that people built here years ago. But we can talk about it later. Right now, Arly and I have a couple more trees to cut down, don't we, Arly?"

George put on his hard hat, goggles, and earmuffs to show off his logger's outfit. He wished now that he had also ordered the chaps, to make himself look more authentic. When they got outside, Arly expressed her admiration of Grampy's outfit. George decided that she should wear the hard hat, goggles, and noise-protecting earmuffs. He almost went back inside to get his camera when he saw how cute she looked. But that could wait until they felled these two last trees. George began with a detailed explanation of how one carefully selected the desired location for the tree to fall before making the cuts. Placing the first cut with precision gave the woodcutter exact control over where the tree landed when it fell. Then he showed Arly how to start the chain saw. She stood back a safe distance while he cut a wedge out of the base of the tree. He began a second cut on the other side of the tree, just above the first one. "Stand clear, Arly." The saw roared, and the tree came crashing down. Another perfect fall.

"Look, Grampy," Arly shouted, "a branch on that big old tree has pushed over one of the little birches. See?"

"Can't have that," George said.

Arly was right. A branch from the fir had pinned over one of his precious birches. "Not a problem for a man with a chain saw. Just cut the branch away from the trunk, and the little birch will pop up free. You see, Arly, birches are very limber and elastic. Remember the poem about birches by Robert Frost? 'When I see birches bend to left and right / Across the lines of straighter darker trees, / I like to think some boy's been swinging them.' I memorized that whole poem when I was in school. I'll tell you the rest of it this afternoon when we're done. Now watch this. No problem at all."

George did not remember anything after that. Not Arly's screams, nor his daughter's attempts to perform mouth-to-mouth resuscitation while his wife called 911. Not even the ambulance's piercing siren when it arrived.

"He's breathing, and he responds somewhat to stimuli, but he's not fully conscious," Arthur said to the other EMT as he assessed the situation. "Boy, he's gonna have some shiner on that left eye, don'tcha think? That little birch tree must have snapped back and smacked him in the face when he cut the branch loose, judging by the blood on the birch tree. Wow! He's got some rapid pulse. We better get him in the ambulance and hook him up to the EKG."

As they slid the stretcher into the ambulance, George began to wake up. While they attached all the EKG leads, George told them he felt fairly normal except for a bad headache. The vision in his left eye seemed okay too, but he saw two of everything whenever he tried to look upward.

"EKG looks pretty much normal to me. What do you think, Arthur?"

"Looks finest kind to me. I better radio it in to the emergency room and see what the ER doc thinks, just in case." He punched up the radio and began his report.

Everyone was relieved to see the sudden improvement in George's condition. Arlene was concerned that he had not shaved that morning. "That's not like you," she remarked. George promised his family he would be all right, and they promised him they would all drive to the hospital as soon as they got themselves properly dressed.

"He's going to be okay, isn't he?" Arlene asked Arthur as he climbed into the cab of the ambulance.

"I don't rightly know, ma'am," Arthur said. "But I promise we'll get him to the emergency room as fast as we can." The ambulance drove off, and Arthur cranked up the siren—a plaintive wail, echoing from across the cove.

Chapter 5

*B*uns of Steel came to mind as Sally caught a glimpse of her tush in the mirror behind her. Her brain had been on autopilot ever since she turned on the hair dryer. She switched out of autopilot. *My butt is my best asset. I could wear thong underwear if I wanted to. Mmmmm. How would I ever manage to launder them? If Sam were to see them hanging out to dry somewhere … I don't even want to think about it.*

She turned slightly to do the other side of her hair. Glancing in the mirror again, she detected a bulge in the flank. *Damned Atkin's diet! You lose the weight but not the bulges. Maybe I could find a plastic surgeon in Florida who would do liposuction while I was on vacation. Not that there's anyone around here who would notice the difference.* She shook her head. *Never thought I'd get desperate enough to consider Club Med. What the hell was I thinking when I moved to Maine? Should have considered my prospects. I must have been in retreat mode. The only things on my mind were getting away from Charlie and getting Sam out of Philadelphia.*

She thought about the gang Sam started hanging with after his father moved out. Most of them were fatherless, looking for whatever it was that guys thought they needed and their mothers couldn't seem to give them. Gang violence was on the rise, with the number of beatings and muggings of high school students increasing. The gang murder of one of Sam's classmates created the final straw in her decision. The memory made her shudder.

Maybe we should have gone back to the farm. She sighed after that thought. Back home in Illinois, moms didn't have to worry about their sons hanging out with gangs. *But then I'd get fat and dumpy, just like my mom. No thanks. I'd rather have a cute butt.*

Sally checked the mirror to make sure she still had it. The phone rang.

"Hello," Sally finally said as she picked up the telephone.

"Sally, it's Charlie. What took you so long to answer the goddamn phone?"

"I was doing my hair. I didn't hear the phone ringing until I happened to turn off the blow-dryer. What's on your mind this morning?"

"Sam. That's what. It's time we firmed up the arrangements for his trip to Philadelphia this summer. When does school let out?"

"Around two and a half weeks, I think."

"I need the exact date so I can make the reservation for his plane tickets."

"Why don't you hold off on that awhile? It's not settled yet whether he's coming or whether he is staying here for the summer."

"Don't gimme that shit, Sally. The divorce decree says he spends summers with his father. It's already settled. Just tell me when school is out."

"Christ, Charlie. Would you just listen for a minute so we can make a decision on what's best for Sam?"

"Look. We already agreed on what's best for Sam. Boys need to spend time with their fathers. Remember what that counselor said about role models and mentoring for boys? You know all that, so quit stalling."

"Charlie, I really need your help here. Please. I know you want what's best for Sam."

"Well, of course I do."

"Well, you know Sam's on the swim team this year. But you are probably not aware of how good he's getting. His coach says Sam has really got a lot of potential as a swimmer. And Sam has finally started to get some motivation in his life. He wants to get his letter in swimming."

"That's great. Sounds like maybe he's finally starting to mature."

"Right. The problem is that they want him to attend swim practice up here all summer long. It's two hours a day, which means he can't come to Philadelphia. So you need to decide which is more important for Sam. I can't do this by myself. See?"

"I get the picture."

"Good. It's the first positive thing Sam has ever focused on. He's starting to develop a little self-esteem from the success that he's already had. So it's kinda nice to see."

"Yeah. I can imagine. Okay, gimme a chance to talk with Sam about it before we make our decision. All right?"

"Good idea. Except he's not here right now. But he should be home this evening. Call back tonight. I think you will enjoy talking with him about his swimming. Bye. And thanks for calling."

Damn! What a pain it is to get a phone call when you're drying your hair. And then to have it be Charlie. What a bummer! It started out to be such a beautiful day. What a great run she'd had—seeing the ospreys, and Tom and everything. It was probably the best she had felt since she moved to Maine. She turned the dryer back on.

After she relaxed a little, Sally regained some insight into her problems with Charlie. Nothing like a little dryer therapy. The therapist she had seen, back when they first started having problems, was very helpful and showed her how to avoid the bitter disputes with Charlie. All she needed to do was to consciously step back. Let Charlie think he was in control. It was called the "one down" position. After Sally got the hang of it, she could practically make him decide whatever she wanted, as long as she framed things so that he thought he was the one making all the important decisions. Charlie was happy and helpful, as long as he felt like she was dependent on him for "husbandly" leadership in their relationship.

Charlie wasn't like that at first. He was very helpful and supportive all through the last years of her residency and during the early years in the ophthalmology department while she was working her way up to associate professor. What a peach of a guy.

Then Medicare cut payments for cataract surgery in half. Her salary dropped proportionally. About the same time, Charlie's career started to take off. He began bringing home more money than she did. Suddenly, Charlie wanted to become the man of the house.

What an ego. It swelled up bigger than his penis. She soon got to where she couldn't stand either one. Charlie wanted her to quit working, have more kids, and become a stay-at-home mother. After spending her entire life studying to become a doctor, and then working up to associate professor, why should she have to spend the rest of her life playing second fiddle, with piles of kids and a house to look after, just like her poor mother? Not in this lifetime.

She turned off the hair dryer and slipped into some jeans and a sweatshirt. Time to finish planting those dahlia bulbs. What a joy. She could already see their blossoms, growing in the secret garden in her mind. She pulled on her gardening gloves. She was back on track for a happy day.

Let's see. A couple of red ones would look nice over in front of the fence, and the pink one can go in the corner. Now where should I put the yellow?

Beep! Beep! Beep!

Oh God! She punched up the pager to stop all the beeping and display the telephone number. She recognized the number instantly. The emergency room. *Damn! First Charlie and then the emergency room. The world is against me today.*

"Hello! Dr. Gardiner? Kyle Libby here. In the emergency room. Say, I've got an older gentleman here who got struck in the eye by a tree limb this morning. CAT scan shows a blowout fracture of the orbital floor. And he gets diplopia on upward gaze. I thought you might want to come in and take a look at him. See if he needs to be fixed."

"Sounds like he probably does. I'll change my clothes and be right in."

"No need to hurry. He ate a big breakfast and had a couple of beers this morning, so anesthesia is not gonna want to put him to sleep any time soon. Probably needs a cardiac eval too. The ambulance driver thought he might have had some kind of tachycardia when they first saw him. So take your time and we'll see you when you get here. And thanks a bunch."

So much for the dahlias. Might as well go in and get it over with. I never fully appreciated how nice it was having surgical residents around all the time to take care of the scut work. What a hassle it is, practicing in Maine, where there is no house staff. You have to do everything yourself. But, in Maine, even though you do a lot more, you still get paid much less by Medicare than anywhere else in the country. It just isn't fair.

By the time Sally reached the hospital, she was beginning to wonder if, maybe, she should have stayed in Philadelphia after all.

～

The Gurnet family felt relieved when they finally arrived at the ER and saw how much better George was looking and feeling. The pain mediation was starting to take effect. Arlene noticed that George had even borrowed an electric shaver to freshen up a bit. The ER doctor's report, suggesting that he might need surgical repair of his eye injury, was disturbing. They were all eagerly awaiting the local ophthalmologist, Dr. Sally Gardiner, whoever she might be, to explain the issues pertaining to the eye injury. Hopefully, the injury would not require immediate treatment so they could get him back to Boston, where the care would be much better.

"Busy place you've got here today," Sally remarked as she walked into the emergency room.

"Yeah. They start pouring in here round Memorial Day every year," Dr. Libby returned. "We'll be out straight like this until Labor Day, when all the summer people go back home. Your man is in room three."

"Thanks. Where is his CAT scan?"

"We can see it right here on the computer screen. I'll get it for you in a second."

"Thank you, but I need the films to show to the patient."

When Dr. Gardiner entered exam room three, she had a large envelope with the CAT scan films in one hand and a cardboard box she had borrowed from the radiologist's office in her other hand. She introduced herself to Mr. Gurnet and his family.

"I understand you got hit in the face by a tree branch. How did that happen?"

"Well, I was cutting off a branch from a tree I had just felled, and something came up and whacked me in the face. I can't see anything in the left eye."

"I see. Would you mind if I had a closer look at that eye for a moment?" Sally pried open the swollen lids of his left eye. "How is your vision in that eye now?"

"Okay, if you keep the eye lids open."

"Good. How many fingers do you see?" Sally held up one finger.

"One finger."

"Now. How many do you see now?" Sally moved her finger slowly upward. The right eye tracked up, but the left eye didn't move.

"Now I see two."

Sally showed the family how the left eye could not move upward but moved normally in other directions. Then she opened the cardboard box and took out a human skull to explain the anatomy of the orbit. When she got out the CAT scans for review, everyone could see the eyeballs and the little muscles that move the eyes around. She showed them the fragmented bone in the floor of the left orbit, all tangled up with the inferior rectus muscle and restricting its movement. They all then understood why the left eye couldn't move in an upward gaze.

"Is that something that can be fixed?" Arlene asked.

"It is a delicate but not terribly complicated or difficult operation. It is done under light general anesthesia. Patients usually go home the same day as the surgery."

"Does this need to be fixed right away?"

"Not necessarily. But you shouldn't wait more than a week or ten days. Otherwise, scar tissue starts to develop around the site of injury, and it becomes much more difficult to repair. The results may not be quite so good."

"I see. Before you came in, we were wondering if it might be better if we could take him back to Boston for something this delicate. Would that be reasonable?"

"I suppose so. If that's what you want."

"Hold on a minute, Arlene," George inserted. "Dr. Gardiner seems to be able to handle this problem. Her presentation was clear and understandable. If we go ahead and fix it now, I'll be able to stay up here and finish off the rest of my tree work and help sail the boat back to Boston."

"Dr. Gardiner, could you please excuse us for a moment so we can discuss this?"

Sally tried to ignore what was going on behind the curtain in exam room three as she wrote up her report in the emergency medical record. She had been warned about summer people and their distrust for any doctors north of Boston. Then an alarm went off and a red light came on above the entrance to exam room three. The nurse rushed in and the alarm stopped. After a while she came out and walked over to Sally.

"Dr. Gardiner, the Gurnets would like to speak with you. They want to go ahead and have the surgery here."

"I see. Wonder what made them decide to do that?"

"When I went in to see why his heart monitor was on alarm, I told them that you were previously associate professor of ophthalmology in Philadelphia before you came here."

"Oh. I suppose I should thank you. But I'm not sure."

Sally went back in and made certain all the family's questions were answered. Then she proceeded to do a complete history and physical exam. The patient seemed rather vague and somewhat evasive around questions regarding his cardiac history. Was he in denial? Or perhaps he was trying to hide things from his family.

"The main concern here, Mr. Gurnet, is the effect of general anesthesia on your heart. You've had some irregular heart rhythms on your monitor this morning. Anesthesia has already asked our cardiologist to come in and evaluate your heart before the surgery. Then the anesthesiologist will go over everything with you. We have to wait until your stomach has emptied anyway before it's safe to put you to sleep."

The operative permit was signed, and Sally went out to finish filling out the hospital record. When that was completed, she asked the ER nurse to page her when Dr. MacMahan finished his evaluation of Mr. Gurnet so they could confer on his case.

Sally left the hospital and walked over to her office in the medical building. Might as well catch up on paperwork. No use wasting time hanging around the emergency room. Besides, she needed to get into a better mood. *It's no wonder they don't like out-of-staters around here. Go back to Boston for surgery. What an insult. No more than a first-year resident case. In Philadelphia, at least I had some respect, even from Charlie. Well, at least in the field of medicine. Here, in Maine, it doesn't matter if you taught in medical school or coauthored a chapter in a medical textbook. None of my achievements seem to be acknowledged by my patients or my colleagues. Should have thought about that when I decided to leave Philadelphia.*

The air near the bleachers at the YMCA pool was rather hot and muggy that morning, especially for people wearing street clothes instead of bathing suits. Cathy stepped out into the lobby for a breath of relief and dialed up her sister on the cell phone.

"Please enter your message after the tone."

"Hi, sis. It's Cathy. Sorry, I was out last night. Didn't check my voice mail until this morning. I got your message about Mom, and I—."

"Hello, Cathy. It's Francie."

"Sis? You're home after all?"

"Just screenin' calls. That's all. Sorry we missed you this weekend. *La Bohème* was awesome. And the party afterward was to die for. Even had several members of the cast attending. My heavens! You would have had a ball. Hey, where are you calling from? You're breaking up."

"I'm at the YMCA, on my cell phone. I've only got two bars. I'll step outside … There. How's that?"

"Much better."

"Now I've got four bars. Must be the metal roof on the Y that was blocking the signal. So what's up with Mom?"

"Turns out it isn't as bad as when I called you last night and left the message. Mom got confused and fell again at the nursing home. They took her to the hospital for X-rays, but they didn't find any new fractures. She's back in the nursing home now."

"Good. Do you think I need to come down and see her?"

"Not really. She might not even know you if you came. Half the time she doesn't even recognize me. I thought it might be some of the drugs they have her on, but the doctor said it was her brain. They are going to keep her in restraints from now on."

"Oh my God! That's scary. I sure hope we don't end up with Alzheimer's when we're her age."

"I doubt it. The doctor says it's not Alzheimer's. Her problem is most likely due to alcohol."

"I guess that shouldn't be much of a surprise. So, how have you been anyway?"

"Doin' okay. Life is good. How is life up in Maine?"

"Pretty limited, when you compare it to Boston. But I'm stuck here, so I'm determined somehow to get a life."

"Well, good luck. I know what you're up against, and I sure wouldn't want to be in your shoes. Any leads yet?"

"Yes. Things are looking up. I might be going back to school next year to get my master's degree. That's one good thing about being divorced. It gives me a lot more free time to pursue my own career."

"Cool. But how can you afford the tuition on the piddling alimony you're getting?"

"Well, now that I am employed again, I am making a few bucks. And I am applying for a scholarship through the hospital trust fund. I should know sometime this summer."

"Sounds great. Are you seeing anyone new these days?"

"As a matter of fact, yes. Actually, we were together last night."

"What kind of a guy is he?"

"He's a doctor."

"Mmm. Is he nice?"

"As doctors go, he's practically off the scale. All the nurses think he's God."

"What's so special?"

"It's the way he conducts himself at the hospital. He is really polished and well educated. A professor of cardiology in Boston before he moved here. But he never talks down to nurses. He treats them like equals. Respectfully. You know, always asks their opinion about patients' conditions. As well as treatment plans, medicines, and outcomes. That kind of stuff. It's called collaborative care. He's good at it. And it makes nursing a lot more enjoyable."

"Sounds nice enough, but what's he like as a guy? You know. Is he good looking? Or some older guy?"

"He's not that old. His wife died last year. But he's still got a full head of hair. And he's very good-looking. When you get him out of his hospital clothes, you can see he's in great shape. If you know what I mean."

"Well, you make him sound too nice. Just don't let yourself fall in love again. You've been burned more than once. I hope you've finally learned."

"Yeah! Don't worry. I've learned my lesson. Believe me. But I don't want to talk about it now. Besides, I gotta run. Swim class is letting out, and I need to help Britney get dressed. Talk to ya later. Bye."

Strolling back into the YMCA, Cathy couldn't get her mind off the hard lesson she had learned her first year in college. She fell madly in love with a boy she had met at the opera. They consummated their relationship after seeing and identifying with *Tristan and Isolde*. The following Sunday, he was killed in an auto wreck. Cathy went to the funeral parlor to see him and, like Isolde, she drank a death potion she had made from her mother's sleeping pills and threw herself on the coffin. After she recovered from having her stomach pumped, she had *Liebestod* tattooed over her left breast. Whatever made her think that a man was worth killing yourself for was something she could still not understand. She placed her hand over her breast as she walked into the girls' locker room.

~

Ah! The therapeutic shower. Tom savored it. Nothing better, after a long run, for soothing aching joints and muscles. It cleared all the spam out of his brain and keened his mind so he could think clearly. One by one, Tom surveyed all the issues currently on his mind, while the hot water rinsed the rest of the world away from his consciousness. The rapturous smile on Sally's face appeared in his mind. Amazing. One glance at her kid, and there it was. Tom's thoughts wandered aimlessly back in life, surveying various relationships and wondering again how he could have missed the importance of bonding in human relationships. *I probably just took it for granted all those years.*

Finally, he forced himself to turn off the shower. *What a treat. No wonder we used to run out of hot water in the mornings back when the kids were still living at home.*

The phone was ringing. Still naked, Tom answered it. It was the emergency room.

"Hi, Tom. Kyle Libby in the emergency room. We got an elderly guy here who was brought in by the ambulance because of an eye injury. Cardiology evaluation is needed because the patient had a rapid tachycardia and was semiconscious when the EMTs first got to him. His present condition is stable, and the EKG looks pretty normal."

"Okay," Tom said. "Why don't you draw some blood for cardiac enzymes, if you haven't already done it. And I'll be there in a while. I was coming in to make rounds pretty soon anyway. Need to fill up my gas tank first. Then I'll be there."

Tom got dressed and drove over to Bailey's General Store to fill his tank. Gas was four cents a gallon cheaper in town, but Tom preferred to do his business locally and let his friends get the profits. Besides, if he bought it here, he could charge it to his lobster business and save on taxes. He climbed out of the cab and started to fill the tank.

"Mawnin', Scotchy," he said. "Nice truck."

"Ayeah. Jes got her. She's only got a thousand miles."

"How come ya to get a diesel?"

"Had one in my boat a couple a years now. New ones all have that fuel injection system like they got on the 18-wheelers. Makes 'em quiet an' easy on fuel too. Don't p'lute so much as reg'lar diesels either. Even less than most gas engines when you figure in the better gas mileage. So when they come out with almost the same engine in a pickup, well, I had to have one."

"Three-quarter ton too, I see."

"Ayeah. They don't put diesel in the half tons."

"What happened to your tailgate?"

"Gut it out back of the garage. Man don't need no tailgate in the fishin' business. Jes gits in the way, draggin' gear in an' out all the time. I put it on ever' now an' then, 'specially if I'm goin' up to camp. So's I can haul back a load of firewood if I need to."

"I see. Seems like ever'body's gittin' diesels nowadays. Saw Crittur drivin' one last week. Almost like yours."

"Ayeah. Only he's got the extended cab."

The aroma of diesel fuel wafted over to Tom's pump. *Smells better than gasoline,* Tom thought. "How's Bert like his Dodge diesel?"

"Finest kind. 'Ceptin' they had to replace the transmission already. Wicked torque in them Cummins diesels."

"You ain't worried 'bout the transmission in that rig, are ya?"

"Oh, God no! GM has Allison transmissions in their diesels, just like in the big rigs. Even got Jake brakes. Handy when you're haulin' a big load. Yes, sir! Some rugged. Ya can't beat 'em. How come you're still drivin' that ole rust bucket anyway?"

"It's paid for. That's why," Tom replied. "You lobstermen can write off your trucks as a business expense. If I could, I'd prob'ly be drivin' one like yours. Besides, I'm still payin' off college tuitions and jeezly real estate taxes. Boy, have they gone up."

"I know. It's them out-o'-staters comin' in here an' drivin' up prices on shorefront property. Won't be long before an honest fisherman can't afford to live on the coast anymore," Scotchy declared as he placed the nozzle back on the pump. "Whatcha think o' these new gas pumps?"

"I like 'em. Haven't seen pumps like that since I was a kid. Must be antiques. I wonder where Hodge ever picked those up."

"Ya never know with Hodge. He's pretty clever," Scotchy observed as he started into the store to pay up.

Tom finished topping off and checked the oil before going inside.

"Say hello to Prissy for me," he said to Scotchy as he was coming out. "Morning, Lorna," he continued as he got inside. "What are you doing behind the till?"

"Oh, hi, Tom. Mom and Dad took the kids up to camp this weekend, so I'm fillin' in. I'm probably going to be runnin' the store this summer. If I like it, I might take it over next year. I'll have enough time in at the post office for retirement benefits by that time."

"It's gonna be just like we were in high school again, what with you workin' in the store and the new gas pumps your dad put in. They're almost the same as you had back when we were in school and you first started working here."

"Some of them *are* the same. Dad had them in the barn the last thirty years. He bought a couple of others in an antique store and then had the whole bunch refitted with modern electronic equipment. Took a long time, but we finally got 'em installed last week. Dad could see the summer people starting to move in this way, and he figured a little nostalgia was good for business."

"Smart man, your dad."

"Ayeah. He's got a degree in business, so he's pretty sharp how he runs the place. See this old cash register? Inside, it's all computerized, just like the big supermarkets. Only Dad has the scanner fixed so the customers can't hear all the items ring when they're getting checked in. Kinda preserves the quaint atmosphere of the place. The whole store is run on a computer. It just looks old-fashioned."

"Christ! I never would have suspected. Looks the same as it always did."

"I know. But believe me, underneath it's a slick business. I'll be taking night classes at business school the next couple of years before I take over. Dad says you have to keep adapting if you want to survive in this world."

"And you're not worried about the new Walmart that's goin' up in town next year? They're supposed to be putting all the mom-and-pop stores out of business."

"Dad's not worried. He's got the same technology and the same buying power they've got. And he knows the market far better than they do. Besides, we've got sort of a niche market down here. And he's right, you know. Like he says, no one likes the Massholes movin' up this way. But you can't stop it, so you might as well figure out how to do business with them. Go with the flow—that's Dad's motto."

"Strange. That's exactly what my dad used to say. By the way, how'd Granville do with his alewives over in Second Creek this year?"

"Pretty good. So he tells me. Says he's got enough alewives in the cooler to bait his traps all summer. 'Course he always makes ever'thing sound good for his mother. Now he's riggin' up for charter boat fishing this summer when he's not haulin' lobsters. He swears there's plenty of summer people who want to go out after the blues and stripers. Dunno how that'll work out."

"I bet he'll do just fine. Pretty ambitious boy, I'd say."

"Well, not all that ambitious. Granville says he's not going back to college next fall."

"He's not?"

"Nope. Says they ain't no use in wastin' three more years studying stuff he doesn't want to know so he kin git a job doin stuff he doesn't want to do, in a place he doesn't want to live. Says he'll make a decent livin' fishin' and stay right here, where he wants to be. Tuition money would be better invested in a fishing boat."

"I dunno but what he might be right. Listen, I gotta get rollin'. I'm due at the hospital. Nice talkin' to ya, Lorna."

The truck backfired with a puff of dark smoke when he started her up. It was about time for a new muffler. It was tempting to think about getting a whole new truck. *One of them diesels would feel awfully good. Might could drive up to Augusta next week and check one out to see how it goes.* An extended cab with air-conditioning, power windows, and a CD player. All the bells and whistles inside. Outside would be plain. He'd take the tailgate off, just like Scotchy. That way no one would know he'd bought an expensive vehicle. It wouldn't do to make people think you had a lot of money. His father had taught him that. "Money makes people jealous. It's them damned socialists, always politickin' against the rich, that makes folks feel that way." Tom wasn't quite sure about that.

It was human nature that made people jealous. Tom was sure of that. And doctors were probably the most jealous people he knew. They couldn't stand it if they thought another doctor was making too much money. He remembered when an orthopedist parked his racy new BMW convertible in the doctors' parking lot. The medical staff buzzed, all wondering who it was that could afford such an expensive vehicle. In the doctors' lounge, he overheard several primary care physicians swear they would never refer another patient to the orthopedist, because he was obviously making too much money. Pure jealousy. Even doctors were not immune to human nature.

When he got to the hospital, Tom parked the truck and went into the doctors' lounge. Nothing important was in his mailbox. *Thank God!* From his locker, he took out a spare tie and tied it around his collar, put on the white coat, and draped the stethoscope around his neck. He quickly glanced in the mirror to check his tie, and he was off to the ER to evaluate his patient.

"My, don't we look professional this morning," said the ER doc when he saw Tom come in. "White coat and tie on a Sunday morning. I'm impressed."

"Well," said Tom, "back when I was in cardiology fellowship, they made a big deal about dress and appearance. In those days, we were all pretty much a bunch of casual slobs. 'Consider the patient's point of view,' they always said. 'He doesn't know you from a hill of beans when you walk in and tell him you're his doctor. If you appear grubby, he's going to wonder what kind of doctor he's getting. If you don't look like you take good care of yourself, how can he expect that you'll take good care of him?' I adopted that approach, and I've followed it ever since."

"Good point. I like it."

"So what's the scoop on this guy anyway?"

"Ambulance brought him in this morning. He's from Boston. Got a place on the shore. Somewhere close to you. Down in the harbor, I think. He was evidently taking down some trees this morning when a branch or something snapped back and hit him in the eye. Really did a job on himself."

"I wonder if that was the same asshole I heard running his chain saw this morning."

"Wouldn't surprise me if he was. The problem we have is a report from the EMTs who rescued him, which says he was semiconscious and had a rapid pulse when they first found him. By the time they got him hooked up to the EKG, he was back in normal sinus rhythm. Here are his tracings."

Tom's mind buzzed as he scanned the EKG printout. *So there is some justice in this world after all. Serves him right for running a chain saw on Sunday morning. Hmmm. Something about the QRS complex doesn't look right. Looks like he may have had an infarct sometime in the past. Better go in and talk with him and see if we can figure this out.*

The Gurnet family had stepped out of room three by the time Tom went in and introduced himself. "So, could you tell me what happened this morning?" he asked.

"Well, I did a really dumb thing. I was cutting down some trees this morning, and I had my granddaughter with me. I guess I was paying more attention to her and not enough to what I was doing, and some branch whacked me in the face. I should have known better."

"Gosh. That's too bad. But fortunately it's something that can be easily fixed. What brings you up to Maine anyway?"

"My wife and I just bought a place down along the shore. I sailed up from Boston yesterday."

"Is that your sailboat I saw anchored out in the cove this morning? Two masts with a blue hull?"

"Yep. That's her. A baby-blue yawl. I had her custom built by a yard in Friendship."

"Marsh Brothers?"

"Yes. That's the one. You know them?"

"That's the same yard that built my boat. They're famous for building a very strong hull," Tom said.

"Have you got a sailboat too?"

"Nope. Lobster boat. Used to belong to my father."

"Is that right? I used to sail my father's boat too. A Friendship sloop she was. Built by the same yard. But my family got too big, so I had to move up to a larger craft. You like her?"

"Oh, yes. She's a nice-looking boat. I've only seen it from a distance. But it has beautiful lines."

"Thanks. Maybe, after I get this thing fixed, we could go out for a sail some afternoon, if you like."

"That might be nice."

Tom finally got down to business and did a full history and cardiac evaluation on Mr. Gurnet. At issue was the significance of the ambulance driver's report. Was he a reasonable candidate for general anesthesia?

It would take six hours for his breakfast and the two beers to pass through Mr. Gurnet's system. Then anesthesia could safely be given for a nonemergent condition. Tom recommended checking the cardiac enzymes and continuously monitoring his EKG to look for evidence that might help them evaluate the patient's cardiac status before starting anesthesia. A moment later, Sally showed up in the ER to hear Tom's evaluation.

"He seems like such a nice guy," Sally concluded. "What a shame this had to happen to him."

"Yeah. It doesn't quite seem fair, does it?" Tom agreed.

"Why is it always the nice guys seem to get it?"

"Don't know. Guess there's not any justice left in this world."

"That's about right."

"Of course, it could be because he drives a blue boat."

"What's that got to do with it?"

"Never mind. It's just an old fisherman's superstition. I'll tell you about it sometime. Anything else we need to cover?"

"Not really. Oh, yeah, what did you think about his family?"

"Never saw them. They weren't around when I went in. Why? What's with them?"

"Oh, they really pissed me off. Wanted to transfer him to Boston, where they could get proper treatment. I can't stand that. Doctors don't seem to get any respect at all around here."

"I know exactly how you're feeling, Sally. I went through the same thing. You might as well face it. Once you leave academia, no one's ever going to give you any more 'attaboys' for how well you practice medicine. No colleagues, or residents, looking over your shoulder while you operate, or counting how many papers you have published, so you can get a promotion. The patients certainly can't tell. If you need kudos for the good work you do, you have to give them to yourself. Self-congratulation in medicine is pretty much a private, inner joy. Once you get the hang of it, it can be very satisfying."

"If you say so," Sally replied. Tom could tell she was not really convinced.

"Okay! Another way to look at it is this. It's a matter of human nature for people when they get sick and really scared. They to want to go to some medical center, like in Boston or the Mayo Clinic. The prestige of those places gives patients a little more hope when they feel desperate. There's no way we can have that kind of prestige up here in Maine. Loss of prestige is a price you have to pay if you want to practice in Maine. I know. I've paid it. But living in Maine is well worth the price."

"Well, I guess, I mean, I hope you're right," Sally moaned. "Think I might as well go home and reap some of the benefits. There is plenty of time to finish planting my dahlias before this operation can get going. Thanks for your help."

She shuffled out to her car and headed for home. *Might as well accept it,* she thought to herself. It was too late. No way could she go back to Philadelphia now. Even if she wanted to. Besides, she had put too much of herself into the house to just let it go.

Working the soil in her garden out in the warm midday sunshine brought back long-forgotten memories of working on the farm as a child. How satisfying it used to feel to be allowed to work with all the grown-ups. Later, she planted the dahlias and listened to the birds. Her mind kept churning. She began to realize that somewhere inside, she had lost the drive, the inner need, or whatever it takes to rise to the top in the Ivory Tower of academic medicine. Her challenge now was to try to get Sam back on track and figure out how to make a life for herself right here in Maine.

Chapter 6

$\mathcal{S}$tepping into the operating room, all dressed in her green scrub suit—complete with paper booties, paper hat, and mask—Sally became pleasantly aware of a significant improvement in her mood. It was a feeling she had experienced many times before, but until now, she never fully appreciated how important it was in her life. The unique environment of the operating room,. A collaborative atmosphere of teamwork, dedication, and purpose. And, for reasons Sally did not completely understand, here in Maine it was even nicer than back in Philadelphia.

And how nice it felt, not having to tolerate relationships dominated by the egotistical strata of academic hierarchy. Everyone here was on a first-name relationship, with the patient's care everyone's prime objective. What she had now was just a close-knit team of highly skilled individuals, each with an important role to play in the shared goal of helping their patient. The self-doubt and disappointment that had plagued her all morning completely vanished when she took her place in the OR crew.

While they were waiting for George Gurnet to be transported into the surgical suite, Sally huddled with the anesthesiologist to review their strategy for this case. The cardiac monitor and related blood test results had all turned out normal. Nonetheless, George was still considered a high-risk patient, and they were playing it safe.

"Pretty nice guy, don't you think?"

"Yeah. I liked him a lot. What a shame to have something like this happen while you're on vacation."

"And to have your granddaughter there to see it all happen. I can't imagine," Sally said. But she *could* imagine. And it felt horrible. Suddenly, she became aware of how emotionally invested in her patient she had become. Back in Philadelphia, she never had the opportunity to get emotionally connected with most patients. Emergency room patients—whose problems were the most dramatic and unpredictable— were usually worked up by residents, who got to know the patients as real persons. Surgical attending professors served more as consultants. To them, the patients were merely cases, not people you personally cared about. But, here in Maine, the cases were all real people. *I wonder if this is what Tom was trying to tell me.*

"I figure we should probably keep this guy's anesthesia as light as possible. Don't you think?"

"Absolutely," Sally agreed. "I plan to inject local anesthesia around the eye, so he can't feel what I'm doing. That way, he won't need any deep level of anesthesia."

"Good. I'll hook him up to the EEG and monitor the anesthesia level in his brain. That way, I can give him just enough anesthesia so he won't know what's going on, and, with the EEG, I can still make sure he doesn't accidentally wake up and move while you're working inside his eye."

"Great! I'm surprised that you've got those EEG monitors here in this hospital. We hadn't started using them yet back in Philadelphia when I left last year."

"Yeah. That's one good thing about the people who run this place. They were quick to see that the cost of this technology is more than offset by savings from decreased complications and shorter hospital stays. Not to mention, it's also good for patients. Oh, here he comes. Might as well get on with it."

While Mr. Gurnet was being put to sleep, Sally reviewed the operative plan with the scrub nurse and helped him lay out all the instruments they would need for the procedure. Then she went out for her pre-op scrub.

Five minutes of meticulous hand washing could seem like an eternity. But the underside of each fingernail needed to be scrupulously scraped and scrubbed to clean off every last remnant of her dahlia garden before she could feel right about making an incision in someone's eyelid. Some of the newer scrub preparations didn't require five minutes of washing. But Sally needed a full five minutes just to prep her mind. In surgery the whole brain needs to be focused. This particular case did not appear to be so very challenging. But she had seen problems before. You cut a small artery while opening the incision. It retracts back under the eyeball, pumping blood and filling the eye socket with blood. Who knows what damage you might do, probing around under the eyeball, desperately trying to grab the artery and get it clamped? Or maybe she would find the whole floor of the eye socket had been destroyed. A bone graft would need to be inserted into the eye socket to hold up the eyeball and prevent it from falling down into the maxillary sinus. In Philadelphia, there was always an otolaryngologist on call to help with that problem. Here there was none. But, with her experience, whatever might happen, she was certain she could handle it. When the five minutes were up, Sally had her mind, and her hands, thoroughly prepped for surgery.

After the patient's eye had been properly prepped and draped, Sally injected the local anesthesia and made a small incision in his left lower eyelid, taking care to hide the incision in a skin crease so the scar would be almost invisible. Bleeding was easily controlled with electrocautery. She separated the muscle fibers underneath the skin with blunt dissection, taking care not to cut any of the little pulsating arteries, and finally exposed the bony rim of the eye socket, just under the muscle. Next, she made an incision in the periosteum, the tough membranous covering attached to the bone. Carefully, she peeled away the membrane, separating it from the bony fragments on the floor of the eye socket, gently lifting the eyeball and surrounding tissue away from the fracture. This allowed her to remove the splinters of bone from the floor of the eye socket that had pierced into the eye muscle and kept the eye from freely moving upward. There was plenty of intact bone remaining in the orbital floor to hold up the eyeball. The whole thing took less than twenty minutes and caused practically no bleeding. Sally announced she was done, except for sewing up the incision.

Just to be sure that the procedure had been successful, she grasped the underside of the eyeball with an instrument and gently pulled it upward to be certain the eye had full range of motion. No problem. Success. Mr. Gurnet would enjoy normal vision again. Everyone in the OR shared the rush of satisfaction that glowed inside Sally. To her it seemed almost as fulfilling as an orgasm.

She asked for a 6-0 nylon suture. *Beep! Beep! Beep!* An alarm sounded on the anesthesia monitor. The EKG automatically began spitting out paper recordings to document the event.

"Oh my God!" exclaimed the anesthesiologist. "There's that damned arrhythmia they've been talking about. Looks like V-tach, I think. Christ, his pressure is dropping. I'm cutting off all anesthetic gases and switching to pure oxygen. You've still got enough local on board to finish sewing him up, haven't you?" Sally nodded.

"And you better page Dr. MacMahan," he said to the circulating nurse. "We might need his help if this guy crashes."

But he didn't.

It took only several minutes for Sally to suture the incision and apply a dressing.

"Thank you, Jesus," shouted the anesthesiologist just as she finished. "He's back in normal sinus rhythm, and his blood pressure is up to normal. Just the same, I'm transferring this dude straight to intensive care as soon as we can get him out of here." He began gathering up the EKG strips to take along for Tom's review.

By the time he reached the ICU, George was nearly conscious. Cathy Dyer, acting head nurse in the ICU, hooked him up to the monitors, checked his vital signs, and did a pain assessment. Everything was close to normal. His headache and eye pain were gone, and so was his double vision. Except for the big shiner on his left eye, he seemed fine. After a brief discussion with Dr. Gardiner, the family was allowed into George's room. They felt relieved by his recovery and pleased with the surgical results.

Soon, Dr. MacMahan came in and assessed the situation. He explained to the family that George was in the ICU out of concern for his heart and the arrhythmias. They did not know for certain what was causing it, but coronary artery insufficiency or perhaps even a mild heart attack was suspected. The stress of the accident and surgery may have been too much for his diseased coronary arteries and may even have injured the heart muscle. They planned to recheck the blood enzyme levels to look for heart muscle injury and monitor the EKG continuously. Optimistically, if the tests all stayed normal, he might be discharged in the morning.

Tom went out to the nurses' station to write notes in the chart, make out all the orders, and confer with Cathy.

"What do you think is going on with this guy?" she asked.

"I think this gentleman is trying to have a myocardial infarction on us. How do you see it?"

"I would have to agree. That seems most likely."

"Okay. Let's keep him on oxygen. Recheck his cardiac enzymes, and draw up a syringe with 25 to 50 mg of lidocaine to have ready, in case he has any more episodes of ventricular tachycardia. Oh, yes, you might as well ask the pharmacy to make up an intravenous infusion of lidocaine to have available, just in case. Can you think of anything else?"

"What about pain meds? He doesn't seem to need any now, but there is no order."

"Good idea. I'll write for some morphine, IV, with adjustable dosing. Then I'm headed for home. I'm starting to feel sore from all that running this morning. Call me if something happens. On second thought, why don't you just call me anyway, if you get a free moment, just for a chat?"

Mr. Gurnet was fully conscious when Cathy returned to his room. He denied any pain. Cathy used a mirror to show him his wound and the fact that his eye now had regained full range of movement, without double vision. The surgery had been successful.

"Why am I in the ICU, hooked up to all these wires and things?" he asked.

"We are concerned that you may have had a slight heart attack."

"Heart attack?" Mr. Gurnet said with obvious alarm.

"Don't get too upset now. We're not sure yet. So far your blood tests have come back normal. But we are rechecking everything and not taking any chances, in case anything happens. That's all. If you start having any discomfort, just push this button and I'll be right here. Okay?"

Mr. Gurnet ignored his television set and seemed to doze off for a while. An hour and a half later, Cathy heard him buzzing. "Are you having some pain, sir?"

"Yes. My eye is starting to throb pretty bad. Do you think something is wrong?"

"I doubt it. It is probably just because the novocaine they put in your eye at surgery is starting to wear off. Don't worry. I'll give you some medicine that will make you more comfortable."

Cathy returned with a syringe and injected one milligram of morphine. "This stuff works pretty fast. We can always add more if we need to."

"The pain is starting to go down into my left arm now. It's in my chest too."

The alarm went off. Cathy looked at the monitor. *Oh my God! Ventricular tachycardia!* She rushed to the med cart and got the syringe of lidocaine. George had already lost consciousness. She slowly injected nearly 25 mg of lidocaine into the IV. The heart slowed back to normal. *Whew! That was close.* She called Tom for consultation. He thanked her for her quick, decisive intervention. They decided to begin an intravenous infusion of lidocaine at 2 mg per minute, or 60 cc's per hour. Gradually, she was to adjust the rate down to the lowest dose that would keep his heart rate normal.

"What happened?" Mr. Gurnet inquired when she returned to his room.

"Your heart started beating too fast, and you lost consciousness for a minute or two. We are giving you some medicine to control your heart rate. Do you feel all right?"

"Well, I'm not having any pain."

"That's good," Cathy said. "Dr. MacMahan is coming into the hospital to look things over and check you out."

"Oh, isn't that nice."

"Yes. He's always great to work with."

When Tom had finished examining Mr. Gurnet and his EKG records, he ordered some additional lab tests and made a progress note in the chart. He looked across the desk at Cathy's smiling face. "Nice job on Mr. Gurnet," he said. "You probably saved that man's life. You know?"

"Yeah. Thanks."

"You're the one who should be getting all the thanks. How does it feel?"

"It was really scary. It's the first time I've ever saved anyone's life. I don't know if I could have done it without all your careful instructions and backing."

"Around here, we call it teamwork," Tom said with a satisfying smile.

"At the hospital where I trained, they had no such thing as teamwork. It was kind of a dictatorial, doctor-knows-best sort of attitude. If you know what I mean."

"Yes, I do. That used to be the standard everywhere. But it has become outdated now. We've found that the team system does a better job."

"Well, I was talking to some other nurses about this in the dining room today. They really love working here because of the modern work ethic and attitude. From what I hear, most of the other hospitals in Maine still operate under the old system. How did we get lucky?"

"You can thank Betty Norton for that. She was way ahead of the curve in recognizing the need to modernize the working relationships among hospital caregivers. It is a real achievement. She was also the one who helped bring in all new, up-to-date, medical technology and equipment we have."

"No kidding? Betty Norton. A woman? A nurse? Taking the lead in hospital affairs? That's amazing. Too bad my mom is so out of it. She would be thrilled to hear about that."

"You're right. It seems pretty amazing when you first think about it. But the truth is, it was nurses that took the leading role in the introduction of the modern approach to error management in medicine."

"I never heard anything about that in nursing school."

"Well, it's all brand-new. It was adapted from the field of aviation. Airlines were able to reduce their accident rate by recognizing the fact that 'to err is human.'"

"To err is human? Well, duh! Everyone knows that. But I still don't get it."

"Okay, look at it this way. Humans provide all critical services for airlines. And, since humans all make errors, errors are inevitable. That's why they introduced a system of checkups on all decisions that pilots, mechanics, and traffic controllers make so that errors could be detected and corrected before they caused any harm. It made a huge improvement in airline safety. So now the health-care industry is beginning to implement the same process in hospitals."

"And did you have any role in instituting all those changes?" Cathy asked.

"Oh, no. It was just pure luck that I even heard about it. I was still in Boston when Betty got this program started. After my son died, my wife and I decided to leave Boston and started looking around for someplace else to raise our family. When I found out about all the improvements she had made here, I could see she was even way ahead of the hospitals in Boston. I felt comfortable practicing here, without compromising any quality-of-care standards. So we moved back to Maine."

"That's an amazing story," Cathy replied, shaking her head. "You know? Back when I first started in nursing, as just a lowly LPN—well, back then, I never would have imagined that nurses, being female, could ever gain so much power and influence in the field of medicine."

"Well, I feel pretty lucky," Tom declared. "Never in my wildest dreams did I think I could end up practicing cardiology back in my own hometown. And I owe it all to Betty Norton. She's probably done more for this hospital than any person around."

On Tom's drive back down to Snug Harbor in his pickup truck, his conversation with Cathy about Betty Norton and the hospital caused him to recall the experiences that had brought him back to Maine. He turned off the radio so he could hear himself think.

Life seemed so enjoyable when they first moved to Boston. Caroline used to love the opera. Tom grew to love it too after time. Plus, he enjoyed gaining esteem as an instructor at the medical school. Such happy days. Caroline was so great. So happy. Having children and sharing them with all of her friends, who were also mothers, seemed to take away all of her earlier anger about the unfairness of life.

And the grandparents. How life changes when parents see their own children become mothers and fathers. They were always driving down from Maine for a visit. What an effect that had on Caroline.

"I just can't believe how great my parents are," Caroline remarked, over a beer one afternoon in Killington. They were having a getaway weekend of skiing while her parents looked after the kids. "I never dreamed they would ever do something like this for us."

"Doesn't surprise me. They love those kids. They're probably having as much fun as we are."

"You're probably right. You know? It makes me sad to think back on how much I used to hate my parents. I can't imagine why I let that happen."

"I always figured it was typical teenage rebellion. And probably drugs."

"Yeah," she sighed. "I can never forgive myself for getting hooked on pot."

"Ah, get over it. Back then, everyone was into pot. Don't be so hard on yourself."

"Then how come you never used pot?"

"Who said I didn't? I just didn't inhale."

"Very funny. Were you smokin' with Bill Clinton?"

"Actually, I was lucky. Drugs never made it up to Maine, back in those days. Or I probably would have tried 'em, just like everyone else."

Life started to change after that. Caroline began to enjoy their trips back to Maine with the kids. She and the kids eventually grew to love Maine.

As far as Tom was concerned, it was his father's death that turned the tide for him. The event was not totally unexpected. His father had consulted Tom once about episodes of chest pain and shortness of breath. Back then, coronary bypass grafts were not yet well established. Tom was not surprised when he got the phone call from Prince, one day in late May, telling him of his father's sudden death.

On the drive back home to Maine that evening, Tom decided to do a replay of his father's response to Tom's brother Michael's death. Tom spoke to Prince as the gathering at his mother's house came to an end that night. "Meet you on the *Shady Lady* tomorrow morning. Five thirty, sharp. We're haulin' lobsters."

"You want to go out haulin' tomorrow?" Prince asked in disbelief.

"Ayeah. That's what Dad and I did after Michael died. That's how he'd want it now."

Tom did not sit out at the end of the dock very long that night. It was too cold. Even the bourbon was not enough, with the cloudless sky and temperatures dropping close to freezing. But the morning sun warmed things quickly, and lobstering was a therapeutic experience. The CB radio was buzzing with tales of good ole Dickie MacMahan all day long. Tom tried to allay some of Prince's guilt over being out alone in the boat with Dickie when he had his heart attack, and there was nothing Prince could do to help but steam full speed for shore. Dad was still alive when they loaded him into the ambulance, but he never made it to the hospital. EMT training was not what it is today, or his father might have made it.

At the end of the haul, Prince insisted they stop off down at the lobster co-op for a visit at the lobstermen's fish house. All the boats in the harbor were tied up there that afternoon. A sincere and unabashed memorial for good ole Dickie, a regular guy if there ever was one. It brought tears to Tom's eyes. After a six-pack or so (Tom lost count), they steamed on home. Prince recalled how Dickie had somehow been revived after Michael's death by a similar gathering at the fish house.

"They are really a great support group," Tom declared.

"Ayeah. Lobstermen Anonymous—that's what your dad used to call 'em."

That experience was the first time that Tom ever considered the values of small-town life versus the exhilaration of climbing up the ladder of academic medicine in a sophisticated town like Boston. Even though he had gone to Yale, he always harbored a little embarrassment about coming from a Podunk town in Maine. He remembered vividly how his feelings about his hometown changed dramatically at that time. But he never considered actually moving back home.

The final straw came shortly after his son, Mark, turned sixteen. Tom would never forget the day Mark got his driver's license. The two of them went for a long drive together, with Mark at the wheel. It was immensely satisfying for Tom to realize that Mark was becoming an adult. He later told Caroline about all the questions Mark had asked about becoming a man. He felt the most joy of all when Caroline told Tom he was a great mentor.

But it wasn't too many mornings after that when she called to Tom, after the kids were all off to school, "Take a look at this!"

Neither of them knew what to make of the sign over Mark's bed: SHIT HAPPENS. Not long afterward, Mark was killed in a motorcycle accident. Tom still remembered exactly how he felt. *I just wanted to be home and go out haulin'.* And Caroline cried, "For the first time I can remember in a long time, I just want to be with my mother."

They decided to move back to Maine. Some things in life were more important than being an opera buff or becoming chief of cardiology at some university medical center. Tom decided to move his practice to Maine. He resolved to bring cardiology care up to standard at the hospital. He felt certain Betty Norton would help. Weeks later, near the end of their trip home, Tom looked out over First Creek and smelled the clam flats. For the first time since Mark died, he felt a dite of happiness as they drove into Snug Harbor. There was no question he had made the right decision.

～

Soon after Tom left the ward, Cathy began rounds on her patients. When she strolled into Mr. Gurnet's room, she saw the sad look on his face. Recognizing his apprehension, she asked him, "Now that your heart is behaving okay, do you mind telling me how you happened to injure your eye?"

"Oh, I did a dumb thing. I was taking down some trees and a big branch pinned over a birch sapling as the tree went down. So I cut a limb off the tree to release the sapling, and the damned thing snapped up and hit me in the eye. I should have known better. Poor Arly. She saw the whole thing. I'll bet it really scared her."

"Who is Arly?"

"My granddaughter. She just turned nine years old last month."

"What day?"

"The twenty-third. Why do you ask?"

"Well, my daughter is nine, and she was born on the twenty-first. She's two days older than Arly. Isn't that something?"

Mr. Gurnet seemed much more at ease after talking about his granddaughter. Cathy suggested he get some rest. Her shift was almost over and she planned to go home and get some rest.

Chapter 7

The following morning, while the Memorial Day parade marched down Maine Street, Dr. MacMahan was at the hospital, explaining to the family all the events from the previous evening.

"When the local anesthesia began to wear off in Mr. Gurnet's eye, his pain returned. The nurse immediately responded with a dose of intravenous morphine. But before the morphine could take effect, the pain, once again, managed to trigger his arrhythmia. His heart beat so fast, they had to put him on a continuous intravenous drip of lidocaine, a heart depressant medicine that slowed the heart rate, so that the heart would have adequate time to refill with blood before the next beat, and normal cardiac output was reestablished.

"However, the latest blood tests now show evidence of cardiac muscle injury, indicating that he is probably having a mild heart attack."

George could not be discharged, as planned, that morning. He would have to remain in the ICU until his condition improved. He was expected to recover, but later, after his heart became more stable, he might need to be transferred to a hospital where he could have a cardiac catheterization for evaluation of his coronary arteries.

When this news got communicated to George Gurnet III, he left Boston immediately and began driving up to Maine to help his mother with the difficult decisions that had to be made. He arrived in town late that afternoon and drove out to the hospital, following directions on his GPS.

"Boy, that's weird," George III said out loud when he got his first look at the hospital. Situated on a point of land extending out into a peaceful, picturesque bay, the hospital's beautiful coastal setting was somehow depressing to the young gentleman. His mental image of hospitals was formed on the busy streets of Boston, and was reinforced by television dramas. This modern building, with its tasteful architecture and cozy, welcoming gardens, was out of sync with George III's concept a of quality medical facility. Old-fashioned high-rise buildings, with an attached parking garage situated on a busy street, and ambulances all over the place, would have been a lot more reassuring.

His mood dropped even lower when he saw how small and relaxed the ICU appeared.

"Looks more like some uptown gallery, with all those colorful paintings and tasteful decor," he grumbled under his breath. "Maybe if they didn't waste so much time and money on artwork, they could give their patients some decent care."

He entered and requested to meet immediately with his father's doctors.

Dr. MacMahan drove back to the hospital. In the waiting room outside the ICU, he met with George Gurnet III, who listened very politely as Dr. MacMahan briefed him on his father's condition.

"And so, Mr. Gurnet," Tom summarized, "your father is presently in stable condition. The damage to his heart from his recent infarction appears to be slight, but the infarcted area is adjacent to a node that controls his heart rate. That is why he sometimes gets these dangerously rapid heart rates. We are able to control his heart rate with an intravenous drip of lidocaine, which must be continuously monitored to ensure proper control."

Beep! Beep! Beep!

George III was startled by the loud noise.

"Sorry. My lousy pager is going off. Please excuse me for a minute while I answer this damn thing."

Tom stepped into an adjacent room and dialed the number on his pager. "Dr. MacMahan speaking. Oh, it is you, Prince. I thought maybe that was your number. What's up?"

George Gurnet III stepped over to the door for a bit of eavesdropping.

"I see," Tom continued, unaware of George's presence. "You'll never be able to buy any of those on Memorial Day. But you might could check out in my father's dooryard. Ayeah. Finest kind! Well, he used to have a bunch of 'em out in the shed. In one of them old hogsheads. Dad never threw anything away. What? Naw, it don't much mattah. Okay, call me if you can't find 'em. Ayeah. Catch ya later. Bye."

George III quickly returned to his seat before Tom saw him. He had no questions when Tom finished his report. George III was informed that Dr. Gardiner was expected momentarily to explain her treatment of the eye injury and answer any other questions he might have.

~

As Elizabeth Norton—vice president of nursing affairs, formerly known as chief of nursing—entered the intensive care unit later that morning, she felt a satisfying improvement in her mood. Gone was the self-pity about missing the annual Memorial Day picnic down at Popplestone Reach, the last festive gathering of locals before the summer people arrived to dominate the social scene.

Her satisfaction in the ICU stemmed from having been instrumental in its establishment and its continued development. Years ago, as a new nurse fresh out of Cornell Nursing School, back when she was still Betty Cross, she recognized the value of having an intensive care unit, even in a small rural hospital. She personally went to the board of trustees and informed them of the newest advances in hospital care, which she had learned at Cornell. At that time, all of the GPs in town were against it. Her only support came from a young internist. New in town, he was very helpful and convincing to the board of trustees. They became the first hospital in Maine, outside of Portland and Bangor, to establish an ICU. Even after she became Betty Norton she continued to lead the hospital in obtaining all the newest medical technology and broadening the scope of the medical staff.

Recently, when they built the new hospital, she organized the committee that invited local artists and sculptors to participate in and contribute to the elegant decor. Through the years, constantly updating technology and maintaining quality of care in the ICU were continuing sources of pride in her life. It was her baby. She could feel the goose bumps every time she walked through the doors. Too bad about missing the picnic, but a woman had do what she had to do.

"What brings you in here on a holiday afternoon?" Cathy asked as Elizabeth Norton sat down at the nurse's desk.

"Well, we were a little short staffed for the holiday anyway. Then Doris called in 'cause her daughter is pretty sick, I guess. So I am covering as nursing supervisor this evening."

"Well, maybe we should thank you for being so dedicated and

responsible. What's wrong with Doris's little girl anyway? Did she say?"

"Fever and throwing up. They don't know exactly why. Stomach flu is what they think. I hear it's going around." Betty took a deep breath and sighed. "Must be tough, taking care of kids and trying to hold down a job at the same time."

"Yeah, tell me about it." Cathy also let out a big sigh.

At that moment, Dr. Gardiner entered the ICU and inquired where she might find Mr. Gurnet's son. "And, Cathy," she added, "thank you for your help last night with Mr. Gurnet. Dr. MacMahan says your prompt intervention probably saved his life. We really appreciate your efforts."

Elizabeth Norton kept on staring at Sally. "Did you see that, Cathy?" she asked after Sally went into the waiting room. "Dr. Gardiner's got her hair up in a ponytail, and she's not wearing any of her frumpy old professor clothes. It's the first time I've ever seen her in a tailored outfit. Not a bad figure she's got, don'tcha think? And she was even wearing eye makeup. Now what do you reckon has gotten into her?"

"It's gotta be a man," Cathy responded without hesitation.

"I'm sure we'll find out who it is eventually. Should be interesting."

Cathy began her report but was interrupted by the telephone. "ICU. Cathy speaking." She listened for a minute and continued. "I paged you to tell you that the pharmacy has some concerns about the anticoagulant medication you ordered for your lady with the hip fracture. Evidently it doesn't conform to their new protocol for that drug. You could call them directly and straighten it out. Then we could get her started on the medicine as soon as possible." Cathy listened again. "Well, you are very welcome. Bye."

"That was Dr. Barter. He's so nice. He even thanked me for picking up that error. Said I probably saved him and his patient a lot of grief. At the hospital where I used to work, if you called a doctor and said he'd made a mistake, he'd get real nasty. It seems like that doesn't happen around here."

"I know," Mrs. Norton replied. "It's so nice to have such a collaborative relationship among the staff. And it's the result of all the new policies we have implemented."

"Yes. I think it's really amazing. And Dr. MacMahan tells me that you were largely responsible for instituting these changes."

"He did?"

"Well, yes. He started to tell me about it, but we got interrupted. It sounded pretty interesting."

"It is. In fact, it's pretty damn exciting when you see what's coming down the road."

"How's that? I mean, do you have time to tell me about it? I've only got two patients in here tonight, and they're pretty stable right now."

"Okay. Let's finish your report first. Then I'll give you the big picture."

After the nursing report, Betty began, "My first years at this hospital were devoted to acquiring and installing all the new technology that medicine has developed in the last few decades. You know, ICUs, monitoring equipment, scanners, fiber-optic diagnostic and surgical techniques, to name just a few. It was so exciting, learning about the features of all that new technology. But the best part was seeing the impact that modern medical technology had on improving health care. You see what I'm talking about?"

"I think so. That stuff has been there since I started, so I always kinda took it for granted. But looking back in time makes you appreciate technology a lot more," Cathy said very carefully.

"Exactly!" Betty responded. "We began to attract all kinds of medical specialists, instead of a bunch of GPs. That was pretty exciting. And to know we made it all available locally for people here in rural Maine.

"Then, just when the medical community was basking in self-congratulation for all these improvements, along came a study from the Institute of Medicine, documenting the tremendous harm caused by medical errors in America today. It was demoralizing, even if it was a little exaggerated, as some critics claimed. But everyone agreed something had to be done. And the first response was to ratchet up the surveillance over negligent physicians. Root out all the bad apples and make them shape up. Or get the hell out of health care. We called it the blame-and-shame game. And it didn't work. Statistics did not improve. All it did was to create a culture of fear and intimidation in the medical community. Some people even say it helped fuel the growing malpractice crisis in this country."

"I know," Cathy replied. "I've had plenty of experience with the blame game in my short career."

"Well, some people began to realize that you can never completely eliminate human error in medical care. No matter what you try. 'To err is human.'"

Cathy nodded.

"So they came up with what's called the systems approach to error management. That view assumes that errors are inevitable, so why not try and develop a system that finds errors and corrects them before they cause any harm. These systems were already well established in the airline industry. Now they are being developed for health care. And our hospital has already implemented most of these management policies."

"And are these policies having any effect?" Cathy asked.

"You mean here? In this hospital?"

"Yes."

"In some ways they have. The improvement in staff morale and productivity was immediate and very gratifying. It's too soon to have a clear and precise measurement on our health-care improvement. But we're tracking it. There have been some studies at large hospitals showing a significant reduction in hospital costs by reducing complications due to medical errors. You probably already know that the costs of medical and surgical complications are a huge problem. They're responsible for much of the rising cost of medical care. So the early results are encouraging. Some people are saying these results will eventually lead to a reduction in malpractice suits and the ever-increasing cost of malpractice insurance. But I'm not so optimistic about that problem yet."

"Me neither. I'm just glad nurses don't have to carry malpractice insurance," Cathy observed. "But I'm curious. However, did you get hooked into this new system anyway?"

"Oh, well I read a lot. And it's in the nursing literature. So I started going to a bunch of conferences, where we learned how to apply this strategy in hospitals. Then I came home and started it here. Now all orders are reviewed and checked by the staff and the pharmacy. There's a computer program that checks everything according to accepted protocols before orders are carried out. Responsibility is shared at many levels."

"I am surprised you were able to get all the doctors to go along with it," Cathy observed.

"Frankly, Cathy, I think it's probably easier to get this kind of thing started in a small community hospital than in some big academic institution, where all the physicians think they are gods. Here, most of the doctors have come to realize they are not really gods after all— only highly trained and responsible human beings who can still make mistakes every once in a while. And I think what they really care about is their patients. In a small town your patients are your friends and neighbors. The doctors have come to appreciate working in a hospital where the entire staff cooperates to make certain that errors at all levels are identified and corrected before they can cause harm to their patients. That kind of collaborative atmosphere is what makes it really pleasant to work here. And it promotes better care for the patients."

"Sounds like something I ought to know more about."

"Well, I have plenty of literature on it in my office. I'd be glad to share. And it's also being taught in some of the graduate nursing programs, in case you're interested."

"As a matter of fact, I am. And that brings up another question I need to ask you," Cathy said. "If you can spare another minute."

"Go right ahead. I have plenty of time."

"Well, I just sent in my application for the scholarship to get my master's degree. I was wondering if you had a chance to look it over yet."

"Yes, I did. Everything looked very good. I will be presenting it to the board of trustees next month. I am fairly certain they will approve it, if that makes you feel any better."

"It really does," Cathy said with obvious delight. "I never dreamed I would ever get an opportunity to ever get my master's degree."

"Listen, Cathy, you have no idea how delighted we are to be able to give you this opportunity. There is such a shortage of nursing talent these days. I'm sure you are aware of that."

"Well, not really."

"Okay," Betty responded. "Back when I was in college, a woman with ability and ambition had only two choices for a career: nurse or schoolteacher. Hospitals were flooded with well-trained, intelligent nurses. In those days, there was such an abundant supply of nurses, the wages were low, and that kept health care costs down. Nowadays, a bright young woman can go into practically any field she chooses. The nursing industry has to compete for talent these days. Good nurses with leadership potential are now in short supply. So when we find someone with talent and dedication like you have, it is in our interest to help her further her training so we can continue to have an ample staff of highly trained, professional nurses. We are very fortunate to have a sizable trust fund to help us accomplish this objective. Believe me, without the trust fund, this hospital would never survive."

"That is so wonderful," Cathy exclaimed. "I never dreamed I would ever get this kind of opportunity. I can't thank you enough for all your support. Someday maybe I'll be able to repay you, in some way, for all your help."

Betty left the ICU in a much happier frame. Not being a mother had some advantages, she surmised. *I could be just like Doris. Fat and dumpy. No time for fitness and the YMCA. No time for anything but doing my shift or being home with the kids. Then who would be here to look after the hospital? And help out people like Cathy? In some ways she's sort of like a daughter to me. Guess I'm just lucky in some ways.*

⁓

After his visit with Dr. Gardiner, George III stepped out of the waiting room, visited briefly with his father, and went outside the hospital where he could light up a cigarette and make a call on his cell phone. He reached a physician with whom he often golfed, back in Boston, and asked for some advice on how to handle his father's problems. He wanted his father out of this hick town hospital and transferred to a reliable medical center. His friend recommended Jeremy Moshier, a cardiologist at Maine Medical Center who had trained in Boston and was highly regarded in his field. George lit up another cigarette and tried to call Dr. Moshier, only to be reminded that it was Memorial Day. The doctor was not on call and could not be reached until Tuesday morning.

The next morning, after a long conversation with George III, Dr. Moshier agreed to call Dr. MacMahan and make arrangements for the transfer of George Jr. to Maine Medical Center, assuming, of course, that it was an appropriate and safe thing to do. Soon he had Dr. MacMahan on the line.

"Hi, Tom. It's Jeremy. How have you been? Good! I got a call this morning from George Gurnet III. He wants his father transferred to Maine Medical right away. What's the scoop?"

"Well, this guy appears to have had a mild heart attack associated with the pain and stress from an eye injury and subsequent surgical repair. His enzymes are not up very much, and he seems to be stable and comfortable except when he gets these arrhythmias. They're all ventricular tachycardias. I've had him on a lidocaine drip now since

Sunday night, and that seems to control the problem just fine. We've been able to taper the dose somewhat over the last twenty-four hours. I was planning to send him to you whenever he gets over his V-tach. That will make his transfer a little less risky. He needs to go to the cath lab anyway and see about, maybe, a stent or two. But we need to watch him a little longer and make certain he's good to go before we ship him. I'll be glad to get him off my worry list."

"Okay, Tom. Look, I've got a bunch of procedures scheduled this afternoon. If he is stable, you might arrange to transfer him so he arrives here after four thirty or five o'clock. That way I can be available when he gets admitted. And by the way, I didn't tell Mr. Gurnet III that you were once my professor when I was in my cardiology fellowship back in Boston."

"It's just as well you didn't," Tom said. "I'll plan to ship him around three if he looks okay. Talk with you later. Bye!"

What a relief. Like a weight had just been lifted from his shoulders. Perhaps now he could put those shoulders to better use, like swimming maybe.

~

Later that afternoon, around three o'clock, he left his office and went to the ICU to see if Mr. Gurnet's heart was stabilized enough to make all the transfer arrangements. He went over everything with the family and informed them of the risks involved with transferring an unstable cardiac patient. He recommended they wait another day or so for his condition to stabilize before making the transfer.

George Gurnet III, bristling with contempt, insisted the transfer be made right away. Tom told them that if they insisted that was the way it had to be, then they would have to sign a paper for "release against medical advice." Then he recommended sending Cathy Dyer, the ICU nurse most familiar with Mr. Gurnet's condition, to ride along in the ambulance as an extra precaution.

George Gurnet III insisted. The family seemed to agree. Papers were signed.

Despite his resolve that living in Maine was worth the trade-off of not getting any respect as a physician, it still hurt inside when he had to pay the price. Tom was not in the best mood as he resigned himself to the task of tackling the mountain of paperwork required for a hospital transfer. When he had finally finished, the ward secretary came over and dumped on one more thick form for him to complete.

"What the hell is this goddamned thing?" he bellowed out.

"It's the new patient transfer form," she answered. "It's part of the new, revised federal EMTALA regulations governing the transfer of patients."

"Jesus," said Tom. "The way things are going, it won't be long before doctors will have to give up practicing medicine altogether and spend all their time doing goddamn paperwork." He filled out the form and went back to the office.

Chapter 8

*W*alking over to his office, Tom managed to delete from his mind most of the wrath about paperwork, only to confront another mound of papers piled up on his desk: Medicare forms. A never-ending chore. Tom just shook his head. He could hardly wait for electronic billing to be installed next month. It had gotten now to where paperwork took up nearly as much time as patient care. Unfortunately, electronic technology offered no help for the growing, unfunded burden imposed by HMOs and all their prior approval requirements. The paperwork they now demanded; before they would approve a lousy CAT scan. Not to mention HIPAA compliance forms. The EMR (electronic medical record) was another frightening hurdle looming in the future. Why should a cardiologist be required to hire an extra employee just to type into some computer all that irrelevant health data that had no bearing on his medical specialty, cardiology? He tried not to think about it. *Just do what you have to do.* Tom was determined to git 'er done."

He was halfway through the stack, when the hospital called. "Your patient just coded in the ambulance," the operator said. "They want you over here stat!"

Tom rushed over to the emergency room entrance and found a mob scene in and around the ambulance. Typical of any hospital code 99. Representatives from every department of the hospital had come to help. They were all standing around, gawking and waiting, eager to be of service in any way they could. The atmosphere was a mix of anxiety, excitement, and curiosity.

Inside the ambulance, the atmosphere was more a mix of despair, frustration, and hopelessness. An endotracheal tube had been inserted into George's windpipe, and a respiratory technician was ventilating him. The ER doc was just removing the paddles from George's chest when he saw Tom climb in the ambulance.

"We've shocked him three times, but his heart simply doesn't respond," he announced with a tone of gloom and disappointment. "I wonder if he might have somehow gotten a big of dose of lidocaine when they made the transfer over to the ambulance."

"He's had a couple of amps of bicarb, as well as several doses of epi, and nothing works," one of the nurses added for completeness.

Tom looked at the heart monitor. The EKG showed a straight line. It looked hopeless. He took out his stethoscope and placed it on George's chest. No heartbeat. Definitely hopeless. Tom pronounced him dead. "Three thirty-seven," he announced, looking at his watch. A nurse logged it in the record.

Cathy stood by, silently sobbing as she put the pieces together in her mind, analyzing what must have happened. The ambulance and all the equipment were brand-new to her, as well as to the ambulance crew. She had supervised the ambulance attendant as he carefully placed the IV bag in the new, state-of-the-art, digital flow rate control device. She instructed him to set the rate at 44 cc's per hour. The program panel looked just like one on a microwave oven. She tried to figure out what had happened. Instead of 44, the dial read 444 cc's per hour, enough lidocaine to shut down anyone's heart. How could that have happened?

It didn't matter. She should have seen it and corrected it before it was too late. No one else seemed to have noticed. During the attempted resuscitation, the IV had been removed from the control meter so it could be used for administering emergency medications. The flow control meter still had 444 on the dial.

Tom glanced at Cathy and tenderly placed his arm around her. Losing a patient was not an easy thing. The staff began the somber job of cleaning up. No one said anything about the flow control meter when it was returned to its compartment in the ambulance.

"What a nightmare," Cathy said after some time. "He was such a nice man. Did you know he had a granddaughter the same age as Britney?"

Cathy excused herself before Tom could respond and went back in the hospital to make her report to Betty Norton. Tom went out to speak with the family.

The Gurnet family listened politely as Dr. MacMahan explained what had occurred. George III asked if there were any unusual circumstances that would possibly explain why this had happened. Tom said he didn't know for certain, but he suspected that the dosage of lidocaine in the IV drip might not have been properly regulated in the transfer of the patient from the ICU to the ambulance. He reminded them that this was one of the risks in transferring patients with arrhythmias, about which he had warned them. It was more difficult to monitor the patient and regulate his medications during transfer than in the stable environment of the ICU. Too little lidocaine or too much lidocaine. Either one could result in cardiac arrest.

"There are other things that could have caused this," Tom added. "The exertion of moving him around may have extended his infarct. We can't really know at this point. An autopsy might be helpful in finding the answers to all these questions."

"If there is an autopsy," George III announced, "it won't be done here."

"If that's the way you want it, then okay. Unless there any more questions, that seems like the end of it."

"Don't count on it," George III stated emphatically. "You have not heard the last of this case by any means."

Tom did not respond. He went back to his office to finish the paperwork and close up for the day.

～

Cathy Dyer knocked softly of the open door of the vice president of nursing affairs and was told to come in.

"Mrs. Norton," she began.

"I thought we agreed. It's Betty. Remember? Now, what's the problem this afternoon?"

Cathy gave a full report of the incident, including the improper entry in the IV flow meter that probably caused it all. By this time, she was sobbing. "The ambulance was totally new. All the equipment inside was fancy new stuff. I have never been checked out on any of it. So I handed the order sheet to the EMT and let him program the control rate for the IV drip. It wasn't until after the patient arrested that I noticed that the EMT had made an error when he programmed the IV control flow meter."

Betty got up from her desk, walked over, and handed Cathy some

Kleenex. "I don't think that was your legal responsibility, if that means anything to you."

"It never occurred to me that I should check the entry. I just can't believe I could have let that occur. What do you think is going to happen?"

"Probably nothing. Listen, Cathy, mistakes happen in medicine. It's all done by humans, and humans all make errors. That is why I have this famous quote from Alexander Pope posted on the wall. 'To err is human, to forgive divine.' Think about that.

"We have such an elaborate and redundant system of checks and reviews in this hospital to detect and correct these things. Just like we talked about the other night. Regardless, there is no possible way to catch every single mistake before any harm is done. So don't be too hard on yourself now, Cathy. More Kleenex? Besides, technically, once the patient entered the ambulance, his care became the legal responsibility of the ambulance attendant. Our hospital system for identifying and correcting errors does not extend into other institutions, such as ambulance companies. You are not responsible for his error."

Cathy's relief was apparent.

"Tell me," she continued, "have you discussed this with anyone else?" Cathy shook her head no. "Not even Dr. MacMahan?"

"No," Cathy indicated.

"Good. You did the right thing, coming and reporting directly to me. I doubt if anything will ever come of this, but there is no use taking a chance that some word of this would get out and cause trouble for the hospital. So it's probably just as well not to mention this to anybody. No use pointing the finger of blame at anyone if it doesn't serve any real purpose. Don't you agree?" Cathy nodded her head yes. "One other thing, Cathy," she added in a very intimate, motherly tone of voice. "The word is out you and Dr. MacMahan are in some kind of a relationship these days. I don't mean to pry, but there are rumors."

"Well, yes. I mean sort of. I've been seeing him off and on, but I haven't totally moved in or anything. I've still got a nine-year-old daughter at home. She's only with her father half the time."

"I see. Well, it's not likely that anything will ever come out of this incident. But just to be on the safe side, perhaps you might want to avoid discussing this with anyone, including Tom. When stuff like this gets out in the community, it often gets distorted, and repercussions may occur. Do you see what I'm getting at?" Cathy nodded her head, yes. "Thank you so much for your detailed and honest report. I don't see any need to fill out an incident report on this, since he was already discharged from the hospital when the arrest occurred. So you can consider the case closed. And, Cathy, if anything further should come up on this, feel free to come to this office if you need help. The door is always open."

∼

Tom was driving out of the office parking lot when he saw Sam Gardiner, skipping stones in the hospital pond. He stopped the truck and rolled down the window. "Tigger! What are you up to?"

"The name is Sam."

"Okay, Sam. What are you up to?"

"I'm waiting around for my mom to take me home. Like, I always miss the school bus on account of swim practice."

"Well, hop in," Tom invited. "I'll give you a ride. No problem."

"Hey, great!" Sam responded. A ride in a pickup truck was too much to resist. He picked up his backpack. "Just let me put a note under my mom's windshield wiper so she won't be worried. Nice truck," he remarked as he climbed into the cab, "I never knew doctors drove pickup trucks."

"We try not to advertise it," Tom replied. "So you're on the swim team, are you?"

"Yeah. It's the only thing good about this place."

"I see," Tom said. "What seems to be the problem around here?"

"Boring!"

"Boring?"

"Yeah. Like school is letting out in a couple of weeks and I'll have nothing to do except, like, sit around playing computer games and weed the garden whenever my mom makes me. Yuck!"

"Why don't you get a job?"

"Can't. It's like I'm grounded. Lost my driver's license."

"How come?" Tom asked.

"Drunk driving. Happened a couple of days ago. I won't get my license back 'til November," Sam admitted, somewhat embarrassed.

"Ooh! I hate it when that happens," said Tom with a slight grin.

"Me too," agreed Sam, a little more at ease. "My dad was really pissed. He's like, not even talking to me now."

"That's too bad. Where is your dad?"

"He's in Philadelphia."

"What's he do?"

"He's some kind of a stock and mutual fund manager. Like, he helps people with their retirement investments and things. I don't really know for sure."

"But you still see him, don't you?"

"Well, yeah. Like, I was supposed to spend the summer with him, but I don't know if I'm gonna go or not now—being he's pissed and I don't want to miss swim practice and all. I might end up here. I guess it doesn't matter which. I don't know."

"See if you can find us some good music on the radio there, Sam."

"Sure," Sam said, and he began testing stations. Soon "Luckenbach, Texas," with Waylon Jennings and Willie Nelson, came out of the speakers.

"Great song," Tom declared. "Didn't expect you'd be into country music, coming from Philadelphia."

"Oh, I get that from my grandpa. He's from out in southern Illinois."

"I see. What does he do out in Illinois?"

"He has a nice farm, and he also runs a grain elevator. And he, like, plays in this bluegrass band for a hobby. That's how come I like country music."

Tom rolled down his window and cranked up the volume a bit. He stuck his elbow out the window and said, "We could use some air in here." Sam did the same on his side. Truckin'. Elbows out the windows. Eyeballing the scenery. Listening to the music. The warm humid air streaming in the side windows and rushing out the back. A smile appeared on Sam's face.

"So, do you see your grandfather very often?" Tom asked after Waylon and Willie were finished.

"We used to go back to the farm every summer. I really liked it. Grandpa is kinda old-fashioned. Know what I mean?"

Tom shrugged his shoulders and raised his eyebrows.

"I mean, like, he thinks kids should work. And he started letting me work on the farm from the time I was in kindergarten. I always looked forward to being allowed to work. Back in Philadelphia, they don't think it's right for kids to have to work, except, like, maybe to clean their rooms."

"I see. Very interesting. Up here in Maine, we are kinda behind the times, just like in Illinois."

"Hey, that's my road there," Sam said as they sped past the dirt road that led to Sam's house.

"Oops! Sorry, I forgot about that. I was thinking about an errand I need to do. It won't take long. Have you got a minute or two?"

Sam didn't object, so Tom drove on a little farther and turned into his father's driveway. He drove around back, on down to the water, and parked next to his father's fish house. The *Shady Lady* was tied to the dock. They found Arthur in the fish house, repairing lobster traps.

"Sam, this is Arthur Prince. We call him Prince. He's my partner in the lobster business. Prince, this is Sam Gardiner. His mom is Dr. Gardiner, the lady who fixed the eye on that fellow you hauled over to the hospital in the ambulance last Sunday."

"Pleased t' meet ya," Arthur said, observing that Sam's curiosity was already focused on the boat. "Go ahead. Hop on board if you'd care to, and look around. Can't hurt nothin'."

Sam climbed aboard while Tom filled in Arthur on the details of George Gurnet's recent and unfortunate demise. Tom thought Arthur would be interested to know that his intuition about the serious significance of Mr. Gurnet's rapid pulse had been correct, especially since that was what turned out to kill him in the end. He promised to bring a piece of the EKG strip for Arthur to examine.

"Not to change the subject or nothin'," Arthur said, "but how'd ya hook up with that kid?"

"Oh, I was just giving him a lift home. I think he's pretty mixed up right now. The only thing he seems focused on is the swim team. But he says he likes to work."

"Can't be all that bad then," Arthur said, grinning and thinking to himself. "Why, I remember you, back …" Sam's return interrupted Arthur's train of thought. "What do you think of the boat, Sam?"

"It's beautiful. I really like it."

"Well how'd ya like to see how she goes, haulin' lobsters?"

"Well, yeah. I mean I'd love to, but like, I have to go to school."

"What about Saturday?"

"Gee, Saturday's great. What time?"

"Five thirty."

"Five thirty? Like in the morning?" Sam was in disbelief, not remembering ever having been up that early before.

"Ayeah! Five thutty. Wouldn't hurt to be five minutes early."

"Okay. I don't know how, but I'll be here. That's for sure. And thanks a lot."

Once they were in the truck and headed for home, Tom said he would be happy to drive over and pick up Sam Saturday morning at 5:00 a.m.

⌒

After a long, grueling day at the office, Sally ambled across the doctors' parking lot toward her car. Her eyes scanned the perimeter. *Where the hell is Sam?* Then she saw the note on her windshield. *Hmmm. Hitched a ride with Tom. How nice.* Sally shook her head as she climbed in the car and started the motor. The unexpected death of her postop patient, Mr. Gurnet, upset her much more than she would have expected. Here in Maine, things in life seemed to affect her differently. But her problems around Sam still trumped all other issues on her mind. Driving home, Sally didn't see all the gorgeous lupine blossoms, bursting out along the roadside. Her mind was completely occupied with how to get Sam motivated in school—and in all the rest of life, for that matter. She was totally unaware of the fresh spring smells in the air. Her windows were shut, the air conditioner was on, and she was driving on autopilot. When she turned into her driveway, she finally came to.

A rusty old pickup was parked by the front walk. *What's going on here?*

The truck door opened. Sam stepped out and waved. Then it came to her. *Oh my God! That's the same truck I saw last week up on Pitch Pine Hill. It's Tom's. I never would have guessed he would drive something like that.* As Sam walked over toward her car, Tom tooted his horn, waved his arm out the window, and drove away.

By the time Sam reached her car and stuck his head in the window, Sally's mind had drifted into another world: memories of aftershave lotion, excitement, and joy—things she hadn't thought about in ages. She wondered what brought all that up. Before Sally could figure out the answer, Sam began relating his exciting adventures on the lobster boat.

Chapter 9

There was something about the boy—Sam, or Tigger, as he didn't like to be called—that Tom really liked. Tom could not quite put his finger on it. His mind cogitated as he drove along the gravel road toward home. Still truckin'. Elbow out the window. Country music on the radio. Redolent scents of spring filled the cab. He took a deep breath and it came to him. *Pooh.* Tigger reminded him a lot of Pooh. Pooh had been the nickname of his own son, Mark, who was about Sam's age when he died. *So there you have it. Pooh.*

New leaves and tiny buds were popping out everywhere. The world was coming to life again. It could be felt everywhere. He could feel it in himself too. *Probably should make a detour over to the general store and pick up some peas to plant in the garden.* Everyone in Maine knew that peas were supposed to be in the ground by Memorial Day. *I'll plant 'em tonight,* Tom thought. *Right after supper. Only two days late. Should be okay.*

It had to be the exercise that was bringing Tom back to life. Or maybe Cathy? Or perhaps it was just that his grief and mourning were finally coming to an end. Who knew? *Maybe it don't much mattah.*

What did matter was that he was not on call, and that meant he could have a beer. He went to the fridge, popped one open, and scanned the shelves for something to eat. Leftover Finnan haddie. That would do. He'd warm it in the double boiler and cook up some boiled potatoes to serve it over. He chunked up a potato and cooked it in the lower half of the double boiler. There was nothing left to make into a salad, so he looked in the freezer and took out a boil-in-the-bag package of frozen spinach. He could toss that into the boiling water when the potatoes were almost done. Only one pot to clean.

After changing clothes, he went out to the barn for some tools and fertilizer. Two rows of peas were more than enough. He just managed to get one row cultivated when the timer went off, and he went inside to put the finishing touches on dinner. He opened another beer and looked through the paper. Nothing. He clicked on the TV. Nothing. Tom didn't feel like being home alone with nothing. Cathy. That was it. She was not supposed to be working tonight. He dialed her up.

"Hi. It's Tom. Guess what? I'm not on call. What are you up to?"

"Doing the mom thing. I picked up Britney a day early. After what happened this afternoon, I was feeling a little down, so I went shopping for a present for Britney. Then I called Frank and asked if I could have her a day early. If I had known you weren't on call, I'd have come over. What are you up to?"

"Planting peas. Starting my garden. That's why I'm calling. I wondered if you might be interested in doing a vegetable garden with me this summer."

"Christ. I don't know a thing about gardens. I doubt if I'd be much help."

"Well, didn't your mom and dad have a garden when you were growing up?"

"My mom never married. I never even knew my dad. We lived in an apartment in town. Nobody had a garden."

"Is that right? Humph. What did your mom do?"

"It's a long story. I don't want to get into it right now. Sorry about the garden."

"Wait. Don't say no 'til you've heard the deal. My garden is more than big enough for the two of us. What would you say if I taught you all about gardening, and we shared the work together? We'll split the harvest. What we don't eat, we'll freeze or can and divide it up. How does that sound?"

Cathy thought about it for a moment. "I think that might work. I'll talk to you tomorrow. Okay? Bye."

Now that's progress, Tom thought. Only tonight he still had nothing to occupy his mind. Then he noticed Caroline's scrapbook. She had created it during the last few weeks of her life, with obvious determination and visible satisfaction. From boxes of unsorted photos, which she and her family had collected over several generations, she sorted and pasted a thick tome, with instructions that Tom could view it whenever he wished, but her daughters were not to see it until they had children. Tom had started to look through it soon after she died, but it made him so sad he had to put it down after going through the first few pages. This was the first time he had felt the urge to look through it again.

He skipped over the dedication and scanned through the family tree, dating all the way back to the first Yorks. He munched on his Finnan haddie. *Mmmm, not that bad. How did she ever manage to come up with all those pictures of earlier-generation Yorks, some as far back as the late nineteenth century? Oh my God!* There was a footnote indicating that one of the York men may have been the illegitimate father of Tom's great-grandmother. Now that was something to think about.

There were lots of freckles on the pages of Caroline's childhood years. Tom had seen many of the pictures before, but she had managed to find quite a few that were new to him. The photos all changed to color somewhere in high school. A family photo in front of the York house caught his attention. Caroline was wearing the same jean shorts that were still imprinted in his memory from their first encounter on the lobster boat dock.

He was surprised to see a picture of the two of them together, apparently at some social event. He was trying to recall when it might have been taken, when a fish bone from the Finnan haddie got caught in his mouth. He fished it out from behind his tongue and searched his memory. From details in the background of the picture, he deduced that it must have been his junior year in med school. Caroline was attending Wellesley. Tom ran into her occasionally at social functions. This had to be the fraternity house party. What a night that turned out to be.

Caroline was actually somebody else's date, but she had gotten so drunk, her date just abandoned her. Tom came to the rescue and took her outside, where he held her head while she vomited several times. When the world stopped spinning, they took a long walk and ended up at a nearby diner. After two Cokes and a few fries, she perked up a bit and started to make sense. They talked as they walked, heading back to the fraternity house.

At first she talked about school and her friends and how much she enjoyed the parties and finally being old enough to get served in a bar. As she became more sober, she began to question why she even bothered to go to college, except for the drinking and social life. Lately, she had come to realize that, in those times, the world situation was pretty dismal.

"With mutual assured destruction as the foundation of international

policy, it is only a matter time before everything on earth is destroyed in a nuclear holocaust."

"Yep. Some people say that."

"Everybody knows it. So why even bother to get an education and prepare yourself for some type of adult career? Nearly everyone I know feels the same way." She lost control over her emotions and cried for a while. Tom took her hand in his and kept on walking.

"I always thought I would meet some fabulous guy at college and get married and have a family and babies, you know?"

"Right."

"Now I can't have them. I can't bear the thought of seeing them die in a nuclear war. What's the use?" She finished with an angry outpouring of profanities intended to convey how utterly unfair everything in life was. Then she wanted to know where she was supposed to sleep.

Caroline woke up with a splitting headache the next morning. Two cups of Earl Gray tea and three aspirin later, it was gone. She avoided her date and sought out Tom. They agreed to skip out on the frat house breakfast gathering and walked back to the diner for a quiet breakfast in a secluded booth.

"Sorry about last night," Caroline began as soon as the coffee was served. "Guess I sort of got carried away with nuclear holocaust."

"That's okay. I think everyone worries about it."

"Mostly, I try not to think about it, you know, and just keep going. But sometimes it overwhelms me."

"I know what you mean. My brother and I often used to talk about it too."

"Nobody I know is willing to talk about it. It's too scary."

"Well, back home in Maine—"

"Look," she interrupted, "do you remember when the Russians put all those missiles in Cuba?"

"The Cuban missile crisis? Sure, I remember it."

"Well, I can barely remember it. But once I got to college, everyone talked about it. And then came the war in Vietnam and the principle of mutual assured destruction. It seems like the world is on the brink of nuclear holocaust. They say, even if you survive the initial blasts, you'll freeze to death in nuclear winter that follows. So why do we bother to go to college?"

"I understand exactly where you're coming from," Tom replied. "But

I look at it this way. I actually enjoy going to medical school. So why not keep going, as long as the world keeps turning? But mostly I want to be able to enjoy life, as long as there is a chance your predictions might be wrong."

"Well, I'd say the chances of that are pretty damn slim." She stood up and went out to the ladies' room.

When she returned, her breakfast was on the table. While she ate, Tom told her about his reaction to the threat of nuclear war. He and his brother used to have hideouts up in the Hundred Acre Woods, their name for the woods behind the York house, when they were kids. It was an escape from the perils of childhood, both real and imagined.

Tom's father had a camp in northern Maine, where they had another hideout. During their early college years, the two boys had discussed the possibility of World War III on many occasions and had made elaborate contingency plans. They intended to gather their friends, along with plenty of provisions, and go live in a cave near their father's camp. They even stockpiled supplies in plastic trash barrels inside the cave and transplanted bushes around the entrance to the cave, so no one would find them. When everything was over, they would be among the survivors to help rebuild civilization.

Caroline rolled her eyes but said nothing

"Okay," said Tom, "assuming your theory is correct, it looks to me as if we've only got two chances in this life. Slim and none. Right?"

No response.

"Well, I choose slim."

Caroline still said nothing, but she paid for the breakfast and held his hand all the way back to the fraternity house.

Tom put his dish and his single cooking pot in the sink and went back out to the garden. He raked in some fertilizer and then made another furrow in the moist cool soil. Peas like cool soil. He gently tamped the soil on top of the seeds. *There.* Then it was time for one more beer and another look at the TV. But he was drawn back to the scrapbook.

He turned the page and found a group of pictures he'd never seen before, dated August 16, 1969. One picture showed Caroline and two other girls, dancing topless on a table, a beer in one hand, a cigarette in the other. There were also some borderline pornographic shots of her with a couple of shaggy-haired hippies. The title at the top of the page read, "Woodstock." At the bottom it said, "Make love, not war."

After the initial shock, the whole message in these photos made sense in context with what Tom remembered, very clearly, had occurred several weeks later.

It was the Saturday before Labor Day. Tom was helping his dad with cleanup and routine maintenance of the Shady Lady. *He looked up and saw Caroline, standing by the fish house. "My God!" he said, "a vision from the past." He waved, beckoning her down onto the dock. "By gorry, how long ago was it when you first came down here? I can still see the red hair bouncing off your butt as you skedaddled off the wharf."*

"Four years ago. And I haven't forgotten either. I remember exactly what you said. And you were right. I am glad we moved to Maine. And my mom and dad did fix up the house really nice. I have my own bathroom, with a shower and all the hot water I need."

"Well, I'm glad to hear it. How have you been? What have you been up to since the house party?"

"I'm doin' okay. Had a great time at Woodstock. You hear about that?"

Tom shrugged. "Well, yes," he said. "It's not my kinda thing. How're your parents?"

"Great. My dad is totally different here. He even said I could have my own horse. Only I probably won't be around enough to ride it much."

"Well, speaking of rides, how would you like a ride in the boat?"

"I'd love it."

Tom checked in the fish house for permission for an evening cruise. "Granted," his dad said, with an I-could-see-this-coming grin on his face. Caroline checked with her parents and was back in minutes, her sweater and a camera in hand.

Tom did not appreciate the clear, late-afternoon weather. It didn't seem to matter that the water was as smooth as glass. His mind was too busy trying to figure out how to pull off a clambake on his favorite island. Caroline was game for anything. The calm seas and brilliant weather put her in excellent spirits. They hauled a few of his father's lobster traps and finally managed to get some legal-sized lobsters. Oh, what the hell? *And he kept a couple of shorts too.* Why not let it all hang out? *He radioed home to get approval for an extended cruise and supper on an island. His father hesitated and then said all right.*

Tom steamed over to the harbor, tied up at the dock behind the general store, and scurried up the ramp and into the store to get provisions. He reached in his pocket, only to discover that he was broke. Not surprising. He usually left his wallet at home when he was out in the boat. Lorna Bailey was behind the checkout counter. She loaned him a dime so he could make a phone call to his date for that evening. He told her there was a major problem on board his father's boat that required his attention and would probably keep him tied up all night. Soon he was back on board and heading out to Mark Island.

"We've got butter, potatoes, half a dozen ears of corn, salt and pepper, and a six-pack of Coke. That should do it."

"You didn't get any beer?"

"Couldn't. I didn't have my wallet or any money, so I had to charge everything to my dad. Well, they wouldn't let me charge any beer. It's a state law. Have a Coke. Won't do you any harm. Leastwise, not like what happened at the fraternity house party."

When they got out to Mark Island, they anchored and went ashore in the dinghy with all their provisions. Tom began digging a fire pit in the sand. He sent Caroline to scout up some driftwood for the fire. First, they lined the fire pit with large, smooth rocks. Then they started a fire inside the pit. Dried-out driftwood burned well, so they built a large fire. Once it was going well, they went over to the other side of the island, where there was a shallow bay. The tide was out. The clam flats exuded a piquant aroma, which provided them with inspiration to dig some clams and gather seaweed. Caroline came to love that smell.

The fire had burned down to coals when they got back to the beach. Tom raked off the coals and tossed on a layer of seaweed, which steamed furiously when it hit the hot rocks. Caroline helped him arrange the lobsters, clams, potatoes, and corn on top of the seaweed. A second layer of seaweed covered the food. Then a piece of old tarpaulin covered it all. Finally, a thick layer of sand was shoveled on top. Steam began to rise out of the sand.

"How long will it have to cook?" Caroline asked.

"An hour and a half, maybe two."

"What are we going to do while we're waiting? I'm already getting hungry."

"How about a swim? The water's not very cold this time of year."

"But I don't have any bathing suit."

"Neither do I. Is that a problem?"

"Not really." She began disrobing, placing her clothes on the rocks next to the blanket Tom had laid out on the sand.

It was a full two hours later that a slight breeze came up and drifted the aroma of steamed lobster over toward the end of the beach where Tom and Caroline were lying on a blanket. Tom put his pants on and went over to check on supper.

"Boy," Caroline said, "I completely forgot how hungry I was. That smells terrific. I can hardly wait."

Their shore dinner was a prolonged, succulent affair, which ended just at sundown. The breeze stiffened a bit, and Caroline put on her sweater. Tom said the breeze was a good thing; otherwise they would be eaten alive by mosquitoes. He was covered with butter and clam juice and wished to get cleaned up. Despite the breeze, another short skinny-dip seemed to be required. Caroline too felt the sudden need to freshen up a bit.

The moon had risen, and there was a chop on the water by the time they had loaded everything back in the Shady Lady and fired up her engine. Caroline hardly said anything on the trip back home. She huddled close to Tom with her hand in the hip pocket of his jeans. He lectured her on the technical features of the LORAN unit and other nautical features lighting up the dashboard of the boat. As they rounded the point and headed into MacMahan Cove, he noticed the lights in his parents' house suddenly go off, except for the porch light. When the boat was fast to the dock, Caroline waited on board while Tom ran up to the house, sneaked a couple of beers from the refrigerator, and returned. They reclined on the deck and watched the stars.

"I had a great time tonight," she said. "Thank you so much."

"Me too. There's nothing like a clambake, as far as I am concerned."

After a pause for reflection, Caroline announced, "You know, that's the first time I ever had sex when I wasn't either drunk or high on pot."

"Was it nice?"

"Oh, God yes." A long silence followed. "I think it was the nicest evening in my whole life."

More silence.

"What's it like?" Tom asked. "I mean, what's different about sex, you know, when you're sober, instead of being drunk?"

Even more silence.

Finally, she had it all sorted out in her brain. "When I'm drunk, it's all about me. You know? Kinda selfish. Like, all I care about is getting off. You know what I'm saying? When you're sober, it's completely different. More open and intimate. Like there's this other person and you're both together inside each other's soul. When you're sober, it's all about us."

Tom reflected on this awhile. Then his thoughts got diverted by another issue.

"You know, if I couldn't charge beer at the store this afternoon, there was no way I was going to charge condoms. That isn't going to be a problem, is it?"

"Well, actually, it could be a problem. We'll have to wait and see."

"What would you do? You know, if you're—"

"I don't know. Maybe I would keep it. And if it's a boy, we could name him Mark, after the island where we had the clambake. How about that?"

"I need another beer. Should I fetch two?"

"Please."

He returned with one beer. "That's all there was. We can share." He gave her the first sip. "I've been thinking. You're not serious, are you?"

"About what?"

"About what we're talking about, that's what. You know, having a baby."

"I just said—I mean, we don't even know."

"Yeah. I know. It's just that I was thinking about last year. At that fraternity party. Remember? You said you never wanted to have any children."

"Well, I didn't mean it like that. What I meant was, I wanted to have children. I was just afraid to have them, because I couldn't stand to see them die. You know, with all that mutual assured destruction ready to blow up the world at any minute? But up here in Maine it doesn't seem so threatening."

"I know. It's like a whole 'nother world."

"It makes me think about what you said to me the first time I was on this boat. Remember that?"

"Oh, yeah. But I don't remember exactly what I said."

"You said life wasn't fair. So, instead of wasting your time trying to make things fair, put your efforts into adapting to reality so you can enjoy the good things."

"Sounds like something I might have said. My dad was always saying stuff like that."

"Well, I thought it was bullshit at the time. But I never forgot it. And recently I have found it seems to work better than anything else in life. Anyway, now I've changed my mind about having kids. Deep down inside, I always wanted to have lots of kids. I was an only child. All my life I wanted brothers and sisters. I guess that must be why I want lots of kids."

Tom sucked down a big swig of beer, which caused him to burp.

Caroline laughed. "Now that was really romantic."

"'Scuse me. But, you know, I was just thinking. What would you think if it turned out you really were pregnant, and we had to get married and it was a boy and we named him Mark, after the island? It's something to think about."

"Sounds really nice tonight, actually … I can't believe I said that. Any more beer? I could use something to drink, if we are going to sit and just talk."

"The beer's all gone, but there's a coffeepot in the fish house. I could perk us up a pot."

"And we'd be awake all night. Oh, what the hell. Let's perk. I've never watched a sunrise before."

And that was how it all started, Tom recalled as he brushed his teeth and slid into bed.

Chapter 10

It was still dark, but the eastern sky was aglow with the rising sun as Tom drove into Sam's driveway, a few minutes before five o'clock on Saturday morning. Sam was seated on the front steps. Tom noticed the boy's head was bare, so he fished around behind the truck seat and found his father's old fishing hat. "You'll be needing a hat out there in all that sun," he said as Sam climbed up into the cab. "Here, this'll do to take along."

Sam put it on obediently and then took it off to adjust the strap in back for a better fit. "Weirdest-looking baseball cap I've ever seen. How come the bill is so long?"

"That's a good question. And honestly I don't really know," Tom replied as they backed out of the driveway and headed for the dock. "Lobstermen have always worn hats with bills like that. Long as I can remember. Guess I never thought much about it. Anyway, that hat belonged to my father. My kids used to argue over who got to wear Grampy's hat whenever they were up here visiting. Eventually, he bought them all their own hats like that. They loved 'em. Always wore those hats when they were out in Grampy's boat."

Sam arrived at the fish house exactly on time. Arthur already had the *Shady Lady's* engine running and was about to put the bait on board.

"Mawnin', Tom. Mawnin', Sam," said Arthur, who was wearing a hat just like Sam's. "Just in time to give me a hand with this crate. Then we'll be off."

"Need anything before I go?" Tom asked.

"Thanks, but we're all set. Got plenty of sandridges and drinks on board. Everything's finest kind." Tom unfastened the lines, and the *Shady Lady* backed out into the cove.

Tom went home, had breakfast, and leafed through Caroline's

scrapbook to see if he could find any pictures of his kids in their fisherman's hats. He found several. One particularly good one showed Mark driving his grandfather's boat. Tom decided he needed to visit Caroline on this morning's run.

He felt a certain satisfaction, because this morning he was able to keep on running when he got to Pooh's house. In fact, he was well past Piglet's before he ran out of breath. As he walked along, he remembered how his own kids had made forts and hideouts back in these woods when they were little. Mark was always Pooh, which got to be a nickname for him. The girls were Piglet and Tigger. He could still see them running, giggling, and pretending. Playing Winnie-the-Pooh was a favorite pastime when they were visiting the grandparents. Later, when they moved back to Maine, they continued, even into their teens, to return to these special places whenever they needed solace. Somehow, hanging onto those fantasies helped them deal with whatever problem was at hand.

When he reached the resting rock, Tom climbed up and looked out over the bay. He immediately spotted the *Shady Lady*, steaming up toward Hornpout ledge. He wished he were stowed away, somewhere on board, so he could see and hear what was happening.

Suddenly, he realized that, without a change in course, the *Shady Lady* was about to slam into Hornpout Ledge. *Oh my God!* Now he wished he were on board so he could grab the wheel and prevent a disaster.

Fortunately, Arthur had his eyes open and looked up in time to scramble over to the helm. "Watch out for the BFRs," Arthur yelled out to Sam, taking the wheel and making a course correction.

"BFRs? What the hell are BFRs?"

"Big fucking rocks!" Prince explained in a very tutorial manner. "It's a navigational term."

"Got it!" Sam responded with glee.

"BFRs like to hide just beneath the surface, where you can't see 'em. If you aren't careful, they'll smack your boat and ding your prop. And that's expensive."

Arthur maneuvered the boat to port and came to a stop alongside a lobster buoy. He instructed Sam to take the gaff and hook onto the pot warp.

"Pot warp?" Sam asked.

"Pot warp is what we call the rope that is tied to the lobster pots," Prince replied. He hauled it up. Then he placed the rope in the snatch block, hanging from the davit, and fastened it to the hydraulic winch. Soon they had three traps on board. Arthur removed the lobsters, measured them, and banded them. Shorts and females got thrown back overboard. Sam watched carefully, trying to learn this part of the operation.

"How long you had this boat, Arthur?"

"You can call me Prince. Most folks do," he said. "You see, I only own half of this boat. Tom owns the other half. It used to belong to Tom's father, Dickie MacMahan."

"I see," Sam said, spearing a wad of herring scraps from the bait bucket with the bait spike and starting to rebait the traps. "So, Prince, how did you get into the lobster business anyway?"

"Well, I used to be a fireman and an EMT on the ambulance way back. But on my days off, I would work for Dickie, as his stern man on the lobster boat. His boys also worked with him part time. But after the boys went off to college, I started in full-time lobsterin'. Later on, when Dickie died, he left half interest in the boat to me, and I've run it ever since. Tom is sort of a silent partner. Course, I still fill in odd shifts on the ambulance now and then, if they need me."

"Boy, that sure sounds nice. You know? I mean the way it all worked out and everything."

Black flies were pesterin'. Tom needed to get off the rock and keep on moving. If he ran fast enough, the flies didn't bother. When he reached the graveyard there was more of a breeze. That helped a little. But he still had to keep after them the whole time he chatted with Caroline.

"I've got a new friend to tell you about. Tigger. Well, he doesn't really like to be called Tigger. His real name is Sam. Lives over in the old Bennings place. And his mom is the new ophthalmologist in town. Anyway, he reminds me of Pooh, you know. I mean Mark. Same age. Same frame. Anyway, he's out on the *Shady Lady* right now. Fishin' with Prince. You know what? He kinda fits in that empty spot I've been carryin' around all these years. Ever since Mark died."

When he had finished sharing that memory, Tom said good-bye to Caroline and continued on his run.

Cathy dropped Britney off at her father's early and headed for the

YMCA. Getting over her period made the aerobics workout seem a lot more refreshing. In the shower, thoughts of a day in the garden puzzled her. She didn't know exactly what Tom had on his mind, but she made certain, before she dressed, that she was adequately scented in Tom's favorite fragrance. *Don't be deceived by a man's proclaimed intentions. Behind all their elaborate plans, they have only one thing in mind.* Her mother had taught her that much. Heaven knew her mom had known more than enough men to be absolutely certain of that fact.

The distinctive nature of men continued to weigh on Cathy's mind as she drove down to the harbor for a visit with Tom. She recalled how Frank was when she first married him—very helpful with household chores when he wanted to be, but underneath all that helpfulness, he was really just setting her up for a quid pro quo. After she got pregnant and had Britney, it took a long time for her to get her knack back. Working and going back to school part time prolonged her recovery. By the time her romantic moods began to reappear, Frank seemed to have developed multiple competing interests: snowmobiles, ATVs, going off to camp, and fishing and hunting with "the boys."

The mail was swamped with snowmobile magazines, Cabela's and L.L.Bean catalogs, and Polaris brochures. They were all over the house, cluttering his bedside stand and piled high on the coffee table and in the bathrooms. It is easy to tell what's on a man's mind by checking out the bathroom reading material. It seemed for a long time that Frank had somehow lost his sexual desire. It was quite a while before she discovered that he had merely transferred that desire elsewhere.

Tom appeared to be different. All that education and professional polish was very alluring. But underneath, he was probably the same as all the rest. As she pulled into Tom's driveway, he was coming out of the barn in tight-fitting jeans and a blue T-shirt. Her image of him suddenly shifted back to her original sighting in the YMCA pool. *What a build. It's hard to appreciate that when we're in the dark and under the covers.*

The Marlboro Man? Perhaps. Definitely not the same guy who wore a white coat, tie, and stethoscope. Cathy sniffed herself to make a perfume assessment. *Should be effective.*

She saw how Tom's eyes narrowed when he saw her, intensifying the steely-blue. The corners of his mouth created little dimples as he smiled. She sensed that he was excited by her arrival. But his embrace felt perfunctory. The kiss. Only a peck. Then he inhaled deeply through his nose.

"Mmmmm!" he said. His delight was unmistakable. She squeezed his hand as he led her into the barn. She could already smell the sweet aroma of hay. Suddenly, gardening seemed more romantic than she had ever imagined.

Then Tom opened the door to the truck and motioned her to get in. He announced that they were headed to the nursery for garden supplies.

She had been to a nursery before, with Frank, who delighted in displaying his extensive knowledge of plants and gardening, giving her an exclusive inside view of a man's world. Tom was different. He explained things a lot more and asked for her help in making choices. It was clear that his garden was not totally a man's province. He actually expected her to participate. *What am I getting myself into here?*

When they finished making all their purchases, Tom drove the pickup around behind the store to load some sacks of fertilizer and bales of peat moss. Cathy browsed the book section and selected a book on organic gardening. *No need to stay ignorant.* She began reading it on the way back to the farm.

The purposeful task of jointly laying out and planting a garden turned out to be a lot more satisfying than Cathy had anticipated. Tom's enthusiastic and vivid descriptions of the anticipated harvests made her hungry. Growing up, she ate mostly canned or frozen vegetables. But Frank had cultivated in her an appreciation for garden fresh vegetables. Getting sweaty, with a little dirt under her nails was not that bad if she drank a few beers along the way. *Beer before lunch? Not so fast.* She'd seen her mom do it and swore she never would. It required some mental adjustment. Tom swore it kept away the black flies. *Oh, well. You live and learn.*

Lunch. At last. She thought Tom would never stop. Homemade baked beans and corn bread never tasted so good. She sipped her beer and continued reading her garden book while Tom tidied up the kitchen. Tom was bubbling over with ideas.

"What about digging clams some afternoon?"

"Forget it. Why bother when you can get them cheap at the fish market? All that stinky, sticky mud. Think of something else, if we must find other activities we can do together."

And bringing Britney along was totally out of the question. The kid would have mud from head to toe. Besides, Britney was to remain unaware of her mother's relations with other men. No way would

Cathy let her child go through what she had experienced with her own mother.

She still remembered. Every night, it seemed like, another man escorted her mother home after the bar closed. And the sounds that came from her mother's bedroom. The walls of the apartment were so thin. *Whatever caused Mama to make all those weird moans and groans? Bad dreams? Poor Mama.*

Eventually Cathy got old enough so that she and her sister figured it out. Those memories were still hard to bear. Britney would not have those memories. Cathy would conduct her affairs, as well as her gardening, away from home.

"Instead of all that chemical fertilizer you're using, why don't we use manure? Isn't organic gardening supposed to be much better?" Cathy asked in an effort to be more engaging.

"Organic gardening is a lot more work, and I'm not convinced the vegetables are any better," Tom replied. "My father-in-law was big on organic gardening. He was the compost king. Used to put horse manure and grass clippings and stuff into what he called a hot compost bed. He worked hard, making good compost. After he died, I never had that kind of time, so I switched to regular fertilizers and peat moss. I couldn't see it made any difference in the vegetables."

"Well, this new book I got tells all about natural and sustainable farming. You might like to read it. Commercial fertilizers have a lot of disadvantages, it seems." She could almost see Tom's brain perking. The expression on his face finally turned to joy.

"I suggest," he said, "we use horse manure on one-half of the garden and fertilizer on the other half. Then we compare our crops when they are harvested to see which is better. Vegetables from the fertilizer side versus vegetables from the organic side."

What a collaborative idea. Gardening was a lot more interesting than she had first imagined. She pushed the wheelbarrow out behind the barn for another load. If only manure wasn't quite so mucky. That shower was going to feel great. *Now what's he up to in his pickup truck? Jesus! Men and their CB radios.*

Squawk, squawk!

She recognized Prince's voice on the speaker, talking from the *Shady Lady.*

"Yeah, Tom, you're comin' in loud and clear. Sam and I are near about finished with our second lunch. We got a few more traps left to haul. Should be home in an hour, I reckon."

"Okay. I gotta make a quick trip over to the nursery. Forgot a bunch of stuff this morning. Meet you at the dock in about an hour, if that's okay."

"Roger! We'll see you in one hour. Over and out!"

Another hour? Will he never stop? Cathy asked herself, still aware of an urgent desire for a romantic shower and a passionate afternoon. Tom shoved her gently into the cab of the pickup and then went around and jumped in the driver's side. She was pleasantly surprised when he pulled her over next to him and buckled her into the middle seat. Her left hand dropped onto Tom's right thigh. A smile appeared on his face. It was the first time she had ever enjoyed riding in a pickup truck.

Out on the boat, Prince hung up the CB microphone and turned to Sam. "Better let me drive for a while. I know where all the traps are. Besides, it gits kinda bony in here."

"Bony? What's that mean? Bony?"

"Lots of BFRs"

"I get it," Sam said. He thought for a minute. "Prince, how do you remember where all the rocks are anyway?"

"Don't have to. All's I need to remember is where they ain't."

Sam thought about that one for a while. Then he tried several times to say quietly to himself, "Ayup, ayeah," sucking his breath in while he said it. No matter how he tried, it didn't sound right. Finally, he asked, "So Tom is coming back to pick me up tonight?"

"Ayup," Prince replied, inhaling as he spoke. "I reckon so."

"You know, Prince, there's something I've been meaning to ask Tom. You see? Like, there's this big sign up on the wall at the YMCA pool. It lists all the swim events and shows who holds all the records. And the winning times and stuff. Know what I mean?"

"Well, there's a Tom MacMahan listed on that sign. It says, like, he still holds two records in freestyle and one in breaststroke. You reckon it's the same guy?"

"Ayeah. That's Tom, alright. He was quite a swimmer."

"Really? Gosh, he must have had to practice a lot to get that good."

"Well, sure. I guess he did practice. But I don't think that's what made him a champ. I think it was hauling lobsters that did it."

"Haulin' lobsters?"

"Ayeah! Haulin' lobsters is hard work. Builds muscles. Nobody had more muscles than Tom did. And it was all from haulin' traps. No question."

"No kidding?" Sam thought for a while. "Prince, was fishing different way back then?"

"Ayeah. Some, I guess," said Prince, thinking back. "Back then, Dickie and I used to run about three thousand traps. Was a lot of work. Nowadays, we're only allowed eight hundred. Got 'em divided up into three gangs. Haul each trap every three days. Haulin' six days a week, every trap gets checked twice a week. You see? Of course, nowadays, the traps are all wire instead of wood. Got vinyl coating so they last seven, eight years. That saves a lot of work too. It's still a pretty good way to make a living."

"And did they used to wear hats like this, I mean, back then? Looks like all the other lobstermen are wearing the same style hat."

"Ayeah. As far back as I can remember."

Later, when they got to the dock, Tom was waiting to give them a hand with the lines and loading the lobsters into the lobster car, which was an underwater cage attached to the dock where the lobsters were kept alive until they went to market. While Sam was busy washing all the gurry off the deck, Tom helped Prince with some routine engine maintenance.

"How'd it go today?" Tom asked.

"Finest kind," Prince replied.

"And what do you think of Sam?" Tom said in a low voice.

"He'll do to take along." That was Prince's highest rating.

When everything was ship shape, Sam thanked Prince for the nice day. Prince offered to pay him. Sam refused. They settled, instead, for a mess of lobsters to fetch home for his mom. Cathy agreed to walk back to Tom's and start her shower while Tom drove Sam home.

"How was the fishing, Sam?"

"Wicked good," Sam replied.

"So did you have a lot of fun?"

"Oh yeah, lots of it was fun. Especially listening to Prince yakking on the CB all day and visiting with all the other lobstermen. What a riot that is."

"That's part of fishing."

"Everyone seems to enjoy what they're doing." Sam paused in thought for a minute and then added, "And I really had a lot of fun today, but fishing, like, it's a lot of hard work, you know? Even harder than working on my grandfather's farm. I never worked that hard before."

"So, which do you like better? Working hard or having fun?"

"I don't know," Sam said. He paused again in thought for a while and then added, "I think maybe working hard is another way of having fun. And it's actually a lot more satisfying, if you know what I mean."

Tom nodded, and Sam took off his hat and sat it on the seat next to Tom.

"Here. Thanks for lending me the hat."

"Well, you're welcome, Sam. Only I want you to keep the hat. Never know when you might be needing it again."

"Gee, thanks a lot. That's really nice. You know, Tom, you can call me Tigger if you like."

Chapter 11

Sitting alone in her office, after her last patient of the day, Sally looked at the picture of Sam on her desk and realized it was time to face up to her problem: figuring out how to get her son back on track, motivated to study and educate himself, so he could become a responsible adult. This was a problem that had displaced all other issues in her life. *How am I going to handle this?*

She took in a deep breath and wondered, as she exhaled, W*hy is it that women are the ones who have to make all the difficult choices in life?* To have the baby or have an abortion? That was the first question. To breast-feed or not to breast-feed? That was next. Women lost either way. If she put Sam on the breast, Charlie got uneasy. The way he acted, one would think he was jealous. Jealous of whom? Sam or her? And try breast-feeding with company around. Forget it. Charlie got embarrassed. About what? What was it he was afraid might show? His jealousy?

Men didn't have to make choices around conflicts between family and career. Only women. Now she was the one making decisions for Sam, even though she usually was able to manipulate things so that Charlie thought he was the one making the decision. Whether she should send Sam back to Philadelphia for the summer or keep him in Maine was a tough decision. There was a lot riding on this one, and she needed more information before she reached her verdict.

It might help if I consulted with Tom about the lobster boat job before I make this decision, she thought to herself. She made a phone call, closed up the office, and headed over to the hospital. Tom was in the ICU, making his evening rounds, when she caught up to him.

"Your office said I might find you over here," Sally said. "Have you got a minute?"

"Sure, what's on your mind?"

"It's about Sam. After his experience working a couple of days on your lobster boat, he's asking if he can have permission to stay in Maine this summer and work on your boat. I have to decide whether to let him take the job or make him go visit his father. Charlie, my ex-husband, is not going to like it if Sam doesn't spend the summer in Philadelphia."

"I see."

"Before I go to battle with him, I need to check things out and make certain I'm doing the right thing. Does that make sense?"

"Sure does. But I can tell you right now it would be a great experience for Sam. I used to have that job myself. Years ago, of course. But don't take my word for it. If you want to see for yourself, why don't you and Sam drop around on Sunday, after church, for dinner. I'll invite Arthur Prince and his wife, Ellie. After dinner, we can all go out in the *Shady Lady* and see if maybe we can find a school of mackerel. You might enjoy catching them. Check out the boat. Get acquainted with Prince a little. You'll get a feel for the whole operation. That might help you make your decision a little easier. And it should be a lot of fun."

"Well, if it wouldn't be too much trouble."

"Not at all. Tell you what. Let me call Ellie and Prince and see if they can make it. I'll get back to you tonight or in the morning and firm things up. Okay?"

"That is very kind of you to offer. I really appreciate it. Thanks."

~

After an early-morning run, Sally was surprised to see Sam already up and reading a book. "Sam, what got you up so early on a Sunday morning?"

"I'm just catching up on a little homework. That's all. Gettin' it off my worry list before we go out fishin'."

Sally was amazed. *Something's changed here,* she thought to herself as she poured herself a glass of water and flicked on the TV to check the weather forecast.

"I just checked the weather, Mom. Should be a perfect day out on the boat. I was hoping we could go a little early. Maybe have a chance to show you around a bit before things get started."

"Okay. I'll go up and take my shower and get dressed. Then we can go."

All throughout her shower, Sally just could not figure out the changes she had noticed in Sam this morning. She did not understand why it seemed so worrisome to her. But once the hair dryer was on, her thoughts turned to Tom. She became aware of a pleasant desire to visit with Tom. His house would be interesting to see. She hoped she would enjoy it as much as the other day, when they were out running together.

Sally could hear Tom singing inside as they knocked on his back door.

"When I'm calling you-ou-ou-ou-ou-ou. 'Indian Love Call' from Rose-Marie," Tom explained as he opened the door. Then he turned the volume down on the record player. "Sorry about the music. Sometimes I get carried away when I'm cooking all by myself."

"That's okay," Sally replied, feeling a little more at ease. "God! I haven't heard those songs in years. My mom was always singing that stuff when I was growing up. She loved listening to show tunes. Only she had a really good voice and could make herself sound just like Jeanette MacDonald. That music makes me a little homesick."

"Is that right? These are all my mom's records. I started leafing through her old cookbook this morning, and her music started popping in my head. So I put on her records."

"What's for dinner?" Sam asked. "I'm starving. I haven't had any breakfast, in case anyone wants to know."

"Okay, Tigger, you're just in time to help with the biscuits. Here." Tom handed him a large ziplock bag.

"What's this?"

"Three cups of biscuit mix and a little bit of powdered buttermilk. You are supposed to add a cup of milk. Open the bag while I pour in a cup of beer, instead of milk. Then you can mush the bag around with your hands and get the biscuits all mixed up for me. My dad always made biscuits this way when he was up to camp. Mixing it up in a plastic bag saves a lot of mess and cleanup. And the biscuits are not that bad, as you'll soon see." He spooned out a batch of drop biscuits onto a cookie sheet, put a dab of butter on top of each biscuit, and then slid them into the oven.

"This house is awesome," Sally observed. "I've always admired it, but until the other day, I never realized that you lived here. Could we, maybe, have a little tour while the biscuits are cooking?"

The luxurious decor, along with all the old familiar music in the background, stirred up pleasant memories in Sally's mind. Her vision of Tom took on a new, and deeply satisfying dimension after he held her hand for a part of the tour. When they returned to the kitchen, she saw that Arthur and Ellie had arrived. Sam introduced them.

"Pleased to meet you, Dr. Gardiner," Arthur declared, his deep-blue eyes sparkling.

"My pleasure too. And please call me Sally, if you don't mind," Sally replied, carefully surveying him. *Looks just the way Sam described him,* Sally thought. He was an older guy with a neatly waxed handlebar mustache. He had a full head of mostly gray hair but no wrinkles. He was still quite rugged and handsome. Then, when he took off his lobsterman's hat, as a polite gesture, she noticed the bald spot on the back of his head. *So that's why he always wears a cap.*

Just then, Cathy Dyer walked in through the door without even knocking. "Good morning, everyone," she blurted out.

Sally had not been informed that Cathy was on the guest list, but it seemed rather obvious that she was there to be with Tom, after she went over and gave him a kiss. Sally's brain went into pause mode for a minute while she rebooted the program in her mind.

Despite the disappointing feeling rising inside her, Sally managed to suppress a deep gasp and put on a gracious smile. "Cathy. What a pleasant surprise. They didn't tell me you were coming. Come right in and make yourself at home."

"Thank you, Dr. Gardiner," Cathy responded. Then she added, with a back-of-the-hand whisper, "Just for the record, I'm already quite at home here. Thank you."

They were all hungry. The appetizing aromas that filled the kitchen only increased their craving, so they all migrated directly to the table and seated themselves, even before all the introductions had been completed.

Ding! The biscuits were done. Dinner was served in the kitchen in front of the old fireplace, with its brick oven.

Tom had prepared his mother's fish chowder and a tossed salad to go with the biscuits. A traditional Maine meal, served in a traditional Maine kitchen. Everyone had seconds, except Sam, who required thirds. But the pièce de résistance was the strawberry-rhubarb pie.

"The rhubarb in this pie came from a patch that's been growing out back here for years. My brother and I used to sneak over here when we were kids and steal rhubarb from this patch. Nobody lived here in those days. We would take it home to Mom and get her to make us a pie.

Finally, we dug up some of the roots and planted our own patch across the road at home."

After they had finished the coffee, Ellie volunteered the ladies to wash the dishes so the men could go down and get the boat ready for their excursion. "You want to come on along, Sam, and help us get things rigged up?" Prince asked.

"No problem. I'm right with you."

"I'll make a quick run over to the general store and pick up some beer and soda," Tom volunteered. "Anything else we need?"

"We might could use a couple more mackerel rigs, if they got any," Prince suggested.

"Finest kind. See ya in a few minutes."

After the men left, Ellie began loading dishes off the table. Cathy headed for the sink. Both were familiar with the operation of that kitchen. Sally put aside her anxiety for the moment and started pitching in to help.

"Isn't that just typical of men?" Cathy shouted above the grinding roar of the garbage disposal. "Walk right out and leave the dishes to the women. Can you believe it?"

She shut off the disposal, but nobody responded.

"And look at this mess," she continued. "That Tom. When he cooks, he uses every pot in the place. Makes everything from scratch. Even the pie crust. I told him to use ready-made crusts. You can hardly tell the difference. But no. He'd rather make a mess. So long as he's not the one who has to clean up."

"I understand what you mean," Ellie said. "But it could be worse. What if they had offered to do the dishes and sent us over to rig up the boat?"

"I'm sure it's a much more pleasant task than dishwashing, don't you agree, Sally?"

Sally shrugged.

"It's pure male sexism. Men taking advantage of women," Cathy continued. "Don't you think men tend to try to take advantage of women a lot of the time?"

Sally shrugged again, but this time with a somewhat sympathetic smile.

"Like at the hospital. You see it everywhere. Male doctors giving orders to female nurses. There is a real pecking order there. It used to be out in the open more. Now it's all covered up with strict sexual harassment regulations so it isn't so obvious, but it's still there."

"Well, I'm not a nurse," Sally said as she picked up a dish towel and started to dry, "so I don't get the same perspective. There may be a pecking order at the hospital, but it's nothing compared to what we had back in Philadelphia. I don't quite understand why, especially since the feminist movement seemed much more visible back there."

"Were you active in the feminist movement back in Philadelphia, Sally?" Cathy asked.

"Not really."

"Why not?"

"I was too focused on medical school and residency to get involved with women's issues. After I got married and started in private practice, I thought I was very busy. Pretty soon I was given a teaching appointment at the medical school, and I got even busier. But I didn't really know what busy was until I got pregnant and had Sam. The women's movement was the furthest thing from my mind. I had no time at all for outside engagements. I could barely manage a home and a career simultaneously."

"That's what I am talking about," Cathy replied. "Women really get a raw deal, having to manage a career and raising children at the same time. We really need to campaign for better child care provisions, don't you think? I mean, however did you manage all that anyway?"

"It wasn't easy, I tell you," Sally answered, beginning to feel somewhat connected. "We had a couple of nannies, and day care, but nothing was ever satisfactory. My husband was always after me to give up my practice and become a full-time housewife. He wanted more children. It got to be a major problem."

"Well, it's a problem for me too," Cathy said. "I'm still trying to get my master's degree in nursing so I can move up. My ex-husband is a real pain. He says that if he has to take care of Britney while I'm in school, he's going to cut off child care payments. What can I do? Men don't have all these problems holding them back."

"Right," Sally agreed. "It's women that seem to have all the problems. But I'll bet it was even worse in the past. What was it like for you, Ellie? You know, back before we had women's lib?"

"Oh, fiddle," Ellie responded. "Guess I'm not very much up on women's lib. When I was growin' up, Maine was kinda behind the times. No one ever heard of women's lib. Everybody knew you weren't supposed to have sex until you were married. Even in college, a girl wouldn't dare to take a chance havin' sex in a small town like this. Can't keep no secrets around here. 'Bout time I reached the breedin' stage, birth control pills were just coming out. Sexual behavior really changed a lot after the pill came along. I think it was the pill that made all these changes possible."

"I'm sure that's true," Cathy opined. "But even after the pill, we still had sexual discrimination, right?"

"Well, it's kinda hard for me to know. I suppose sexual discrimination was not so easy to see in a small town. Everyone knows everyone else. Men were men, and women were women. And that was life. When birth control came along, people were kinda slow in adapting to the new realities. Still, I always figured it was the pill that brought about all the changes in women's lives. You know? And maybe dishwashers and automatic dryers helped too. Family planning and less housework changed women's lives and created better opportunities for careers. And women's lib tried to take all the credit."

"I can't believe it," Cathy gasped. "You must be looking at the world through rose-colored glasses. If it weren't for the women's movement, we'd all be washing diapers and scrubbing out pots and pans full-time, not just when we get invited out to lunch. Right, Sally? She wouldn't be a doctor. I wouldn't have prayer of getting my master's degree. We wouldn't have our right to sexual freedom or abortion or anything. Wouldn't you say, Sally?"

"That's what I have always been told. But I've got to admit, Ellie does have an interesting point."

"Well, I really don't know enough to say one way or the other," Ellie began again. "It just seemed like birth control made life a lot easier for me compared to what my mother went through."

"Sure, the pill made it all possible," Cathy countered, "but society would never have changed if it weren't for women's lib. We would still be living under those same antiquated customs, just like the Muslims. Don't you think?"

"Where do you keep the Saran wrap around here?" Sally interrupted.

"Bottom right-hand drawer. What do you need it for?"

"Wrap up the rest of this pie. It was too good to let it go to waste."

"I'll say," Cathy declared. "Let's split it three ways. A fitting reward for cleaning the kitchen, don't you agree?" The motion passed unanimously. Ellie dug out some vanilla ice cream to go along with the pie.

"Anybody need a little coffee?" Ellie started the pot, and they all sat down.

"The way I see it," Sally said, "it doesn't really matter who takes the credit. What matters is that we are all living a lot better today than our mothers did."

"True. And thank God for that. But you still can't make me believe that society's attitude would have changed without the women's movement."

"Well, around here lots a folks don't see it that way," Ellie chimed in again, still not willing to get off her pedestal. "You're a bit young to remember. But back when I was in grade school, my mom spent all of her time cooking, cleaning, washing clothes, hangin' 'em out to dry. She had no time for a career. When I was in high school, if a girl got caught having an affair, it usually led to a shotgun marriage. For my two daughters, it's entirely different. Around here, they grew up without much, if any, exposure to the women's movement. Somewhere—in high school, in college, or from their peers—they learned the facts about birth control and made their own decisions about sex. Each of them called home and had a little chat with Mom before making their final decision. Their behavior was based on the existing medical and social opportunities, just as my behavior was guided by the realities that existed back then. As far as I am aware, women's lib never had much effect on either of them.

"And what's even more amazing is now that both girls are in a relationship with a guy—one of them is now formally engaged to hers – they bring these fellows home with them and sleep with them in our house, and we don't say a word. Arthur takes the guys out in the boat and enjoys having them around, almost like they were his own sons. Can you believe that? I'm sure women's libbers never got to Arthur. He just accepted the new reality. And he's not scared that one of the girls is going to get pregnant and ruin her opportunities to have a happy, normal life. I think that's what really frightened parents so much, back when I was growing up. People are just adjusting to the new realities of life."

"Excuse me," Sally said, "hadn't we better pay attention to the time? They'll be wanting us down at the boat soon, won't they?"

"Don't worry, Arthur will blow the horn when they're ready for us,"

Ellie said, getting up and pouring an extra half cup of coffee. "Anyone need a refill?"

Before long, they heard a few hopeful toots on the *Shady Lady's* horn. Ellie hustled out to her car to fetch a tote bag for the trip. She told Cathy and Sally to start on down to the boat. She'd catch up.

"Wow!" Cathy remarked. "Sorry I got her so wound up. Did you ever hear such a distorted bunch of bullshit as that?"

"No. Not really. But she said it so logically, it almost makes you wonder if she possibly could be right."

"No way! Look, in our sexist society the men have all the advantages. I can't go back to school and get ahead. You couldn't pursue your career in academia. Why? Because we have the responsibility of raising children. Men are free to do whatever they want. They don't have to make the difficult choices women do. Is that fair?"

"I won't argue with you on that one," Sally said. "But do you think the women's movement can change all that?"

"Well, if my mom is right, we're in for a big change in the near future."

"How's that?"

"Women are already taking over society. They've broken through the glass ceiling to head many large corporations. Mom says women will eventually run everything. And men will become what evolution designed them to be. Drones. Like bees. Good to have around for sexual pleasure, and handy for when you decide to have a child. My mom wouldn't even tell me who my father was. She only assured me that it wasn't at all an accident. She selected him and seduced him, strictly for his genetic superiority."

The conversation ended abruptly as they neared the boat. Not a topic to be discussed within earshot of men.

Look at that boat, Sally thought to herself as she started down the ramp to the dock, her mind now totally distracted from Cathy's monologue. All-white, wooden hull, with a sharp, high bow up front and low gunwales aft. Much bigger than she had imagined, despite Sam's lengthy and idyllic descriptions. She stopped for a moment at the bottom of the ramp to take it all in. A low cabin, forward. Then came a broad windshield, with a roof extending back over the helm. Mounted on the roof were two antennae, a radar dome, and a lobster buoy. Just to the right of the helm was a sturdy post with a pulley of sorts, hanging out over the water. She was trying to imagine how it all worked, when Sam appeared, wearing his lobsterman's hat. How strange it felt to be helped aboard by her own son.

"Whadaya think of her, Mom?"

"It's huge. How big is this thing?"

"Forty-two feet. Didn't I tell you about her?"

"Yes, but somehow all I could picture in my mind was some grimy little old work boat, filled with fish guts and fishing gear and smelling of rotten fish. I never dreamed it would be so clean and tidy."

"It's 'cause every night, when we get back to the dock, we scrub her down and hose her off. Get everything all set up and full of fuel, so she's good to go early the next morning. All's we have to do is put the bait and some lunch on board and we're off."

"My! Look at all that complicated electronic equipment on the dashboard."

"Yeah. An' it's all neat stuff. This is your compass. That's the GPS. Has a screen with a chart that shows your current position and course. That's the radar screen, and that's the sonar. It shows you what's under the surface, all the rocks and ledges 'n stuff. Gives you your depth, and you can even see schools of fish."

"It'll take you a long time to learn how to use all that stuff."

"I already know how to use it, Mom. Prince showed me, and he gave me all the manuals to read. And I read them all."

My God, Sally thought, *too bad he never puts that kind of effort into his schoolwork.* This was her first time on a boat that was headed out into the ocean. Her unfamiliarity with the nautical environment brought on a nagging anxiety that something unexpected and awful might happen. She couldn't imagine what it would be.

As soon as Ellie was on board, Sam unfastened the lines and jumped aboard. Prince backed her out and headed the *Shady Lady* toward the Marks, a couple of islands where the mackerel had been showing up in the last few days. He gave the helm over to Sam and told him to follow the navigation buoys out of the bay. Prince went back to the stern and poked around in a tub of ice until he found a can of soda that pleased him and opened it.

"Anyone else need a drink?" Prince asked the group.

"I'll take a beer," Cathy said.

"Sorry," Prince explained, "but we're not allowed to drink beer on this boat until someone catches a fish. It's called the beer fish. I'm hopin' we won't have to wait very long for someone to catch it."

"Are you sure it's okay for him to be driving this boat? He's still just a kid," Sally whispered to Prince, nodding toward Sam.

"He's all right. That boy's a fast learner. An' he ain't really a kid no more. He's just shy of bein' a man. Besides, I'm watching things. When we get into trickier water, I'll take over. Don't you worry. I've been in this business a long time, and I've taught many a young man how to run a boat."

"Well, that's nice to hear," Sally replied, not certain whether to believe him. Sam's drunk driving episode was still fresh in her mind. And people always tend to flatter moms about their children, especially if they want to hire them for the summer. A bit of caution seemed appropriate. "But tell me, Prince," she continued. "I'm just curious. Why do you have that lobster buoy mounted on the roof?"

"That buoy is painted the same pattern as all the buoys we use to mark our traps. It's supposed to show everyone which traps belong to this boat. Ya don't really need it, but it's kind of a tradition. If ya know what I mean?"

Sally felt a subconscious sense of relief when Prince took the helm so Sam could watch while Tom began his tutorial on the basic technique of mackerel fishing. It all sounded pretty straightforward to Sally. Apparently, finding a school of mackerel was the hardest part for sport fishermen. But for lobstermen, evidently, that was not a problem. They kept a pretty current inventory of what was swimming around in their areas.

The mackerel rig consisted of a four-foot length of heavy nylon leader that branched out to a series of four or five hooks attached to very simple, brightly colored lures. At the end of the leader was a weighted jig to take the line down. No bait was needed. Just drop the rig in the water, let out some line, and jig it up and down. No problem.

Before long, Prince cut the engines. "There's a school of 'em up ahead," he said, "right off'n Mark Island. Same place as yesterday. I'll cut the engine and we'll drift into 'em so as not to make a sound."

Cathy had no problem hauling in the first ones. Three fish were on her rig.

"Beer fish on board!" Tom hollered out. By then Sam and Sally were also hooked up. Sally refused any assistance in the landing of the four fish on her rig. She even took them off the hook. She declined a beer and cast out her line again.

"I can see you have fished before," Tom observed as he returned her beer to the cooler.

"A long time ago," Sally said. "When I was a kid. I used to go fishing for catfish on the river with my dad and grandpa."

"That sounds like fun."

"It was. I used to love it. But then, when I got older, I was informed that ladies don't go fishing. Only men and boys go fishing. Women cook the fish when the men get home. I had almost forgotten how much fun it is," she said, working her rod up and down to attract the fish. "Oh! I've got one. Whoops! I can feel another one hit it."

"Leave your line out a little longer before you reel it in, and see if you can get a fish on every hook."

Sally jigged her pole and line up and down a few more times, delighting in the feel of the rod as it bent a little more each time another fish was hooked. Memories of a fifty-pound catfish flashed through her mind as she struggled to crank in all the shiny, wiggling mackerel.

"Wow! Five fish. Way to go, Mom!" Sam cheered as he went over to help her unhook elongated, silvery, streamlined critters with dark, blue-green, vertical stripes along their backs, flopping and slithering over the deck. "Aren't they beautiful? Huh, Mom? When you compare them to an ugly old catfish."

"They're gorgeous," Sally observed. "Hey, Tom, are these good to eat?"

"Not particularly. Kinda fishy. But the spawn are to die for."

"Spawn?"

"Yeah. Fish eggs. The roe. You know, like shad roe. Only better. Wait 'til you taste 'em. You'll see."

Tom and Prince kept busy for twenty minutes with the steady job of taking fish off the lines and loading them in plastic trays. Finally, Tom called a halt and went over to open up a few beers for those who were thirsty. "Don't you just hate it when the fishing is so damn good you don't even have time to drink beer?" No one disagreed. They filled two bait trays with mackerel before the school disappeared.

The *Shady Lady* began the scenic route back to port, with Sam at the helm. Tom and Prince had their knives out, opening the fish's bellies and removing the spawn, little sacs of fish eggs that had the appearance of pale little sausages. Prince raved on about how tasty mackerel spawn were as he carefully stored them in an iced cooler. He gave some to Sally to take home for supper and explained how simple it was to prepare them: Boil them for a few minutes, split the thin skins, and add plenty of butter, salt, and pepper. Sally reluctantly agreed to try them, constantly returning her gaze up toward Sam at the helm.

How could they ever let him drive this big boat, with all these people on board? He's just a kid. Her intuition that something bad would happen still haunted her.

Prince glanced over at Sally when he finished cleaning the fish and immediately got the message. He went to the helm to be with Sam. Tom hosed down the deck and got out some fish crates and pails. He turned them over so people would have places to sit for the ride home. Everyone sat back, sipped their beers, and enjoyed the ride.

A warm, sunny day on the ocean. Nothing like it. Islands and lobster pot buoys slipped by as the boat glided through the water. A noisy flock of seagulls followed the boat overhead. Tom threw them some mackerel bits. Howling gulls skirmished for fish. Sally was no longer in angst. Aware of how much fun she was having, she went over and helped herself to a beer. She stepped back to the stern, where everybody congregated away from the noise of the engine and the overhead exhaust up forward. She sat down on a fish crate, next to Cathy, leaned her back against the gunwale, opened her beer, and felt some of her anxiety slip away.

"Sally," Cathy said, "since our conversation this morning, I've been wondering. Whatever made you decide to become a doctor anyway?"

"It's a long story," she began. "My grandfather was a doctor. And I really idolized him. I always liked to mess around in his office when I was a kid. He loved showing me things. You know, equipment, and pictures of anatomy, and stuff under the microscope. And he took me fishing."

"I see," Cathy replied with a questioning look on her face that reminded Sally of a psychiatrist, probing for more information.

"Well, yes. But it was really my mother that convinced me I should become a doctor. You see, I was her last kid. And when I got into high school, I became aware that—was that a seal?"

Prince told Sam to slow the boat. Two seals, looking for lunch, were into a small school of fish. Prince could see the school of fish on the sonar screen. The seals splashed around on the surface for a few minutes, until the bait fish swam away. Tom threw out a couple of mackerel to prolong the seals' performance. When the seals disappeared, Sam got under way again.

"As I was saying," Sally continued, "I could see that my mother was bored with her role in life. After she got married, all she ever did was work in the kitchen, take care of kids, and go to church. With all the kids out of the house, her life seemed sad and empty. Actually, I think she was probably depressed. I didn't know anything about depression at the time. All I knew was I did not want to be anything like my mother. I think that thought alone was what eventually made me decide to become a doctor."

"Isn't it just amazing," Cathy said after a moment's reflection, "what it is that affects how people make decisions in life?"

"Yeah," Tom said, "it's very interesting. My kids are just now making those decisions. But you know, Cathy, I often wondered why you didn't go to medical school. You certainly could have been a very good doctor."

"At the time, it never occurred to me to think about medical school. There was no one around to guide me or suggest that I might even be capable of doing something like that. I'm not sure I could have ever made it through. Besides, I'm just glad I don't have all those huge debts to pay off."

"So, Tom," Sally said, "whatever made you decide to become a doctor?"

"Oh, my dad always wanted to be a doctor himself, so he encouraged me. I was headed in that direction ever since I can remember. Never figured I'd end up practicing back here in Maine. But it's worked out well for me."

A restful lapse in the conversation allowed Sally to appreciate how smoothly this boat slid though the white-tipped waves, with only the rhythmic chopping sounds as the waves smacked the hull. A far different sensation from what she recalled of her childhood experiences, bouncing along in three-seated rowboats with outboard engines. The warm, moist sea air felt good. Or was it just the effects of the beer? She finally lost her feeling that something bad was about to happen. That's when it happened.

"Ouch!" Sally yelled out, smacking her right calf. "What the hell is that?" On her hand she found the culprit: a green-headed fly with flat, triangular wings. She stepped up to the helm and showed it to Prince. He nodded his head knowingly.

"Ayeah," he said, inhaling as he said it. "I hate it when one of them flatbacks muckles onto ya."

"Flatbacks?"

"Some folks call 'em deer flies, but round here we call 'em flatbacks."

"They sure are vicious, aren't they? I'm surprised you guys let him drive this huge boat all by himself," Sally said, pointing to Sam at the helm.

"I could see, a while back, that you were a bit uneasy," Prince replied. "But no need to fret. Comin' ashore is the easiest part of the trip. Besides, Sam is a fast learner. And a good captain always keeps a close eye out, even when he's not at the helm. Sam, show your mom here how to bring a boat into harbor."

"You see, Mom, the entrance to the harbor is all marked with buoys. See? Coming in, you keep the *can* buoys to port. The *nun* buoys—those are the cone-shaped buoys—are kept to starboard."

"However, do you remember all that stuff?"

"Easy, Mom. The nun buoys are all red. All's you need to remember is red-right-returning. Simple."

When they reached the dock, Sam jumped out and carefully fastened the boat to the dock, under Tom's supervision. Then he helped move the mackerel trays out of the heat so they could be used the next morning for lobster bait. He wouldn't let his mom leave until he had washed the rest of the gurry off the decks, so the boat would be all set to go out in the morning. Sally stood on the dock, amazed at how smoothly everything had gone this afternoon. *I can't believe I actually had fun today. It's been a long time since I've had this much fun. And, except for the fly bite, nothing went wrong.* On the way home, she promised Sam she would call his father as soon as they got back.

Charlie was not at home, so Sally left a message on his phone. He returned the call just after dinner.

"Charlie," Sally began, "I thought we should talk about Sam's plans for this summer's school vacation."

"It's all set," Charlie stated. "I've got him a job lined up at the club. He'll be a lifeguard at the pool. That way he can have plenty of opportunity to train for his swim team. Is he there? Put him on the phone and let me tell him."

"You can talk to him in a minute. Let me get a word in first. Okay? Sam has a really nice opportunity right here in Maine this summer. The lobster boat he'll be working on is only two miles away. He can ride his bike to work. And Prince, the guy he's working for, says he'll drive Sam to the YMCA after work every afternoon in time for swim practice until he gets his driver's license back. We had dinner with them today and went out on the boat afterward. They are really nice, and I think it's an excellent opportunity for Sam."

"Put Sam on, will you?"

"Hi, Pop. What's up?"

"Hey, Tigger. Your mother and I were just talking about your summer plans. You don't really want to stay up in Maine this summer, do you? I've got a really plush job lined up for you this summer. Lifeguard at the country club swimming pool. Plenty of girls. Not much hard work. Can't beat that, can you, Sam?"

"Sounszz triffish," Sam replied, with an audible gulp.

"I can't understand a thing you're saying, Sam. You must be talking with your mouth full. What are you eating anyway?"

"Biscuits and mackerel spawn. And boy are they good They are called camp biscuits. We got the recipe from one of the guys who owns the lobster boat."

"Your mom's into making biscuits, is she? Whatever got into her?"

"Mom didn't make these biscuits, Dad. I did. It's really simple, and they're wicked good. I'll teach you the recipe when I get down there, if you let me."

"Maybe I will. But right now we need to decide what you're going to do this summer. Are you staying in Maine or coming back home? It's your decision."

"I'm sorry, Dad, but I really want to stay here. Lobstering is real work, not just setting around, like lifeguarding. I think, like, it will be a lot more satisfying, if you know what I mean."

Sam heard a long sigh over the phone, followed by a period of silence. "Okay, Sam," his father finally said, "here's the deal. You promise you will apply to college this fall, and I'll let you stay. Okay?"

"Okay, I'll do it. Thanks a lot, Pop. Bye." And he hung up.

"I can't believe I just did that," Sam said afterward. "He made me promise to fill out applications for college. You gotta help me, Mom. I'll never be able to do it alone. Thank God he did not make me agree to actually go to college. He'd bust a gut if he knew I was going full time into fishing as soon as I graduate from high school."

Chapter 12

ernard Appledore—of Nomans, Appledore, and Hull, Attorneys at Law, in Boston—sat at his desk one Monday morning in July. "Yes, Miss Pasque?" he spoke into the intercom.

"The Gurnets are here."

"Please show them in. And, Miss Pasque, could you bring us some coffee?"

"Yes, sir. How many cups?"

"Please, no paper cups, Miss Pasque, real china cups. Get the tea set out of the closet. Put the coffee in a pot, so we can pour it out. And Mrs. Gurnet likes plenty of real cream and sugar. Okay?"

"I get it. No problem. Have it in right away."

George Gurnet III and his mother were shown in to the large, mahogany-paneled room. After appropriate greetings and introductions, they were seated in plush leather chairs facing an ornately carved, oak desk. Frederick Naushon, a new addition to the firm, well versed in medical malpractice litigation, was presented and seated.

"First, let me extend our most sincere condolences for your late husband's unexpected passing," Bernard began. "I understand that there are issues concerning faulty standards of care, which may or may not have had something to do with his death. Is that correct? Could you give us a report of what happened, as you saw it?"

Arlene related what had happened. George III started to speak but was quieted by a quick motherly glance. "I see," began Bernard again, "and exactly what kind of a person did this Dr. MacMahan seem to be?"

The door opened and a silver tray with coffee was brought in. Mr. Naushon served.

"He seemed like a capable and pleasant doctor," Arlene explained, her coffee cup in hand. "His appearance was very professional and refined, and he was always very kind and sympathetic. He tried to explain everything as best he could. It's just that George was perfectly fine before the accident. And all the rest of the afternoon, before they took him to surgery, he seemed fine too, except for a black eye. But something happened during surgery. They said it was a heart attack." George III started to interrupt again but retreated after another maternal glare. "Then, when they started to transfer him down to Maine Medical Center, something else happened, and he died. It seems to me that things just weren't being done properly; otherwise, George wouldn't have died like that."

"And so, I presume, you are considering bringing a malpractice suit against whomever is to blame. Is that correct?"

"Well, I'm not sure yet. I'm really not comfortable with the idea of being involved in a malpractice suit. It feels a little—" Arlene was interrupted by her son, who started to speak. Once more, a motherly glare settled him back in his chair. "It's just that the whole family is pressing me to find out if that might be appropriate."

"I can well understand your reluctance to get involved in litigation," Bernard said. "Let me first reassure you that public perception of malpractice suits is ill founded. The main purpose of malpractice suits is to compensate victims for damages that result from errors in medical practice. But the whole of society benefits in other ways from malpractice litigation. The threat of legal action is the main incentive that prevents negligent doctors from injuring even more patients than they now do. Does that perspective make this a little more palatable?" Arlene sipped her coffee and nodded yes.

"And what is your perspective on all this?" Bernard asked, speaking directly to George III.

George III stood up and walked over to where an ashtray stood on a pedestal, near the right side of the desk. "Do you mind if I smoke?" he asked.

"Go right ahead." Bernard reached into a bottom drawer, pulled out a box of cigars, and offered him one, but George III declined. Bernard picked up the sterling silver lighter from his desk and lit George's cigarette and a cigar for himself. A few puffs later, everyone seemed a little more relaxed.

"And so, what kind of useful information do you have to add to this story?"

"That Dr. MacMahan didn't fool me any. He sounded very educated and all, especially when he talked with the family. He was dignified and even somewhat eloquent, you know, like he'd been to Harvard or Yale maybe. But it was all just an act. I overheard him talking with someone on the hospital staff on the telephone. You could tell he was a real Bubba. I remember he said, 'You might could try' something or other. 'And it don't much mattah.' That's when I knew. Anyone who says 'might could' is a Bubba. That's why I made arrangements to transfer him out of that hick hospital as soon as I got there. The only trouble is I should have gotten there sooner. That's all."

"Well, it sounds as if there might possibly be a basis for a malpractice case here. We'll have to investigate a bit before we can make a recommendation. There are a few questions with which you may be able to help us. First off, prior to the accident, your husband was in good health. Is that right?" Arlene nodded. "I'm sure his medical records will confirm that. And he was still employed at the bank? Vice president, I believe?" Arlene nodded again. "And exactly how old was he?"

"My father just turned sixty-one, and he was in excellent health." George III stood up again. "He planned to continue working another nine years and retire when he became seventy, just like my grandfather did." He looked over at his mother. Arlene nodded again. "See? And with his salary being nine hundred thousand dollars a year, that's over eight million dollars my family will never see. And it's all because of Dr. Bubba. Don't we have a constitutional right to sue him?"

Both lawyers nodded in the affirmative.

Frederick then produced some medical release forms for Arlene to sign, and Bernard told them it might take some time, but they would make a thorough investigation of the matter before advising them as to whether a malpractice suit was reasonable or not. After they left, Bernard asked Frederick what he thought.

"It's hard to see how we could make much money on a malpractice suit up in Maine since we'd have to hire someone licensed in Maine to file the papers and do all the front work, and they would take a chunk of any award."

"Absolutely right, Fred. I very much doubt if there is enough money involved here to make it of interest to us. The thing is, though, that this firm has handled the estates of three generations of Gurnets. That kind of business we can't afford to lose. So we need to at least make a show of having looked into the matter in order to pacify George the Turd."

"I see what you mean. I could go up to Maine on Monday, if that's okay."

"Good. If it does look promising, give me a call. I'll be out of the office next week, but you can still reach me on my cell phone. And if we decide to ask for the records and file a suit, get in touch with Sturdivant and Cushing in Augusta. We've worked with them in the past. And thanks a lot for sitting in this morning. Now you'll have to please excuse me. I don't want to be late for my squash game."

∽

"Hi, Cathy."

"Sis? You're not screening your calls anymore?"

"Don't need to. I got caller ID now."

"I see. I wondered how you knew it was me. Anyway, I was just calling to see how Mom was doing."

"About the same, I'd say. Spends most of the day out on the porch in her wheelchair. It's the only place they're allowed to smoke. Every time I visit, the first thing she asks is, did I bring any booze? One day, last week, her mind was pretty clear, and she asked about you and Britney. But she didn't remember you were divorced. Not much of any change, I'd say. But she's all recovered from her fall."

"Good."

"You still seeing that doctor?"

"As much as I can."

"You're not letting yourself get hooked again, are you?"

"No freakin' way."

"Good."

"But he has really got his tentacles out. I tell you. He's always trying to get me to join him in all sorts of activities and ventures."

"Sounds like he's trying to get you into a relationship or something."

"I know he is. He's pretty up front about it. Wants to get to know Britney too."

"Not a good idea."

"Don't worry. I can handle myself."

"Is he good-looking?"

"Oh, God yes. He was out in the barn the other day wearing a T-shirt and jeans. Here I'd been sleeping with this guy for a month and I'd forgotten what a build he has. I got so excited. I wanted to make hay in the hay."

"Sounds ecstatic."

"Mmmmm! Isn't it sad that men just aren't able to maintain close relationships with women?"

"I suppose so. But they can't be trusted."

"I know, but there are some marriages that seem to last."

"Yeah, but only because the women are docile and put up with a lot of crap. Men are all the same. They only want three things from a woman. And the other two are cooking and looking after the kids. And that's life. Believe me. I've been around. And so have you. But *you* keep on trying."

"It's hard sometimes, when you see on TV or read in books and magazines about pleasant, romantic relationships, and you can't keep from dreaming and wishing. Somehow?"

"You're sounding just like you did with Terry. Remember? And when he got killed in the auto accident, and you wound up in the emergency room, getting your stomach pumped out."

"Yeah. But back then, I was just a freshman in college. Now I've got Britney, and she needs me. Besides, I know better now. But I can still dream, can't I?"

"I suppose. Okay! I'll be talking to you. Bye."

"Bye. And say hi to Mom for me, will ya? Bye."

On Monday morning, Fred Naushon, Esq., was up in Maine, looking for information on property values at the county courthouse. When he finished there, he drove out to look over York Farm and adjacent properties. He drove slowly around, scanning each MacMahan property and making notes on the map he had printed out from his GPS. Then he went on into Snug Harbor to scope out the fishing village. The only restaurant was Eddy's Wharf. He went in and ordered a lobster roll for lunch. From his table, he got a panoramic view of most of the harbor and the adjacent shorefront properties. Amazing! There was hardly any development at all along this part of the Maine coast. Lots of beautiful shorefront properties with only modest, and in some cases even run-down, houses. Many were covered with weathered gray shingles. What a disgrace.

A pair of binoculars stood on his table next to the salt and pepper. He picked them up and began making a more detailed inspection of the real estate. *Hmmm. Interesting.* Up away from the shore, in some prominent locations, were a few old, Federal–period homes. One was quite stately. *What is that?* His eye picked up something gliding through the sky. A bird. An osprey, no question. The bird had something in its talons and was taking it to a nest on top of a nautical tower, out in the water. Soon, another osprey arrived with food. Fuzzy little white heads with open beaks appeared, eagerly waiting to be fed. Just then, the waitress arrived with his lobster roll.

"Mmmm. Looks good," he said. Motioning to the nest, he added, "I wonder if what they're serving out there is as good as this."

"I'll bet they think it is. Enjoy your meal."

Fred watched the ospreys all through lunch. *Impressive, how hard both parents work at caring for their babies. Thank God human beings have evolved to the point where men no longer have the burden of raising children.*

After lunch, he drove once more past the MacMahan-York Farm and its stately Federal house. He checked to see how far out along the shore the other property extended. It looked promising. He called the real estate developer in Kennebunkport, who agreed to meet with him in the morning.

After his meeting with the developer, Fred called the office. They called him back on a conference call, with Bernard Appledore, out on Martha's Vineyard. "What's it look like, up there in Maine?" he asked.

"It looks like we may have hit pay dirt," Fred replied. "This guy, MacMahan, is loaded. Not with money but with property. From his father he inherited a beautiful strip of shorefront on a cove, all the way out to a scenic point. It's priceless. From his wife he inherited a 250-acre farm that starts on the shore, goes up and across the road. The property slopes gently upward to the crest of a hill that looks way out to sea. It's breathtaking."

"What's it all worth?"

"Well, for tax purposes, it's only assessed at two hundred and twenty thousand for the shore piece and six hundred thousand for the farm. But don't let that fool you. The shore piece gets some kind of tax break because it's used for a commercial fishing operation. You know, lobstering. The other place gets a break too, because it's still classified as a working farm. I had your developer friend from Kennebunkport look it over today, and he said it would easily sell for well over two million. He said he'd give three million himself."

"That sounds promising," Appledore replied, "but it's a long way from nine million."

"I know, but listen to this. That developer guy is really hyped about this place. He says a creative developer could easily get five million in profit out of this place. If it were developed properly, maybe twice that much."

"No kidding. And I'm pretty sure that guy knows his stuff. Very interesting."

"This is how I've got it figured. Say we win this case with an award in the millions. Then we agree to settle for one million from the insurance, plus the assessed value of his property. That's a total of one point eight million roughly. If we gave the insurance money to the client and threw in another hundred grand cash, that would give them two-thirds of the settlement. And we could keep the property ourselves."

"Right! And then turn around and sell it to the developer for a cool three million, which is the same as what we'd make if the case was settled for nine million."

"You get it?"

"Sure do.

"And, I might add, the profits on that deal would only get taxed at capital gains rate. Another huge savings."

"Excellent, Naushon. You pull this off, and we'll make you full partner," Bernard exclaimed. "There's one thing I forgot. Any mortgages?"

"Only 120 grand. I did some checking around. Evidently, this guy MacMahan doesn't make much money for a doctor. Actually, from what I managed to finagle out of the tax collector's office, none of the doctors around here make a decent salary, as far as I can learn. Anyway, he has a hard-enough time just paying his taxes. He had to take out a mortgage to put his kids through college."

"How about the hospital? It sounds pretty rural. I don't expect there's much there we can touch outside the standard one million in insurance."

"Actually, the hospital has excellent opportunities too. They have a huge trust fund that we might be able to access, depending on whether we can find something in the medical record we could use to show probable cause."

"I don't know if we could persuade a jury in a small town to award a huge settlement against their own community hospital, even if there is probable cause. In a large city, it would be a lot easier, don't you think? Doctors are easy picking everywhere."

"Absolutely," Naushon said. "So far, the doctor looks like the best target."

"Good work, Fred. Why don't you go ahead and ask Frank Cushing to request the records and get things ready while we figure out how to make a case out of all this."

Ten days later, a registered letter requesting copies of all the records on George Gurnet Jr. arrived in Betty Norton's office. She called medical records and asked them to bring everything up to her office for a review before the records were copied and sent out. She studied them carefully for more than two hours, checking every note for accuracy and cross-checking all medical orders with doses actually administered. She was pleased at the overall quality of the record-keeping skills of her staff. She had worked hard to bring them up to that level. Only one problem failed to meet her standards. An entry on the new EMTALA hospital transfer form did not look right to her. The doctor had written 44 cc's per hour for the IV flow rate, but she knew from the nursing report that the actual rate administered inside the ambulance had been 444 cc's per hour. An easy thing to correct. But was it ethical? Or even necessary? Questions that required a little time and consideration.

She locked the records in the safe, went home, and changed into her old clothes. Then she loaded both dogs, a chocolate lab and a yellow lab, into the back of the Mercedes, put the top down, and drove to the shore for a walk on the beach.

Things in life seemed a little clearer when she was near the water. Perspectives improved. Contrasts were more apparent. Betty had made many of her most important decisions in life on this beach. Lou had proposed to her here one moonlit night, long ago. They still came here to discuss important issues or settle personal differences. And sometimes to rekindle smoldering desires. She needed to think things over before she made a decision.

Betty had come to realize the hospital was her whole life. *When I look back at all the time and effort I've put into that hospital. What it took* to penetrate the glass ceiling to become the vice president of the hospital corporation, with its network of nursing homes, elder-care facilities, and bulging trust fund. I never imagined I could be so successful. If Mom could only see me now. She wouldn't believe what her daughter has accomplished.

But the best part is seeing the evolution of new relationships among the staff at the hospital, doctors and nurses working together so harmoniously. They're the only family I've got. A lawsuit against the hospital would tear them apart. Bitterness will develop when lawyers attempt to divide the staff over issues in their testimony and then dramatically pit one side against the other to impress a jury. Unbearable. They'd dig up all the dirt they could find and spread blame everywhere to make a jury think the hospital was no good.

And the publicity. All that community good will,__down the tubes. Damn lawyers! What if people stop paying all their pledges to the trust fund? It's our lifeblood. We need that trust fund to provide benefits and bonuses to key members of our professional and administrative staff. We could end up like many Maine hospitals that are seeing their staff leave for better-paying positions in other states. I can't just sit here and let that happen.

But altering the medical records? No. It just didn't seem possible.

These thoughts ricocheted through her mind as she walked all the way to the end of the beach, where a winding, marshy stream emptied into the ocean. Offshore she could see a school of fairly large fish, feeding on whatever food was drifting out in the current of the stream, often jumping completely out of the water. Bluefish? Yes, the bluefish were in. She peered for the longest time into the water of the stream but could not determine what it was the larger fish were finding to eat. She tossed some sticks of driftwood out into the water for the labs to retrieve. Their jubilant splashing did not disturb the fish's feeding frenzy. It must be blues. Lou would be pleased to know that the bluefish were around.

She gradually became aware of the sound of a lobster boat, approaching from the east. The boat stopped at some lobster buoys near the school of bluefish. She recognized it: the *Shady Lady*. A boat she knew well, from way back. A boat she actually hated.

Something about the distraction of the *Shady Lady* refocused her mind. Now she could see her problem from a different perspective. She was not consciously aware of why her mind was suddenly so clear. It seemed obvious that her decision must meet the needs of the institution and the people it served. She, as an executive officer, had to make the decision, and she would. Let the chips fall where they may.

It was amazing how much better she felt after finally making a difficult decision. Betty raced along the beach, keeping up with the labs, almost until they reached the Mercedes. Back home, she fed the dogs and took a shower. Lou was out of town so she might as well go back to the hospital and finish her job that evening, when no one was around.

Driving back to the hospital, she became aware that someplace in her brain was still churning, trying to find some logical rationale to support her decision—put everything in perspective, so to speak. Errors in medical care—that was the central issue, currently a hot topic in the media and in medical literature. It was becoming widely recognized that the blame game was not a productive approach to reducing the effect of human errors in medical care. The new computerized order entry system they were presently installing should be much more effective. All orders entered directly into the computer eliminated the problem of doctors' notoriously lousy handwriting. The bar code on the patient's wristband must match the code on the medicine container, insuring that the right dose was delivered to the right patient. It would be very satisfying to get that system up and running.

However, the threat of litigation put a different spin on things. Even though this error had occurred outside the technical responsibility of the hospital, there was still considerable risk of a suit. Lawyers were extremely skilled at the blame game, taking advantage of a unique part of human nature, the emotional satisfaction of finding and punishing wrongdoers. Lawyers called it justice. They might easily convince a jury that the hospital was really to blame for Mr. Gurnet's death. Somewhere inside of her she could actually feel her own need to find someone to blame for this situation.

As far as she was concerned, it was George Gurnet III who was at fault. He had insisted that his father be taken from the safe environment of the ICU to Maine Medical Center via ambulance, which could not provide the same level of sophisticated medical supervision as the ICU. Deciding who was at fault did not help solve any of her problems. Often the person who was at fault was not the same person who got the blame.

It was past dark when she arrived at the hospital. From the safe, she took out the medical record and looked for the EMTALA transfer form. She found the carbon copy in the hospital record and matched it with the original from the transfer file. In matching blue ballpoint pen, she added another four so that the order read 444 cc's on both copies. "Everything looks ship shape," she thought to herself as she replaced all the sheets of paper in their proper places. *Ship shape*. What a fitting adjective for a mission that had been decided by the sighting of a lobster boat. She returned everything to medical records, where it would be copied and sent out the next morning. If someone ever found fault with that flow rate, the blame would fall squarely on the doctor, not the hospital. Any claims would be paid by the doctor's insurance company and not the hospital trust fund. She still remembered how to play the blame game. And it could be very satisfying. *What a relief!*

On her drive back home, the *Shady Lady* still floated in her thoughts. An inspiration came to mind that might solve another of the problems still confronting her, an idea of how she might lure Tom away from Cathy and reduce the risk of any communication between the two of them that might reveal the corrections that had been made in the medical record. As she sipped on her double martini that evening, it occurred to her that maybe God had not given her children because she had in mind a more important mission for Betty Norton.

Chapter 13

A rusty old pickup was already parked at the end of the bumpy dirt road down to Back Cove. Bald tires. No tailgate. The truck bed was filled with junky old tools, plastic fish trays, and another bald spare tire. *What a disgrace*, Cathy thought. *Even more disgusting than Tom's truck.* She scanned the scenic cove all the way out to the blue ocean waters. The truck was still on her mind.

That heap of junk spoils the beauty of this nature preserve, she thought as she placed an arm around her daughter, Britney. The tide was completely out, just starting to come back in. Cathy looked way out across the mud. Near the water's edge, she could see a man bent over, digging in the mud. It had to be the pickup's owner. Something about him bothered her.

Tom parked his truck, and they all got out.

"Pee-you-wee!" Britney howled. "What's that smell, Mommy?"

"That's the clam flats, Britney. You'll get used to it."

"You might even learn to like it," Tom added, pulling down the tailgate and climbing into the truck bed to put on his hip boots. He dug around and found another pair of rather roomy boots.

"Here, Cathy. These boots will probably fit, to use the word loosely."

Cathy got the pun but managed to hold back any response.

"We've got two clam hods and two clam rakes. I could only find one rake this morning, so I went to the general store to get another rake, and guess what I found? A special pair of knee boots, just for you, Britney. Let's see if they fit."

They did. Cathy said hers were a bit loose. Just as Tom figured.

Tom picked up the gear and started on down toward the flats. Cathy was still kicking herself for letting Tom talk her into bringing Britney along. She held Britney's hand and helped her stump down the banking, through the puckerbrush, stopping to smell the pink blossoms of the rugosa roses along the way. Just like a puppy, she was, checking out all the smells. Maybe this wouldn't be such a nightmare after all.

Britney let loose of her mother's hand and took off along the sandy strip of beach that ran around the perimeter of the mud flats. Stomping in her new boots, she hopped over driftwood, singing to herself and stopping to look at seashells, heading toward the water's edge.

"Don't go near the water, Britney! Tom, who is that guy down there? He makes me nervous."

"Can't tell from here. But the tide's coming, so he'll be moving up this way in a bit. We'll find out who he is in a while. Don't worry. He won't bother Britney."

"How can you be sure?"

"Don't know. Round here, I never heard of kids being bothered." Tom shrugged.

Digging clams was more fun than Cathy had expected. Thinking about how good they were going to taste made it even more fun. She saw the clams beginning to accumulate in her hod. Tom's was already half full. If only she didn't have to keep one eye on Britney and whoever that was down by the shore.

"Tell me, Cathy, if you don't mind, exactly what does your ex-husband do?"

Christ! Here comes the third degree again. "He's a lineman for the power company. Why are you concerned?"

"I don't know. Just curious, I guess. Tryin' to get to know you better, I suppose."

"You already know me better than anyone else I know. I'm easy. What you see is what you get."

That Tom doesn't seem to have any boundaries. I should have recognized that before. She pondered exactly how to manage this. Britney came running up with her yellow plastic pail extended.

"What have you got there, sweetie?"

"Some shells and a starfish. He's dead though. Why are you guys digging all those clams?"

"We're going to eat them."

"Yuck! They're all mucky. I don't like clams."

"Yes, you do. You eat fried clams when we go to the seafood place. Remember?"

"Looky here," Tom said, holding out a clam. "First we wash them clean. Then we take them out of the shell before we cook them. How's that? I like 'em boiled in the shell. But for you, we can batter them and deep-fry them. They're awful good that way too."

"Oh, I see. Can I dig some?"

"I thought you might want to, so I brought along a little kid-sized clam hod that my dad made for his grandchildren when they were your age. Bring your shovel and I'll show you how to find clams."

Cathy stood back and watched as Tom showed Britney all the little holes that clams made in the surface of the mud. Britney was amused to discover that she could stomp in the mud with her shiny new boots, and if water squirted up out of the hole, it meant a clam was down there. Excitedly, she dug down with her little shovel and found the clam.

"Look, Mom, I found him." *Stomp! Stomp! Stomp!*

The day was turning out much better than she had expected. Who would have guessed a child would like clamming? The little boots and pint-sized clam hod were what did it. *Look at her dig.* Cathy suddenly understood the origin of that famous old saying, "Happy as a clam." She began to experience that contagious feeling of happiness, oozing into herself. She scanned the horizon and shook her head. What a poetic place, except for the lone clammer, coming in with the tide. An inspiration came over her.

> Tom, oozing charm.
> Britney, entranced.
> The flats, oozing mud.
> Cathy, swamped with angst.

Still, the day was turning out better than expected. It had been a long time since she'd seen Britney this happy. *Sis will never believe this. If only I had a picture. Damn! Why did I leave the camera in my backpack?* She headed back to the truck to get it. *What a great photo this will make.* She found the camera. Then, as she closed the truck door, she heard it.

"Mommy! Mommy!"

Oh my God. Where the hell is Tom? Britney had one foot stuck in the mud, up to her crotch. Tom was sloshing his way across the flats toward her. *Oh, no.* The loan clammer was heading toward her too. *Hurry Tom. Please!*

Too late. The loan clammer picked up Britney, reached down in the mud to retrieve her boot, and headed for shore.

"Walter! I thought you were still in prison, up in Thomaston."

"They let me out. Tom! Well, I'll be. Didn't expect t' see you out here. Is this your grandchil'?"

"Naw. Just a friend. When did they let you out?" Tom took Britney and started trying to wipe off some of the mud. Then he shook Walter's hand.

"Thanks for the rescue."

"Welcome, Tom. Glad to be a help. Ayeah. They let me out early on account of my wife bein' sick and needin' someone at home to look after her. Jeez. I figured this was your grandkid. This her mama?"

Tom introduced Cathy and handed Britney to her mother.

"Whatever happened out there?" she asked, glaring at Walter with hostility.

"The young lady got fetched up in a honey pot and couldn't drag herself out."

"A honey pot?"

"Ayeah. It's a big mucky hole, hidden in the mud. Jes waitin' t' grab a holt to ya an' fetch you up."

"Honey pot. So that's what it was. You all right, Britney? Mommy will watch out for you. Don't you worry."

"Yes, Mommy. But I lost my clams."

Tom went off to rescue the clams, but Cathy never thanked Walter, so he went back to his clamming.

"That guy makes me feel creepy," Cathy complained as Tom handed Britney her clams. "Let's get out of here."

They loaded up, backed the truck around, and headed for the harbor.

"You know this Walter guy?" Cathy asked when they were under way.

"Oh yeah. Known him for years. Walter Crowley. Used to work on my father's lobster boat, way back."

"Boy, he sure smelled bad. What a yucky guy. I can't stand it when guys wear their pants down so low you can see their crack sticking up above their belt."

"Yer talking about a plumber's butt?"

"Plumber's butt. Is that what you call it?"

"Ayeah. They are almost a Maine tradition. Prob'ly have one myself someday."

"Oh, gross. Did that guy say he was in prison?"

"Yep! Thomaston State Prison. The Crowley clan was always in trouble with the law. Short lobsters. Over the limit in clams. Shooting deer out of season. Nothin' vicious or violent. Still, everybody in town likes Walter, 'cause he's not mean or anything. Very friendly and kind. Just a reg'lar old down-homer."

"Yeah, sure. If he was so nice, why did they send him to prison?"

"A few years back, they caught him on the game preserve, guiding some out-of-state hunters. That really cost him."

The *Shady Lady* was tied up when they reached the dock. Prince helped rinse off the clams in the salt water. "How did you like clammin', Britney?"

"Wicked good."

"Wicked good? Wherever did you learn that, Britney?"

"At school, Mommy. Everybody says it. Prince, I got stuck in a honey pot today."

"You did? Just like Winnie-the-Pooh?"

Britney looked confused.

"That's another kind of honey pot, dear. I'll read you the story about Pooh when we get home. We need to get going anyway. You could use a bath."

"Sorry you guys can't stay and help cook up the clams tonight. I'll put them in a mesh bag and hang them in the lobster car, where they can stay fresh and clean themselves in the sea water. We can eat 'em later. Thanks for coming clammin' with us today." He stuck his head in through the car window as Cathy started the engine. He tried to kiss her, but she backed away, throwing a glance over at Britney.

As Cathy roared off, Tom stepped back onto the dock. Sam and Prince were loading lobsters out of the lobster car and into the boat. "The price on lobsters is back up," Prince announced. "We're fixin' to sail over to the co-op and sell 'em. Wanna come along for the ride? Maybe have a visit with the boys over at the fish house?"

Sam was visibly pleased but kept silent, driving the boat, while Tom and Prince yakked endlessly. He sat next to Tom in the fish house, with a smile on his face. No support group dynamics today. It was all jokes and teasing that afternoon. Sam felt pleased to take his own share of razzing, along with everyone else. Just happy to feel "reg'lar" and one of the guys.

Walter Crowley dropped in and told everyone about the honey pot mishap. Later, on the trip home, Sam felt comfortable enough to ask

Tom a lot of questions, some of them quite like the ones Mark asked after he got his driver's license. His last question was "Would you take me clamming sometime?" They agreed to go soon, when Tom's daughters got home for a visit.

Tom showered and went over to Eddy's Wharf for dinner and the Red Sox game. It had been a really lucky day for him. Not for the Sox, however. They lost again. But their luck could change. Unfortunately, so could Tom's.

The change occurred on the following Wednesday. "Oh my God! Why didn't I see this coming?" Tom groaned as he signed for the certified mail. Stepping inside his private office, he was pretty certain about what he would find inside the menacing envelope that read PERSONAL AND CONFIDENTIAL in huge red letters. TO BE OPENED ONLY BY ADDRESSEE. "Sturdivant and Cushing, Esp. P.A., Attorneys at Law" was written in a stylish ecru font on the return address.

Tom sat down before opening the envelope. Inside was a copy of a letter addressed to the county superior court: a notice of claim of professional negligence, 24 M.R.S.A. section 2853, regarding Arlene Gurnet versus Dr. Thomas P. MacMahan.

The claim alleged: 1) Dr. MacMahan had failed to provide an adequate preoperative evaluation for a patient with a documented cardiac arrhythmia. A board certified cardiologist should have been consulted prior to surgery. His condition merited transfer to a higher-level medical center, where the surgery could have been carried out more safely. 2) He failed to administer additional medications, which were indicated during the postoperative period. 3) He had prescribed an improper dosage of lidocaine for the transfer to Maine Medical Center. It alleged that these failures to meet the standard of care led directly to the death of Mr. George Gurnet Jr., the late husband of the plaintiff. She was seeking damages amounting to eight million dollars for loss of wages, plus one million for pain and suffering.

Nine million dollars! They must be dreaming, Tom thought, still unable to accept the reality of it all. *George Gurnet III. He's got to be at the bottom of this.* Tom could smell it. Then reality began to set in. Better call his malpractice insurance company and report it. They'd know how to handle this.

The insurance company agent was courteous, respectful, and gave straightforward instructions about their role in protecting him. They would arrange an attorney, who would contact him in a few days. He was reassured to learn that most cases that were filed never went to trial in the state of Maine. But it was extremely important, for reasons unexplained, he was not to mention a word about this case to anyone until he had talked with his attorney.

"Except, of course, you may always talk with your wife. She can't be forced to testify against you."

"I know. She died last year."

"I'm very sorry to hear that, Dr. MacMahan," the insurance lady said in a very pleasant, empathic voice. "Have you ever been sued before?"

"Never. In twenty-four years."

"Well, we're here to help you. Please feel welcome to call back, anytime, for questions or support."

He felt a little better when he hung up. The matter was in their hands. There was nothing he could do. So there. But the sense of relief did not last. Not being able to take care of his own problems was a problem in itself. It made Tom feel helpless, a feeling Tom had seldom experienced in life. He became extremely uncomfortable. If he couldn't take care of himself, how could he expect to take care of his patients? He started to stand up, but his knees were flaccid. *Nine million dollars! Holy cow! How could this happen to me? Right here in Maine? And there's not a goddamn thing I can do about it. Oh my God!* He reached over and called his secretary on the intercom. "Cancel the rest of the afternoon, Marcie. Something big has come up, and I won't be able to see any more patients today. I'm not on call, so sign me out."

The rushing, throbbing noise, pounding in his ears, distracted Tom as he climbed into his pickup truck and drove out of the doctors' parking lot. When he finally reached the top of Pitch Pine Hill and began coasting his way downhill, toward Snug Harbor, he became aware of a new, even louder noise coming from the tailpipe. It was time to give in and get a new muffler. That thought finally diverted Tom's mind from the horrible mess that had been occupying his brain. It allowed him to take his eye off the road and quickly scan the peninsula spread out below him, all the way to Lobster Cove and the nearby islands. Most of the boats were out of the harbor, hauling traps or dragging. Odors from the sardine plant drifted in through the window and helped reprogram his mind with peaceful thoughts of being on his lobster boat, out to sea amid the myriad of scenic islands. A six-pack of beer might help. He swung by the general store on his way to the dock.

Damn! The *Shady Lady* was not yet back to the dock. He cranked up the CB radio and, after a long and frustrating delay, finally reached Prince.

"What the hell is goin' on out there, partner?" he asked.

"Some trawler or dragger went through here last night. We're not sure who it was, but the guys figure it was prob'ly a couple of them Russian ships that slipped in here after dark and went draggin' for the large school of cod that's been hangin' around here the last week or so. Anyway, their rigs hooked onto a whole mess of everyone's traps. Moved 'em all over the place. Tangled 'em all up. It's a real mess. Everybody's out here, workin' hard to straighten things out. We'll be lucky if we can get the job done by sunset.

"Worse things have happened at sea," Tom replied. "That's what my father would have said."

"Yeah, I can hear him now," Prince replied. "Ole Dickie managed to stay pretty cool most of the time. But if he lost it and blew his top, it was not a pretty sight. I'm sure you can remember. Oops! Sorry, Tom, I gotta go. The boys need me. Over and out."

Tom thought for a minute, recalling his father's smooth, logical, and optimistic approach to life's problems. "Jes keep on keepin' on" was another of his favorite mottoes, handed down from Tom's grandfather. But a streak of wicked temper also ran in the family, and an occasional tantrum was known to slip past the emotional safeguards, especially during childhood. Tom recalled how he always felt during one of his childhood temper tantrums. His father's response was always the same. "Go to the rock!" was what he yelled. Much like "Go to your room!" But since Tom and his brother shared a bedroom, it wasn't private enough to give that necessary feeling of solitary confinement. So he sent his kids to a huge rock, way out in the backyard, where their property extended into the bay and ended on a large rocky knoll, rising out of the water, adjacent to a stretch of sandy beach. Sitting all alone on the rock, with such a spectacular vista, and the salt air blowing in, had a stunning effect on a person's emotions, much stronger than a large dose of Prozac.

Tom finally recognized that the veneer of emotional protection—insulating him from the helpless frustration caused by his malpractice suit, and especially the restriction from talking about it with anyone—put him on the verge of an old-fashioned, childhood temper tantrum. It had been a long time since he'd been there, but he knew he needed to *go to the rock*.

The comfy flat ledge had been carved out of the rock in some previous geologic era. He sat down and leaned back against the granite. Tom couldn't remember the last time he had been out here—probably forty years ago, at least. He'd forgotten what a sensational vista it presented: across the entire shorefront of his property, partly beach, but mostly rocky, extending out to another rocky point that separated him from Second Cove and the Gurnet property. He could just make out the roof of their cottage. It made him sick to even think about them and the threat they presented to him.

Tom opened a beer and tried to rinse away his anxiety and fear. Two seagulls flew over and roosted on the rock to keep him company. He shared a few of his smoked potato chips with them and enjoyed their company. By the time he had finished his second beer, Tom felt much more at ease and able to cope with the problems he faced. Nothing like a little rock therapy. Now he could go home and keep on keepin' on.

He was about to pick up his beer cans and leave, when he glanced over at the huge pile of oyster shells next to the rock. Those shells had been there for thousands of years, put there by Native Americans who inhabited this area back when the climate and the local sea water were much warmer. Nowadays, the sea was much colder, and oysters could not survive much north of Chesapeake Bay. *Wouldn't it be nice if global warming came and brought back our native oysters?* Then it occurred to him that he should throw his beer cans onto the pile. The shell piles along the coast of Maine had been declared archeological sites by an old patient of Tom, who was the state archeologist. He had told Tom that the shell piles contained remnants of primitive human cultures, scattered down through the layers of shells. They were on the list for archeological digs. No one was allowed to disturb them. Beer cans would make a good representation of today's cultural era. Tom added them to the pile and went on home.

He managed to get through the evening by polishing off two manhattans and a bag of corn chips while watching the Red Sox game on TV. The Sox's luck had changed too. Tonight's victory made it a four-game winning streak. Cathy showed up when her shift was over, at the finish of the eleventh inning. With her help, Tom had no problem falling asleep.

At 2:00 a.m., he was awake. Getting back into bed after a quick trip to the bathroom, he felt like he could fall right back to sleep. But he didn't. The letter with the menacing markings kept floating through his consciousness He just couldn't find a place in his brain where he could comfortably park this malpractice case so it wouldn't bother him. He wasn't angry. Well, maybe a little bit. Uncomfortable was more like it. Uncomfortable and unable to sleep.

With a couple cups of coffee and a stroll through the garden the next morning, life seemed normal again. The beets and Swiss chard looked happy and prosperous. There were plenty of zesty-looking weeds on the organic side of the garden. He lifted his gaze to survey the cornfields. The corn didn't seem to mind all the lawyers. The little ears were fattening every day. He tied up a few tomato vines to their stakes and pulled out all the rest of the dying pea plants before he left for work. He would get the rest of the weeds after work.

Missing a few hours' sleep at night was an occupational hazard for a physician, something one learned to accept and adjust to. An extra cup or two of coffee and a catnap between patients could keep one functioning, as long as he caught up the next night. Tom was under thirty minutes swimming his mile at the YMCA that day, his fastest time in years. He sailed through the afternoon in fine spirits. "When the going gets tough, the tough get going" was one of his father's many sayings. Tom adopted it as his motto. It got him through the days just fine, but it didn't help him get back to sleep in the middle of the night.

Neither did the upcoming meeting with his lawyer. It was pretty scary, just thinking about it—yielding control of one's life to someone else. What would this guy be like? What would he think?

They met in Tom's office. Tom was seated behind his desk with a white coat, regimental-striped necktie, and stethoscope all in place. He was vaguely aware of a desperate need to be at the helm and in command of his own ship, as he seated the lawyer in the patient's chair.

The attorney appeared nonjudgmental and didn't talk much about the case itself. He said, "The purpose of this meeting is to get acquainted with you and to inform you about the rules and procedures involved in malpractice cases. Discussions and judgments about the merits of the case will have to wait until after all the depositions and evidence are gathered.

"Tort law is a civilized process for resolving disputes, clearing up misunderstandings, and compensating victims. Nowadays, most doctors can expect to encounter this process from time to time. They all seem to get through it just fine. So try not to take it personally.

"The most important thing is not to talk about the case with anyone outside the legal process. Otherwise, that person could be subpoenaed and deposed to find out what has been said.

"Plaintiffs' attorneys love it when this happens. It's easy to use this against you. They can depose the various parties involved and easily twist any inconsistencies in front of a jury so that it sounds like some kind of a cover-up. This could mess things up and interfere with a clean resolution of the case."

"I get the picture," Tom said. "I will keep my mouth shut and my feelings hidden."

"It will take some time for the plaintiff's attorney to gather all the information and review it. They will probably send me a list of questions for you to answer. It's known as the discovery process. It takes a long time and a lot of patience. But I'll be with you all the way and keep you informed of all the information as we get it. We will meet periodically to go over the records and reports throughout the process."

"Thank you," Tom said. He shook the attorney's hand and showed him to the door.

The legal requirement for silence had some positive effects. No one else knew he was being sued. The matter never found its way into the hospital gossip mill. Also, not talking with anyone, and maintaining an outward state of denial, helped his internal process of denial. Keeping busy at work and in the garden, along with disciplined exercise, kept him going throughout the days. Cathy helped with the evenings. It was in the middle of the night that he awakened and could not rid his mind of the thought that someone was out to get him and everything he had. Even worse, the idea that he had been falsely accused. The anger. The helplessness. The fear. All of it kept him awake. Never before in his life had he experienced a problem with sleep.

Missing a few hours, night after night, began to take its toll. He was aware of increasing difficulty being patient with people. His fuse became shorter. He consciously began to avoid certain people whose political and social views might overtax his diplomatic resolve.

Cathy became suspicious of his slight alteration of mood, disturbing changes in sleep patterns, and decreased libido. There might be a problem. She had encountered this before with her ex-husband. *Another woman?* These thoughts kept her from enjoying the job of pulling weeds in the garden. Everything was growing so nicely. And they hardly had to water, with all the rain they'd had this year. Tom was probably right about the manure.

"Next year, if we want to use manure again, we had better compost it first, so we don't have so many weeds."

"Good idea," said Tom, half in a daze.

"What's the matter with you anyway? Seems like you've been in another world for a couple of weeks now. It makes me suspicious when a man loses interest in sex. What are you doing anyway when I'm home with Britney, huh? Don't tell me you're home reading *Hustler,* or *Victoria's Secret.* I've been around, you know."

"Christ. Give me a break, will you? It's nothing like that. I've had a lot of problems on my mind these last few weeks. That's all. One of the girls is having problems, and I have to be the mom."

A plausible lie, he thought. *Oh, Christ! Here I am lying. But there is no way I can talk to her about the malpractice case. She'll probably be a witness. My God! If they ever found out I'd been talking to her, they'd fry me. Good-bye close relationship.*

"Plus, there is stuff at the office you don't want to hear about. Bottom line is that I'm not able to sleep. Haven't had a good night's rest in weeks. Right now, I don't exactly know what I'm gonna do if something doesn't give."

Then he found Xanax, a mild tranquilizer. Half a pill at bed time furnished the denial necessary for a good night's sleep. Gradually, a veneer of happiness returned to his life. And to Cathy's.

It was always a happy day when the first batch of corn came, ready for harvest. Prince and Ellie invited Tom and Cathy over for dinner. Tom did the corn, tender and sweet. Prince cooked up a few of his lobsters. Cathy harvested some of her lettuce for a garden fresh salad, and Ellie added a blueberry pie. They drank beer and played cribbage until late in the evening. Cathy announced that her scholarship had been tentatively approved, and she was making arrangements to switch to a part-time schedule at the hospital so she could begin classes at graduate school. She expressed her gratitude toward Betty Norton, who had encouraged her through the whole process. Ellie was especially pleased, since Betty was her sister.

"I used to feel sorry for Liz when we were younger," she related.

"Growing up, we always called her Liz. When she got to high school, she decided she wanted to be called Betty. Anyway, she and Lou wanted to have children, but she never could get pregnant. She was beside herself. They went to Boston to some fertility clinic, but it turned out Lou had a low sperm count or something like that. They tried everything, I guess, but no luck. I thought for a while she would crack, but she's pretty tough and resourceful. So, instead of having a family, she devoted her energy to her career. Lou was very supportive and helped her all through graduate school. Over the years, she's developed that hospital and its staff to an amazing level of performance, especially for a rural hospital. And she's now a vice president. Not bad for a country girl."

There were cheers for Betty. Everyone toasted.

"Cathy," Ellie continued, "you remind me of Betty in lots of ways. It kinda looks like, maybe, you are following in her footsteps."

"I haven't dared to let myself dream that high yet. One step at a time is how I'm taking it. But I wouldn't mind having her job someday."

There were cheers for Cathy as the evening drew to a close.

Tom slept well that night but woke with a bad headache, a very unusual occurrence. Maybe it was the booze. Aspirin stopped the pounding for a while, but it kept on coming back over the next few days. Finally, one of the office nurses checked his blood pressure: 190 over 110. Hypertension. That's what. The result of too much stress? It wasn't booze that caused his headache. He let a colleague prescribe the blood pressure medication. A day later, his blood pressure was normal, and he didn't have a headache. No problem.

Betty Norton had many things on her agenda as she opened the gate to Ellie Prince's front walk. When her sister opened the door, Betty handed her a large bouquet of flowers.

"These are for me? They're gorgeous! Thank you very much. Who gets the other bouquet?"

"I thought maybe later we might take a walk over to the church and place them on Mom's grave, if that's okay with you."

"Oh, I'd love that. Would you care for some coffee?" she asked as they strolled out to the kitchen. "Or I could make a pot of tea, if you prefer."

"Let's make it tea. For the good old days."

Ellie lit the gas under the tea-kettle and went into the dining room to fetch the pewter tea service. "Anything special that brings you down to the harbor? Gosh, you haven't been down for months."

"Yeah, I know. I've been meaning to come down ever since Memorial Day, but we've been straight out at the hospital all summer long. I'm kinda short on upper-level nursing staff these days, but I still have to let them all take their summer vacations. Otherwise I'll lose the ones I've got. So I've had to cover lots of shifts myself all summer long. But that's all part of the job."

"Well, I'm sure it's worth it," Ellie said as she started brewing the tea and cutting up a lemon to put on the tray with the spoons and cups. "Shall we have this out on the porch? The black flies are all gone now, so it should be nice." Betty held the door as her sister carried the tray outside. "Thank you," Ellie said. "And you are forgiven for not coming sooner. I must admit, though, I am a little bit jealous that you are still active and have such a challenging career."

Ellie paused for a minute and admitted to herself that she had always been somewhat jealous of Betty. She was still pretty, she still had her terrific figure, and in high school all the boys were hot for her—something a sister finds difficult to forgive.

"Now that I have quit working at the library, we can go to Florida in the winter. And with the girls all grown up and gone, frankly I've been a little bored of late."

"I can't believe that. The fact is sometimes I'm envious of you, Ellie. Two grown daughters, plenty of time for hobbies and projects, and now winters in Florida. I would trade places with you any time you want."

"Thanks, Liz. There's no way I would ever trade, especially now that I'm going to be a grandma."

"No kidding. Who's pregnant?"

"Laura. She and David have been planning to get married for some time."

"So when is the big wedding?"

"They don't want a big wedding. They want to get married down at our place in Florida. That's where they like to visit us. His parents live close by, so it'll probably work out nicely. And it won't be all that expensive. I'll let you know as soon as they set a date. They want you and Lou to come, if you can take the time."

"Wouldn't miss it. So when does the baby come?"

"Not until April. I can hardly wait." She began stacking all the cups onto the tray, and they headed back into the house. Betty went to the sink and started to clean up the tea service.

"Just leave those. I'll do 'em after we get back from our walk. Oh, dear," Ellie said and sat down on a nearby chair. Her face broke out in red blotches, and she began to sweat profusely.

"What's the matter?" Betty asked with alarm.

"Nothing. It's just a hot flash. That's all. It'll be gone in a few minutes."

"Well, it looks horrible. How long have you been having them?"

"Oh, three of four months now. You don't get them? I'm surprised. You're a year older than me. How did you luck out? You still look young, with a terrific figure and smooth skin. I'm starting to get wrinkles."

"Well, I work out pretty religiously, and I watch what I eat. You know. No red meats, whole grains, and lots of organic fruits and vegetables. And I'm also on estrogen."

"How can you dare take estrogen when Mom died of breast cancer? I'm afraid."

"You forget. Mom smoked. And she also ate red meat and lots of fats. Not me. I'm not so worried. Besides, I get my mammograms twice a year. You feeling better now?"

"Yeah. I'm okay. Shall we go?"

They picked up the flowers and started off toward the church. "Ellie, you'll never guess who I saw at the grocery store the other day. Virginia."

"Virginia Morse?" Her sister nodded. "What's she doing back here?"

"Well, her name isn't Morse anymore. Her husband just got out of the navy, and they are retiring back here. She told me her married name, but I can't remember what it was. Anyway, you ought to see how fat she is now. I almost didn't recognize her. I just can't understand how she could let herself get that way."

"It's hard to know," Ellie said, shaking her head. "Why, I remember back in high school she had the best figure of anyone. You used to be so jealous of her."

"I was not."

"Oh, yes, you were. She used to date Tom MacMahan, and you were always kinda crushy on Tom. Remember?"

"I was not crushy on Tom," Betty insisted. "I did go out with him a few times, but I wouldn't say I ever had a crush on him." They reached the graveyard and placed the flowers on the grave.

"Speaking of Tom," Betty continued when they were on their way back home, "what kind of relationship is he having with Cathy Dyer anyway? I mean, you see them from time to time. What's going on there?"

"So that's why you came down here to visit. To snoop on Tom MacMahan. Pretty sneaky. You never change, do you, Elizabeth?"

"Okay. I admit you're partly right. I am snooping. But it's not about Tom. It's Cathy I need to find out about. You see, I am recommending Cathy to the board of trustees of the hospital for a scholarship so she can get her master's degree. If they find out she's about to marry Tom or something, we might not want to invest our money in her. You see?"

"Well, if that's it, my personal opinion is that this is just Tom's rebound. You know, just coming out of mourning after Caroline died last year. Besides, she's way too young for him. I can't see it ever lasting."

"That's more or less the way I figured it, but I needed to be certain," Betty said as she started to climb back into her car. "I've got to be getting back. Thanks for the tea. I'll see you next week maybe at Janice's party. You are going, aren't you?" she asked through the window as she drove off.

On her way back to town, she drove past Tom's house and pulled off the road when she got to the cornfield. She thought about the evening, years ago, when she had parked in this same spot to reconnoiter the MacMahan property after getting a phone call from Tom, canceling their date that evening. Something in Tom's message had made her suspicious, so she drove out and checked the MacMahan dock. The *Shady Lady* was not in port that evening. Her suspicions increased.

It was impossible to keep secrets in a small village. Her friends at the general store were right. The provisions Tom had purchased were more suited to treating the shapely redhead they could see sunning herself on the deck of the *Shady Lady*. Not for repairs on the boat.

By the next morning, nearly everyone in the village had a pretty good idea of why Tom had broken his date that night. Betty was not the type to engage in revenge, but even at this late date she felt a sense of justice at last as she contemplated her plans to split Cathy from Tom.

She needed to break up their relationship and prevent them from ever talking about the malpractice case and figuring out what had really happened. Maybe this time she would be successful in saving Tom from the clutches of a sexually aggressive female. She might actually be doing him a favor—not that he would ever thank her for it.

Betty took notice of the large stand of sweet corn growing in Tom's field. Since he had planted none the year before, she took this as a sign he was recovering from his wife's death. She had left him a wealthy man. What a great property. Betty couldn't help thinking how differently things might have turned out if today's sexual morals had been in place back when she was dating Tom. Her niece was pregnant before her marriage, and nobody thought a thing about it. That couldn't have happened when Betty was young. No way! But who knew? Maybe if she had let herself sleep with Tom, things might have turned out differently. Maybe she would be getting ready to have a grandchild of her own right now. *Oh well.*

At least she had found out enough information to know her plan might work.

Betty invited Tom into her office that afternoon and reminded him that it was time for the annual hospital fund drive. Tom listened patiently to the old, familiar sales pitch. Maintenance of a large trust fund was essential for continued operation of the hospital. Most of Maine had the lowest Medicare fee scale of any place in the country. Hospitals lost money on most Medicare and Medicaid patients. Without a large trust fund to offset the operating deficit each year, they would be unable to retain their skilled nursing staff and might possibly have to close. He'd heard it all before.

She wanted Tom to head up the doctors' portion of the fund-raising drive. He agreed to help, and that meant he got invited to the kickoff dinner party at her house on Labor Day weekend. Tom offered to provide fresh corn for the party from his abundant crop.

It turned out to be a gala affair. Many of Tom's friends from the hospital board of trustees attended, and so did Sally Gardiner, who had been enlisted to assist Tom on the doctor's drive. After cocktails, she found her place card on a table near the pool, seated next to Tom. The other two seats had place cards for the Browns. Tom thought that was strange. Most everyone knew the Browns were in California, visiting their new grandchild. Sally seemed quite pleased with having Tom all to herself for dinner. She had some things on her mind.

"I really want to thank you for everything you have done for Sam this summer," she began after they were seated. "I don't know if you can fully appreciate the change that has occurred in that boy over this past summer."

"That's nice to hear. Prince and I both enjoyed having him work for us this summer. He's a hard worker and really a lot of fun to have around."

"That Arthur is such a prince, if you'll pardon the pun. He's been a real mentor for Sam. Sam has matured greatly over the summer. He gets such satisfaction out of working. It's quite amazing to see."

"I am actually not very surprised to hear this. Prince has mentored a lot of young men over the years. He's a natural."

"And you. You are his ideal. Or more like a role model, maybe." Sally was so sincere in her feelings that, without even realizing it, she reached over and touched Tom's arm. A flashbulb flared as the local news photographer captured the moment. "He tells me you were evidently some record-holding swimmer in high school. Is that right?"

Tom shrugged, with raised eyebrows and a coy smile, but did not deny it.

"Anyway, he wishes he could be just like you. Although he knows he can't."

"I wouldn't sell him short. I think that boy could be just about anything he wants to be, if he just puts his mind to it."

"Unless he pulls his grades up a lot, I don't think there is much chance that he'll ever get accepted to any college. His father—and I have to give Charlie credit for this—managed to get Sam to promise, at least, to apply to college this year."

"That's a step in the right direction," Tom observed. "It's nice that his father still has a positive influence on Sam."

"Yes. I suppose, overall, that it's a positive thing. But it's hard, trying to raise a kid in a divorce. I think it's really hardest on the kid."

"I don't doubt that. Whatever made you get divorced anyway, if you don't mind my asking?"

"Alright, I suppose I can tell you. See, when we first got married, I was earning most of our income while Charlie was just getting by— selling a little insurance, doing some estate planning, and selling a few mutual funds. He spent a lot of time playing golf and schmoozing up potential customers. But we got on just fine. When Sam came along, Charlie pitched in and took a lot of responsibility for his care. It was a pretty good arrangement at first. I worked full time, and he took care of

Sam. Took him everywhere. Even the golf course. Strapped him in his car seat so he could ride in the golf cart. But he never got the hang of managing a household like a woman can. Know what I mean?"

"Not exactly."

"It's the little things. For example, can you imagine how absolutely infuriating it is to be sitting on the toilet with no toilet paper? Not a goddamn roll, anywhere in the house, and Charlie went to the grocery store that very afternoon. Not a big thing, but it was the little things that drove us up a wall.

"Well, there were some big things too. Charlie wanted to try for another kid, but that was not very realistic from my point of view. Then two things happened. Medicare cut back payments for cataract surgery. I mean drastically. That was my biggest source of income. So my income plummeted. I mean nearly 50 percent. Plus, I was putting in a lot more time at work with my new teaching appointment at the medical school. At the time, I was looking at possibly going full time into academic medicine.

"Charlie, on the other hand, saw his income skyrocket. Retirement plans, 401(k)s, IRAs, and the like, exploded about that time with all the baby boomers starting to save for retirement. Charlie was selling mutual funds and making big bucks. A breadwinner, at last. Money was coming in, but we had no life together. He wanted me to quit my career and become a stay-at-home mom and, of course, have more kids. Our goals in life were so completely divergent, we finally decided to go our own ways and got a relatively peaceful, uncontested divorce. Neither of us really wanted it, but we just couldn't figure out a way to make the marriage work in a mutually satisfactory arrangement. I still don't know the correct choice for a woman: career or children."

"The way you frame it," Tom said, "it sounds like a dilemma in which there is no absolutely correct choice. What I—oh, pardon me?" Tom was interrupted by the bartender from the catering service, asking if they cared for another drink. Sally declined. Tom asked Sally if she would mind driving him home that evening. That way, he could have another drink. She said yes, and Tom ordered another manhattan. Soon a steaming plate of lobster and corn was placed in front of them. Everyone dug in.

"Where were we when the manhattan interrupted us? Something about the nature of dilemmas, I believe."

"Forget that," Tom said, butter dripping off his chin. "Because of that diversion into your divorce, we never finished talking about Sam and college. That's what really interests me."

"Well, I'm not sure whether he just doesn't want to go to college or whether he's really afraid of being rejected. And as for bringing his grades up, he's not very motivated by that right now. Says he'd rather be a lobsterman."

"He could do a lot worse, I'll tell you," Tom said. "My father was a lobsterman, and he made a lot more money than I'll ever make."

At that point, Betty Norton stood up and began by thanking everyone for attending and extending credits to various people who had contributed to the evening's occasion.

Tom's corn was acknowledged as the best ever. He stood up to speak and say he was flattered but declined to take all the credit. The main reason the corn tasted so good was that it was fresh. He had picked it that very afternoon, just before he drove over to Betty's. It was old man York, his father-in-law, who was really responsible for the delicious corn. He was the one who had gotten Tom into farming.

He sat down and continued his story for Sally. A few years before he died, old man York had begun raising sweet corn on a commercial scale in the same fields where his ancestors had grown it. It was a York family tradition, which, Tom hoped, would be carried on by his daughters someday. The cornfield also qualified the property as a working farm and reduced real estate taxes, a much bigger financial yield than what he made selling the corn. The farm would someday be back in the York family when his daughters inherited it. He was only a temporary steward for the land. Tom shut up, realizing that he had gotten too carried away from all the manhattans.

On the way home, Sally thanked Tom several more times for his help with Sam. "It's very depressing," she admitted, "to take an honest look at your only child and realize that, somewhere along the line, you made some big mistakes. At first, I blamed everything on Charlie. Later, I decided it was the school system in Philadelphia, with all the drugs and alcohol use that was to blame. So I scanned the Internet and found that Maine has a relatively low incidence of drug problems in its schools. And ophthalmologists were scarce.

"I moved to Maine to get Sam away from all those negative influences. And what happens? He gets tagged for drunk driving. Charlie was furious and, of course, blamed me. It had a terrible effect on Sam."

About then, they came to the scenic turnout at the top of Pitch Pine Hill. Sally pulled in and switched off the motor.

"Whatcha stopping here for?"

"Oh, I can't drive and talk about this stuff without getting upset, so I decided to stop for a few minutes. You don't mind, do you?"

"No problem. It's a beautiful view. Lobster Cove sure looks gorgeous with the moon on the water, don't you think?"

"Sure does," Sally replied. She paused for a while in thought. "Lately I have come to believe that I am partly to blame for this whole mess. Looking back, I can see where I made mistakes as a parent. Lots of them, in fact. My whole life has been devoted to perfecting my technique so that I wouldn't make a mistake during cataract surgery. I was always so careful. Then all of a sudden I find out that, as a mother, I've been making one mistake after another. How could I do that? Possibly too much devotion to my career. Maybe I should have had another child. Other mistakes, I don't even want to think about. And poor Sam paid for it all. That's what really hurts."

"Well, we all make mistakes," Tom said as he rolled down the window to let in some aromatic ocean air. "I have been guilty of some of the same things as you. And believe me, it still hurts. You see, by the time I finished medical school and residency, we already had our kids. Caroline. All she wanted to do was be a mom. She loved it. Ran the house, chauffeured the kids, and hung out with all her friends, who also had kids.

"I enjoyed the kids too," Tom continued. "But so much of my time was taken up with medicine and cardiology research. I was always getting called into the hospital at night or on the weekends to supervise the residents or consult on patients. Not that I minded it all that much. I enjoyed the work. I could see myself in line for associate professor and eventually department chair at some medical school. Back then, I was ambitious. Also, I guess, part of it was that I wanted to make my father proud."

"I can relate to that," Sally observed as she rolled down her window and pushed her seat back.

"Well, after Mark died, my whole perspective changed," Tom continued. "Looking back on those times, I realized that the memories I treasured most were when we were on vacation with the kids, especially when we were up here in Maine, visiting with the grandparents. Spending more time with the kids was very satisfying. Knowing that part of me was in each kid. Watching them grow. Helping them learn. Seeing parts of Caroline in them. It was very satisfying. Caroline said I was more like the man she thought she was marrying when I was home. I finally saw the mistake I was making, and that's when we decided to move back to Maine."

"It's hard," Sally said, "when you look back at the mistakes you have made."

"Excuse me," Tom said, stepping out of the car. "I need to go out behind the bushes for a minute. Be right back." After he returned, he said, "I've been thinking—nothing clears your mind like emptying your bladder—Sally, at least you recognize your mistakes. So many people fail to even recognize their own mistakes, or much less acknowledge them. I once had an art professor back at Yale who had been an apprentice at the Louvre. You know, the art museum in Paris. They had a saying at the Louvre that the sign of a good apprentice was not one who didn't make mistakes, but one who found his own mistakes and fixed them up before the master could ever find them."

"Humph! Now that's really savoir faire."

Tom gave a big nod of agreement and continued. "Think about it. You have already gotten past the first, and probably the hardest, part in that process: finding your mistakes. Now that you have found them, you still have plenty of time left to fix them up before Sam becomes an adult."

"But he is so far behind in school. What can I do? I've been thinking about sending him off to prep school for a year, after he finishes high school. Do you think that might get him moving?"

"We considered sending our girls to prep school. Caroline went to prep school. But it was expensive, and we both felt they weren't quite mature enough to leave home. Or maybe we just weren't ready to kick them out of the nest yet. You know? After what happened to Mark. I don't know.

"Anyway, what we did was to start spending a lot more time with them in the evenings while they did their homework. Not just tutoring them, but taking interest in their studies. Letting them teach us new things we didn't know. Keeping them engaged in the learning process. That was probably the main thing. Sometimes we were able to teach them things their teachers didn't teach. It was actually very rewarding. They got a lot out of it, but I think Caroline and I probably got more. That kind of approach might work with Sam."

After a very long silence, Sally finally said, "I don't know if it will work or not, but it is an excellent suggestion. I would never forgive myself if I didn't try it." The next thing Tom knew, he was home.

～

Tom was still in bed when Cathy showed up the next morning. She opened the morning paper to show him his picture, sitting beside the swimming pool, with Sally's hand on his arm, plastered on the society page. Rumors were all over the hospital about how he had left the party with Sally Gardiner. Cathy demanded an explanation.

Tom had another headache, but he managed to laugh. It was all a part of some radical right-wing republican conspiracy, he said. To get him drunk and embarrass him. Betty Norton kept on putting manhattans in front of him all through the evening. At the end of the evening, she pronounced him inebriated and insisted that Sally drive him home. In fact, he was hoping that after his shower, Cathy would drive him back over to the Nortons so he could pick up his truck.

In the car, Cathy continued her interrogation. She wasn't interested in details about the angry phone calls, the blame game, or guilt trips that Tom had patiently listened to Sally talk about. She was more concerned about the kiss. The hospital was a rumor mill, so he wasn't too surprised that Cathy knew about what happened at the party, but how in the world, Tom wondered, did she find out about the kiss? Totally on the defensive, Tom confessed.

"When Sally pulled into my driveway to let me out last night," Tom confessed, "she said to me, 'I know I'll never be able to repay you for everything you've done. All I can say is thank you.' She reached over and gave me a big smooch, just before I got out of the car to go in the house."

Cathy told him, when she dropped him off to pick up his truck, that he'd better wipe the lipstick off his cheek before he got home.

Tom followed Cathy home in his pickup truck. Driving the truck always seemed to calm him and help him focus. It had been a fun night overall. Maybe he had gotten a little carried away about the York Farm. But he was so in love with the place. Suddenly it occurred to him. He needed to get in touch with his family lawyer and put the farm into some kind of a trust for his daughters. Make sure it was out of the reach of greedy, malpractice lawyers. Not that there was much likelihood of that happening. But no use taking chances.

He pulled the truck into the barn and met up with Cathy, sporting a brand-new cowboy hat. "What do you think, pardner?"

"Mighty fine," Tom replied.

Cathy led him into the tack room to show him the new western saddle she had just bought. She recently had started riding Caroline's Morgan horse and had gotten fairly good at riding after taking a few lessons. But she didn't care for the English saddles that Caroline had left behind. She had seen too many cowboy movies, growing up. Tom was amused by the saddle.

Starting out of the barn, they got into brighter light. Cathy looked up at his face and suddenly tackled him and slammed him onto a hay bale. She scrubbed the lipstick off his left cheek with a Kleenex, like he was a little boy. "If you're gonna insist on wearing lipstick on your cheek, it had better be my shade." Then she proceeded to cover him with the proper color. And in some pretty exciting places.

Chapter 14

The smell of fall was in the air. The subtle fragrance completely reprogrammed Tom's perspective on life. He took in another deep breath and bent over to pick up the morning paper off the front door stoop. Glancing first at the weather report, he noted that low-lying areas in the northern part of the state could expect frost tonight. As he poured out some coffee, the screen in Tom's mind flashed prompts about getting ready for autumn, a mental list of chores that needed to be finished so a man could go off to hunting camp with a clear conscience: finish harvesting the garden, can or freeze all the vegetables, put another load of hay in the loft for the winter, dig up the dahlia bulbs—his list would grow over the next few weeks.

Tom sat at the breakfast table, drinking his coffee and leafing through a stack of hunting catalogs. He was looking for a hunting vest to give to Sam. Tom and Prince had invited Sam to join them up at camp for a little partridge hunting. The season opened in less than a month. Tom was eager. He had missed the whole season last year, with Caroline's death and all. He took out his notebook and started a list of things to accomplish that day:

1. Call estate lawyer. Tom wanted to set up a trust to put York Farm in safekeeping for his daughters. A million dollars was supposed to be more than adequate for malpractice coverage in Maine. Still, there was no use taking any chances with tort lawyers.

2. Call Alfred. He needed to check about harvesting the apples. Ever since Caroline's father had his stroke, they had subcontracted the apple orchard work out to Alfred. Tom thought it might be fun to do the harvest himself, maybe run off a batch of cider, but he simply didn't have enough time.

He gazed out the picture window and got a glimpse of Cathy, coming back from her early-morning ride, wearing her cowboy hat. He had cunningly lured her into the world of horseback riding. She seemed to enjoy the relationships she was forming with other women who rode. And she found great satisfaction in learning how to care for horses, although she could never make herself stoop to mucking out the stall. But Tom didn't mind doing that job himself.

It amused him to see her different approach to riding, compared with Caroline's style. The people Caroline rode with were equestrians— the "horsey set," as Tom liked to call them, people who preferred to ride in the proper, traditional manner. They used English saddles and wore English riding clothes. Cathy had somehow fallen in with what Tom liked to call the "hossy crowd," people who rode western style with cowboy clothes and matching manners.

He looked through his pile of catalogs, full of riding clothes and equine equipment. Some of them were still addressed to Caroline. A nice western shirt to go with her new hat would make a great birthday present. After going through the pages, he decided instead to order a lady's leather riding vest. He made that number three on his list.

3.   Get two boxes of mason jars and a new pressure cooker. They planned to can most of the tomato crop this year. It was a good thing he had noticed Cathy stop to stake up a few tomato vines or he might have forgotten about the canning supplies.

Tom managed to take care of most everything on his list in between patient visits that morning. His afternoon was taken up by a meeting with the malpractice lawyer. It was time to go over details of all the medical issues, in preparation for the depositions, which were scheduled to begin in November. The lawyer drove up from Portland, and they met in Tom's private office again. Tom decided, this time, the attorney should sit in the doctor's chair to see how it felt to be in that position. A feeble, last-minute, strategic ploy devised purely by instinct.

The lawyer's affect was noticeably altered by this new perspective. He carefully scanned the walls, appraising all the degrees, board certifications, and awards that were not quite so apparent when sitting in the patient chair. He made inquiries about members of Tom's family pictured on the desk.

"I was surprised to discover that you are a board-certified cardiologist," the attorney said and congratulated Tom on his impressive curriculum vitae, which, he said, would help in the presentation of his case. "The expert witness for the plaintiff was not nearly so impressive."

Tom had never heard of the guy, a fellow with a Middle Eastern–sounding name who practiced in New York. The attorney said he was well-known to malpractice lawyers. He testified frequently for plaintiffs' lawyers and regularly advertised his services in one of the tort law journals.

Tom had done considerable prep work for this meeting and tutored his attorney on the medical issues involved in the case. They went over the preoperative test results, which showed no objective evidence of any heart disorder. He furnished written criteria for the diagnosis of coronary artery disease from the American Cardiology Association. He also offered a copy of a paper from the CDC, stating that most fatal heart attacks strike unexpectedly, without any recognition of early warning signs. The attorney felt that this information would be helpful in disputing the expert witness's first allegation.

Tom then showed him a section from a textbook that stated that digoxin was not indicated for the acute management of ventricular tachycardia because it took three hours for the drug to achieve its therapeutic effect. The issue about the improper lidocaine dosage was a "crock of shit" in Tom's view.

When the lawyer showed Tom the nurse's note that recorded a flow rate of 444 cc's per hour, taken from the digital display on the flow pump, and compared it with the 444 rate on the EMTALA transfer order, Tom nearly collapsed.

"I tell you what. Something's awfully fishy here," Tom started out softly, but his vocal projection quickly increased, almost to a scream. "There's no fucking way I could have written 444 cc's per hour. Do you hear me? It's ridiculous. I'm going right over to the hospital to get this whole thing straightened out, once and for all."

"That's exactly what you had better not do," the lawyer protested. "If they ever find out you have been discussing this case on your own, outside the legal process, it will impair your chances for a favorable settlement in this case. Leave this dispute up to the legal process. It is designed to resolve these things.

"Now calm down," the attorney continued. "Fortunately, we've covered pretty much everything, so I can leave you alone now."

Tom apologized for the outburst, but the attorney reassured him.

"Don't worry. These kinds of reactions are common in this business. And they seldom cause any problems in these private meetings. But, out in public, you need to keep yourself calm, cool, and collected." He picked up his briefcase and left.

Tom had no choice. He knew enough to keep his mouth shut. He could handle it. Thank God he had taken action to set up the trust and get all his property out of the reach of the tort lawyers. That thought, together with his growing anticipation about the upcoming hunting season, kept him pretty happy throughout the busy days in the office.

In his free time, he enjoyed harvesting his garden and canning the tomatoes. They still had another big batch to put up before the frost came. Sunday, he planned to do it by himself. Cathy had Britney for the weekend. She never came around anymore when she had Britney. Tom was out in the garden, harvesting tomatoes, when Cathy drove up and got out with Britney. Tom was overwhelmed.

"What an unexpected pleasure. Nice to see you again, Britney," he said and gave her a big hug.

"Are we going to eat the clams?"

"I'm afraid not. They kinda disappeared. But we can get some more if you like." Tom suggested that Cathy take Britney into the barn and check out the horse.

"I was planning to do that. Maybe we could go for a quick ride while you finish picking the tomatoes. We'll be back in time to help out with the canning. Okay?"

"Sure. Take your time. I'm all set here. I wasn't expecting any help today anyway."

From time to time, Tom looked up from his harvesting to watch the horseback riding. Britney rode in front of her mother, wearing the cowboy hat. After a few turns around the ring, they headed out on the trail.

Tom was getting things started in the kitchen when they returned. Britney was still wearing the cowboy hat. "Did you guys ride up by Pooh and Piglet's house, up in the Hundred Acre Woods?" he asked.

"Yes, but Britney wasn't very interested. Winnie-the-Pooh was kinda dated when she came along. It's just a bunch of cartoons on TV now."

"Can I help can some of the tomatoes?" Britney asked.

"How would you like to be the peeler?" Tom responded. "Here's how we do it. I put the tomatoes in this wire basket and drop them in boiling water for a minute or so. See? After I cool them off in cold water, the peel comes off easy. See that? Think you can do it?"

"This is easy. I can hardly wait to show my dad. Maybe he'll let me help can his tomatoes."

"Your dad's got to be a regular guy if he cans tomatoes," Tom said.

Cathy let out a frustrated sigh.

"Well, I don't really know about that, but he sure likes it when I help."

Production got into full swing. The jars were all filled. *Heavens! One o'clock already. Time flies when you're having fun.* Tom opened a beer. Cathy and Britney shared a Coke.

"You guys will never know how much I appreciate all the help you've given me in getting all these chores done before partridge season opens next week."

"Partridge? My daddy hunts partridge. He's a great shot. When I get older, he's going to teach me how to shoot. I love partridge."

"Your dad's a partridge hunter? He must be a terrific guy," Tom remarked without thinking. A huge crash occurred as Cathy dropped the jars into the pressure cooker. Scalding water spilled on her shin. Fortunately, the skin was barely burned, first degree at most. The last batch went through without a hitch. Cathy and Britney left after the kitchen was cleaned.

Tom spent the rest of the day laying out everything he needed for the opening day of partridge hunting.

Friday afternoon, before Tom was scheduled to leave, he got a call from the estate lawyer. "Are you involved in some kind of a malpractice suit or something?" he asked Tom.

"I'm not permitted to talk about that."

"I thought so," said the lawyer. "Well, I've a bit of bad news. It turns out all your property has had a legal injunction put on it. You are prevented from selling or otherwise disposing of your holdings pending settlement of whatever suit is pending in county superior court. I'm very sorry, Tom. They probably had that injunction in place before you were even notified of the case. You never had a chance."

Tom had to cancel his plans for partridge hunting. There was no way in the world he could enjoy hunting in this state of mind. Prince and the boys would have to go without him. He could barely keep his anger and fear under cover enough to keep on functioning. It just wasn't fair!

That thought dominated Tom's mind all day long. Come night, half a Xanax wasn't enough. He took another half at one o'clock. The next day, his head was pounding. This time he took his own blood pressure and adjusted the medication himself. He had some measure of control left, but it made him angry when his time in the mile swim was significantly slower—probably because of the higher dose of medication. The loss of libido was the least of his worries. Given enough time, Tom felt he could find a way out of this mess. In the meantime, he would keep on keepin' on, just like the old-timers used to do.

But it didn't work. Yielding control over the resolution of his personal problems to some law firm made Tom anxious. Loss of control frightened him. He recognized depression setting in. As time went on, Tom began to realize that, regardless of his lawyer's insistence on silence, he needed to talk with someone about this lawsuit before he could face a deposition or, even worse, maybe a trial. He needed some validation of his outrage, some reassurance about his medical management, something to help put all his emotions and ideas into perspective so he could cope with the impending ordeals as skillfully as possible. Plus sympathy—he needed some of that too.

Whom could he ask? Someone he could trust to keep their mouth shut. Without Caroline, he had no one left for heart-to-heart talks. He usually felt like talking to Prince whenever he was bothered by something. But Prince did not have the medical background to digest the meat of this complex enigma. Cathy? There was no doubt she could help him figure things out. But it was too risky. If the lawyers ever found out that he'd been talking with her, he'd be duck soup. Besides, despite his best efforts, there still was a certain distance between them he just couldn't bridge. Cathy was out of the question. It had to be another doctor. He considered various colleagues, even Sally Gardiner.

Hmm. Sally Gardiner. Now there was someone he might be able to talk with. Logically, she might not seem like the ideal choice. He didn't really know her all that well. But something inside him persuaded him to call and ask her anyway. She should help him out. Didn't she owe him big for everything he had done for Sam? They could take a Saturday and drive up to camp. With no one else around, they could talk freely. Besides, he really needed to get off the tar.

Sally agreed to go. She was not completely certain she liked the idea of going way up in the boondocks to a backwoods camp with no indoor plumbing, but Sam encouraged her and said he wished he was going. From talking with Prince about camp, he was thoroughly enchanted with the place. He was disappointed that he had not been able to complete the hunter safety course in time for hunting season because of conflicts with swim practice. He told her she was lucky to have been invited.

Saturday morning, she packed some warm clothes, her running clothes, and a book in her backpack. A day reading and chatting in front of a campfire might not be too bad.

Sally could not recall having ever ridden in a pickup truck since she left the farm. Sitting up so high, with all that noise from the big off-road tires, took some adjustment. Heading out of town in moderately heavy traffic, Tom pulled to a stop and allowed a lady in an SUV to pull onto the road from a side street.

"Say, that was very polite," Sally opined. "I've noticed people here in Maine do that a lot."

"I suppose you're right. It's just common courtesy, I suppose."

"True. But what is it that makes it so common in Maine?"

Tom thought for a moment and then replied, "I guess it's because bein' courteous makes a driver pleased with himself. Kind of an inner satisfaction. I think that's what makes me do it. And if the other driver smiles back or waves a thank-you, that intensifies the pleasure of being courteous."

Sally just shook her head and pondered. *Guess I've still got lots to learn about life in Maine,* she thought to herself.

"I need to get off the tar," Tom announced as soon as they were on the interstate.

"Excuse me?" Sally obviously had no clue.

"Gittin' off the tar?"

"Yeah. I never heard that one before."

"It's a local expression for getting away from it all. You see," Tom explained, "drinking and driving, it seems, is not legal on Maine public roads. Sam can tell you about that. However, on the unpaved private roads of paper companies, the rule is not enforced. As soon as we turn off the tar road and onto the dirt road that leads to camp, we can have a beer and keep on driving. It's great! Feels like going into another world where you can completely escape from all your problems of normal life. That's gittin' off the tar. Wait and see. You'll love it."

As they drove on the paved state highways, Sally and Tom thrashed over the malpractice suit from every angle. Sally was almost in tears when she learned how the lawyers had arranged to seize all of his property if they won a big settlement. Neither one could believe that anyone would make a mistake such as 444 cc's. Someone must have fudged the records. Tom wished he could do his own detective work. He'd snoop around, get the facts, and deal with this problem. Get it over, once and for all. But that wasn't allowed in the legal system.

"And it's starting to overwhelm me. First the suit. Then altering of the medical records. After that, they put an injunction on all my property. Who knows what's coming next? I understand perfectly well," Tom explained, "that I have no choice but to keep on treading water and contend with each issue as the legal system deals them out to me. What I need from you is some help in gathering all the resolve necessary for me to keep my head above water until this thing is over."

"Well, I'm not sure what I can do, but I'm more than happy to help. I mean, he was my patient too. And after all you've done for Sam, I owe you a lot."

When they turned off the turnpike onto a Maine country road, Sally noticed an immediate change in Tom. He seemed more relaxed, slouched down a little behind the steering wheel. His right hand rested comfortably on the top of the steering wheel. Whenever they passed an oncoming pickup truck, he would lift the fingers and palm of his right hand in a casual wave to the passing driver. Soon she realized almost all of the passing pickup drivers were giving the same subtle signal back to Tom. The right hand never left contact with the top of the steering wheel. Sally tried to remember if rural pickup drivers back in southern Illinois did the same. She didn't recall. Back then, ladies didn't ride in pickup trucks. Her pickup days ended when she got too old to go fishing with her grandfather.

Tom disappeared somewhere inside himself, listening to country music on the radio. Sally stared out the window. Rural northern Maine landscape was hardly what she would have expected. The farms were all so small and run-down. Lots of broken-down stone walls everywhere. *Years ago I bet they probably were the boundaries to fields and pastures. Now they are overgrown with trees and brush. People everywhere, living in trailers or double-wides, with old broken-down cars, trucks, and even skidders out in the yard. Amazing. Not at all like the prosperous, well-managed spreads back home in Illinois.* She had never imagined seeing farms without windmills and silos.

"Ahhh," Tom sighed as he turned onto a dirt road that led to camp. "This is it. We're finally off the tar roads. Need anything to drink?" He pulled off to the side of the road and got out of the truck.

"No, thanks."

Tom came back with a cold can of Coke and popped it open.

"I thought you would be getting a beer."

"Well, usually I do. But this is bird-hunting season, and it's eleven miles to camp. I might see a partridge on the way. Drinkin' and drivin' is okay, but drinking and hunting don't mix."

"Look!" Sally shouted just as Tom let out the clutch. "There's a deer."

It just stood there and looked curiously at the truck.

"Ayeah. Look at him, just standin' there, the gravy drippin' right off'n him. Too bad deer season doesn't open 'til next month. Otherwise, I just might tip him over."

"Well, listen to you. You sound like a redneck and a lot like my father, as a matter of fact," Sally observed. "I never hear you talk like that when you're at the hospital. Where did you pick up that kind of talk?"

"This is how I've always talked, just like everyone else around here. At the hospital, I have my doctor's suit on."

"Doctor's suit? What in hell is the doctor's suit?"

"When I put on the white coat and lay that stethoscope around my neck, that's when I've got my doctor's suit on," he explained. "So I talk doctor talk. People expect their doctors to look and act properly. They don't want to think their doctor is some casual redneck. While I'm wearing my doctor's suit, I behave like a doctor and talk like a doctor. But that's not who I really am. I'm Tom MacMahan, son of a lobsterman. Born and raised in Maine. Get the idea?"

"More or less. I guess it's okay, if it works for you."

"Well, it does work for me. At least here in Maine. Back when I lived in Boston, I was a doctor all the time. It was different. Bein' a doctor is more important. It says who you are. So ever'body knows your status."

Sally said nothing for a long while. Tom could tell she was still engaged when he looked over at the expression on her face. "You know," she finally said, "I went to medical school to change the kind of person I would become. Really! A whole new me.

"Then, when I took the Hippocratic Oath, it felt like I had completely changed who I was. There were new and higher standards to live by for the rest of my life. It felt good. Very satisfying."

"That's exactly how I felt at first," Tom replied. "But now it seems different. I look at it this way. When you become a priest, you're a whole new person. For the rest of your life. Wouldn't you say? But all getting your MD means is you've got a new trade. You're still the same person. It took me a long time to figure that out. After Mark died and we moved back up to Maine, it finally hit me. Suddenly, it seemed, my life got a whole lot better. I'm happy being just plain me. Make sense?"

"Well, sorta."

"Look, everybody at home has known me since I was a kid. No use putting on an act just because I went to medical school. You know, pretending like I'm somehow better than everyone else."

"I see," said Sally. "I really do. Now that I think about it, when you were discussing the malpractice stuff, you sounded like a normal doctor. But after we finished our discussion and you turned onto the unpaved road, it was like a whole 'nother person was driving the truck. Listen to me. Now you've got me talking that way too. I sound just like my dad."

"See? Gittin' off the tar will do that to you. The words just slipped out of your mouth when your back was turned."

"Lord! What have I gotten myself into? Growing up, I always wanted to get off the farm. Maybe I figured I was too good to wear the farmer's suit."

"How does it feel?"

"How does what feel?"

"Wearing the farmer's suit," Tom replied. "How does it feel now?"

"Actually, it's a lot more comfortable than I remembered."

"Well, the guy driving the truck now is the real me. Problem is the goddamn lawsuit is messin' up both of me."

Tom drove along very slowly, scanning the road and adjacent woods, for signs of partridge, his brain reprogramming itself to relax mode.

"While I'm at it, I should tell you about another suit we MacMahans sometimes wear. It's called the asshole suit. It's my favorite suit. Wanna hear about it?"

"I guess I don't have any choice. I'm gonna hear about it, right?"

"I'm sorry, but yes. My dad, you see, he loved manhattans. He mostly never drank them except up at camp. Well, two of them would completely change his personality. He talked loud and told raunchy jokes. Didn't matter who was around. He didn't care. He just told everybody he had his asshole suit on. Mom could hardly stand it. But we all thought he was a riot. Anyway, he always asked if anyone else wanted to try on one of the suits. See how it fits. Then he would mix them a manhattan. He usually announced that he never added any bitters to his manhattans when he was up at camp. 'Cause a man don't need no bitters when he's roughin' it, you see?

"When Dad saw that your first drink was near about finished, he'd always ask, 'How's your suit fit? Don't be shy there. Speak up if'n it don't fit right. We always give free alterations.' Then he would pour them a second manhattan. Lucky for you I didn't bring my asshole suit along on this trip. But you saw me in it the other night at Betty's party. If you know what I mean."

"Actually, you were really funny and very charming. A bit outspoken, maybe, but I think everyone enjoyed you."

Suddenly Tom slammed on the brakes and brought the truck to a stop. "Partridge!" he shouted.

"Where?"

"On the right side of the road. Up ahead. See? Two of 'em." He jumped out of the truck and fished a double-barreled twenty-gauge shotgun out from behind the seat and loaded both barrels.

"You're not going to shoot them, are you?"

"You bet your ass I am." He left the engine running and started slowly walking up toward the birds, all the time looking down the barrel of the gun at them. As he got closer, the birds became nervous and began sticking their necks up and looking around. Tom fired two shots. One bird fell over in the road and wiggled around spasmodically. The other bird flew off into the trees. "Damn. I shoulda had 'em both."

"Well, I'm glad at least one of them got away," Sally announced, getting out of the truck to get a better look.

"My brother woulda shot the both of 'em," Tom declared. "He was a great shot." Tom picked up the bird and threw it in the back of the truck.

"What exactly is a partridge anyway? I thought they only grew in pear trees."

"Actually," he said, "it's really a Ruffed Grouse. In Vermont they call it grouse hunting, but around here we call 'em partridge, 'ceptin' if you shoot one in the air. Then it's a bloody grouse."

"Sounds pretty gross to me."

"Yeah, ha-ha! Wait 'til you taste 'em. You'll change your tune."

"No, thanks."

Sally was pleasantly surprised when they reached the camp. Situated near the bank of a river, surrounded by woods, the camp was constructed of logs. It was a two-room affair, with a fieldstone fireplace and chimney, plus a metal stovepipe for the wood stove. But no electricity or indoor plumbing. In front was a small screened porch.

Tom soon had the inside lit up with gas lamps. A deer head was mounted over the mantle. Numerous deer antlers decorated the walls, along with old pictures of crusty-looking campers from years past. Red-and-white–checked curtains were hung around the tiny windows. He started a fire in the wood cookstove and went out to the well to fetch a couple pails of water.

"Sit down. Make yourself comfy," he said as he started building a pot of coffee in the percolator.

"In case anyone wants to know," she said, looking out the window, "I was wondering which one of those buildings out there might be an outhouse. I presume you don't have a ladies' room."

"The one on your left, down that little path. Watch your step now, and enjoy yourself. You might want to wear a jacket. The shitter's not heated, and it's startin' to get cold. Might could even snow later on."

A sense of urgency overwhelmed Sally's distaste for outhouses. She hadn't used one in years. Fortunately, because it had not been used for a long time, the dreaded smell was absent. Inside, the place was rather cozy, with humorous decorations on the walls. When she returned, Tom was outside in his T-shirt, chopping wood. "Paul Bunyan, I presume?"

Tom gave her the finger and handed her a load of wood to take inside.

Sally put her load in the wood box and plumped herself in the rocking chair next to the wood stove. *A pretty cozy little camp,* she thought to herself as she began to relax in the warmth of the stove. Tom came in and poured them both some coffee and then put a large container of water on the back of the stove to heat. From the other bucket of water, he filled two canteens. Then he dressed out the partridge, put the breasts in the cooler, and pinned the bird's tail, all fanned out, onto a piece of wood shingle and gave it to Sally for a present.

"It's gorgeous. What do I do with it?"

"After it dries, it'll stay all spread out like that. You can take it off the board and use it to decorate a shelf or a mantle. I think there's one on the wall in the bunk room if you want to peek in there." He nodded at the door beside the fireplace. "I'm going out to the shed and get out the canoe paddles and life jackets. I think a canoe trip would make a good expedition for today. With all the rain we've had, the river is not so low as it usually is in October. No better way to get a feel for this part of the country than a river trip. Won't take but a couple of hours, and we'll still have time for a partridge supper before heading home."

Tom showed Sally, in the *Maine Atlas and Gazetteer*, exactly where their canoe trip would take them. Then they loaded the canoe and all their gear onto the pickup and drove up a winding dirt road until they came to a bridge over the river. Tom parked, and they put the canoe in the water, just below the bridge. Tom went back and locked the cooler inside the truck cab, and they were ready to shove off. Sally had very little experience in a canoe, so Tom gave her an introductory lesson.

"Any fish in this river?" she asked.

"Very few. The wormers hit this place pretty heavy in the spring. It used to make my dad mad 'cause this is a fly-fishing–only river. But so many people canoe this river in the spring, and lots of 'em bring worms and take home fish, it's pretty much been cleaned out. But there are plenty of other good spots to fish around here, so it don't much mattah as far as I'm concerned."

Sally was immediately taken by the river. Long-forgotten memories of joyful childhood experiences chimed in harmoniously through her mind. She could feel the anticipation kindling in her brain. Going around a bend in the river was exciting, with the anticipation of new and breathtaking landscapes. The trees, although not quite at their peak autumn colors, still displayed a rich spectrum. Lovely yellow and reddish-brown hues decorated the mountainsides. When the sun occasionally broke through the clouds, Sally would stop paddling and stare in awe.

"I moved to Maine to be on the coast," she said. "It's what you always hear about when people talk about Maine. I never dreamed the rest of Maine would be so beautiful and unspoiled."

"We try to keep it a secret as much as possible." Tom chuckled.

Around one bend they came upon a large, flat, boggy expanse where the river widened and the current slowed. Sally had to paddle a little harder. A large cow moose brought her head up out of the water and gave them a careful appraisal as they paddled by. Over near the shore was her little calf, also staring at them. "I've never seen a moose so close up before. They're huge."

"Wait 'til you see a bull up close. Then you'll know what huge is."

They kept on paddling down the river, enjoying the brisk but gentle current that carried them past the constantly changing scenery. Eventually, after they had passed the camp, Tom steered them over to the shore for a rest and a drink of water.

"Is this the end of it?"

"Not necessarily. There's another mile and a half or so left. But sometimes we take out right here. A woods road comes in where that old washed-out bridge is. We can get the truck in there to load up the canoe." He could see by Sally's nonverbal response that she was having too much fun to quit now.

"Okay then. It gets kinda bony on this next stretch, but it's really the most fun part of the trip. In the spring, when the water is up, you've got class three and sometimes even class four water in there. That's why this river is so popular, especially with the kayakers."

They paddled back into the current, and Tom started his advanced-level instructions on white-water canoeing. Sally mastered the new strokes quickly. She was a little concerned when she heard the roaring sound from the rapids up ahead.

"It gets pretty tricky in here, but don't worry. Just do like I showed you, and you can make it." Tom reassured her as he paddled them into a little back eddy where they could chat. "You know, when Caroline first started coming up here years ago, well, she hated those rapids. Her idea of a canoe trip was cruising down the river on a Sunday afternoon, if you know what I mean."

"Yes. That's how it is back home. The country is pretty flat compared to here."

"Well, Caroline thought it was unfair that the state didn't come in here and move all those rocks and boulders so everyone could have a quiet, peaceful canoe trip. My dad set her straight about white-water canoeing. He loved the sport. Grew up canoeing these waters and competed in the big white-water canoe races when he was young. One year, he and his buddy were way ahead in the race, when they hit a rock and turned over their canoe. Several canoes went right past them. Dad lost his paddle. He was totally defeated and ready to quit. But his partner always kept a spare paddle fastened inside the boat. He told Dad to get back in the boat and get paddling again. Well, they did. And they ended up winning the race anyway."

"No kidding."

"I kid you not. Dad always said it was the biggest lesson in his life.

He used to say white-water canoeing was a lot like life, don'tcha know? Things get going fast and furious, and there's lots of hazardous obstacles in the way. A reg'lar person works hard trying to achieve their goals, but their canoe gets turned over by a BFR. They cry about how unfair life is. Dad believed that life was not supposed to be fair anyway. 'Whenever a BFR upsets your canoe, just bail it out, get back on board, and start paddling. Get back in the current. If you go with the flow, you'll find a new way to achieve your goals.' That was one of Dad's favorite rules for life. Go with the flow."

"Go with the flow?"

"You got it. Dad was always grousing about out-o'-staters—Massholes, he called 'em. They move up to Maine, and the first thing they want to do is change the flow. Said they were gonna ruin the whole state."

"Go with the flow? So that's how it's done in Maine?"

"I know it's a bit much. I bet I've heard that a hundred times in my life. But getting back to white water, things go so fast you don't even have time to think. You just have to react. All's ya need to remember is two things: Keep away from the BFRs. You know what those are, don't you?"

"Oh, yes. Sammy could hardly wait to educate me on that subject."

"Anyway," Tom continued, "all's you need to remember is: Try to keep from running into the BFRs, and go with the flow. That means try to stay in the mainstream and don't make waves, if you know what I mean."

"I think I got the picture."

"Anyway," Tom continued, "after she learned how to do it right, Caroline grew to love the white water. I think you will too." He guided the canoe back into the fast water.

They made it through the rapids, past Carrying Point and down through Dead Man's Rip, without a scratch.

"Wow! That was fun," Sally said, catching her breath as they pulled the canoe to shore at the edge of a large calm pool.

"You ought to try it in the spring, when the water is really pouring through here. It's even more exciting. 'Course you got to wear wet suits when the water's up high. It's wicked cold." Tom hauled the canoe on shore and rolled it over to let all the water out.

"I think I might like to try it," Sally said with much enthusiasm. "How do we get back to the truck now?"

"That's why we brought our running clothes. It's three and a half miles. You want to go? Or you can wait here if you prefer." Sally shook her head. "Okay, jump in the bushes and change." He handed her the canteen and went in the bushes to change into his running clothes. Soon they were jogging at a comfortable pace along a gravel woods road.

They spotted five partridge and one bull moose before they reached the bridge where the pickup was parked. Tom regretted not having his Contender along so he could have shot a couple more birds. Sally was amazed when he told her how he often carried the Contender, a pistol, with a four-ten shotgun barrel, when he went out running up at camp. Occasionally he returned from his daily run with a partridge for the pot. She was also glad when Tom unlocked the truck and pulled out a couple of cold beers from the cooler. They both had a few gulps and then jumped in the truck and headed on down the gravel road to pick up the canoe.

"How do you like drinkin' an' drivin'?" Tom inquired after a swig of beer.

"It's not that bad," Sally said, recalling an expression Sam had picked up from Prince. "Only don't ever tell Sam about this. He just got his license back."

Sally was starting to feel her second beer by the time they got the canoe back to the camp and onto its rack behind the shed. The camp was warm and much more hospitable than Sally had remembered. The dank smell was gone, replaced by a fragrance from the wood stove. She made another trip to the outhouse.

When she returned, there was a roaring fire in the fireplace. Tom was working on his third beer and getting all the food for their dinner out of the cooler. He had prepared the salad and garlic mashed potatoes ahead, so there was minimal work remaining. Sally declined a third beer. She asked what he was doing, pouring all that hot water through the big funnel and into the large rubber bag.

"Getting things ready for our bag showers," he said. "See? This tube fastens onto the bottom of the bag, and the nozzle on the end hangs down and makes a showerhead." He showed her how to operate it. "Now you go in the bunk room and take off everything but your shoes and wrap a towel around, whilst I go out and hoist this bag up on the cross pole in those trees. Underneath is a wooden platform to stand on. There's soap and shampoo on a shelf between those trees. I'll have everything ready for you in two shakes."

"But it's starting to snow," she protested.

"Trust me. That makes it even better. You're gonna love it."

Sally would not have gone through with it if it wasn't that she desperately needed a bath after all that running. Despite the falling snow, she made herself go out, take off her shoes, and hang the towel on a branch. She was pleasantly surprised that cold and snow did not bother her as soon as the warm water began drizzling down over her naked body. It kept her quite warm and comfy. She shampooed her hair and soaped all over, and then she let the delicious warm water rinse her off.

That's when she became aware of the large, lacy flakes of snow, floating gently down in the windless night. They glittered brightly in the soft light coming through the cabin window. It felt so pleasant. So alive. Never had she experienced anything quite like it. The soft, spongy coolness of flakes felt so good against her warm skin. So sensual. She kept on rinsing. Then the shower bag went dry. Sally reached up to check the nozzle and see if she could get any more water. The nozzle came off in her hand. She quickly dried off, wrapped up in her towel, and made a beeline for the camp.

"You were right," she said as she stepped inside the cabin. "It was fabulous. Really sensual. Sorry I used up all the hot water. I think I may have broken the shower." She handed him the nozzle.

"No problem. It's happened before. I can fix it. And there's plenty more hot water on the stove."

Wrapped only in his towel, he retrieved the bag, refilled it, and went out for his shower. When he got back inside the camp, Sally was still in her towel, seated in front of the fire and working on her third beer.

"How come you're not getting dressed?' Tom asked, a bit puzzled.

"Well, there's no use putting all those things on if you're just going to have to take them all off again."

"I see. And just what brought on all these ideas?"

"Well. When a girl gets a glimpse of a gorgeous set of buns like that, she starts to get ideas. Then when she sees those pecs and abs, I mean, what do you think?" She reached around and gave his buttock a gentle squeeze.

"Oh! You peeked."

"And you didn't, I suppose?"

"No. I didn't." He could see immediately he wasn't making any points. "Just because I'm not wearing the doctor's suit doesn't mean I'm no longer a gentleman."

Sally scowled.

Tom was getting nowhere. "It's not like I even needed to look. I've already made an appraisal. Spandex doesn't leave much to a man's imagination, if you know what I mean."

Sally retreated to the bunk room in a huff. Tom tried to follow, but Sally put her foot down and blocked the door. Through the crack that remained, Tom pled his case.

"Please don't get me wrong, Sally. That was the nicest, most sincere compliment I can ever remember. And believe me when I tell you that I would really love to respond. You understand?"

No response.

"It's just that I can't. I mean it would not be fair to Cathy. I'm just not the two-timing sort."

Still no response.

"And even if I was, it probably wouldn't do you any good anyhow. I'm not in the rut right now."

"Not in the rut? Now I've heard it all."

"I'm serious. This goddamn malpractice case has got me so wound up, my blood pressure went sky high. The high dose of blood pressure medication I'm on is causing a problem in the rut department. I'd probably have to drive in town to a drugstore somewhere and get some Viagra. I'm not kidding."

"Thank you for sharing that with me."

"Sorry, guess I got carried away. But it is true. How about if I just said I had a headache? Would that work? I'm sure when this goddamn lawsuit is over I'll be able to go off all this lousy blood pressure medicine. I haven't been sleeping much of late, and they say that not getting enough hours of REM sleep every night is all it takes to raise your blood pressure. I've seen patients get completely off their blood pressure medications after they were treated for sleep apnea and started sleeping again. So I'm not too worried about the long run. Get your clothes on. I'm starting dinner right away."

The smell of partridge breast frying in hot butter brought her right to the table without further invitation. After a few "Mmms" and an "Oh my God" or two, she finally said, "I really should have come on this trip with your brother."

"What do you mean? 'Cause he wouldn't need Viagra?"

"No, silly. Because he's a better shot than you, and he would have shot both those birds, and we'd have more meat on the table."

"Now you're talking. Here, have this last piece. We can stop at McDonald's on the way home if need be."

"Question?" Sally asked.

"Okay. Go ahead."

"Tell me again, what's the difference between a partridge and a ruffed grouse?"

"Well, if you shoot it in the road, like I did today, it's a partridge. But if you shoot one in the air, it's a bloody grouse."

"Ha-ha!" Sally groaned.

"Ah, but there's more. When you cook a partridge, you should serve it with beer. But a grouse tastes better with a martini."

"Boy," Sally said, shaking her head. "Up here at camp, you get almost as silly as the folks in my family, when they're off to camp. But I've got one more question for you. While I was pouting in the bunk room, I looked through the little bookshelf at the window by the bed. And I noticed a very early copy of Winnie-the-Pooh. Where did that come from?"

"That was my book. My brother and I had it when we were kids."

"Well, why do you keep it up here in camp?"

"It's been here for years. My mother brought it up to read to my kids when they were little. She had another copy she kept at home. My dad liked to read to them too. It sort of got to be a tradition. I still read Pooh to them at bedtime, whenever we're up at camp. Especially Kristen. Even at her age, she still likes to snuggle up with me and listen to Pooh at bedtime. The girls came up to camp with me after Caroline died, and we all snuggled in. Only that time, they read to me."

Sally just sat there and shook her head back and forth. Finally, she said, "That's nice."

After the dishes were washed, Tom announced that he needed a couple hours of sleep before he was ready to drive home. Sally said she could stay the night if necessary. Tom said no. He had to be on call at 8:00 a.m. on Sunday. He tucked her into one of the bunks and began reading the story of "What Tiggers Like Best." When he was finished, he gave her a fatherly good-night kiss and hopped in his own bed.

By 11:00 p.m., they were all packed up, with a fresh thermos of coffee on board. Ready to hit the road. Sally felt a little anxious. Four inches of fluffy snow covered the road. But with four-wheel drive, it was no problem. The windshield wipers ticked, and the evergreens were all decked out in white. Beautiful. Every time they turned around, it seemed, the scenery in Maine changed. Sally enjoyed the trip.

When they got back on the tar road again, Sally's cell phone went off. It was Sam, checking in. He wanted to make sure it was okay for him to stay at a friend's house for the night. She had no objections and said she would be there when he got home the next morning.

"So how did you like being up at camp?" Tom asked after she got off the phone.

"It was a lot more fun than I expected. In some ways it reminds me of home."

"How's that?"

"Well, our family always had a camp, back when I was growing up. Only we never said we were goin' up to camp. We always called it going 'down to the river.'"

"Down to the river?"

"Yes. My grandfather owned a big chunk of woodland, down along the river. They had a small cluster of family camps there where they could fish for catfish in the summer and go hunting in the fall. It was great fun when we were kids."

The tar roads had all been plowed, and Tom shifted back into two-wheel drive. He immediately became lost in his own thoughts. Sally broke the silence with "I'm curious, Tom. Not that it's any of my business, but whatever happened to your wife?"

"You want the summary version or the whole nine yards?"

"I guess anything you feel comfortable telling would be okay."

"It's a long story," he began. "I don't think I have ever told anyone the whole story before. It all began," he went on, "with Mark, our first child. Mark developed warts on his vocal cords when he was very young. They are caused by human papillomavirus. Kids usually catch them from their mothers. They checked Caroline and, sure enough, she had vaginal warts—a sexually transmitted disease caused by the same virus. They figured she picked up the disease sometime before we ever got married. Who knows, maybe at Woodstock. But she stopped all that *make love, not war* stuff after we got married.

"Anyway, neither of our daughters, nor I, developed warts for some reason. We all were treated with interferon. Maybe that did it. The whole problem faded away for a while. But Caroline always held onto a portion of that sixties mentality. She was never really comfortable with doctors, it seems. Perhaps it was all the in-your-face embarrassment over having a sexually transmitted disease. I can only guess. But, unbeknownst to me, she completely stopped going to doctors. She still appeared to care about health. She faithfully took the kids to the pediatrician. She was always in the health food store after the current holistic remedies. But she never had a PAP smear. I was totally unaware of this until she began with persistent vaginal bleeding and was finally diagnosed with cervical carcinoma. By then it had already metastasized, and it was too late."

"What a bummer" was all Sally could manage. "Imagine. No PAP smears. And it's pretty clear, isn't it, that cervical cancer is caused by human papillomavirus?"

"Absolutely," Tom said, "but the amazing thing about it was, she never once complained that it was unfair. Most of her life she complained how unfair life was, but she never complained about her cancer. She just accepted it. Sort of like it was her own fault, I think. All she did was work with the girls and try to help them adjust to the reality of it all. And she was determined not to be a burden on anybody, right up to the end."

"Sounds like she must have been a pretty strong person."

"Strong? I guess, maybe, she was. Started out weak and gathered strength over the years. I could use some of that strength right now. I really miss her."

"I suspect you may be stronger than you think."

"Thanks. I hope you're right."

Tom slipped back into reverie and hardly said anything the rest of the trip home.

What a day, Sally thought to herself in the silence. *More fun than I expected. Probably should never have taken that shower. But what a rush. All those cold snowflakes touching my warm skin. Ooh.* She felt a shiver of pleasure go down her back. *I can't believe I let myself get carried away like that. Must have been the shower. Never again.* She glanced over at Tom. *Look at him, driving along in his own world. I wonder what he's thinking.* Before she knew it, they were almost to her house. Tom thanked her for being so patient and listening to all his problems. Said it helped a lot.

"Getting off the tar always helps."

She promised not to tell anyone about any of their conversations until after the case was over, and she thanked him for an unusual adventure.

Tom went home and snuggled in with Cathy.

Chapter 15

"My, you're in a good mood this morning," Cathy said, feeling a pleasant little caress on her bottom as she slipped out of bed and headed for the bathroom.

"A day up at camp always sets a man straight. You know, Cathy," he shouted into the bathroom, "you really ought to come up there sometime. We could bring the horse. You'd love it."

"Not during hunting season, thank you. Maybe next spring. I'd like to try out the canoe." She stuck her head out the door. "You didn't shoot anything, did you?"

"One partridge, and he was some tasty."

"Yuck!" The door slammed shut. Minutes later it swung open again. Cathy posed in the doorway, wearing her new western skirt and cowboy boots, along with the new vest Tom had given her. "How do you like it?" Tom smiled and raised his eyebrows. "While you were at camp, I did some shopping. Goes good with the beautiful leather vest you bought me. Don't you think?" She waltzed over to the bed and gave Tom a big kiss. "Thank you so much. I just wish you weren't on call so you could come to the horse show with me."

Tom struggled out of bed and over to the bathroom. "I gotta get moving or I'll be late." He went to the downstairs bathroom to shave and take his medicines. Cathy made coffee and brought a cup in while he shaved.

"Guess what. While you were at camp, Betty Norton called and said the trustees had agreed to sponsor me for my master's degree. Isn't that great? And I won't even have to work part time unless I want to. I just have to agree to work for the hospital for at least five years afterward. How's that for a great deal, or what?"

She gave him a kiss as he went out the door. Tom drove Cathy's car to the hospital for his morning rounds. She needed his pickup truck for towing the horse trailer.

She hitched the trailer up to the pickup and was backing it up toward the corral when she spotted something on the floor in front of the passenger seat. A cell phone. Definitely not Tom's. *I wonder who left it there.* She turned the phone on. A telephone number was displayed on the screen. She went inside and used the house phone to dial the number on the cell phone screen. Soon she was connected to the cell phone. She let it ring until a recorded message announced that the person she had reached was currently unavailable. To leave a message press one. She pressed one.

"Hello. You have reached the cell phone of Dr. Sally Gardiner. Please leave a short message and your number. I'll get back to you as soon as I can. Thank you."

Cathy could not resist leaving a message. "Sally, this is Cathy. You and your friend Tom can go fuck yourselves. I know that's what you've been doing for some time now."

So that's who went to camp with Tom yesterday. I should have known. She left the cell phone on the kitchen table, squarely on top of her new leather vest. When Tom arrived back from the hospital, Cathy was at the edge of the driveway, seated on her saddle, next to a suitcase and several boxes. One contained a dozen quarts of canned tomatoes.

"Don't say a word," she ordered. "Go in the house and look on the kitchen table." She threw everything in the car and screeched out of the driveway.

By the time she neared the top of Pitch Pine Hill, Cathy could feel some of her anger starting to subside. She slowed down to the speed limit and then felt the need to pull over into the roadside turn at the top of the hill and get her mind in control so she could drive safely the rest of the way home. What a romantic village Snug Harbor was, nestled into the shore, with all its neighboring islands. Still outwardly untouched by urbanization. They almost sucked her in. The close-knit community nearly had her convinced that two people could live together harmoniously, that a relationship with a man could be satisfying, honest, and open. A dream. The product of wishful thinking. An idea that had sold millions of dollars' worth of women's magazines.

I almost thought my dream was coming true, Cathy said to herself. *Those people down in the harbor still believe in it, like in Brigadoon. They are only fooling themselves. Underneath the carefully crafted facade, the men down there are still the same. Only, down in the harbor, all the fooling around gets swept under the rug or kept out in the shed by the ladies who run everything. Some of it gets rinsed off the dock at Eddy's and goes out with the tide,* she thought, recalling her first social encounter with Tom.

Suddenly, she found it easy to forgive herself for letting herself get so closely involved with Tom. It really wasn't her fault. When she thought about it objectively, she was merely the victim of a slick con job.

She drove home and loaded her things into the apartment. Thank God her whole life was not going to fall apart. She still had her job, her scholarship, a promising career, and Britney. Men were like alcohol. In small doses, they made life more enjoyable and were probably good for one's health. But if one let herself get addicted, life became a disaster. Sis was right. It had been a close call, but she still had it all together. No use even telling Sis about it either. There would be no sympathy from her. That was for sure.

Cathy found a card from the post office as she sorted through all her mail. Now, who would be sending her a registered letter? She wondered about it all the way to the post office. Maybe it was something officially notifying her of her scholarship. *Oh, brother!* It was a subpoena, calling her to testify in a deposition for a malpractice suit. Someone was suing Tom. *That bastard. He must have known for ages. Never said a word. All that pretense about closeness and intimacy. And he never even bothered to tell me he was being sued. It figures. I'll do double workouts at the YMCA, and I'll be over it in a couple of days.*

By the time she went over to pick up Britney at her ex-husband's house, Cathy felt she had pretty much gotten over most of the anger. She had cleaned up the mess from all the jars of tomatoes she had smashed. She regretted that incident more than she expected after she tasted some during the cleanup. What a shame to waste all those delicious ingredients. But she probably never could have really enjoyed them anyway, knowing that Tom had a part in the processing.

"Are you mad at me, Mommy?" Britney asked before they were halfway home. Cathy was amazed at how astutely she detected her mother's altered affect. Cathy had consciously tried to be pleasant and motherly. It was not like this was the first time a man had cheated on her.

"No, Mommy's not angry. She's just worried about some stuff, but it has nothing to do with you. Mommy loves you very much. What if we stop at McDonald's for supper and enjoy ourselves? That way you won't have to help with the dishes, and we can watch TV before you go to bed."

"Goody! McDonald's. Can I have a Happy Meal?" Then she added, "What are you so worried about, Mommy?"

"Oh, Mommy has to testify at a deposition later next week, and it's kinda scary. That's all. Nothing for you to worry about."

"What's a deposition, Mommy?"

"It's like all those lawyer programs you see on TV."

"Yuck. I can't stand lawyer shows. I always zap onto another channel." She started in on her hamburger.

When Britney was dropped off at her father's later that week, she kissed her mother and gave her a tender hug. "I love you, Mommy. And don't worry about those lawyers. They act nasty on TV to make an exciting program. None of that stuff is real, just like *Sesame Street* and the soaps." The girl was amazing. All week long she had been so helpful and cooperative. Not once did she have to be told to pick up her toys or her room. And how cute she could be when she snuggled up for her bedtime stories. Somehow, she could feel her mother's anxiety about the impending deposition.

Early Monday morning, Cathy went into Betty Norton's office to meet with the hospital attorney.

"As you are now aware, Miss Dyer," he began, "the Gurnet family has filed a suit against Dr. MacMahan for the wrongful death of George Gurnet. How long have you known about this suit?"

"Only since I was notified that I would be a witness, you know, when I got that letter last week."

"And have you spoken with anyone about this case or any of the events that led up to it?"

"Only to Mrs. Norton, when I gave her the report immediately after the accident. That's all."

"You haven't ever discussed the case with Dr. MacMahan, have you?" Betty asked. Cathy shook her head no. "And is it true that you are no longer seeing him?"

"That's right. We broke up over a week ago. And that was before I even got the notice about the malpractice case. But I'd rather not talk about it, if you don't mind."

"That's not a problem," the attorney assured her. "What I want you to understand is that the issues discussed at the deposition on Friday and any testimony you may have to give at the hearing, or possibly even a trial—none of it is to be discussed with anyone outside of this room as long as the suit remains open. Is that clear?"

"I understand."

"The reason this is so important is that if the opposing attorneys ever discover that you have been talking with anyone else who may have been present at the time, it will be easy to twist that person's testimony around so that it sounds to a jury like there may be some kind of a cover-up going on. As it stands now, no charges have been filed against the hospital. Fortunately, the event occurred after the patient had been transferred to the responsibility of the ambulance. But that's a fuzzy line. They were still on hospital property. So any hint of a cover-up, or anything like it, could put the hospital at risk of being drawn into the case. You do understand that?"

"Yes."

"You should be aware that the damages they are seeking far exceed the limits of our malpractice insurance. We could stand to lose heavily from the trust fund if the hospital should become a defendant in this case. That must be avoided at all costs. You are probably aware that the trust fund is what's paying for your master's degree program, so I am sure you will be very discrete. Am I right?"

Cathy nodded.

"As it now stands," Betty added, "the hospital is not at risk for losing any money in this case. We want to keep it that way. Mr. Winslow, here, will be with you to help you all the way during the deposition. He will object to any line of questioning that is unfair. Do you have any questions at this time, or is anything bothering you about next Friday?"

Cathy shook her head no.

"Very good then," Betty continued. "We will meet again on Friday morning just before the deposition and go over everything with Mr. Winslow, so you will have it all fresh in your mind when you testify. In the meantime, Cathy, if anything about this case bothers you and you need to talk to someone, feel free to come in if you need help."

As far as Cathy could tell, nothing about the deposition bothered her much. *What bothers me are men*, she thought to herself as she headed back to the ICU. *Why are they such philanderers? See a cute ponytail bobbing up and down, and off they go. Are all men like that? Or do I just have bad luck in picking men?* Never would she have guessed that Tom was the type to fool around with other women. Now Frank was another story. He had fooled around on her from the beginning. It took a long time for her to finally admit to herself that enough was enough and file for a divorce. She still could not understand how a man could be such a good husband and a caring father most of the time and keep on having affairs with other women at the same time. It was beyond understanding.

What if I try to think out of the box? What if it isn't the men who are at fault? Perhaps all men are just naturally vulnerable to seduction. And some men are so sexually attractive that women are always hitting on them. What if it's women who are really to blame? All morning long she couldn't get these thoughts out of her mind—and her mind back in the box.

At lunchtime she was carrying her tray through the cafeteria when she passed by Dr. Sally Gardiner, dressed in surgical scrub clothes and having lunch. Maybe it was she who had seduced Tom, and not the other way around. When they made eye contact, Cathy gave her a look that only women understand. It put the entire blame for their affair squarely on Sally.

Sally couldn't stand it. She went over to Cathy's table and said, "Why don't you and I go outside to the smoking area for a minute?"

"Bug off. I don't smoke, thank you."

"Neither do I. I just thought it would be a nice place where we could talk in private for a minute."

When they got outside, Sally told Cathy she felt terrible that Cathy was so hurt by this huge misunderstanding. "I'm not so concerned about what you think about me," she said. "I just want to correct your misunderstanding about Tom. I want to assure you that he never laid a hand on me during that trip up to his camp or at any other time, for that matter. He is too much of a gentleman for that kind of behavior. Besides, I know he cares deeply about you. You're all he talked about on the way home from camp."

"So you were up to camp with him. I thought so. What the hell were you two doing anyway?"

"Well, I probably shouldn't be telling you this. I'm sure Tom has never said a word. But Tom is involved in a horrible malpractice suit, and they have all his property tied up in the courts. It's been driving him insane. I think he is really scared to death. His blood pressure, I understand, is way up. And he desperately needed to talk to someone about it.

"But with you directly involved in the case, there's no way he could mention it to you. And he really needed to unload. He couldn't sleep at night. All that lack of sleep caused his blood pressure to go sky-high. He was lonely and about to explode. Finally, he asked me if I would go to camp with him. That's the only place where he felt comfortable and safe enough to talk openly about his feelings and anxiety. I didn't really want to go, but after all he's done for Sam, I just couldn't refuse trying to be of help when he asked."

Cathy began to cry.

"Please don't tell anyone I said he was being sued. Okay?"

"I just found out about the lawsuit last week." Cathy sobbed. "I have to testify at a deposition on Friday. Maybe you are telling the truth. I don't know. I guess I'm sorry about the message on your cell phone."

"Under the circumstances, it was probably understandable. Anyway, I just wanted to make certain you didn't have any wrong ideas about Tom, that's all. He's too nice a guy to be treated that way."

"Okay. Okay! Now please go away. I'm really upset right now."

"I could tell you were pretty upset. But I've got to get back to the OR now anyway. I hope everything goes well at your deposition."

Cathy's mind was back in the box again. And it felt like the lid had been nailed shut. *If only I could call Tom. Maybe we could still patch things up. This damn malpractice suit is messing up everything. But there's no way Tom and I can talk until this thing is over. Lousy lawyers. I thought they were supposed to protect people's rights. Not control your life. How am I ever going to get through that deposition? If I didn't have that scholarship and Britney, no telling what I'd do. Get as far away from here as I can. Guess all I can do is wait 'til this mess is over and try not to worry too much.*

But over the next few days, figuring out how to repair her relationship with Tom was the only thing on her mind, right up to the time her deposition began.

Chapter 16

"The whole truth and nothing but the truth, so help you God?" Cathy's mind cleared just in time to reply, "I do." It didn't seem as bad as she had feared. The hospital lawyer had carefully instructed her only to answer the questions that were asked and not to volunteer any information that was not specifically requested. Also, she was not to speculate or guess about anything that may have happened, if she was not absolutely certain about her answer. Most questions would be phrased so they could be answered with a simple yes or no. If she thought it was some sort of a trick question, she was to request to have the question rephrased. He was seated beside her to help if things got awkward in any way.

The questions usually followed the events in the medical record and served mostly to validate what was already in the record. From the questions he asked and the facts he carefully avoided, Cathy could easily see where the lawyer was leading her. Then, suddenly, he called for a break.

During the recess, her thoughts went right back to men. *I'll bet those lawyers fool around all the time. Look at them. Lawyers from both sides, schmoozing each other like they are one big fraternity. Men are just like bucks in the rut. Why is it that only women are interested in having a solid, lifelong relationship with children and family and things? How is it that some women manage to form a relationship with a guy based on family values? Like it used to be in the old days. Or was it all the same back then? Maybe men were just the same as today, only nobody used to talk about it. No way was it women who were mostly to blame. Perhaps, after I finish my master's degree, things will get better.*

They filed back into the hearing room.

"Remember, Ms. Dyer," the attorney said, "you are still under oath."

Cathy nodded yes.

"Now, Ms. Dyer, do you recall Dr. MacMahan's altered state of mind when he was filling out the EMTALA transfer orders?"

The hospital lawyer objected, saying there was no way Cathy could know what was in Dr. MacMahan's state of mind.

The question was withdrawn.

"Ms. Dyer, another witness has testified that Dr. MacMahan had yelled out, 'What the hell is this damn thing?' when he was handed the EMTALA form. Did you hear him say that?"

"Yes," she replied.

The remaining questions revolved around the entry in the nursing notes, summarizing what had taken place when Mr. Gurnet suffered his cardiac arrest after he was transferred to the ambulance.

"Your statement in the nursing notes says that the ambulance attendant had entered 444 cc's into the flow control monitor's program by mistake. Is that correct?"

"Yes," Cathy replied.

"Is there any possible reason to think that it might *not* have been a mistake?"

"No."

The lawyer then showed her the doctor's orders on the EMTALA transfer form and the carbon copy that remained in the hospital record.

"Could you please read for us exactly what the doctor's order states?" he asked, ever so politely.

"Four hundred and forty-four cc's per hour," Cathy said with a gasp, not believing what she had just seen. She started to try to explain something, but, under the table, the hospital lawyer's leg slammed painfully against hers.

"Please. Only answer the questions as they are asked," he whispered. "Nothing else, remember?"

"Ms. Dyer, is it possible that Dr. MacMahan's angry outburst, at the time he was filling out the EMTALA transfer form, was the cause of the erroneous medical order that caused the death of his patient, George Gurnet Jr.?"

Cathy felt her attorney's leg again as she started to speak. "I have no idea about that."

"I have no further questions. Thank you Ms. Dyer. That will be all."

"You did very well today," Mr. Winslow said as they left the hearing room. "You should feel pleased with yourself."

"It wasn't fair! That's what I think."

"I am sorry you feel that way, Ms. Dyer. Perhaps you may wish to talk more about this. I would be happy to meet with you sometime next week in Mrs. Norton's office, if that's all right. Call me on Monday, and I'll fit it into my schedule somehow. But remember, don't speak a word about this matter to anyone. Is that clear?"

"Yes, sir," Cathy replied and then headed directly back to the hospital and Betty Norton's office.

"Excuse me, Mrs. Norton," she inquired, knocking on the open door. "Do you have a moment?"

"Of course, Cathy. Come in and have a seat. And please call me Betty." Cathy sat down. "Mr. Winslow just called and said you did very well in your deposition today. Did everything seem to go well for you?"

"Not really. That's kinda why I need to talk to you."

"What seems to be the problem, Cathy?"

"Someone altered the medical records to frame Tom. That's the problem."

"Oh, dear! What makes you think the records were altered?"

"The transfer order sheet they showed me today said 444 cc's per hour. Tom would never have made a mistake like that. And, even if he had, I would have picked it up. After the way we've been trained to carefully check orders, there's no way I would have missed something like that."

"I understand what you are saying, Cathy. Tom is a very excellent doctor. But he's still human. Even the great Dr. MacMahan can make an occasional mistake."

"Well, I don't buy it. That Mr. Winslow. He smashed me in the leg to make me shut up when they showed me the order in today's deposition. I think he changed the records to place the blame on Tom."

Betty Norton said nothing for a while, watching and waiting for Cathy to calm down a bit. "I can see how it might seem that way to you under the circumstances. But I can assure you Mr. Winslow would not alter the record. He's a good lawyer. Lawyers know better than to alter evidence. I have reviewed that chart myself. I can assure you that carbon copy of those orders in the hospital record reads exactly the same as the original you saw this afternoon. Face it, Cathy. Even the best doctors occasionally make mistakes. That's why they all have to carry malpractice insurance, and we all have to learn how to deal with it."

"You might be right, but whoever wrote 444 on that order sheet did not make a mistake. That was done on purpose, to shift the blame to Tom MacMahan. And if that lawyer didn't do it, it had to be you, Elizabeth Norton. The question is, why? What have you got against Tom? What was he, one of your old boyfriends or something? Snug Harbor's not a very big place. Shouldn't be too much trouble to find out. I'm going to dig around until I find out who had access to these records and get to the bottom of this whole rotten mess."

"Calm down, Cathy," Betty Norton implored. "I know this is very disturbing to you. But before you do anything you might regret, I want you to take some time out. Think about the big picture. I want you to think carefully before you say anything to anyone that might shift the responsibility of this unfortunate event onto the hospital. If we lose a big chunk of that trust fund, it will create a huge problem. We use earnings from that fund to offset the annual losses we have, because Medicare and insurance payments are so low in this state compared to the rest of the country. That trust fund allows us to pay the competitive wages that you have been receiving. And I can assure you there'll be no funds available to send you back to school for your master's degree. You are a smart young lady, and I think you will appreciate the wisdom in what I have just said, once you've given it some consideration."

Cathy said nothing. She just sat there, fuming and thinking. Betty Norton braced herself for the onslaught. Cathy took a deep breath, as if she was about to talk. Only a hopeless sigh came out. Then she picked up her backpack and shuffled out of the room. On her way out, she slammed the door in a way that said, *You ain't heard the last of this yet!*

Betty got the message. What if she had underestimated Cathy Dyer? *No. She'll come around when she cools off. Actually, she's a lot like me. Puts her career ahead of everything. When she gets back in focus, everything will fall in line. Grudge against Tom MacMahan.* How did she ever come up with that? She looked at her watch. *Hmm. After five. Lou should be mixing martinis about now.*

⟡

Cathy was glad they needed her to work the evening shift in the ICU. Keeping busy would help keep her mind off the deposition and Betty Norton's thinly disguised threat. The ICU was a madhouse that evening. Working nonstop improved her mood immensely. But during her break, she couldn't help slipping into the equipment room to check out something on one of the hospital's new IV flow control machines. It was the same exact model as the one she had seen in the new ambulance. She turned it on and placed her finger on the 4 button. It was pretty darn easy to let 444 slip onto the monitor screen if you kept your finger on the button an instant too long. No doubt about it. That had to be what happened. She should have checked it at the time. She might have prevented this whole thing, if only she had been more careful. As a team member in the error management system, she should have picked up the error before it caused a problem. Maybe it was *her* who was really to blame for what happened to Mr. Gurnet.

How could that be? She always tried to do her best. How could a person be to blame if she had tried her best? What would Tom say? What if the lawyers found out and pinned the blame on her? Or maybe the hospital?

If that happened, she could forget about the scholarship for her master's degree. She couldn't deal with that. She thought about Frank. She had really tried hard to make her marriage work. But she had always blamed Frank. Could she have been even partly to blame for that? Hardly. *Whatever will become of me? No career? No husband? Just like my mother? I can't believe it. I almost had it made, and I blew it. No one to blame but myself. Impossible. How can anyone live with all that blame and hopelessness?* Even though she had tried the best she knew how, it was no use.

Her beeper went off. They needed her back at the nurses' station right away. Cathy quickly went back to trying as hard as she had always tried, to help other people.

⟶

In the middle of the night, Tom got a call from Jim Freese, a sergeant on the police force. He asked Tom if he could come into town and over to Cathy's apartment. She had killed herself.

Tom got there as quickly as he could and ducked under the yellow police tape out front.

"Thanks for coming, Doc. We needed a doctor to pronounce her dead anyway, so I figured it might as well be you, because there are quite a lot of questions, and I thought maybe you could help answer some of them."

"Oh my God! When did this happen?"

"Tonight. Sometime after midnight. All we know, so far, is she called her ex-husband around midnight and asked to talk to her daughter. There was an argument, and he got a hint of what she might be up to. He called us, but we got here too late. She was already dead."

Tom just stared. The photographers were getting pictures of Cathy in her bed. Her right arm had an IV needle inserted and connected to a bag of fluid, which was hanging from the closet door on a bent clothes hanger. Her face was covered with the bedsheet. Tom pulled it back, just to be sure.

"How well did you know this lady, Tom?"

"We were dating off and on for several months, but we broke up a couple of weeks ago. At the time, I knew she was pissed. But something else must have made her do this. I mean, we liked each other a lot, but we were never that close. Close enough, you know, that it would make her want to do something like this. Not two weeks later."

The IV tubing was running through an IV flow control monitor on her bedside table. She had obviously borrowed it from the hospital. The flow rate on the meter read 444 cc's per hour.

"What exactly is lidocaine anyway?" Jim Freese asked. "That's what the label says on the bag."

"It's a medicine to control your heart rate, but that big of a dose would kill a moose."

"Well, it's obviously a suicide. She must have had music playing while she died. It was still playing when we walked in here. The CD looks like some Wagnerian opera, *Tristan and Isolde*. Does that strike any bells with you?"

"Oh my God! That was her favorite opera," Tom said, pulling down the sheet to expose her left breast. "See that tattoo? *Liebestod*. It's a song from that very opera. In German it means 'love's death.' Isolde commits suicide at the end of the opera."

"Is that right? Boy, she must have been some strange lady. She also left a couple of suicide notes. This one is addressed to you, Tom."

The envelope had already been opened.

Dear Tom,

I am sorry to end it this way. But I have come to realize now that I have reached a hopeless dead end in life. However, there are some things I want you to know.

They took my deposition today, and that's when I found out that you have been framed. They showed me the EMTALA order sheet. Somebody has altered those orders. I'm sure you didn't write them that way. Besides, I would have picked up an error like that. I tried to tell them the truth today, but the lawyers wouldn't let me speak. If they find out the truth, the hospital will get sued and I'll lose my scholarship and a chance to have a real life. And everything I've been dreaming of, including you. But there is no way I could live with this lie. It's hopeless. Sally told me that you two were not fooling around after all, so I guess I blew that too. I can see now I ruined the only chance I've ever had to live a happy, normal life. I have no one to blame but myself.

I still love you,
Cathy

Chapter 17

What a night. Tom left Cathy's apartment feeling empty. A major shake-up of his perspective on life—or death, as the case may be. Emotions in free fall, he got in his truck and headed back down to the harbor. The whole thing made him sick, washed out, and unable to even care anymore. He thought the police would never stop asking questions. It was hard to cope with his sorrow and grief amidst all that interrogation. Driving the truck helped. Somehow, it always did.

A warm pinkish glow lit up the eastern sky as Tom drove back to the harbor. Two deer appeared in the headlights. Tom hit the brakes. A doe and a large buck crossed the road ahead of him. They jumped the stone wall and disappeared into the woods on his property, probably heading up to his apple orchard for breakfast. He stepped on the accelerator again.

When he got home, he could see that a heavy frost had finished off everything green in the garden. He probably should be digging out the rest of the carrots, turnips, and dahlia bulbs. He needed coffee. And some peace and quiet. He tried lying in bed for a while, but sleep would not come. In desperation, he picked up Caroline's scrapbook just to get his mind off of Cathy. On the final page she had placed the poem by Henry Scott Holland, 1847–1918.

Canon of St. Paul's Cathedral in London.

Death is nothing at all.
I have only slipped away into the next room.
I am I and you are you.
Whatever we were to each other,
That we still are.

Call me by my old familiar name.
Speak to me in the easy way which you always used.
Put no difference into your tone.
Wear no forced air of solemnity.

Laugh as we always laughed at the
Little jokes we enjoyed together.
Let my name be ever the household word it always was.
Let it be spoken with effect, without
The trace of a shadow on it.

Life means all that it ever meant.
It is the same as it ever was.
There is absolutely unbroken continuity.

Why should I be out of mind
Because I am out of sight?
I am but waiting for you, for an interval
Somewhere very near,
Just around the corner.
All is well.

It was the same poem as he had up over his bed. Beneath the poem
was a note.

> Tom, thank you so much for helping me to get my life back.
> I will soon be gone, but I will not be entirely dead. Part of
> me will still exist, in our children. The fact that they were once
> inside of me and an integral part of my own self is the single
> thought that has kept me going this last, difficult year. Thank
> you for giving them to me, and please take care of them. Even
> as you took such good care of me. And always remember, my
> love for you will live forever.
> Caroline

He reread the poem and felt the soothing effect it had on the rubbish
heap in his emotions. Caroline had done her utmost to help her family
deal with their grief before she passed. She always expected to die. But
she was grateful for having had enough time for a full and satisfying

life, instead of being wiped out in a nuclear holocaust. Tom refocused his perspective. Living in a close-knit community helped him to keep going. But it could not fill the void he felt when his wife died.

Right now he didn't feel anything. Just empty. He waited for it to hit. He knew it would, the same as when Mark died and when Caroline died. A big piece of his heart was ripped out. The wind blew through, and there was no way to stop it. He felt hopeless and helpless. *This must be how Caroline used to feel back in the sixties.* And anger. He had some of that too. Anger at what? Probably a lot of things.

Caroline's letter contained the same message as Cathy's letter. *I knew someone framed me for George Gurnet's death. It's outrageous! What kind of justice is that? When I find out who did it, I'll kill them. Goddamn lawyers. Take away the farm and turn it into a subdivision for yuppies. I know that's what they'll do. If only they'd let me do my own thing, I'd get to the bottom of this. Rotten lawyers have all the power. And they don't give a hoot about what happens to other people. Look what they did to Cathy. Look what they've done to me.*

It suddenly felt like everything he had tried to do in life had not succeeded: become a professor, maintain a marriage, raise a family, and run a farm. Nothing happened like he planned it. He knew that going out for a run would help, but he could not make himself do it. Getting drunk was a possible way to escape these feelings. Caroline tried that at Woodstock.

I really should dig up the rest of the bulbs and carrots and onions and things before the ground freezes solid. Oh, screw it! The bulbs can wait. If not, let 'em freeze. There is no way someone would intentionally try to frame me. There has to be some other explanation.

It was all very confusing. But suddenly he became aware that, for some unknown reason, he did not feel the wind ripping through his heart like he expected. It was not the same as when his dad died. Or Mark. Or Caroline. It was totally different. Still, he knew he needed support. But where could he go to help him get a grip on these feelings?

He looked out the front window and viewed the ocean and the shore. That it was still unchanged from when he was a child was a stabilizing anchor for a mind in troubled waters. Smoke was coming up from the chimney on his father's fish house. Prince must be in there.

Prince. He needed to talk to Prince. Tom went across the road and down to the dock. Inside the fish house, Prince was knitting pot heads and repairing lobster traps. The place was messy but warm with the smell of a wood fire. The pot belly stove was glowing, and Hank Williams was singing on a radio over in the corner.

"Hep y'self to some coffee, Tom. They's a fresh pot on the stove."

Tom helped himself and carefully kept the conversation to small talk. Prince was full of ambitions. He had to get all his lobster traps and equipment ready for next spring, before he and Ellie left later in the month to spend the winter in Florida. He was still hoping to get his deer before the season closed. He'd seen a few, but they were always on the road and never around his deer stand. Tom just nodded in agreement but said nothing. Finally, Prince cut the small talk.

"What's on your mind this morning, Tom? Sumpin'. I kin tell."

"Nothing, really." Tom took a long swallow of coffee and leaned over to check something crawling on the floor.

"Don't hand me that line. I've known you so long, I can read you like a book. Cathy's dead, ain't she?"

"How in hell did you find out?"

"It was on the police scanner all night long. That's how I found out. Ain't no secrets in a small town like this. I heard they called you in too. Kinda figured you'd be showin' up this morning. That's how come I made up a full pot of coffee."

"Yeah, Cathy killed herself. She called her ex-husband sometime after midnight and asked to talk to Britney. They had some kind of disagreement about waking the kid up. After they hung up, he got to thinking about what she had said. That's when he called the police, and they started checking."

"What do ya reckon made her do somethin' like that?"

"Hard to say," Tom replied as he stuffed another stick of wood in the stove and freshened up his coffee. "Cathy, she, uh. Y' know, I really never could figure out what it was that made her tick. She was a lot of fun, and I liked her a lot, but I never got to know her well enough that I could understand how she was thinking most of the time."

"Mmmm. That's too bad."

"Yeah. Guess I'll never know why. It's hard to say for certain. Well, anyway, from the note she left, it seemed that she got involved in this malpractice case. They took her deposition yesterday, and the lawyers somehow backed her into what seemed to her like a hopeless situation. I figure that's prob'ly what pushed her over the edge." Tom shook his head. "It's a big mess, I tell you."

"Malpractice case? Hmmm. Don't know nothin' about that."

"I tell you, Prince. I shoulda been a lobsterman. I don't think I can take too much more of this malpractice crap."

"You sound just like your dad," Prince allowed.

"No way, pardner. My dad was a lobsterman."

"Well, he always used to say he shoulda been a doctor. Sounded just like you when he said it too."

"Well, lobstermen don't have to put up with the government and lawyers, always messin' in their affairs. I'm not supposed to say anything about this, but they are trying to pin a malpractice case on me and take away the farm and everything. Who knows? Maybe even our lobster boat. And I don't have a clue as to how to stop 'em."

"Well, you're dead wrong about one thing," Prince said, shoving a few chunks of soft wood into the stove and freshening up his coffee cup. "The gov'ment is always messin' with the fisherman too. You shoulda seen your dad when they cut us back from three thousand traps to eight hundred was all we could haul."

"Is that right?"

"Ayup! Your dad was ready to shut down. There wasn't no way a man could make a decent livin' off'n eight hundred traps. Ole Dickie, he fumed and swore for a day or two, and then one morning the two of us sat right here in this fish house and started figuring out a bunch of ways we could do things slicker and cut expenses. Pretty soon we were back in business and makin' as much money as ever. Your dad was awful good at figurin' things out, once he got over feelin' sorry for hisself. I figure that's why lots of folks can never get themselves out of a fix. They never get over their self-pity long enough to look for a solution to the problem. Just keep on lookin' around for someone else to blame."

"Well, I don't have to look very far. It's lawyers that's to blame for all my troubles."

"You sure about that?" Prince asked.

"Absolutely. Lawyers remind me of fishermen. They are kinda like you used to be, you know, back before you and Ellie started spending your winters down in Florida. Remember how it was during the shrimp season? You would be cruising around, way off shore, with your sonar scanning the water. When you located a big school of shrimp, you'd come after them with your net. If I were a shrimp, I'd be plenty pissed. But being pissed wouldn't help me much to figure out how to escape the net. I reckon the lawyers spotted me in their sonar and have lowered their nets."

"Humph! I get the picture," Prince opined. "Strange, ain't it? Usta be, lawyerin' was an honorable profession. Helpin' out folks whenever they had legal problems. You know? Wills and estates, and maybe a speeding ticket. Or some ornery game warden. Nowadays, seems like they're usin' the law just to scoop up people's money for themselves. No wonder people call 'em sharks."

"Sharks! That's what they are, sharks," Tom concurred. "I wonder why lawyers don't go after lobstermen. Lobstermen usually have more money than doctors. Doctors just don't know enough to keep it hid. Yep. I shoulda been a lobsterman. No doubt about it."

"Your dad used to tickle me, ya know? After he'd been off hunting with old Doc Harwood for a coupla days. They'd get into the hooch and start bragging' 'bout how much money they was making. Then your dad would come home, happy as a clam at high tide, 'cause he was always making more money than Doc. He'd say, 'Glad I never made a doctor.' But I think he was just foolin' himself."

"Ayeah, he really wanted to be a doctor. Just never got the chance. That's kinda why he made it so I would have the opportunity. Don'tcha think?"

"Ayeah. Your dad was full of ambition and goals back when he was young and we was both in the fire department together. Wanted to be a doctor. But things didn't work out. You came along, and he didn't have the money. So he looked around for other opportunities besides bein' a fireman. Went into lobsterin'. He believed in having goals in life. But if there was no way of makin' that goal, well, instead of givin' up altogether, he'd start looking around for some other opportunity. Life is full of 'em if you keep your eyes open. He'd keep on looking until he found another way to succeed in life. Then he'd set a new course and keep on sailing. 'You gotta go with the flow.' That's what he'd always say whenever he ran into some obstacle in life. I learned a lot from your dad."

"Jesus, I wish he was here now to help figure a way outta this mess."

"Maybe we don't need him," Prince opined. "Your dad trained you pretty good. You're actin' more like him all the time. I've seen you goin' with the flow for quite a while now. What exactly is the hitch anyway?"

Tom outlined how someone had probably altered the records to make it look like he had prescribed an overdose of lidocaine when he wrote out the transfer orders for the ambulance trip to Maine Medical

Center. "Four forty-four it says on both copies of that goddam EMTALA form. Don'tcha just hate them jeezly new forms they've got?"

"I hate all them forms. They make us keep a copy of everything now. Big waste a time. Got a huge file cabinet, down at the fire station, overflowin' with them EMTALA forms."

"No kidding." Tom rolled his eyes upward, thinking as he gazed at the roof of the shack. "That means all those new forms must be in triplicate. I never noticed that. I might could drive over to the firehouse and see if the dose got forged on their copy too." He stood up and started putting on his coat. "I'll be back," he added with Terminator inflection and a slight chuckle.

"Wait for me," Prince replied. "Soon 's I turn down the damper on this here stove, I'm good to go."

They had to drive all the way into town to the main fire station to find the ambulance company file cabinet that contained the forms they were seeking. Prince knew right where to find them.

"Look here. *Forty four* cc's an hour. Just like it I wrote it. Plain as can be," Tom announced triumphantly. "Whoever changed the hospital records must not have known that the new forms have three copies. I'm calling my attorney."

The attorney told them to stay put and not let that form out of sight until he got there.

After he arrived, he stared at the EMTALA form almost in disbelief. There was no doubt that 44 cc's was the intended order.

"I think this form is going to get you out of a lot of trouble, Tom," the attorney said.

"Good. Does that mean the suit is finally going to be dropped?"

"I wouldn't go that far. We are still in the discovery phase of this case. More depositions are scheduled. Who knows what other surprises may appear. But you guys can go now. I'll get hold of the judge and get a court order to take this document into protective custody. Things like this have been known to disappear, you know."

Tom and Prince got in the pickup and headed back down to the harbor. They planned to head over to Eddy's Wharf to celebrate with a few beers. When they reached the edge of Tom's property, their plans changed. Tom pulled off the road for a minute.

"There's the place," Tom said, pointing to the stone wall at the edge of his farm. "That's where I saw those two deer go across the road this morning."

"Christ, I seen 'em crossin' there a dozen times, I'll bet. Mostly on the way home from work. Sometimes there'll be three of 'em. Ya know, Tom, now that you've unposted your land, we might could sneak in there and tip one over this afternoon. There's still three hours of huntin' before closin' time."

"Right. We can always drink beer later."

Back home, Tom changed into his blaze-orange hunting clothes and took out his thirty-ought-six rifle and some ammo. He headed up through the Hundred Acre Woods and across the meadow to the apple orchard. Prince had agreed to come in from the road over the stone wall and find a stand in the woods on the opposite side of the apple orchard from Tom. Any deer, feeding in the orchard, would be covered, whichever way they went.

Tom took his time, walking slowly, looking for deer signs along the way but finding little. He whispered a greeting to Caroline as he passed the graveyard and then moved silently toward the upper edge of the apple orchard. That was where he expected to find the deer sign.

Soon he found a deer run. It looked like a venison superhighway. Hoof prints and deer droppings were everywhere under the apple trees. Every so often he found places where the bark had been scraped off of small saplings along the deer run. They were called rubs, made by the horns of some buck in the rut. Finally, he found what he was hoping to find, a fresh buck scrape. All the leaves and grass had been scraped away, leaving a wide swath of raw earth about one yard in diameter. In the middle of the freshly scraped dirt was the hoof print of a huge buck, the work of a buck in the rut. A little puddle of what Tom figured must be doe urine was next to the hoof print, a clear signal the doe was in heat and intending to return to the area.

Tom surveyed the orchard, looking for a clear vantage point for a good shot at the buck scrape area. He found an apple tree about thirty yards away, with large branches just a few feet above the ground. It was easy to climb and comfy to rest in. He had an open shooting lane all the way to the buck scrape area.

He climbed up and loaded his gun. Tom found a position in the tree that was quite comfortable and began to relax. A light breeze was blowing in off the bay. It came across the road, over the woods, and up through the apples, blowing his scent up over the hill. Except for an occasional flock of chickadees, the woods were pretty quiet. How much better he felt compared to this morning. *Cronk! Cronk!* A raven was flying overhead. The *whoosh, whish* from his wings disappeared as he flew over the hill.

What was that? Something rustled in the crisp, dry leaves. Tom went into full hunting mode. All senses were highly tuned into his consciousness. There it went again. A flash of movement in the corner of his eye caught his attention. *Damn! Just a red squirrel. How could such a little critter make so much noise comin' through those leaves? Musta been wearin' snowshoes. I just knew it had to be a deer.*

Tom's body stayed completely relaxed, but his hearing and visual senses remained on high alert. He felt extremely aware of being alive. Even his sense of smell was carefully analyzing every breath he took. Yet, as alert and tense as his senses were, he still felt quite relaxed and completely alive. He was in a very pleasant state of mind. *How is it,* he wondered, *that the process of hunting creates such a pleasant sensation? Is it the anticipation of killing something to eat? Or perhaps it is the intensely interactive relationship with the environment that creates the pleasure? Maybe it is all part of some primitive mental program I inherited from my hunter-gatherer ancestors?*

Then he heard them coming. *Crunch. Crunch. Crunch.* An occasional twig snapped. It was definitely a large animal, moving through the woods on the farside of the orchard. And coming his way was more than one deer. No doubt about it. His heart beat rapidly in his ears. Two deer, a doe and a small spikehorn, maybe ninety to a hundred pounds. The doe stopped frequently, looking behind her at something. Then he heard a snort.

Aha! Just as Tom figured, a large buck was coming along behind, maybe eight points. He couldn't tell for certain, but Tom felt himself go suddenly calm and determined. Slowly he pulled the sights up just behind the forward shoulder and squeezed the trigger. *Wham!* He didn't even hear the shot, nor did he recall taking off the safety. It all happened automatically. The spikehorn dropped in its tracks. The buck and doe took off back through the apples and down into the woods toward the stone wall. The last thing Tom saw was their white tails flashing through the trees.

He climbed down and went over to check out his deer. Might go a hundred pounds, dressed. *Should be tender and tasty meat all the way through,* he thought with mouth-watering satisfaction. He fastened his tag on the horn and started to carve the guts out of the deer.

Wham! Wham! Two shots rang out from somewhere down beyond the orchard, maybe near the dirt road.

"Oh, Thomas," he heard Prince yell out. "I got him, Tom."

Tom quickly finished dressing out his deer and hustled down the hill, where he soon found Prince, hunched over, searching for something in the leaves.

"Look here. Hair. See? On the trunk of that alder, and on the leaves is some more. I knew I hit him."

"Which direction did he run?" Tom asked.

"Downhill towards the road. Look. A drop of blood. Stand here and mark this spot while I scout around. Oh boy. A really big glob. He's pumpin' blood big-time."

They tracked blood through the leaves and swamp for over a hundred yards until they came across an eight-point buck, easily 180 pounds. "Sorry you missed him, old buddy. Lucky thing I was backing you up," said Prince, grinning like a Cheshire cat.

"After we finish gutting out your deer, come on back up in the apples a minute and I'll show you why I didn't hit him," Tom replied with smugness he could barely contain.

When Prince saw the small spikehorn deer, the first thing he said was "What happened? You didn't see the buck, right?"

"Oh, I saw him, alright. Coulda shot him. But some people shoot to kill. I shoot to cook. And he's gonna eat some good."

"That's for sure. Now let's drag these critters outta here. And thank you for saving the buck for me."

They loaded the deer into Arthur's pickup and hauled them over to the tagging station. Then they went home and hung both deer in the barn. "Too bad Sam couldn't be here. He'd really enjoy this."

"No reason why he shouldn't be here," Tom said. "Why don't we have a big feed tonight? I'll make a call and invite him and his mom over for supper."

"Good idea. I'll ring up Ellie and see if she'll whip us up a fresh apple pie for dessert."

Tom surveyed the pantry and fridge while Prince spoke with Ellie on the phone. He composed a list of supplies that were needed for a festive dinner.

"We need to make a run to the general store for some provisions," he announced.

"Might 's well stop in over at Eddy's while we're there. Have a beer with the boys. They'll need to hear all the details. Reckon they prob'ly got wind of it already from some of the guys over at the tagging station."

~

The music was unusually soft for a Saturday afternoon at Eddy's. No one was watching football. Only the drone of multiple conversations from the bar crowd and the occasional clink of glassware could be heard. A rowdy game of cribbage animated four men at a corner table. Everyone stopped for a minute to welcome Tom and Prince as they seated themselves at the bar. Two draft Buds appeared in front of them before they even ordered. Walter Crowley came over from his usual perch at the end of the bar.

"Heard you boys both got lucky today," Walter announced, loud enough that everyone could hear.

"How'd you find out, Walter? Over at the taggin' station?"

"Ayeah. Jus' come from there. Boy, that was some nice buck, Prince. A hundert an' ninety pounds. Guess you kinda outshot ole buddy Tom here." Walter comforted Tom with a little hug.

"Yeah. I hate it when he does that," Tom admitted with a slight grin. "But what are ya gonna do?"

Prince gave a detailed account of the hunt for the enjoyment of the whole bar, thanking Tom for saving the buck for his old buddy.

"A hundert and five-pound spikehorn is okay," Walter assured them. "He'll eat good. That's for sure."

Noticing that Walter's glass was empty, Tom ordered him a draft. The barmaid had a question when she served the beer.

"How you guys can ever shoot a cute little deer is something I just don't understand."

"Ma'am, if God hadn't meant for us to eat deer, he wouldn't have made them out of meat." Walter raised his glass. "Thanks for the beer, Tom."

"You're welcome, Walter. And thank you for rescuing little Britney from the honey pot last summer."

"It was a severe pleasure. Say, was that her mom I heard about on the scanner last night?"

"Yeah, it was. But this is not the place to talk about it."

"How 'bout we go out to the smokehouse?" He glanced over his shoulder. "Ain't nobody out there now. I got a nice cigar somebody give me. Prince could smoke it."

They went through a sliding glass door out onto the wharf. A three-sided lean-to, with a U-shaped bench inside, had been created for smokers. A ceramic chiminea fireplace was lit to keep smokers warm if they were puffing on cold nights. They picked up their beers and went out to light up. Tom enjoyed being around cigar smoke, because the smell brought pleasant memories of his grandfather, who used to smoke cigars up at camp. He stood by the stove, where he could stay warm but not get too much smoke.

"How come that lady killed herself? Any idea?"

"Nothin' for certain yet. She left a couple of letters, but I wasn't allowed to read all of them. I never figured she'd do something like that."

"Didn't s'prise me none. Sumpin' told me she wasn't quite right when I first saw her out on the flats there. Ya know? After bein' round all those crazies up at the prison, a fella gits a feel for these things."

"Is that right, Walter? What exactly was it that tipped you off about her anyway?"

"There was sumpin' about her attitude. You could tell right off she didn't trust men. Actually, once I figured that out, I was kinda surprised to see you with her. Didn't seem your type somehow."

"Turns out she wasn't."

"Musta been quite a shock just the same?"

"Ayeah. At first. But it wasn't anywhere as bad as when your wife or kid dies. I'll get over it." He looked at his watch.

"Reckon we better be gettin' back," Prince suggested, snuffing out his cigar and replacing it in its plastic cylinder. "Thanks, Walter. I'll smoke the rest of this after supper."

Tom and Prince went home and loaded the groceries into the kitchen. They built fires in the wood stove and the fireplace. Coming in with an armload of wood, Prince opined, "A manhattan would taste some good right now, don'tcha think, Tom?"

"My clock don't say five o'clock yet. Cocktail hour starts at five. Sorry. House rules. Grab yourself a beer out of the fridge. And while you're in there, I could use one too."

Tom put a large skillet on the stove and started melting butter. Prince knew exactly what to do. They had cooked together at camp for years. He began slicing mushrooms. When the butter got hot enough to foam and was just starting to turn brown, Tom threw in the mushrooms. By the time he had them nearly cooked, Prince had the onions and garlic finely minced, and they went into the pan. Prince took over cooking and stirring. He deglazed the pan with port wine when everything was cooked. He set the mushroom pan on the warming shelf for later use.

Tom rifled through the freezer and came up with a one-cup package of brown sauce, à la Julia Child. He kept a supply on hand for precisely this sort of occasion. He thawed it in the microwave and put it on the warming shelf.

Shortly before six, the guests arrived almost simultaneously. Sally brought in a basket with ingredients for a Caesar salad and set it on the counter. Ellie followed with her pie and a half gallon of French vanilla ice cream. Tom and Prince had the music cranked and were trying to see if they could yodel. A supply of premixed manhattans was on the counter in a large Coke bottle.

"I see you boys already have your asshole suits on," Sally observed.

"Yes, we do," Tom replied. "And would you care to try one on and see how it fits?"

"I'd be delighted to model one."

Tom filled a tumbler with crushed ice, added a cherry, and poured in some of the mix from the Coke bottle. "What's that you're fixing there?" Sam asked.

"Cherry Coke," Tom answered. "Sorry, but you have to have an ID to get a cherry Coke in this joint."

"It's okay. I don't much think I'd like it anyway. Got any regular Coke?"

"They're in the fridge, Sam. Help yourself."

Sam looked over at Prince as he popped open his Coke. "I don't need no friggin' cherries," he said to Prince, who was making a production with the maraschino jar, offering to make a Shirley Temple cherry Coke for Sam. Sam was more concerned about whether his mother had heard the word that had accidentally slipped out of his mouth. Fortunately, she was yakking with Ellie and apparently hadn't heard him.

"Don't worry, Sam," Prince consoled. "There'll be plenty of time to drink after you turn twenty-one."

"Yuck! I don't even like booze," Sam insisted.

"Then how did you manage to get picked up for DUI?"

"Oh, I was out with the guys, you know, and everyone else was drinking, so I did too. But I don't even like the taste of alcohol. Yuck."

"Too bad you had to get picked up for drunk driving."

"Ayeah, well, that's one mistake I'll never make again. That's for sure!" Sam vowed.

Everyone went out to the barn to inspect the two deer that were hanging. Sam was fascinated, but Sally kept her distance. She was still uneasy, expecting Cathy to show up but hoping she wouldn't.

"I don't see how you can ever make yourself shoot a poor little deer like that," Sally declared as she sucked on her cherry Coke, surprised at how quickly it was working on her mood.

"This may surprise you, but I completely understand how you feel," Tom replied with empathy. "I can never make myself pull the trigger 'til I feel the drool running out the corner of my mouth."

"Hey, Mom," Sam yelled from one of the stalls. "Check out this barn."

"Yeah, c'mon, Sally," Tom said. "Let me show you around. Whatcha looking at there, Tigger?"

"This tractor. See, Mom. It's a John Deere, just like Grandpa's. I used to love it when he let me drive it. Makes me homesick."

Sally was suddenly aware of all the familiar smells of a barn: the hay, diesel fuel, and horse manure. "I smell a horse," she announced. "Have you got a horse, Tom?"

"Right this way." He gestured, leading them to the farthest stall at the end of the barn. "Jerry Garcia, I'd like you to meet Sally and Sam Gardiner."

"Jerry Garcia? Who gave him that name?"

"My wife. He was her horse. Poor thing still misses her."

Jerry nickered and came right to Sally. She stroked its head. "He's a Morgan, isn't he?"

"Yep. Six years old. I can't believe that. He came right to you. Just like he used to do with Caroline. You like horses?"

"I did a long time ago. Had a Tennessee Walking Horse when I was in high school."

"You never told me you had a horse, Mom."

"I must have at some time. Don't you remember seeing the pictures from the horse shows in the big album at home?"

Sam shook his head.

"I can't believe I didn't show you," Sally continued. "Oh, yeah. I did it all. Brushing and grooming. Picking out their hooves. Mucking out the stalls. Everything."

"You really used to shovel horse manure, Mom?"

"You bet I did. 'If you want to handle the bit, you have to shovel the shit.' That's what we used to say."

"Mom? You never talked like that when you were a kid."

"Well, only when your grandparents weren't around." She gave Sam a gentle hug and a tender kiss.

There was that radiant smile again, Tom noticed. How did Sam do that to her? Some connection to him lit up her whole face. Her eyes. It was her eyes that smiled. So beautiful.

"Sally, if you ever get the urge to start back riding again, feel free to come over and ride Jerry. He needs the exercise."

Prince returned from the house with the Coke bottle full of refills for their manhattans. He allowed as how he was getting hungry and asked if everyone wanted to get started with supper.

Back inside, Sally felt a wave of happiness swoop down on her. Was it because Cathy was apparently not going to come? Or was it just the manhattans, doing their job? She threw together a big salad, and Prince made his special garlic mashed potatoes with crushed rosemary mixed in it. Ellie and Sam set the table. Tom cooked the venison tenderloin cutlets, rare, in a mixture of hot bacon fat and butter. He deglazed the pan with port wine. He then added the mixture of onions and mushrooms and the brown sauce to make the gravy. Everything was ready. Dinner was served.

"Oh. Oh my gosh!" Sam spurted. "I never imagined venison would be this good. I always heard it was strong and tough. This is really tender and mild."

"It pays to carefully choose which deer you shoot," Tom said. "That is, if you are lucky enough to have a choice."

"I'm impressed too, Sammy," his mother said with a mouth still half full. "But if you think this is good, wait 'til you try partridge. It's to die for."

"That does it," Sam decided. "When the swim team is over next spring, I'm putting the hunter safety course at the top of my agenda."

"I might take the course with you," Sally declared. "I have an idea it just might be fun if I could learn to outshoot Tom on partridge."

"Gee, Sally," Tom remarked, "your asshole suit fits real good."

Sam and Tom helped clear the dishes and stack them in the dishwasher while Ellie dished out the pie. "How is school this year, Sam?" she asked.

"So far, things are great this year. When you get to be a senior, they finally start to make the courses interesting. In fact, I don't even mind doing my homework. Can you believe that? Even Mom thinks it's interesting. Right, Mom? Most evenings she sits with me while I'm studying. Asks me questions and stuff. She's learning all kinds of new things. Guess lots of new stuff has come along since way back when she went to school. At least that's what it seems like. Having her around and all probably helps me get a better grade on my homework, I suppose. Anyway, this year I am starting to like school, and the swim team is awesome."

"Why don't you tell her about midterms?" Sally asked.

"Oh yeah, I got all As. First time ever."

After supper, Ellie started right in on the rest of the dishes. Tom insisted he'd do them later, but Ellie kept cleaning, so Tom and Sam pitched in to help.

Prince slipped out to the porch to finish off the rest of his cigar. Sally felt the need to go out and talk to him.

"After that little conversation," she said, "I couldn't pass up the opportunity to tell you how grateful I am for all the help you have been in getting Sam moving in the right direction. Without you, I don't think this would have happened."

"Well, thank you, Sally," Prince replied, blowing out a puff of fragrant smoke. "It was a pleasure. I can assure you."

"It feels so good to see him starting to develop this way. He's even happy about applying to colleges. And I don't think it could have happened without your friendly guidance last summer."

"Well, Sally, it's been a great satisfaction to me too. He's almost like my own own."

"It's so nice to hear you say that, Prince. I don't know why it took me so damn long to realize that having children is so important. I wasted a lot of time over the years, trying to be a doctor instead of a mother. But there's just not time enough to do a good job at both all at the same time," Sally declared, surprised at how the cherry Cokes had loosened up her tongue. But she could not stop herself. "There are hard choices to be made. And some of them I've made were wrong. Can you understand that, Prince? Men are lucky they don't have to make all those difficult choices."

"Is that right?"

"Yes. Somehow it doesn't seem fair. Tom says it's a dilemma."

"He does?"

"Yeah. A dilemma. No matter which way you chose, you're gonna lose something."

"Well, I can think of one woman who probably thinks it's unfair because she didn't have to make that choice."

"Oh, yeah? Who's that?"

"My sister-in-law, Betty Norton. She and Lou tried everything, but she couldn't get pregnant. All she had left was her career. No other choice. I guess maybe she's happy, but I always felt kinda sorry for her."

"You're talking about Betty Norton, at the hospital?"

"Ayeah. She's Ellie's sister. She always wished she could have children. You see?"

Sally nodded.

"And come to think about it," Prince went on, "I can remember once, wishing that I could have babies."

"You're putting me on."

"No. I'm serious. Back when Ellie was pregnant, I never saw her look so pretty. Bein' pregnant made big changes in how she looked and how she felt. She was so happy, all the time putting her hand on her belly and feelin' the kid moving inside her.

"Then, when she got to breast-feeding, she was even happier. Kinda made me jealous, don'tcha know? It's part of life I'll never experience. The relationship that develops between a woman and her child is maybe the most precious feeling in life, I reckon."

"Wait a minute here," Sally interrupted. "Are you telling me you wish you were a woman?"

"Gosh, no. I guess I'm just kinda envious of women who choose to have children. That's all. The way I see it, having children and raising them is the most satisfying experience in human life. And men are not given the opportunity to choose to have that experience. Now, I ask you. Is that fair?"

"Oh. I never thought about it like that before."

"Women are damn lucky they can choose to have children."

"You know, Prince?" Sally said. "I'm going to give that idea a whole lot of thought. But it'll have to wait until these cherry Cokes have all worn off."

"'Course it's a good thing men can't have children," Prince observed.

"Why's that?"

"'Cause they'd make lousy mothers. Women are lucky they have an inborn talent for motherhood. When I see how close and intimate they get with their kids, it's amazing. You see the same thing with cows and their calves, or does with their fawns. I used to try to imagine what it would be like to breast-feed my kids. It must be like an expansion of your life that you can actually feel. You know what I mean? Ellie and I have talked about this a lot. My only relationship that's anything like that close is with Ellie. And as close as I am to our girls, even now, when the girls call home, it's always 'Hi, Dad, is Mom there?' They love their dad, but somehow it's just not the same as Mom. Ayeah, women are the lucky ones. And some of you are lucky enough and talented enough to be both moms and have a career."

Sally gave him a kiss right on the cheek. Prince snuffed out his cigar.

It was time for cribbage. Prince informed Sam that learning cribbage was just as important as the hunter safety course if he wanted to go up to camp next year. After several raucous games, everyone agreed it was time for bed.

"Interested in jogging tomorrow morning?" Tom asked Sally as they were leaving.

"I might be. Give me a call in the morning and see how I feel. Thank you so much for including us in the sumptuous feast. I had forgotten how good venison can taste. We had a marvelous time, didn't we, Sam?"

"Oh, God yes. It's the first time I ever partied with grown-ups. What a riot."

"Oh, yeah? How's it different from partying with high school kids?"

"When kids are drinking, it's like they're way out. You know. Like chill out, dude. Far out. Like that's all they do. Grown-ups seem to have a lot more fun when they're drinking. Mom, I never knew you were such a hoot. Just the same, I'm driving home. It wouldn't do for you to lose your license too."

Chapter 18

B arns. Hmm! That's odd, Sally thought as she struggled to wake herself up. The topic was still fresh in her mind. *I must have been dreaming about barns. How strange. I haven't dreamed about horses or barns since I was a kid.* She added another pillow to raise her head and became aware of a slight throb in her temple. The barn was soon displaced from her conscious thought by the need for coffee and maybe some aspirin. She made two extra cups in that morning's pot and went out for the Sunday morning paper. While the pot perked, she drank a large glass of orange juice and made herself drink two glasses of water. She was aware of slight dehydration from last night's partying and did not want to suffer a flame-out on this morning's jog with Tom. He was supposed to call anytime now.

The coffee had the hoped-for beneficial effects. The wood stove purred with fresh logs. Sally sat in the rocker, the paper in her lap, a fresh cup of coffee in her hand, and the phone on the table, ready for Tom's call. Her mind went into roam mode. What a fantastic evening. The first time she had ever partied with Sam. Amazing how he joined in with the adults so smoothly and appropriately. And the barn. The whole scene in the barn played a rerun in her mind, and she savored the pleasant memories that it evoked. The phone rang. Sally told Tom to come anytime.

"Which way you want t' go?" Tom asked as they started off. "Back towards my place, or out in the country?"

"How 'bout the country? Dirt roads are easier on the legs."

"This could be the last day of jogging this year," Tom announced after they were on the road. Each word he spoke formed foggy little puffs from his breath. "S'posed to snow today."

"In November? It didn't snow last year until after Christmas."

"Last year was an exception. Most years we start getting snow in November. We need it."

"You need snow?"

"Sure. Plenty of snow means we'll have a white Christmas. It's a Maine tradition."

"I guess you're right. A white Christmas is everyone's dream," Sally said with a sigh. "But I'm sure going to miss jogging with you. You're the only person around here I feel like I can really talk to. And running seems like the best way to get you alone."

"Humph! That's kinda how I feel. And I owe you big for all the help you gave me commiserating about the malpractice suit."

"You are very welcome, Tom. And by the way, any word on Cathy these days? I saw her at the hospital the other day. She seemed pretty stressed out."

"That's just why I asked you to go running today. To talk to you about Cathy. She's dead."

"Are you serious? She's dead? What happened?"

"She committed suicide Friday night."

"Really? You know what happened?"

"Yep. They called me in the middle of the night and asked me to come into town and pronounce her dead. Her obit was in the paper this morning."

"Is that right? I never read the obituaries. Whatever made her do it? Do they know?"

"Not really. She left a couple of notes, but they only let me read one of them. Judging from the way she killed herself, I'd bet she must have been feeling guilty in some way about George Gurnet's death. From what I could gather, she gave her deposition on Friday, and they sort of trapped her into lying about the order for dose of lidocaine that killed him. They claimed it was 444 cc's per hour. That must have really got to her, because she killed herself by starting an IV on herself and administering the same dose that killed Gurnet."

"I can't believe it!"

"Neither could I when I first found out."

"Oh my God, Tom, I feel awful. You must feel horrible."

"I'm pretty much over it now. When I first found out, I expected this huge empty feeling to descend on me, like what happened when Caroline or Mark died. But it never came. I've been thinking about it, and I figure I partly got over her when she up and left last month."

"Well, maybe," Sally said, "but—"

"Yes, but. But what I really think is that I was never really close enough to Cathy so her death would take that much of a toll on me. Infatuated? Yes. I tried like hell to draw her in, but she somehow couldn't tolerate too much intimacy. Physical intimacy was okay but not emotional. Get it?"

"Yeah. It does make sense."

"But there's more," Tom continued. "With all that weighing on me yesterday morning, I had to talk to someone. Or bust. So I went over and unloaded to Prince about the whole mess. He was unaware of the malpractice suit, but it turned out he knew something very helpful. There are evidently three copies to those new EMTALA forms. The government now requires a third copy of the new form, which is to be kept on file in the ambulance company office. So we went over to the fire station in town and found it. And guess what?"

"What?"

"The third copy reads 44 cc's per hour. That shows that someone at the hospital altered the records to protect the hospital. How about that?"

"Amazing!"

"I was dying to tell you last night, but I held back because there were too many people around."

"So do they know yet who altered the records?"

"Not yet. My lawyer—whew! I'll be glad when we get upwind of them critters," Tom said as they jogged past a barn with both horses and cows out in the feedlot. "My lawyer said he would talk to me later this week, after he had a chance to look into things."

"What was that again?" Sally asked. "Sorry. My mind drifted off there for a minute."

Tom repeated himself.

Sally apologized. "I didn't mean to ignore you, but passing that barn made me think of something that's been bugging me. And I finally realized what's been digging at me all morning."

"What's that?"

"The smell of the horse manure. I think the smell of horse manure is making me homesick. Is that crazy or what?"

"Don't ask me."

"Anyway, I woke up this morning and knew I felt strange. I figured it was the drinks I had last night. But now I realize that I feel homesick.

For the first time in I can't remember when. For years, I have tried to put my life on the farm behind me, because I was afraid of turning out to be like my poor mother. Bored and unfulfilled. And also fat. So I sort of denied my whole childhood. But being in your barn last night and smelling the hay, and the tractor smells, and the horse did something. It brought back all kinds of pleasant memories and feelings. Just like that horse manure back there did.

"I haven't been anywhere near a horse in over twenty years. Those old familiar smells triggered memories of stuff I must have been suppressing for all this time. Last night I didn't understand exactly what was happening, but I could actually feel the pleasure of being around a barn again. But now I get it. It was the smell of horse manure that did it."

"No shit?" Tom's face broke into a smug grin.

"Jesus, Tom. You're too much. I'm serious. It's probably the same thing that happens to you when you smell a clam flat. Don't you see?"

"Incredible! Is that what they call aroma therapy?"

"It must be."

"Well, you're welcome to come over anytime and spend time in my barn whenever you need another treatment. And give Jerry a ride, if you want. Like I said, he needs the exercise."

"Thanks. I might just do that. But don't you see why the visit to the barn set me up to have such a good time last night? I really enjoyed myself. I think Sam did too."

Tom acknowledged her with a nod, but neither said a thing for a long time. They jogged along, each deep in thought.

"So who do you think changed the hospital records?" Sally finally inquired.

"Right now, I don't give a boulder," Tom answered. "I'm just so damn glad to finally get the record straight. I never believed I could have made a mistake like that. But sometimes, when I would see those depositions where the lawyers maneuvered the nurses to say how upset I got over those new EMTALA forms, I often believed that—just maybe—I might have actually done what they said I did. I became haunted by a lingering doubt."

"Jeez … That's awful. So what's going to happen now?"

"I'm not sure exactly. First thing I'm going to do is get myself off of those lousy blood pressure medicines, now that some of the stress is off."

"That's progress. But won't they have to drop the malpractice suit now?"

"I can't imagine why not. I'm supposed to meet with my lawyer after Thanksgiving. He's going to reassess the whole case next week. And speaking of Thanksgiving, are you interested in getting together over the holiday?"

"Well, right now I'm not certain. Sam'll be in Philadelphia with Charlie. And I'm not on call. All this homesickness has got me thinking about goin' back home with Mommer 'n 'em."

"Okay. Hmmm. Ya know? I like the way you said that."

"That's good ole boy's talk. I kinda got carried away."

"I know how that feels. Anyway, let me know if you change your mind about Thanksgiving."

About that time they reached Sally's house. She thanked him and gave him a little pat around the back of his waist before she went inside to shower. He drove off in his pickup. A few large flakes of snow began to flutter on the windshield.

～

It was more than a week after Thanksgiving when his lawyer called and asked to meet with Tom. Forty miles per hour was all the traffic was moving along I-95 as he drove to Portland. It was no use trying to pass the snowplow, even in four-wheel drive. Tom was over an hour late. The lawyer didn't seem to mind. He could still bill for that hour anyway.

The lawyer said he had been to the hospital and personally examined the original documents. There was little doubt that they had been altered. A forensic examination seemed unnecessary. Nonetheless, he had subpoenaed the original documents, so they would all be in court custody for security and easy examination for everyone. And also for dramatic effect.

He had talked personally with Frank Cushing, the Augusta lawyer who was representing the Boston law firm's interests in the Maine courts. Cushing was tied up in court until Christmas but agreed to come down after the holiday to review the documents himself and then make a report to Boston so they could reassess the case, considering all the new developments.

"Now who do you suppose changed the records?" Tom asked when the lawyer finished his summary.

"I have no idea at this time."

"The hospital lawyer," Tom guessed, with obvious disgust.

"I doubt it. He would know better than that."

"If I find out that's who did it, I'll kill him," Tom replied, surprised at his own anger.

"It might be just as well if no one ever knew, Tom. Consider that. And while you are thinking about it, keep in mind that your exposure in this case has been significantly decreased by these developments. So be patient."

"And what happened to justice? Doesn't someone need to be brought to justice?"

"Justice?" said the attorney, pulling himself up in his chair in an authoritative pose. "Let me tell you something about justice. Justice is a politically correct word for vengeance. And it is often not a pretty sight."

"Oh, yeah? Gimme a break," Tom replied, his eyebrows raised, vacantly gazing out the top of the window at the snow, still falling in tiny crispy flakes.

"The original meaning of the word justice, if you look in the dictionary, is *the settlement of disputes by administration of the law, with fairness and impartiality*. But for most people, the idea of bringing someone to justice means punishing him. To make him pay for the suffering he has wrought on someone else. You know, an eye for an eye, a tooth for a tooth. That's not really justice. That's vengeance, a way of dealing with anger. It's a part of human nature. Do you see what I'm getting at?"

"Well, maybe. I really never thought much about justice before."

"Seeing someone getting punished, you know, like in a public hanging, or maybe beheading, was a common way of letting go of some of that anger. A process known as justice. True justice is our society's way of dealing with people's anger in a more civilized manner. Our legal system, while not perfect, is a method of resolving disputes among people, as fairly as possible. When you consider the killings and bribery that years ago were commonplace out in the Wild West and, for that matter, still go on in places like the Middle East, to settle disputes among people, you can begin to appreciate our legal system, even with all its imperfections."

"Killings and bribery? Are you serious?"

"Okay. I'll give you an example I read in the paper last month.

Over in Pakistan there was a tribe of Afghan refugees. And it seems a woman left her husband because he was abusing her, and she went back to her own family. Well, this is strictly taboo in the Muslim culture. But, evidently, the abuse was so bad that the family accepted her back anyway. Well, her husband's family was so offended, they had one of the woman's brothers assassinated. How's that for justice?"

"Wow!" Tom uttered. "You're not making this up?"

"No, sir. But the Muslims are not all that primitive. They didn't think that was justice either. The tribal elders feared a bloody feud might be starting, so they called a meeting with the heads of both families. And here is the agreement they made to settle the dispute. The father who killed the other man's son paid the other father the equivalent of two thousand dollars, American money. Plus, he gave one of his own daughters in marriage to another of the other man's sons. In return, the woman went back to her husband. How's that for justice?"

"That's hard to believe," Tom replied.

"I know. Most Americans have come to take our legal system for granted. But it's only been around a few hundred years. Much of the world still uses more primitive forms of justice. Now consider the Gurnets' viewpoint in this case. That family is very angry with you."

"With me? Why me?"

"Because their father is dead. That's why they're angry. And to help them deal with their anger, they need someone to blame. And that turns out to be you."

"But I was trying to help him."

"I know. But when people are stricken with grief and anger, they often don't respond with rational thinking. Blaming the person who appears to them to be responsible for their father's care, even though he was not the person who actually made the error, is not unusual behavior."

"Unbelievable."

"Not really. Most malpractice suits are based in anger. And Mr. Gurnet's son is almost out of control with anger."

"How can you be so sure about that?"

"I took his deposition. You'll get a copy eventually. You won't miss it. Listen, the Gurnets are a rich and powerful family. Back in the Middle Ages, instead of trying to sue you, the Gurnets would have sent a hit man up from Boston. He would have killed you and taken your property.

There are many countries in the world where that kind of justice still exists."

"That's a bit of a stretch," Tom replied. "America is a totally different culture."

"Perhaps. But consider the Wild West. All the western movies, with their range wars, gunfights, and duels. That was not so long ago. And even today, amongst the street gangs and the Mafia, many of their disputes are still settled with violence. The resolution of disputes by *fair and impartial administration of the law* helps assuage people's anger in a less destructive manner. In a way, this malpractice suit has protected you from the Gurnets' anger. Think about that on your drive home."

The snowplows had done their usual superb job while Tom was talking with his lawyer. He drove home at nearly the speed limit. But he just could not make himself deal with the problem of Gurnet anger. When he got home, he mixed himself a manhattan and tried to see justice from a new perspective.

There were only five more days to Christmas. Sally was already depressed by Christmas carols. Bing Crosby, crooning "I'm Dreaming of a White Christmas" on the car radio, did not help her mood. Christmas in Maine was not as appealing as Sally had once anticipated. Being on call, and with Sam off visiting his father again, she would be home alone at Christmas for the first time in her life.

When Tom called and invited her to join him and his two daughters for Christmas dinner, it was more like a sense of relief that she felt, not really a sense of joy.

Then, on Christmas day, there was a gentle snowfall on the drive over to Tom's house. Large, fluffy flakes on the windshield evoked pleasant memories. Christmas carols didn't seem quite so sad anymore. She went in through the back door. The smell of roast beef in the oven and fires in all the hearths made it feel almost like home. Christmas in Maine was getting better.

Tom was on the phone with the hospital, so the girls introduced themselves and put her pecan pie in the dining room. She was seated in front of the fireplace, next to the Christmas tree. She accepted a hot toddy and showed the girls how she made her "on call" cocktails.

"Mix the toddy first, without any booze. Then gently add a

teaspoonful of rum on the top. That way you can taste the booze and not get all liquored up."

"You need to teach Dad that trick."

They relaxed a little, but the situation felt somewhat awkward to Sally. Growing up, she always dreaded having to pass the boyfriend's parents test. Having to take the boyfriend's daughters test was even more awkward. But feeling awkward was better than feeling alone on Christmas.

Petite little Kristen sat prim and proper in a chair and sipped from her teacup. Sherry plopped her ample frame on the floor in front of the fire and leaned back against the sofa. "So, how long have you been in Maine?" she asked as she popped open a can of beer.

"This is my second year, but it's my first Christmas in Maine. It sure is beautiful."

"Yeah. There is no place as nice as Maine for Christmas."

The conversation continued on a superficial level, until Sally presented pictures of Sam at the helm of the *Shady Lady*.

"Oh he's the kid who lobstered with Prince last summer. Dad never told us you were his mom. He's wicked cute."

"Yeah, he went clamming with us one time last summer. He's getting to be a real hunk."

Sam? A hunk? Impossible. He's still just a kid. Sally could only smile a muted thank-you.

After that, things got more relaxed. Kristen revealed she was applying to medical school, and Sherry told about her experiences studying computer science in graduate school. Sally accepted another half of a toddy just as Tom finally got off the phone.

"Merry Christmas, Sally." Tom rushed in and gave her a warm embrace. Sally responded with reserve, not quite trusting her emotions in the presence of the girls.

"Where is the goddamn mistletoe when a man needs it?" Tom added.

Sally remembered the Christmas presents she had left in the car. She wiggled out of Tom's embrace and went out to fetch them and place them under the tree. The girls were buzzing around like bees, lighting the candles, pouring wine, and setting up the coffeemaker. Tom put the finishing touches on the gravy. Dinner was served.

"So, how does this compare to Christmas back in southern Illinois?"

"Remarkably similar in many ways," Sally decided. "Only the scenery here is much more beautiful. Illinois is pretty flat, and we don't get snow very often. But I *am* surprised at how much at home I feel."

"Well, it's nice to have someone sitting in that chair again," Sherry observed. "It was empty last Christmas."

"Thank you very much. You've made me feel very special today."

After dinner, the girls offered to clean up, but Tom said he and Sally would take care of the dishes. He knew the girls were eager to go ice-skating with some of their friends. "Your skates are out in the barn," he said when they were ready to go. "They are hanging on the wall in the tack room. Come on, Sally. Let's have an eggnog in front of the fire. I want to open my presents. We can knock off these dishes later."

"What do you think of the girls?" Tom asked, adding another log to the fire.

"They are amazing. I kept thinking to myself, 'If only Sam could someday hook up with someone like one of your girls.'"

"Don't worry about it. Sam will do okay for himself. By the way, how was your trip home for Thanksgiving?"

"Wonderful. It was great to be back home with Mommer 'n 'em, if you'll pardon a Midwest expression. I can't remember Mom ever being quite so happy back when I was growing up. She gets this unbelievable smile on her face every time she looks at one of her grandchildren. And she looks beautiful. It's amazing. I never noticed that before. Anyway, the day after Thanksgiving, most of us went down to the river for a few days at hunting camp. Things have changed a lot since I left. Now they let women come during hunting season."

"Did you go hunting?"

"Didn't have a license. Mom and I just visited while they all went out. I haven't had a good talk with Mom in years. I finally got kinda caught up with her a bit. Seems like life has been a lot better to her than I figured. She got depressed, you know, back when I was in high school. Her last kid, leaving the nest. She completely withdrew. Now she's more open to talk about it."

"That's probably good."

"You bet. Mom thinks it was mostly the change of life that caused her depression. And with all the kids off in college, she started feeling lonely before I even left. Thought she'd lost everything: her youth, her beauty, her children. She felt like she wasn't attractive to anyone anymore."

"Humph. Wouldn't surprise me if that was a pretty common feeling for women at her stage of life."

"Wouldn't surprise me if you were right. Fortunately, it didn't last long. With all the kids out of the house, Mom began to notice how much Dad still cared for her. Didn't matter to him how she looked. They felt closer than ever. Then the grandchildren started to appear. Mom really started to feel loved again. When the grandchildren are around, it completely changes her. It's like she goes into grandmother mode. Starts acting like a kid herself. I've never seen her so happy and alive. I guess there are some good things about getting old, after all."

"Like what?"

"Like knowing people can love you without having to worry all the time about how you look."

"That makes sense."

"She also told me she gets a great deal of pleasure out of seeing a piece of herself in each of the grandkids, something she really never appreciated in her own children. She feels like part of her will still go on living inside the grandchildren. A sense of immortality, I think."

"That's interesting," Tom replied. "Caroline had the same ideas when she was preparing for her death. Made it a lot easier on all of us when she shared that idea with us."

"It's nice to know there may be good times ahead, even when you get old. Say, isn't it about time to open your presents?"

The first present Tom opened was for Jerry Garcia. A new horse blanket. The second present was a new shower bag for the camp.

"It's to replace the one I broke back in October," she said.

"Thank you very much. You didn't need to replace that bag. It's been coming apart like that for a long time. I've been too lazy to buy a new one."

"Well, I want you to have it. I think about that shower often. Sort of hoped I might get another chance to use it sometime."

"Ahhhh. Well, isn't that interesting. Uh, maybe it could be arranged. Let's see. The girls are both leaving after a few days. I'm not on call for New Year's. Maybe we could celebrate New Year's up at camp, if you're not on call. What do you think?"

"Sounds good. Sam is going out west with his father to ski next week. Doing some makeup time for staying here last summer. He called this morning. Said he was having a great time with his father and new stepmother. Really pissed me off."

"How come?"

"Jealousy, I suppose. And it pisses me off even more, because I allow myself to get so jealous."

"Sounds like you need to get off the tar."

"You might be right. Let's go up to camp."

∼

Two days after Christmas, Frank Cushing called Frederick Naushon, Esq., at his office in Boston. "Fred, this is Frank Cushing, up in Maine. How are you?"

"Fine. And you?"

"Just fine. Did you have a nice holiday?"

"Splendid. How was Christmas up in Maine?"

"Snowy, as usual."

"So how much snow have you got up there now?"

"About two feet on the ground right now."

"Nice. I'll bet the skiing is good."

"You bet. We're going up to Sugarloaf over New Year's. Say, the reason I'm calling you is to bring you up to date on some surprising developments in the MacMahan case."

"Okay! What's new?"

"Well, it seems that there are three copies of those EMTALA transfer orders. Another copy of the doctor's transfer order sheet has been discovered in the ambulance company's file. And it shows that someone has evidently changed the hospital records, after the fact, to make it look as if this Dr. MacMahan wrote an improper dose of lidocaine for Mr. Gurnet. It looks to me like the record has been altered, and that's going to ruin our case against MacMahan."

"I'm not convinced. I'd have to see it myself. Maybe we should arrange a forensic evaluation to be certain."

"I think you'd be wasting your money," Frank Cushing replied. "Why don't you drive up and look at them yourself. MacMahan's attorney arranged to have all the original copies taken into protective custody for safekeeping. It looked pretty clear to me when I saw them today that they had been altered. But that's not all," Cushing continued. "You know that nurse, Cathy Dyer, we deposed last month?"

"Yeah."

"She committed suicide."

"No. Any idea why she did that?"

"It had something to do with the deposition. I don't know all the details. Anyway, I think we may need to reconsider our options."

"Like maybe going after the hospital?"

"Exactly. I've been doing some checking around. The hospital has a huge trust fund we might be able to tap. More than enough to cover the nine million in damages."

"Yes. And with all that record tampering, there could be substantial punitive damages on top."

"Right. I was figuring another million, easy."

"Well, I'll get in touch with you after New Year's and arrange to come up and reevaluate things."

"Sounds good. But there is one more thing. MacMahan's lawyer wants to arrange a deposition with the ambulance attendant."

"So?"

"Well, I just thought you might want to wait 'til you found out the date of the deposition before you made your plans. That way you could inspect the records and attend the deposition, all in one trip."

"Good idea. We'll be in touch. And happy New Year!"

Sally was already dressed in her new long underwear and her new insulated hunting boots. Tom had recommended she buy them at Renys discount department store, where she got them at bargain prices. Sally felt pleased with herself. She was finally beginning to get the hang of living in Maine. It was snowing lightly when Tom picked her up, shortly after noon. He had a thermos of coffee on the front seat and Andrea Bocelli on the CD player when she climbed up in the cab of the truck.

"I can see you're in a good mood," she observed.

"Ayeah. Closed the office at noon. Signed all the Medicare forms, and I'm good to go. Are you ready to git off the tar?"

"Well, I was in great spirits until just before you got here. Sam called this morning from Aspen to say he and his father were having a great time. Of course, I got pissed again."

"Get over it!"

"What do you mean?"

"Get over it! That's out of Lobstermen Anonymous."

"I still don't get it."

"Sorry. Guess I was being a little obtuse. I'm talking about forgiveness. You know, forgive and forget. And sometimes your own self is the hardest person of all to learn how to forgive. Know what I mean?"

"Well, not exactly."

"Look, you can't help feeling that way about your ex-husband. It's normal. So learn to forgive yourself and forget about all that self-blame, guilt, and self-pity. I know what you're going through. I put myself through the same scenario after Mark died. Decided I was to blame. Prince straightened me out after I whimpered to him. He pointed out that, being human, we all make mistakes. But just because you make a mistake doesn't mean you're bad. 'Cause everybody makes mistakes. So learn to forgive yourself."

Sally raised an eyebrow.

"It's something all lobstermen have to deal with. You see, they all love their boats, but there is no way they can tend all those hundreds of traps in Maine waters without occasionally running into BFRs every now and then. Put a big gouge in the bottom of your boat, or get a ding on your propeller. Gets expensive. Makes a man feel terrible. Unforgivably guilty. Self-pity. Stuff like that."

Tom glanced over at Sally, who gave a nod of understanding.

"So they developed Lobstermen Anonymous therapy to deal with it. It was originally a twelve-step program. You know, like in Alcoholics Anonymous. Now they have it down to two steps: Step 1: Get over it! Step 2: Get, the fuck, over it! See? Try it. Once you get the hang of it, you'll learn how to forgive yourself."

"Okay. I'm over it."

"There, now. Don't you feel better?"

"Well, of course I do. I'm over it. Thanks. I needed that."

The Maine turnpike was well plowed, so they made good time on the road. While they were under way, Tom brought Sally up to date on the recent developments in the case. He had talked briefly with his lawyer that morning. Sally felt a noticeable sense of relief in Tom's voice when he gave her the news.

"So, have they figured out yet who it was that changed the hospital records?"

"No. The lawyer mentioned that this morning. He has not reported it to any of the authorities yet. He figures an investigation would not have much bearing on the outcome of this case at this point. But it could drag things out for a long time. He left the decision sort of up to me."

"So who do you think did it?"

"At this point, I have no way of knowing for sure. But if I had to guess, I'd say it was the goddamn hospital lawyer. I'd skin him alive if I could. What do you think?"

"You can call it woman's intuition if you like, but I'm fairly certain it was Betty Norton."

"Hmmmm. Actually, you could be right. I don't know."

"Well, I think there ought to be an investigation. Somebody ought to be held accountable for doing such an awful thing."

"You're talking about justice?"

"Yes, justice."

"I'll tell you what my attorney said about justice. He said that justice is a PC word for revenge. And it can sometimes get pretty ugly. He's got some cockamamy idea that this malpractice suit is a civilized way to protect me from the Gurnets' desire for revenge."

"He said that?"

"Ayeah. He says that when people get angry, all that anger makes them feel miserable. So, in order to get relief from their misery, they find someone to blame and then seek revenge. And the person that gets the blame is not always the person who's at fault."

"Sounds pretty primitive."

"Right. But if you substitute the word *justice* for *revenge*, it suddenly sounds respectable. So I've been thinking about who it is I want to seek justice on. It's lawyers. Especially plaintiffs' lawyers."

"What's that got to do with justice?"

"Haven't figured it out yet. Right now, all I know is I'm angry at all lawyers."

Sally decided to drop the subject. She became aware that Tom's attention was focused on his driving. They had turned off the turnpike and onto a county road that had not been well plowed. She was just as glad to get off that topic anyway.

Handel's "Messiah" was on CD player, and they were playing one of her favorite parts. Sally poured them both some hot coffee and settled into her own reverie. The trees were stunning, all decked out in a blanket of snow. Most of the houses still had quaint Christmas decorations displayed. Even though she had been along this road once before, with all the snow, everything looked new and peaceful. In the snow, Maine was even prettier than Illinois. Suddenly, Tom made a hard left turn onto a narrow dirt road, threw the truck into four-wheel drive, and came to a stop.

"We are off the tar," he announced. "Want a beer?"

"I'll split one with you," Sally replied after a moment's hesitation.

The snow was deep, and the paper company road hadn't been plowed in days. They did okay until they got to the turnoff at camp. The camp road hadn't been plowed at all. There was no hope of getting through two and a half feet of snow, even with four-wheel drive. Two miles left to go.

"What do we do now?" she asked.

"No problem," Tom said. He dug out a shovel from the back of the truck and cleared a spot on the camp road where he could park the truck and leave it, out of the way of the snowplows. Most of their things were in backpacks. The rest of the provisions Tom loaded into an old toboggan. Then Tom got out two pairs of snowshoes and showed Sally how to maneuver them. The recent snow squalls had not quite reached this far north, and there was a firm crust on top of the snow cover that made the going easy. Once she got the hang of it, Sally found snowshoeing very satisfying. It did not take long at all to get to camp. It was cold and musty inside, and Tom lit up the gas lights and built fires in the wood stove and the hearth while Sally loaded in the gear and some more wood. Then they cleared a path to the outhouse and primed the pump with warm water so they could pump a supply of water for the camp.

"What now?" Sally asked.

"Well, while it's still light, I suggest we put on the snowshoes and explore around a little bit. Maybe work up a little appetite, don't you think?"

"I'm good to go. Is that the way you say it?"

"Ayeah. You're soundin' like a real Mainer."

"Got that one from Sam. He's really picking up the Maine dialect."

"That's not surprising."

"I suppose not. Actually, it's a lot better all that rap and jive stuff he learned at school back in Philadelphia. And thank God he's stopped saying the word *like* in front of every sentence. It was driving me crazy."

By then they had their snowshoes on, and off they went.

"Look," she said, not long after they were into the woods. "Bunny tracks. Can we follow them? Maybe we can find the bunny. Don't they turn white this time of year?"

"Go right ahead. It don't much mattah where we go. I can find the way back to camp. Besides, the girls got me this new GPS for Christmas, and I'm hot to play around with it."

Sally tracked rabbits for what seemed like miles, behaving more and more like a little kid as time passed. "I don't think we're ever going to find one of those little critters," she finally admitted to herself. "All we ever find are their little bunny poops. But I've had a good time snooping around. And it's great exercise. I'm bushed."

"It's just as well we head back to camp. Soon be dark anyway."

The camp was warm and smelled good when they got back. It was only four thirty, but it was already getting dark. "It's not five o'clock yet," Tom remarked, "but I don't see any wardens around, so maybe we could get away with starting cocktail hour a little early. What do you think?"

"Good idea. Actually, you remind me of my dad on that subject. He has moved cocktail hour up to four o'clock these days, whenever the grandkids are around. Says you need to start early so you can finish by five o'clock. That way, you can have supper with the grandkids before they have to go to bed."

Tom poured the premixed manhattans from a Coke bottle over the glasses of ice and added a cherry. "One cherry Coke on the rocks," he announced as he served. "Of course we don't use no bitters in our manhattans when we're roughin' it, in case anyone wants to know. Cheers."

"Cheers. Mmm, this hits the spot. Guess what. I think I told you about going to Dad's hunting camp when I was back home for Thanksgiving. And how nice it was, just being there and finally feeling like I fit in. Well, being here feels even better."

Tom smiled. He had two huge kettles of hot water on the back of the stove, heating up for their showers. Toward the end of the second manhattan, Sally was lying back in her chair, obviously in some peaceful trance.

"What are you thinking about?" Tom asked.

"I was thinking about hunting."

"Interesting. Whatever brought that up?"

"A number of things, I suppose. First off, seeing you shoot that partridge last fall kinda put me off. But then when I ate it, my perspective changed. Know what I mean?"

"Yeah. I think so."

"Then, after you shot that deer, and it tasted so good. Plus, that great party we enjoyed that night. I think that also had a big effect. Well, at Thanksgiving, when I went down to the river on our family hunting trip, I began to really enjoy the hunting process a lot."

"Yes," Tom replied with a nod.

"But the whole thing kinda came together this afternoon, when we were out there looking for those rabbits. This strange new feeling came over me as I was following those tracks. It was so exciting, trying to stalk that bunny. All my senses were on high alert, so aware of every sound, every smell. And the vision thing. My brain was tracking not only where my eyes were focused, but also everything in my peripheral vision fields. I just felt so connected with the environment. I don't ever remember feeling so alive and glad to be that way. Ya know? A couple of times I almost wished I had a gun, so I could shoot the bunny if I found him. Is that strange?"

"Sounds pretty normal to me."

"Well, it seems a bit primitive to me."

"You're probably right about that. It's the primitive predatory instinct that you have been experiencing. We prob'ly inherited it from our Paleolithic ancestors. That's prob'ly how they were able to feed their families."

"I suppose so. But it seems strange that that instinct could cause so much pleasure, even when you don't actually end up killing anything. Know what I mean?"

Tom took a sip of his drink and thought a minute before he came up with the answer.

"You know, I've wondered about that myself at times in the past. But I never came up with an answer until you framed the question so clearly. I'd guess that hunting is similar to another primitive instinct called sex, which is necessary for the continued reproduction of humans, just like the hunting instinct was essential for human survival."

"Okay, I suppose so."

"And I'm sure you'll agree there are some very pleasant experiences in sex, even if you don't have an orgasm or get pregnant, and you can still enjoy the hunting experience, even if you don't actually kill something and eat it."

"Oh my God!" Sally replied with a huge smile. "You are amazing." Then she paused for a moment, staring out the window in solemn thought. "If only it would snow," she added. Her mind was in another world.

"How come you want snow?"

"Well, for weeks now I keep thinking about the shower I took the last time we were up here. Standing out there, with no clothes on and the snowflakes falling on me. It was so pleasant. All the warm water drizzling down and keeping me warm. Mmmmmm. It was nice. Been a long time since I've felt that sensual."

"Well, even though it's not snowing, maybe we could think of a way to make it even nicer this time," Tom contemplated.

"I've already thought of a way," Sally replied. "We've got two shower bags. What if we showered together?"

"Hmmm. I'd need another cherry Coke for that."

"Good. I'll have one too. All I can say is I hope you're in the rut tonight.'"

"I can hardly wait to find out," Tom replied.

The next morning Tom was working on a crossword puzzle and enjoying a cup of coffee by the wood stove, when Sally returned from a visit to the outhouse. She said nothing, just poured herself some coffee and sat down in the rocker with a sigh and a far-off look in her eye.

"A penny," Tom said.

"A penny?"

"Yeah. A penny for your thoughts."

"Oh. Well, while I was out there, in the john, I somehow got to thinking about all the changes in my life, since I moved to Maine."

"Oh, yeah! Like what?"

"When I first came up here I was on the run."

"On the run?" Tom interrupted.

"I was in a rush to get Sam out of Philly and away from the unwholesome environment at his school, with the rotten gang of kids he was always hanging around with. And I really needed to get away from Charlie too. We were always fighting over something. Usually Sam."

"Well, you couldn't have selected a better place than Maine," Tom said.

"Actually, I didn't really choose it. Maine was the only place that had a job for an ophthalmologist that wasn't in some city and far enough away from Charlie. I really wanted Sam in a more rural environment. Maine was what was out there when I needed to move."

"I see. So now that you've been here for a while, what do you think?"

"Well, for one thing, being a doctor in Maine is a totally different experience from what it was like back at the university."

"That doesn't surprise me," Tom observed. "What do you see as the most important differences?"

"The goals and rewards of medicine are totally different here. You'd think medicine would be the same everywhere. But it's not. In academic medicine, it seemed like the goal of everyone was to have a reputation of being the best in your field. Or, at least, maybe become an authority in some small area of medicine. Prestige and respect were the rewards we were all seeking. Know what I'm talking about?"

"I sure do. Been there, done that."

"Back there, most all patients were just cases. Everyone was after good cases. The hard ones that nobody else but you could handle. And the high-paying cases. Work that either fed your ego or your wallet. That's what gave you satisfaction."

"I know exactly where you're coming from."

"Well, here in Maine, you can forget all that stuff. It's just not available. But I've discovered an entirely new side of medicine that I never saw in medical school or academic practice."

"Oh, yeah? What's that?"

"It's patients. I think you've probably discovered that yourself," Sally replied as she saw Tom nodding. "I think that there is a certain aloofness in academic medicine that separates doctors from their patients and prevents them from ever getting to know their patients as real people. Many of the patients, you barely get to speak to. You only see them on rounds, with the staff and med students. Most of the face-to-face dealings are done by the interns and residents." Tom nodded again.

"Here, I do everything myself. So I really get acquainted with every patient. And most of them are very nice. They appreciate everything you do to help them. And you know what? Doing even the simplest treatment for a patient you really like, it turns out, is even more satisfying than doing some great case on a patient you hardly know."

"I couldn't agree more. I almost told you that myself, one time last summer. But I figured it was the kind of thing you were better off discovering for yourself, if you know what I mean."

"That's just what I said to Mom. It's one of the things we talked about when I was home at Thanksgiving. Another thing I told her was how proud of myself I had always been, because I advanced so much further in medicine than my grandfather ever did. It's only recently that

I learned what it really was that made medicine so satisfying to him. I figure, really, that I'm only just now catching up to him."

"That's very interesting," Tom said, getting up to fetch the coffeepot. He filled their cups. "I can see you are starting to feel good about being in Maine?"

"Very good. I had forgotten how many fun things there are in life, besides just being a doctor all the time."

"Like what?"

"Like fishing and horses. And planting a garden. Things I enjoyed growing up. That got put aside when I went into medicine. And, of course, going to camp."

"Exactly!"

"It feels good, being up at camp. Being totally away from everyday life. Just relaxing. Away from all the rules and standards society imposes on us."

"I know what you mean. That's what camp is all about."

"It's more than just camp I'm talking about," Sally said, sipping her coffee. "It's about taking off the doctor's suit. This is the first time, since I graduated from medical school, that I have ever taken the doctor's suit totally off."

"Really? How's it feel?"

"It feels like I need to do it more often."

Sally never put the doctor's suit back on the whole time they were up at camp. She felt comfortable telling Tom her whole life story. Seated in front of the fire, out tromping around in snowshoes, and after they made love, she shared her most intimate feelings about life. Tom was entranced but not yet fully aware of the therapeutic effect her openness was having on the damage caused by the malpractice suit—and Caroline's death, subjects he still could not quite handle, even up at camp.

They drove home the day after New Year's. The whole time at camp, no mention was made of Tom's malpractice suit. Sally finally asked him, "Have you given any more thought to what you are going to do about whoever altered the medical records?"

"To tell the truth, I haven't thought about it at all, the whole time we were at camp. But I have decided what I'm going to do."

"How can you make a decision without thinking about it first?"

"Easy. I'm going to do what feels right. I've had it with rational thinking. Whatever makes me feel good, that's what I'm doing. And I'm gonna drop the whole thing and be done with it."

"Drop the whole thing? After all you have been through? And without any rational consideration? I don't believe it."

"I didn't mean to insinuate that I haven't given the matter a lot of thought," Tom replied. "It's just that rational thought never gave me an answer. Not one that gives me any comfort. The people I'm really pissed at are the ones who sued me in the first place and then put my family's property up for the taking. The plaintiff's lawyers. And they are all immune to justice. I figure whoever changed the hospital records was only trying to protect the hospital from the same scumbags that were after me. It wasn't their motives; it was their methods that were wrong. And I almost suffered some collateral damage. Leading a vindictive investigation against the hospital will only make a lot of other people angry, and it won't do anything to assuage my anger at the plaintiff's lawyers and give me a sense of revenge. Or justice, if you prefer. If the hospital wants to pursue the issue of altering records, let them. I only hope I never find out who it was that changed those records."

"You can't be serious. Why don't you want to know?"

"It would probably make me angry. I don't want any more hate and anger."

"I don't blame you," Sally replied.

"Well, I've decided to try to get rid of my pain and anger by some method other than punishment and revenge. I'm worn out with this affair."

"So, what else can you do?"

"Lobsterman's therapy, that's what. Look, I managed to get through this mess without any real personal damage. I need to put this behind me and get on with my life. The time has come to just get over it. So I'm gettin' the fuck over it."

"Come to think of it," Sally said, "that may be a pretty good way to deal with it, after all."

Chapter 19

THE PROXIMATE CAUSE

*Smiles never go up in price
Or down in value.*

For Fredrick Naushon, Esq., the ambulance attendant's deposition was devastating.

"In all my days as a lawyer," he said, "I have never seen anyone testify in such an honest and straightforward manner. That guy had balls. It's hard to believe."

"I know how you feel," Frank Cushing replied. "But some Maine people are just like that. There's no getting round it."

"Can you believe it? That little bastard just sat there and told the truth, the whole truth, and nothing but the truth. And nobody tried to stop him."

"I just hate it when that happens. You lose control over what a witness says, and it can ruin everything. I don't know about you, but I could use a drink."

"Me too. Shall we do lunch?"

"Good idea. Where do you think we should go?"

"How about Eddy's Wharf? I went there when I was up here last summer. It's pretty good food, and the drive down to Snug Harbor should be gorgeous on a day like today."

"Sounds good to me."

Driving along in the car, they went over the ambulance attendant's testimony. He had testified that, during the transfer of Mr. Gurnet into the ambulance, he had connected the IV bag to the ambulance's flow regulator himself. The order said 44 cc's per hour, and that's what he intended to set the rate at. He figured that his finger must have lingered on the 4 button an instant too long and caused a wrong flow rate of 444 cc's per hour to get entered. By the time he discovered the error, the patient was dead. It was a new piece of equipment, and he didn't know that it was so tricky to set. Both attorneys agreed that this testimony, along with the finding of the unaltered copy of the EMTALA order form, put this case in a whole new perspective.

"I can't help wondering what kind of law school that guy must have gone to."

"How's that?"

"Well, didn't they teach him you're never supposed to ask a witness an open-ended question like he did? Otherwise they're likely to start talking, and who knows what kind of evidence they might reveal? And you have no control over the testimony. Like what happened with that ambulance driver today."

"I see what you mean."

"I mean, didn't they teach him to pose all questions in a declarative statement? So it can be answered with a simple yes or no?"

"Sure beats me."

"Another thing. It's really frustrating, trying to bring a malpractice suit in the state of Maine."

"How's that?"

"Well, having to present every case in front of a review panel before you can go to court and present it to a jury really sucks."

"I know," Cushing replied. He suddenly stepped on the brake. A pickup truck in front of them stopped to let a car pull into the traffic from a side road.

"Boy! What a crazy driver that guy is," Naushon remarked. "That's something you won't see in Boston. Folks know better than to stop the traffic just to let some jerk in from a side road."

"Happens all the time in Maine. Drivers are pretty polite around here, 'specially pickup drivers."

Naushon just shook his head all the way to the restaurant. They parked the car and went in.

"If we could only get this case in front of a jury without having to go before that lousy review panel. I would present a flood of spicy testimony about the relationship between Dr. MacMahan and that Dyer nurse. That, along with the altered medical records, could be woven into a persuasive case for a cover-up that would make any jury award us a million in punitive damages on top of the nine million."

Naushon ordered a double martini. "I'll have the same," Cushing requested, "and bring us an order of your deep-fried parsnips to go with it. I like this joint," he added after the waitress had gone.

"I know. I can't believe it's so busy this time of the year. There are almost as many people in here now as when I was in here last summer. That guy Eddy must be making a mint."

"Mmmm. These are good. Try some," Frank said after parsnips were served. "It looks to me like our chances of getting a settlement out of either the doctor or the hospital were pretty much wiped out today, wouldn't you say?"

"Yes. It's too bad," Naushon replied. "All we got left is the ambulance company. After today I expect they'll agree to an out-of-court settlement, if it's not too big."

"Well, it won't be big, that's for sure. State law limits suits against ambulance companies to three hundred thousand dollars, max."

"Three hundred thousand dollars!" Naushon almost choked. "That's all? Boy! Maine is still back in the dark ages. I can't believe how unfair malpractice laws are here in Maine. All malpractice suits have to go before a review panel before they can go to a jury. Suits against ambulances are capped at three hundred grand. Doesn't the Maine Bar Association have any clout in the legislature? You guys should get these laws changed. They are really unfair."

"We keep trying. I think eventually we'll win. In the meantime, we'll have to settle for a measly three hundred grand."

"I guess so. Too bad. I could almost taste that nine million."

"Me too. Another martini?"

"Make it a single. I've got to drive all the way back to Boston this afternoon."

From Tom's perspective, the revelation that the medical record had been altered had little effect on the momentum of the legal process. Somehow, despite all the new developments, a nagging worry never completely left Tom's mind. He adopted the unusual practice of grabbing the mail every day, as soon as it was delivered. He searched through the letters, looking for envelopes marked PERSONAL AND CONFIDENTIAL. Inside would be the latest deposition of some witness, some additional scrap of medical record that might possibly serve as evidence for one side or the other. There was no indication that someone was reviewing the facts to assess whether or not the case had any substance worth continuing. The legal process, once in progress, could not be derailed.

Any day that one of the specially marked envelopes was not in the mail was a day of relief. The arrival of one meant a week of bedtime Xanax so Tom could remain functional.

At last, the deposition of George Gurnet III arrived in the mail. Taken back in November, many weeks had passed while the transcriptionist typed the first draft, which, during the holiday season, slowly circulated among the attorneys' offices for review and corrections before the final draft was typed up and mailed out. Tom scanned it and then stuffed it in his briefcase so he could take it home to read that evening. He knew he would need help from a manhattan to suffer through it.

That evening, as he read though George III's deposition, he finally began to appreciate the level of anger behind this lawsuit. *Scary.* The attorney was right. Anger was behind this whole suit. And, of course, tort lawyers manipulated that anger for their own benefit. Tom began to reconsider his perspective of this whole case as he prepared for bed.

It was 2:00 a.m., and Tom was awake. He made a quick trip to the bathroom and then back to bed. But sleep would not come. He tried desperately to delete the deposition from his mind as he tried to get back to sleep. Then George Gurnet III suddenly appeared with a scowl on his face. "Definitely one of the fiercer animals," as Piglet would say. Tom awakened and realized he'd been dreaming. *Glad it's the lawyers that have to deal with him and not me. Imagine what would happen if we didn't have litigation to settle our disputes?*

With that calming thought, he drifted off to sleep. George III was back again, this time wearing his cowboy hat. The scowl was still on his face and, as usual, a cigarette dangling from his lips. He was stalking down the vacant street, a six-gun on his hip. A few bars from "High Noon" were played. As George reached for his gun, Tom suddenly opened his eyes. Three o'clock. It was all a dream. A nightmare. Yet, so real. Finally, it came to him. *If you stop and consider the alternatives to our legal system, lawyers are really not all that bad.* Tom dropped into a deep sleep for the rest of the night.

∼

One afternoon, late in January, and soon after his two-week visit in the Virgin Islands, where he attended a three-day conference on legal issues followed by a charter sailboat cruise, Bernard Appledore, of Nomans, Appledore, and Hull, sat at his desk and spoke into the intercom.

"Miss Pasque, please show the Gurnets in now."

"Yes, sir. Shall I bring in coffee on the silver tray again?"

"Please, Miss Pasque. It is after noon. No coffee. It's tea time, so serve us a proper tea."

"Not a problem. I'll have it right away."

Arlene Gurnet and her son, George III, were ushered in and seated. Shortly, Frederick Naushon came in, carrying the tea service. Mr. Naushon poured out.

"And so, Arlene," Bernard began, after the pleasantries and formalities were complete, "we invited you here today to bring you up to date and summarize the latest developments in your suit against Dr. MacMahan. And, hopefully, to make some decisions that will help bring this endeavor to a conclusion."

"We understand," Arlene replied, casting a glance at her son. "Please continue."

"Mr. Naushon will explain things. He is more familiar with the details in this case."

Fred cleared his throat twice. "We have just completed the discovery phase of this case. Our most important finding was the revelation that someone had altered the hospital medical records to make it appear that Dr. MacMahan had prescribed the improper dose of lidocaine, which was what caused the death of your husband. Our people have done a careful forensic evaluation of the original documents, and there is no question that they have been altered. Our careful investigation led to the discovery of a third copy of the transfer order sheet in the ambulance office file. This copy was unaltered. These findings make our case against Dr. MacMahan very weak."

"Well, what about all the other mistakes the expert witness said that hick doctor had made?" George III asked.

"Those allegations were put forward, mostly, to bias a jury, in case this ever came to trial. It's likely they aren't even true. And it doesn't matter whether or not they could be proven. Their purpose was to question the overall competence of the whole medical treatment so that the error in dosage would fit into a pattern of substandard medical care, rather than an unintentional mistake by a good doctor. This kind of strategy usually leads to larger settlements. In this case, even if we could prove these other allegations, which is doubtful, they would not constitute proximate cause."

"Proximate cause?" George III exclaimed. "What the hell is proximate cause?"

"Proximate cause means that in order for some action to constitute malpractice, it must have been the actual cause of the undesirable outcome and damages. None of these other allegations, even if they were true, were the actual cause of your father's death. Dr. MacMahan was not the proximate cause. It was the improper dose of lidocaine, administered by the ambulance attendant, that did it. Plain and simple. And that's the proximate cause."

"Well, who altered the records?"

"We don't exactly know for sure. It was likely someone in the hospital. No one else would have access to the records."

"Then why don't we sue the hospital?"

"Proximate cause," replied Mr. Naushon. "Altering the record must have happened after the fact. Although it was wrong, it was also not the proximate cause of your father's death. Your father died because some ambulance attendant inadvertently entered the improper dose of medication on an IV control meter. And that's that, wouldn't you say, Bernard?"

"Yes, Fred. I'd say you have covered everything pretty well. Don't you agree, Arlene?"

"I suppose so. But is that the end of it?"

"No. Not at all. We have some very good news for you. We have arrived at a tentative settlement with the insurance company for the ambulance—subject, of course, to your approval."

"How much is the settlement?"

"Three hundred thousand dollars. Would that be acceptable, Arlene?"

"Well, if that's the best we can do, I suppose we'll have to take it."

"Your share of three hundred thousand dollars, added to the huge profit you made on the sale of your shorefront property in Maine, will allow you to buy a very nice place down in Florida. Don't you think?"

Arlene nodded in agreement. She stood up and shook hands with both lawyers, thanking them for all their good work. Then she started for the door.

"Wait a minute," George III said, also standing up and popping an unlit cigarette in his mouth. "What happened to our nine million dollars? And what's going to happen to that hick doctor? Where is the justice?"

"You don't want justice, Georgie. You're just out for revenge."

"Justice or revenge? What's the difference anyway? And when are you going to stop calling me Georgie?"

"When you get a job and start earning your own money. And if you want to know the real proximate cause of your father's death, it was you, insisting that he be transferred with his unstable heart. If you had just left him where he was, there is a good chance he might have survived." She dragged him out the door.

When they had left, Bernard said, "Nice job, Naushon. Too bad we didn't get a shot at the doctor, but three hundred grand is better than nothing. Don't you agree?"

"Absolutely."

"And one other thing. Make certain you get the settlement with the ambulance company all locked up before we close this case."

"Of course."

∽

Shortly after Valentine's Day, on a Friday afternoon, Tom's attorney called to say the suit had been dropped. Tom immediately phoned Prince in Florida to give him the news. He could hardly wait to tell Sally. She was over at the YMCA, where the high school swim meet was about to begin.

Sally was not all that easy to find, tucked way back on the farthest end of the spectator gallery at the pool. The familiar damp, chlorine smell was soothing to Tom and stirred up pleasant memories from years of swimming and competing in this pool. He wormed his way through the crowd of parents and spectators until he finally found her.

"How come you're sitting way the hell over here?"

"Charlie and his new wife are supposed to be up here this weekend. I'm hoping they won't see me. I don't feel like watching the meet with them."

"Guess what." Tom told her, "They finally dropped the case."

"At last." She hugged him and kissed him. "Whatever took them so long?"

"My lawyer said that it took a long time for the plaintiff's lawyer to finally determine there was no hope of getting a lucrative settlement from me or the hospital. I was told they have made a settlement with the ambulance company."

"That's interesting. Did they ever find out who it was that altered the record?"

"They did. But, according to my lawyer, that apparently was no longer an issue, as far as this case is concerned."

"Boy. That's a load off you, I'll bet," Sally said as they sat down to watch the first race.

"I'm relieved that it's finally over. Going through that suit was rougher than when my wife died," Tom confided. "Not being able to talk about it. That's what kills you. I don't think I could have made it without your help." He gave her a big hug.

Sally filled him in on the schedule of swimming events. It was the district finals. If they won this meet, Sam would get to swim in the state championship meet. The opposing team had won the state championship last year. Sam was swimming in the 50 free and the 100 free, plus one of the relays. "One of the guys he's swimming against in the 100 freestyle was the state champion last year. That's gonna be a tough race."

Sam's first event was the 50-yard freestyle, only two laps. It was not a long-enough race to build much tension and excitement. Sam won by an impressive margin. After the race, he came up into the stands and found his father. Then he looked around until he spotted his mother and began leading the way toward her.

"Oh my God, here they come," Sally gasped. "And look! Jesus! She's pregnant. I can't stand it."

Sam used all his charm to make proper introductions. "That was a great race Sam swam, don't you think, Sally?" Sam's father asked. "He really knows how to make his father proud. Mother too, I'm sure." He smiled at Sally, but she did not respond.

"Nice race, Tigger," Tom added, "in case anyone wants to know. You made us all proud."

"Thanks, Tom. I was hoping somehow I might break your record, but no way."

"You came close though. And you'll get another chance in the 100 free. I still hold the record for that one too. If it ever gets broken, I'd be happy if you were the one to do it."

"So you're the guy Sam has been telling me about," Sam's father interjected. "You and that guy Prince. Say, I can't thank you guys enough for all the help and encouragement you've given Sam. Just look at him.

My own son. Look at all those muscles. He's going to make some lucky kid a wonderful big brother, right, Gloria?"

"Are all those muscles just from swimming?" Gloria asked. "Or do you lift weights and things?"

"Nope. Haulin' lobsters. I reckon that's what did it. Right, Tom? Oops! Gotta go now. I'm up in the relay, next race." He disappeared.

Charlie sat down next to Sally and tried to start a conversation. *Good luck,* Tom thought to himself when he saw Sally's reaction. The gun went off for the relay. Sam's team won again. The swim meet was getting pretty exciting. The scores were very close. But all the cheering and hollering made it difficult for Tom to eavesdrop.

"I was dead against you bringing Sam to Maine," he overheard Charlie say as he stood there, pretending to watch the meet. "I must admit, however, that it has really worked better than I would ever have imagined. The change in that boy is just amazing."

Whatever else they said, Tom could not make out.

"The next event will be the 100 yard, men's freestyle" was announced over the loudspeaker. Sam and five other boys were introduced as they each climbed onto a starting block in the six-lane pool. The crowd grew silent as the official called out for the swimmers to get ready for the gun. *Blam!*

On the first lap, Sam was neck and neck with the swimmer in the next lane. The other swimmer gained half a length on the turn. It was turning into a two-man race. Sam remained half a length behind in second place through the second and third laps.

Tom glanced over and saw Sally with her hand clutching Charlie's arm in the excitement. Both were intent on the race.

At the beginning of the fourth lap, Sam turned it on. The crowd roared as he passed his opponent and took first place. The officials announced that a new record had been set in the men's 100-yard freestyle.

Tom looked over and saw Sally and Charlie in a joyous celebration embrace. He looked at Gloria. She had seen it too but just shrugged her shoulders, raised her eyebrows, and smiled in amusement.

When the meet was finally over, Charlie asked Tom and Sally if he could take them all out to supper before he went off with Sam for a weekend of skiing at Sunday River. He was hoping to find someplace where they served lobsters, if anyone knew of a good place.

Eddy's Wharf, down in Snug Harbor, seemed like the place. After the meet, Sally rode in the pickup with Tom, and Sam followed, driving the rent-a-car with his dad and stepmother. As they walked out on the restaurant pier, the tide was going out but was not quite slack yet. The place seemed fairly busy, considering there were no summer people around. Only locals, drinking beer, eating supper, and watching a hockey game on TV. Jimmy Buffet was playing in the background as they were seated in the back dining room, formerly known as the "no smoking" section.

Conversation was awkward at first, and Sally began to wish they hadn't come. When the cocktails arrived and everyone had had a few sips, Tom proposed a toast to Sam for his outstanding performance in the swim meet. Finally, there was something they could all agree on.

"Thanks, Tom," Sam replied. "Sorry about breaking one of your records, but I couldn't help myself."

"That's okay, Sam. I always knew it would be broken someday. But I can't think of anyone I'd rather have do it than you. And I was there to see it with my own eyes. I'm not at all sorry. I couldn't be prouder. Or happier, for that matter."

Sally breathed a sigh of relief and finally had a sip of her manhattan. The ice was broken. Everyone joined in, adding their own congratulations for Sam. Sally announced that Sam had gotten straight As last semester. After the congratulations, Sam reiterated how his mom had spent many evenings last fall, keeping him company while he did his homework, stimulating his interest and teaching him some things he hadn't picked up in class.

"Of course, I sometimes taught her a few new things too. Turns out school is a lot more interesting than what I used to think."

Unconsciously, Sally reached out her hand and touched Sam's wrist as her face broke into a smile. Dinner turned out to be much more enjoyable than Sally had anticipated. Gloria's explicit recognition of the power of positive parenting elicited another smile from Sally and a nod of thanks for the approval. But Charlie. God only knew. He just sat there silently, with a look of amazement on his face. Did he even get it?

The good food and pleasant conversation allowed everyone to relax as they all got better acquainted.

"Gloria," Tom inquired, near the end of the salad course, "what kind of work do you do, back in Philadelphia?"

"I'm a licensed clinical social worker. Right now I'm working at the university mental health clinic. But I haven't decided yet what to do after the baby comes. I'm considering taking off a couple of years so I can enjoy being a full-time mom."

"That's probably a good idea," Sally blurted out without even thinking. "There have been times when I wished I had done the same thing."

Another awkward moment.

"Sam, are you still planning to be a lobsterman after you get out of school?" Gloria quickly inquired, skillfully changing the subject. Sally downed the rest of her wine.

"Well, I kinda changed my mind and decided to go to college next."

"Well, your father has been telling me he didn't think you really wanted to go to college. What made you change your mind?"

"Actually, it was Prince. He's the lobsterman I've been working for. He convinced me I ought to have a try at college while I have the opportunity. He said that, at my age, I should prepare myself for all the opportunities that may arise in life before I make any decisions about a career. He said he would have gone to college if he could have. Guess he didn't have the money. Said you can never know what's gonna come along in life, so prepare yourself the best you can. A good education is probably worthwhile, even if I do finally decide to go into lobsterin'."

"That makes a lot of sense," Gloria continued. "Your dad says you did promise him you would make some college applications. Have you heard from any of them yet?"

"I was saving that for a surprise," Sam said, "but I guess now's as good a time as ever to let it out. I got accepted at all three colleges."

"Isn't that great?"

"Oh, God yes. Bringing up my grades helped me a lot, but I'm pretty sure my success in swimming was what really got the colleges' attention. I haven't made any decisions yet, but I was planning to ask Dad this weekend to give me some help with that."

"It will be my distinct pleasure, I can assure you," Charlie said as the waitress arrived to clear away the dishes and take orders for dessert. "It would also be a distinct pleasure if we all ordered something great for dessert. I hope they've got something chocolate that's good."

"I don't know if it's okay to say this or not," Sam interjected, "but having everybody together like this is really nice for me. Partially because I never thought I would get accepted to a college, and partly because I never expected I would be this lucky in swimming. But mostly because

I never ever expected to be lucky enough to be having dinner with my mom and my dad at the same time. It feels really good."

When the chocolate orgy was finished, the waitress walked over and presented the bill.

"Remember, this one's on me," Charlie reminded.

"Thanks," Tom replied. "I'll get the tip."

They all wandered over toward the cash register while Sam's father handed his credit card to the cashier. "Tell Eddy we had a great meal, and thanks for everything."

"Eddy ain't here right now. The tide's out," she responded. "Glad you enjoyed your meal."

"What the hell was that all about?" he asked Tom as they stepped outside, waiting for the girls to get out of the ladies' room.

"You just made her whole day," Tom said. "They love it when out-o'-staters ask for Eddy. You see, Eddy is never here at high or low tide. The eddy current is only present when the tide is rushing in or out. This restaurant is not named after a man. They named it after the eddy current that forms off the end of the wharf when the tidal current is flowing hard. In or out."

"Well, I'll be," Charlie said, shaking his head. A huge smile remained on his face until the girls finally emerged from the ladies' room.

When Sally stepped out, Charlie took her off to one side for a private word.

"Before we take off, I just wanted to finish saying what I started to tell you back at the YMCA pool. You see, Gloria has been a tremendous help in getting me to see a lot of things I never understood about family and relationships. You know what I mean? Then add in everything that happened at dinner tonight. It has helped me a lot to understand and get over my anger at you for taking Sam away from Philly and off to Maine. It's turned out to be good for him. Better than I ever expected. And that's what I care about most of all. Now, I can only apologize and say thank you for such a fine job."

"Thank you, Charlie. It means a lot to hear you say that. I hope you guys have a really great time at Sunday River."

"I'm sure we will. But there's one more thing I found out tonight, and I just have to tell you."

"Oh, yeah? What's that?"

"I want you to know I still love you."

"Charlie."

"I'm serious. Not in a sexual way. I'm quite certain. But I know I still care about you, and I'm grateful for all you've given me. I wish the very best for you. And I hope we can maintain a friendly and meaningful relationship in the future."

"Thank you, Charlie. I think I want the same. And have a great time at Sunday River."

Sam kissed his mom good-bye and then hopped in the rent-a-car and drove off with his father and stepmother.

"What took you so long in the ladies' room?"

"Oh, Gloria and I got into a long discussion about women's issues. You know? How difficult it was for her to make the choice between spending her time raising kids and pursuing her career. You are aware of that issue, aren't you?"

"Oh, yeah! You're talking about how unfair it is that only women have to make those choices?"

"Yeah. Well, I told her about Arthur Prince's perspective on this subject, and turns out she agrees with him."

"Hmm. That's interesting. And what, exactly, is Prince's perspective on this subject?"

"Well, remember that venison feast we had at your house, last November, after you guys shot those deer? Well, Arthur and I had a little private conversation out on the porch while Arthur smoked his cigar. And he told me that, from his observations of life, having children, breast-feeding them, and raising them was probably the most rewarding and enjoyable experience in human life."

"You know? Arthur could very well be right about that."

"I know. But Arthur put a fresh new spin on it. He said women were really lucky to be able to choose to have that experience. You might could say that life was actually unfair to men, because men are never given the choice."

Tom just shook his head in amazement.

"Later on, after I thought about it, I finally realized that the process of having a kid and raising him was the most valuable experience in my life. I was lucky to have that opportunity."

Tom nodded, with a smile on his face that showed his agreement.

"Well, when I told that to Gloria, she slapped herself in the head and wondered why she hadn't ever figured that out herself. She completely agreed with Arthur, as I do, and she said that settled the question she had been struggling with. She was definitely going to take some time off from her career and enjoy being a full-time mom. It really makes you appreciate the advantages of being a woman.

"Then she asked me what kind of a guy Arthur was. I reminded her that he was the lobsterman that worked with Sam, and he was also the one who had convinced Sam to go to college. She kept on shaking her head in amazement. She just couldn't believe it. After all those years of college and graduate school, this was the most valuable lesson she had ever learned. And she learned it from a goddamn lobsterman."

"That Arthur is a pretty clever guy," Tom observed. "He was also the one who finally got me out of that damn lawsuit. Can you believe it?"

"Well," Sally said, "I told her, from my experience so far, people from rural Maine have the most realistic experience and understanding of life compared to anywhere I have lived. And they really seem to appreciate the privileges that only women have been granted."

"That's amazing," Tom replied. "So, I take it, now you're happy, wearing the mother's suit?"

"Well, most of the time."

Tom picked up a discarded newspaper from an empty table. "Did you see this?" he asked as he showed it to Sally.

"On my!" BETTY NORTON ANNOUNCES RESIGNATION FROM HOSPITAL, CITING HEALTH REASONS. "Do you know anything about this?"

"Well, yes. There's a lot more to it than what's in the paper. The CEO of the hospital called me around lunchtime and apologized about the hospital records being changed and all the grief it brought me. He asked me not to tell anyone. It seems he and the executive committee of the hospital board have been aware for some time that it was Betty who altered the hospital records. They've been waiting for the malpractice case to be resolved before taking any action, because they were worried the lawyers might take advantage of any negative publicity and use it against the hospital.

"This morning, they found out the case was settled, so they called a meeting and decided it was time to take action. As far as they could tell, Betty had changed the record only to protect the hospital and not out of some selfish motive.

"So, because of that, they let her resign instead of firing her. That way she can still get her retirement benefits. You know, health insurance and pension. After all, over the years, she has done a world of good for the hospital. Besides, if she hadn't turned the tort lawyers onto me for a while, they would have gone after the hospital and cleaned out the trust fund. The way it turned out, ethics aside, her maneuver probably kept millions of dollars of this community's money out of the lawyer's pockets."

"I just knew she did it."

"You were right."

"Doesn't it make you angry?"

"Not anymore. If I had known about it last fall, I'd have gone ballistic. But now that the pressure is off, all I can feel is … I don't know. Kinda sorry for her, you know?"

"Sorry for her? How can you feel sorry after all she's done?"

"It's just that all my life I have been very close friends with Liz. I mean Betty. Growing up, she was always Liz. I can't imagine what she's going to do with herself now. She has no kids. The hospital was her whole life. Now she's got nothing."

"Oh, yes. Actually, you do have a point," Sally said with a sigh. "Suddenly I finally get the picture. For the past year I've been feeling sorry for myself because of all the difficult choices and problems I've had to deal with. You know? Balancing career and family. But poor Betty is like a man. She was never even given a choice."

"Exactly! And when I think how she taught us all a better way of managing errors in medicine. Then she goes and makes one herself. Just tryin' to save the hospital. That's all she was doing. Fortunately, her mistake was found before it could do any real damage. So what do they do? Fire her. Is that justice?"

"I reckon so. Sometimes justice can be pretty ugly, can't it?"

"Ayeah. The lawyer was right about that. It seems like the uglier it is, the more people like it."

"That's for sure."

Tom took Sally by the arm, and they walked slowly out toward the end of the wharf.

"Turned out to be a very nice dinner tonight. Don'tcha think?" Tom reflected.

"Very nice. In fact, the whole day has turned out better than I expected. How are you feeling, now that the malpractice suit is finally off your back?"

"Better than you can ever imagine. And the bulk of the happiness hasn't even totally sunk in yet. Until now, I didn't even realize how much that suit was dominating my life, suppressing all the rest of my emotions and feelings about everything else."

"I know exactly what you mean. I'm feeling the same way. Today is the first day I have allowed myself to accept that Sam is going to turn out all right. His performance at the Y this afternoon, and even more at dinner tonight, was so unbelievable. I have finally accepted the reality in life that being a mother is much more satisfying and important than being a doctor."

"So how did it feel, seeing Sam tonight and watching him drive off with his father?"

"Good. And I'm not pissed off for a change."

"Now that's progress."

"Yes. Charlie apologized tonight for all his anger over my taking Sam away."

"That's good. I'll bet seeing what a good job you have been doing with Sam probably helped a lot."

"I think so. But I think it was Gloria's influence that made the big difference. In our little chat in the ladies' room, she said she's been actively reprogramming Charlie on this issue. I got the impression Charlie's anger was bothering her almost as much as it was me."

"That doesn't surprise me. You can see she has great people skills."

"I'll say. I bet if I had had her understanding of interpersonal relations, I probably would not have had to get divorced."

"Well, I'm kinda glad you didn't have those skills."

"You are?"

"Yes. If you'd had those skills, you might never have moved up to Maine, and I never would have had the chance to fall in love with you."

"Do you really mean that?"

"I think I do."

"That makes me so happy. Funny, isn't it, how different things seem when you look at them from the opposite perspective? I think I have probably been in love with you for a long time. Only I never could see it with all these other problems occupying my mind."

"I know just how you feel," Tom whispered in her ear as he drew her in close for the start of an embrace. "And, come to think of it, we should probably forgive Betty Norton and maybe even thank her too."

"Thank Betty Norton? Tom, what the hell are you talking about?" she asked, pushing him away. "And how can you ever forgive her too?"

"Well, it just now came to my mind. If she hadn't set me up for that malpractice case and then seated us together at her party, in her effort to break up my relationship with Cathy, we probably never would have gotten to know each other like we did. It was her scheming that led to my breakup with Cathy. The case also created the need to form a relationship with you, in order to help me deal with all the anxiety from the malpractice case. Without her nasty maneuvers, I don't think it's likely we would have ever fallen in love."

"You know? I think you're right."

"Yes. And for all the trouble she has caused us, it's been worth it. So I forgive her."

"If that's true, then, according to Alexander Pope, you've got to be divine."

Their embrace was long and tender, full of love and devotion, more like two people who had been married for years. It was only at the end of the last kiss that passion began to take over.

Hand in hand, they strolled out toward the end of the dock. The tide was at full slack. Some of the larger rocks and ledges had a light cap of snow where the high tide couldn't quite reach. Most of the rocks had no snow because they were covered up at high tide. A foggy blanket of Arctic sea smoke was forming offshore, and they could hear a foghorn from an island out to sea. The moon peeped out from the rapidly drifting scatter of clouds overhead and lit up the harbor with a romantic glow.

"Even at this time of the year," Sally observed, "you can still get a faint whiff of the clam flats. Think I'll ever get to like that smell?"

"Well, for anyone who gets homesick at the smell of horse manure, it shouldn't be too difficult."

"Don't think I've ever seen it when the tide's so far out. Look at all those big rocks sticking up out of the water. At high tide, you wouldn't even know they were there."

"That's right. Fishermen and boaters have to be mighty careful to follow the buoys and stay inside the channel whenever they come into this harbor. Lobstermen who moor their boats outside the channel know where all the submerged rocks are. And even then, a lot of them hit the rocks every year, it seems. It's a lot more challenging than just getting in and out of the harbor."

"I can see why your dad liked to philosophize about hitting BFRs and going with the flow."

"Yeah. Low tide kinda bares it all."

"You know, looking back now at our lives over this past year, it's sorta like the tide is out and now we can see things a lot better. We both have managed to scrape a few rocks along the way, but overall it seems like we've been pretty lucky, when you look at all the big ones we missed."

"That's sorta how I feel," Tom replied, taking in a deep breath and then exhaling. "So now that Sam is off with his father, what do you plan to do the next couple of days?"

"Well, now that I've learned how good it feels to take off the doctor's suit, I think I'll try taking off the mother suit for a while."

"Good idea. Then maybe you might see how you'd feel about getting married."

"Am I to consider this a proposal?"

"Oh my gosh. I think it is."

"Good. Consider it accepted."

She put her arm around his waist and laid her head on his chest. Tom looked down at her. There it was again. That rapturous smile. Her face completely transformed. Beautiful. Only, this time, Tom was the proximate cause.

Printed in the United States
by Baker & Taylor Publisher Services